THE UNTAMED DUKE

THE TAMING SERIES, BOOK TWO

APRIL MORAN

The Untamed Duke – The Taming Series, Book Two

Copyright © 2018 by April Moran

All Rights Reserved

Cover by: Amanda Walker PA & Design Services

Formatting by Christina Butrum

Editing by Karen Boston Editing & Proofreading

ACKNOWLEDGMENTS

A wealth of knowledge comes with the writing of a second book. I've learned so much during this last year since publishing *Taming Ivy*, and there are new friends in the writing community who have offered advice and encouragement along the way. I would be remiss if I didn't mention them here.

Amanda Walker, you always have the perfect teasers and covers. Having you on my side is an amazing gift, and I'm so grateful. Christina Butrum, your formatting skills are so professional, I can't imagine anyone else doing it for me. Thank you, ladies, for making my book look so beautiful.

Cindi Medley, your encouragement always lifts me up. You are one of the most generous people I've had the pleasure of becoming friends with. Michelle Windsor, girl, I swear we were separated at birth, LOL. Thank you for always including me. You've inspired me to try my hand at writing a contemporary... we'll see how that goes. Jennifer Trethewey, my sister in the historical romance world, thank you for always answering my questions and for the encouragement! And Nicky F. Grant, you are always sharing the love-you are a sweetheart.

Thank you to Karen Boston Editing & Proofreading, for polishing my work and making it shine bright.

Gary Swearingen, love you for always doing live Facebook readings on a Friday night with me. Karen Pike, Beth Garvey, Kathryn W. Haley, and Melony Bowden, I adore ya'll. Thank you for your enthusiasm and the love and support. Karen and Kathryn, your GIF wars on Facebook are legendary and always crack me up. Dan Pike, special thanks for joining in on the craziness with us! My sweet sister, Jodi Moore—thank you for always sharing my books and encouraging your friends to read them.

I cannot forget my #1 Alpha reader, Ladyne Swearingen. You didn't care for Nicholas, or the book in general, but you loved me enough to read it and still give me your honest opinion and multiple suggestions to make it better. I think I changed your mind by the end. I hope I did, anyway. Thank you for always having my back. I love you.

My Beta and ARC readers, you guys are amazing. Thank you for the feedback, love, criticism and encouragement. You help me write better books.

And last, thank you to my Readers. Every time you choose one of my books, I'm humbled.

XOXO

April

For James.
Always on my side. Always up for adventure. Always my best
friend. Always my love.
For Alyssa ∼ Best Daughter Ever.
For Trey∼ Best Son-in-Law Ever.

For our very own Winter Wolf
∼BLUE∼
RIP
10*22*2009 ∼ 07* 20* 2018
I couldn't leave you out.
Callie's waiting for you over the Rainbow Bridge. Y'all be good
dogs until we come for you. We'll bring your favorite blue ball and
lots of treats.

The wolf howled
Lost in winter's desolation
A gilded wilderness
She offered him
The curve of her neck
Her wrist
Her heart
Her soul
Herself
That he might feast
That he might trust
That he might love
And become hers

———————————

A.M.

CHAPTER 1

*M*en were confounding creatures. Prone to capricious moods and jealous displays, and mulish behavior. It was the only explanation for Tristan Buchanan's dogged pursuit.

"Will you run from me again? As you did yesterday?"

Lady Grace Willsdown sighed, the solitude of the ivy-clad gazebo evaporating like wispy smoke as Lord Longleigh's voice penetrated it. Blast. He must have cut across the perfectly manicured lawn, the warning crunch of his footsteps on gravel unnoticed while she was immersed in her book.

Only yesterday, Tristan practically chased her about Calmont Down's garden maze. She avoided disaster by kicking his shin, scolding his behavior as unseemly for such a respectable viscount. The tall, green walls of the hedges had swallowed his curses as she zigzagged down narrow paths in escape. Later, when he limped into the main drawing room where she took tea with the viscount's own mother, Lady Darby, and their host, Lady Calmont, Grace did not ask if he'd spent the entire afternoon searching for the maze exit.

No matter how many times Lord Longleigh declared an adoration lasting until the end of time or how often he plaintively insisted, "I love you", she repeated her refusal. The tactful rejections probably qualified her as an expert on the subject, something other women might study and learn from. Tristan simply ignored them.

Grace refocused attention on the hefty tome detailing Viking invasions during the medieval era. Lately, she'd begun ignoring the viscount when he became overly persistent.

Ignore the behavior. Eventually, he must give up.

Sometimes the tactic sent him stomping away in angry defeat. Yesterday, it resulted in a bruise on Tristan's shin and a telling limp.

"Why do you avoid me? Our time together is so enjoyable. Other than those unfortunate moments when you kick me."

His slur-laced words compelled Grace's eyes up. Lowering the book so it rested in her lap, a finger serving as a temporary bookmark, she blinked as guilt stabbed her. These rejections would be much easier if only she didn't care for him. He and his sister were very dear, like the siblings she never had.

Was he intoxicated? She couldn't imagine he was. Tristan never over-indulged. The man was a walking example of self-possessed, abundant charm. Capable of holding his liquor with admirable skill. How many times had she heard it said? *How clever Viscount Longleigh is! Such a charming rogue. So handsome!* And he was. A clever, charming, handsome rogue she had no desire to wed. A pity, that. Someday, a lucky woman would gain an absolutely wonderful husband.

Not her, for God's sake. But somebody.

Grace turned the book over and untied a scrap of black ribbon from her wrist. Gathering her hair into a loose ponytail, her lips pressed thin with growing discomfort. An intoxicated Tristan was an unknown element. It was best she prepare for whatever arose.

One foot on the gravel path, the other planted on the first of the gazebo steps, Tristan faltered. But his face darkened when Grace cautiously flipped the book upright and resumed reading.

"Good God!" Flinging an arm wide, he nearly lost his balance. Embracing a marble pillar steadied him. "Does nothing interest you other than books, horses and that godforsaken heap of stones you call home?"

Grace calmly finished perusing the page until reaching its last word. She recognized his mood. He would needle and prod until she snapped back with a response.

"Don't be silly," she said, finding a second bit of ribbon in the pocket of her gown.

Laying it against the seam of the current page, Grace closed the heavy tome with a wistful frown. Her forefinger traced the title's gilt embossing. Considering the numerous interruptions over the past few days, she doubted finishing the book. Perhaps Lord Calmont might consider its loan.

"I have other interests. And please, do not call Bellmar Abbey godforsaken."

"What are they? These interests." Tristan's tone bordered on petulant. "Tell me. What amuses you? Entrances you? Tell me what you like, and I shall transform myself. It appears the only way I'll gain your attention. If I thought it mattered, I'd have words tattooed all over my body. Then you could read *me* like one of your damned books."

Grace ignored the scandalous suggestion, but her lips twitched. *Croquet.* She liked croquet. Envisioning Tristan as a round little ball, she imagined his surprise if she ever whacked him with a wooden mallet.

She swallowed her giggle when he released the column and advanced another riser, hands clenched. These past few nights he'd scowled at any man approaching her, even those merely following a gentleman's code of polite interest in her wellbeing.

During today's outdoor festivities, he hounded her steps until it was either escape or scream aloud.

Every nuance of Tristan's body exhibited exasperation as he gazed at her, uncomprehending her lack of enthusiasm for his courtship.

Grace could not understand his fixed interest when she'd never encouraged anything more than an affectionate, platonic relationship. His interest was truly puzzling. Oh, she considered her own features pleasant enough, but she held no illusions that stick-straight blonde hair and direct brown eyes qualified her as an extraordinary beauty capable of ensnaring a man's devotion. And while it was true she possessed the capability of carrying on an intelligent conversation, many girls managed the same, so she was nothing special.

All talent as a conversationalist aside, others considered her an outsider. A terror on horseback and a bluestocking. A strange girl far more concerned with horses and dusty books than how many suitors trailed in her wake, which until recently consisted solely of Tristan Buchanan, Viscount of Longleigh.

"Let your hair back down," he muttered, feet shuffling wide in a bolstering of his stance. Another tread conquered, and he stood within the cool shade. "It's so damned lovely..."

"Tristan, you are not yourself." Grace rose from the bench, nerves stretched tight, her skin prickling. Tiny beads of sweat marked Tristan's brow, his eyes bright with glassy sparks. He was definitely foxed.

What should I do? Escape or reason with him?

"We shall discuss this later."

"I wanted to discuss it yesterday—"

"No!" Grace snapped. Taking a deep breath, she continued in a calmer tone. "No, yesterday you chased me around the fountain in the center of this maze."

"Was it this one? They all look alike, I'm afraid." Tristan

4

regarded her blankly, then breathed, "Had I caught you, you'd understand why I chased you."

The hair rose on the back of Grace's neck while considering his cryptic statement. Something felt...odd. An electric current floating along the breeze, at once both disturbing and exciting. She glanced toward the thick bushes. One of five gazebos scattered about the estate, this particular one sat well-hidden, nestled amongst rhododendrons and boxwoods. Paired with a twisting gravel path and the backdrop of the maze, she and Tristan were effectively concealed from view.

Surveying the abundant greenery, Grace half-expected movement, a rescuer perhaps, but no one emerged. She hugged her book, disturbed by the unsettling sensation of being watched.

"*That* would not have ended well." She brushed past Tristan. "In light of this pointless conversation, I shall return to the house."

"Damn it," he groaned. "How will you understand my dilemma if you are forever running away?" Before Grace reached the steps, he snagged her arm, spinning her against him. Deft, masculine fingers tugged the ribbon from her hair. "You are driving me insane." A hiccup marred his fierce declaration.

"Your ills are of your own doing. I've not encouraged you. Tristan...oh! Let me loose!"

"Not until I have a kiss. Just one. *Blast it.* Hold still." He embraced her tighter, crushing the book between them. Its hard edges bit into Grace's collarbone when Tristan squeezed her.

"Tristan, stop! Don't make me—"

"Will you just let me give you a proper kiss?" He grunted, attempting to hold her still.

The book thumped the side of his head, but Grace might as well have used a dandelion for a weapon, for it did no good at all. A pain immunity woven of alcohol had developed around him, and her resistance was merely a pesky deterrent.

Although his head surely swam from the blow, Tristan's

mouth clamped over hers, muffling a shriek of feminine outrage. Redolent with spirits, his breath made her dizzy. Even as she batted at him, he buried a hand in her loose hair, kissing her until Grace thought he'd never come up for air.

When he finally drew back, his drunken ardor proved far more disturbing than inebriated frustration. "I'm a fool, waiting so long to do that." His brow furrowed. "You taste like—like lemonade. Delicious, but not at all what I expected. It's the damnedest thing."

With an anguished groan, he dove in for another kiss. Grace squealed in protest. She struck him multiple times with the book until he grasped her wrist. Breathing an exasperated curse, he forced her hand open, and the tome landed with a heavy thud at their feet.

Squirming with useless ferocity, Grace realized that reasoning with Tristan was impossible, drowning as he was in an alcoholic haze. Desperate tactics were required if she wished to extract herself.

It's for the best...really. And if he lands on me, that will be most unfortunate. Oh, why did I not study Celia's technique more thoroughly? Should I faint forward or swoon backward?

SHE SAGGED LIKE A WILTED FLOWER IN THE HEAT OF summer, her full weight falling against Tristan in a lifeless slump. Startled, he gave her a rough shake, but when she did not rouse, he carefully lowered her onto the gazebo floor.

Her wrists were smacked; stinging strikes that almost had her yelping aloud.

"Damnation, girl. I only kissed you." Using the back of his hand, Tristan briskly tapped her cheeks.

Grace bit her tongue in outrage. If only she could return the favor; she would box the viscount's ears until they rang like church bells.

She realized a tactical mistake when a gentle hand brushed the bangs fringing her forehead. Pretending unconsciousness could end badly. Tristan might take advantage of the staged swoon. Perhaps kiss her more thoroughly. Or, bloody hell, decide her unresponsive form invited exploration. A new strategy was devised, one involving fists and teeth should his intentions turn in that direction.

"Oh hell," Tristan muttered after a few moments of silence, his absent conscience finally peeking out. "Stay here. I'll get Celia."

Grace breathed through a grimace at the unnecessary order.

As if I'll patiently wait for your return. Drat. You might have laid me on the bench at least.

Gravel scattered beneath Tristan's heels as he rushed from the gazebo and trotted around the path's bend. Grace remained as he placed her, slightly curled on one side, arms limp and crossed over her stomach. Seconds slipped by, with only the chirping of birds filling the silence. Relief escaped her lungs in a tiny sigh. She cautiously opened her eyes.

"Do you require assistance?"

The man's voice was deep. A bit annoyed. A subtle hint of clean linen mixed with sandalwood and mint wafted on a slight breeze.

Grace's eyes slammed shut. *That's not Tristan.* No, someone else had stumbled across her. Was Longleigh seen kissing her? *Dear God, I hope not.*

Approaching in a leisurely fashion, hard boot heels punched out a restrained staccato on the marble floor. Grace's insides spiraled in frantic eddies of suspense. She dared not move a muscle. Not even when tiny hairs on the back of her neck shifted, each wisp arching, lifting from her skin. They leaned and strained toward that husky voice. The hair on her arms did the same.

What the devil...?

You've no more fainted than I have. Get up. Now."

Indecision froze Grace's muscles. Should she continue this subterfuge? Or obey the quiet command? How inconsiderate he was, forcing such a choice on her. The cad. Temper sparked with panic at the impossible situation.

Oh, please go away. Please.

"You obviously require my assistance after all. If one can consider it such." The interloper's voice dropped a noticeable degree, cold and hot all at once. His offer did not convey the impression of benefiting the situation at all. "I won't be as gentle as Longleigh. Of that, you can be certain."

Gritting her teeth at the man's rudeness, Grace rolled onto her back, moaning in what she hoped was a convincing act of someone recovering from a faint. Her eyes screwed shut as he crouched beside her and something inside her stomach clenched at the overwhelming sense of power emanating from him.

Lashes fluttering, she blinked a few times. "Wh-what happened?"

Piercing and cold, the greenest pair of eyes Grace had ever encountered stared back. Pinned her in place as if she were a helpless rabbit at the mercy of a hungry wolf. In some vague corner of her mind, she registered the ruthless beauty of the masculine visage looming over her.

"How very... theatrical." A thin line of impatience stretched his mouth.

"Wh-what?" she squeaked.

Those emerald eyes narrowed. "What a waste in this refined setting. The stage is your calling, I think. Are you an actress? I've not much luck with actresses, unfortunately."

While he spoke, gorgeous mouth forming words, Grace considered his stunning features. With such long legs, he was undoubtedly tall. As tall as Tristan, possibly more so. And definitely muscular but contained in a lean, sleek frame, with broad shoulders blocking her view of the gazebo ceiling. She almost expected a graceful spread of gilded wings to unfurl behind him. He could be a fallen angel, with that head of dark, tousled gold hair and those magnificently colored eyes.

As if contemplating what to do, the man leaned on his haunches, his hand rubbing over a scuffed, well-defined square jaw. Thick, black eyelashes concealed his thoughts.

"Longleigh has no inkling of the deception you're capable of."

Grace's senses rebounded, and with them came indignant outrage. "An actress...are you mad? I'm not... oh, my God. You—you watched Longleigh attack me."

"Attack?" A smile that wasn't really a smile, then, "A trifling of a kiss. I'd say the viscount got the worst of the encounter." His arm draped casually over an upraised knee. "And if not an actress, you must be one of the annoying offerings on the marriage mart this Season." He casually switched topics with barely the flicker of an eyelash. "This is quite tedious, you know, kneeling in this manner."

Grace's jaw clenched. *Did he truly insinuate kissing me is worse than being mauled? After calling me an actress? And annoying?*

"I should have struck Longleigh harder. He certainly deserved harder." *And so do you!*

"Quite the performance, regardless." An overtly masculine brow lifted. "Do you intend on lying there all afternoon? If so, I'll join you and make this incident worthwhile."

"Oh! How dare you!"

Her skirts were hopelessly tangled— to the point that shifting her bottom to get her legs beneath her was necessary. Rolling sideways, face flushed pink with embarrassment and annoyance, Grace gave the excess silk pinned under her arse a twitch, followed by a desperate, furious tug.

Her mouth formed a startled "Oh!" of surprise when she was snatched to her feet. Released in equally rapid fashion, she stumbled, but the stranger readily caught her. While he held her upper arms, steadying her, Grace experienced a strength that left no doubt of the man's authority. Beneath her palms, which landed somehow on his abdomen, there was a smoldering power. Power granting him the key to anything he wanted.

Those muscles contracted with her touch, and his hands constricted around her arms. Tight, yet exquisitely gentle, those large, strong hands told Grace everything in the compacted space of a few seconds.

Possessive. Restrained. Any lesson will be swift, explicit and unforgettable. He will handle his horses in the same manner...

The next thought sizzled her brain.

...and his women.

Wearing a slight frown, the stranger released her, bending to retrieve her book. The title was examined before he handed it over.

"Studying up on battle maneuvers for your next encounter? Viking invasions were rather brutal affairs."

Goodness, the man was sinfully gorgeous, his suit coat stretching across bulges exquisitely restrained beneath black cloth. Grace was reminded of a large, tawny wolf, his air of authority leaving her nerves in a puzzling tangle. He was slightly taller than Tristan, so it was necessary she tilt her head when meeting his gaze. She did not care for men so much taller than she. It resulted in an awful crick in her neck when carrying on a conversation for any length of time. However, she didn't mind at the moment, and she was breathless just looking at him. His features could have been sculpted by a master artist. With those high cheekbones and his straight nose, she'd never before seen a man so insanely handsome.

"By nature, invasions are a bloody business," she replied, a little shakily. "I've no intention of allowing one against my person. Since the Vikings failed me, I shall call upon *Barbarians of the Roman Empire and Subversive Tactics* for my next offensive." When he gave her a blank look, Grace smiled. "It's a much thicker book, you see."

"If Longleigh had any sense, he would be terrified." Full lips quirked for the briefest second, but he did not truly smile back. "Your next spree of mayhem will probably require an alibi. Although I risk finding myself at the pointy end of a spear, or in your case, the flat side of a treatise on ancient warfare, introductions are necessary in such dire circumstances. Nicholas August Harris March, at your pleasure, my lady."

Grace's knees wobbled. Good lord, it was him. The Winter Wolf. Nicholas March...Duke of Richeforte, Earl of Landon, along with a multitude of other titles. Cold. Heartless. Ruthless. At twenty-seven years of age, the new duke was the youngest, most powerful man in all of England. He was Celia's latest obsession and good friends with Tristan. He'd also once been close friends with her own cousin, the Earl of Ravenswood.

Once. Long ago.

"Well," she blew out an exasperated sigh, "that explains it."

"Of course it does," Richeforte drawled. "Now, explain it to me. I fear I've missed something vitally important."

"Why you didn't stop Tristan. The two of you share some manner of awful code, adhered to most reverently by equally awful rakes. One must never interrupt the undertaking of a misdeed by a fellow rake. Or something of that nature."

"Indeed."

"Indeed, my lord."

"Your Grace," was his soft reply.

"Of course, I'm Grace. And Tristan may steal a thousand kisses. I'll still not marry him!" Grace vowed heatedly. "I won't do it—"

"My title." Glittering, green eyes bored through her. "*Your Grace*. Don't tell me you are unaware of the proper way to

11

address a duke. One might think you purposefully fail at it. And I've no interest who Longleigh weds. Nor who you wed, for that matter."

"Oh." Deflating in chagrined embarrassment, Grace recognized the boredom in his tone. Teeth tugging at her lower lip, she meekly admitted, "There is a proper way to things, and my reluctance in learning them will no doubt be my undoing. Lady Darby says her greatest despair is my unruly nature. She fears it will never be mastered. But if I may be honest, my lord, I pray I never find myself so tamed."

The duke's eyes darkened on her last word, her entire body subjected to a thorough assessment in the space of time it took him to blink. Heat flushed Grace while she self-consciously brushed her skirts free of dust. Every inch of her—her toes, the tips of her fingers, her stomach—felt as if on fire. Even her lips, for God's sake. With a shaky hand, she discreetly traced their outline, abruptly aware she was babbling like a crazy person.

"Ah, you're the Earl of Darby's ward. What is it they call you?" Richeforte's voice was low, husky, a soft feather brushing her senses. "I recall now. The Cornwall Storm."

Grace swayed a little. Had the earth shifted beneath them? Was the gazebo suddenly unsteady upon its foundation? She felt so odd. Perhaps she struck her head during that stage-worthy faint.

"I prefer to be known as the Earl of Willsdown's daughter," she corrected him, ignoring his last observation.

Where might he have heard that nickname? The moniker was slapped on her during those first few weeks in London, but it died away as she found her bearings amidst the social whirl of the elite. And once the Countess of Ravenswood and the new Countess of Bentley took her under their wings.

"Nothing against Lord Darby, he and his family are very kind, but I was a daughter before I became a ward. In six months,

I shall reach my majority at age twenty-one and I'll not be anyone's ward."

Richeforte's gaze was tinged with amusement. "Longleigh's frustration is understandable. What a honeybee you are, all sweetness and stingers."

Grace sucked in a breath. She couldn't comprehend why his words left her wanting to preen and cry at the same time.

"I doubt you understand anything at all, my lord. Particularly matters between myself and the viscount."

CHAPTER 2

Where my heart should reside
in this cage of a soul
rests a block of ice
black
cold
wicked
~Nicholas August Harris March
Ninth Duke of Richeforte

"*Y*our Grace," Nicholas prompted again, resisting an urge to grind his teeth. Was the girl deliberately obtuse in the use of his title, or could she not help it?

Grace regarded him as if debating her next move. A slow smile curved her lips.

"Yes, I'm Grace."

"And I'm Richeforte." Had he fallen? Struck his head? Did they not suffer this same conversation just moments ago?

"Well, of course you are. Is there any doubt you are Richeforte and I am Grace?"

"There seems to be some confusion on the subject."

"Have no fear." Bestowing a condescending pat on his forearm, it seemed she found a mischievous delight in his puzzled irritation. "It is a recent title for you. No doubt confusing, leaping from plain old earl to exalted duke in such short order. And all those names! How can you be expected to remember each one? However, you seem an intelligent enough fellow. I'm sure you'll manage eventually."

Nicholas was dumbfounded to the point of speechlessness. Something wicked stirred inside him seeing her benign expression. Lady Grace Willsdown was a vexing creature, and she could not possibly know the aversion for his new title stemmed from an actual hatred of his own father.

He feared discovering a perverse pleasure in reminding her of his station, should she continue blithely ignoring it. A sudden yearning swamped him. Hearing that despised title dripping from her lips would greatly please him. How best to accomplish it?

Kissing that cheeky grin away would be a logical start. He could smother that wide, lush mouth of hers with his own. Drink her in. Swallow her up with a sweep of his tongue. She probably had the unmitigated nerve to taste of strawberries, or something equally ridiculous.

You taste like lemonade...

Goddamn. Longleigh knew how she tasted, which seemed vastly unfair. An abomination. During their years of friendship, Nicholas never suffered a thimbleful of jealousy toward Tristan Buchanan. Until now.

Against his will, his gaze lingered on her mouth. Yes, definitely strawberries. Overly ripened, decadent, sweet strawberries. And that tumble of hair? It was soft as gossamer; he knew because it had spilled over his hands and through his fingers when he jerked her up from the gazebo floor. He could wrap that shiny mane about his fist, use it to pull her mouth against his own. Why the hell was it down, anyway?

Because Tristan demanded it, remember? While you stood silent. While Tristan demanded that kiss. Bloody hell, while you watched and did nothing to stop him from taking it.

"What a strange creature you are," Nicholas remarked with a tilt of his head.

Grace smiled. "If that was meant as a compliment, I've heard it before, and if not," here, she waved her hand in breezy acknowledgment," the same still applies. I've heard it before, my lord."

"And brash, too. I've always admired a bit of fire in a female."

"Another compliment?" Merriment danced in her golden eyes. "At this pace, the gossips will have our wedding taking place in St Paul's Cathedral six months from now. You'd best restrain yourself."

Horror must have shown in his expression because Grace burst out laughing. "Have no fear. With a reputation such as yours, I would never accept your offer if you ever put one forth. I'm merely teasing you."

Nicholas frowned. "I'm unsure if I should be relieved or insulted."

"I was given this advice once: go with the strongest feeling that's in your heart. I hope, as a gentleman, you will not tell me which emotion you feel most keenly at this moment."

Excellent advice, Nicholas mused.

Only, he felt slightly insulted this vexing creature would dare reject his courtship. If he ever pursued a courtship. With her. Insane, because he would not because of her very strangeness, which for some reason fascinated the hell out of him. She seemed undaunted by his notorious reputation. Unconcerned that he could devour a little innocent like herself in one bite.

"Who imparted such sage advice?" he murmured, admiring the pink softness of her lips.

"Ralph, the baker's son in the village. I was nine years old and could not decide between a lemon tart or the chocolate eclair. I chose the lemon because I'd had a chocolate eclair only moments before. Too much sweetness can turn a stomach very quickly. At any rate, I still utilize his advice." Grace cleared her throat. "Well, this was very entertaining, but I must go now. Lord Longleigh will return soon with Lady Celia in tow."

Nicholas took her elbow, an utterly foreign jolt shuddering through him. Beneath his fingertips, her skin was warm velvet. Reckless thoughts, an overload of erotic images, assailed him. What if she were naked against him? What if he pressed his lips against the pulse beating there in the hollow of her neck? Slid his tongue up and traced the delicate ear where she just nervously tucked a sheath of honey-colored hair.

He could fill his hands with those pert breasts mounding above the bodice of her lavender-hued gown. Lift them to his mouth, bite at their peaks. Were her nipples peach or rose shaded? Would she cry out her pleasure or simply moan in word-less encouragement? Would she like his brand of lovemaking, rough and bittersweet with an edge of pain balancing the plea-sure? Or would she expect soft, gentle caresses and murmured endearments?

He was hard as stone just thinking of her reactions.

"Don't go." His voice was raspy. Which was hardly surprising since he'd never used it in a plea before. "Not yet."

Grace's low laughter sprayed thrills along his spine. A slight bump in the middle of her nose marred its otherwise arrow-straight elegance. It appeared to have been broken in the past. She wrinkled it at him now.

"You should know I cannot save you from Lady Celia's atten-tions. She's spoken of you incessantly since the Warner's Ball, and my presence will not deter her. Her affection for you, while fickle, is sincere."

Nicholas scowled. Celia was a recent development and annoying as hell. Tristan, damn his hide, only chuckled at his grumbled complaints. "It's best to ride out her infatuation," his friend serenely advised the month before. "Celia will grow bored if you show no encouragement."

As if Nicholas ever would encourage his friend's sister. She was off limits. As was the woman whose elbow he currently gripped.

"Why were you not at the Warner's Ball?" he asked softly.

Grace hesitated, appearing unsure of the subject matter. "I was visiting my cousin and Lady Ravenswood at Beaumont."

"I'd heard Sebastian ran across a bit of trouble concerning his aunt around the time my father passed away. I've been assured of his full recovery."

Her head tilted. "I'm afraid to ask how much you know of the incident."

Nicholas's features were a mask of blank politeness. "Then you shouldn't ask." He knew everything. Now that he was a duke, few things of note were kept secret from him. All manner of spies and informants scattered about the country took care of that. "I can't imagine Longleigh was happy with your absence from Town. Is he very smitten with you?"

"It's hardly a secret. I think all of London knows of his courtship." Sly devilment danced in Grace's expressive eyes. "If he discovers I eluded his advances and finds you here in his stead..."

Nicholas barely comprehended her words, too busy wondering what level of sweetness the fullness of her lower lip contained. What might happen if *he* kissed her? Submission or Tristan's fate? How hard would she strike *him* with that enormous book on Viking invasions? He was very tempted to find out.

"Stay," he murmured.

Grace swayed toward him, and every blood vessel, cell, vein, and nerve...everything alive inside him tightened with anticipation. Sweet fires of hell. He wanted her. He had no idea why, having just met her. But he did. It bewildered him.

"Why would I do that?" Grace smiled.

"Because I said so."

"I suppose you are accustomed to having your way in all things," she said softly.

His response was a noncommittal grunt.

"Richeforte?"

"Yes?"

"You're holding my arm rather tightly."

Nicholas glanced down at her accusing whisper. Where he gripped her, his hand was dark in contrast, but her skin was not the pale white sported by ladies of the *ton*. This girl was a luscious, golden hue. Hair, eyes, skin. As if she was spun from drops of sunlight. Some might consider her hair an ordinary shade of blonde, but a poet would describe it differently. Neither amber nor champagne, the silky straight mane glowed like late summer honey. Rich and shimmery, a tousled fringe of bangs brushed dark, chestnut eyebrows. The playful afternoon breeze sifted through those layers with the gentleness of a lover's fingers.

Grinding his teeth, Nicholas pondered her allure. He despised blonde women. Neither trusted them nor liked them. He certainly did not find them attractive. But something about this one was proving irresistible, even if her family associations made her dangerous. Her cousin, Sebastian, would truly finish him off if he ever learned of their meeting.

"You could encounter Longleigh on your way back," he said, unwilling to release her.

Grace nodded. "I've experience in dealing with him. You've probably precious little when it comes to Lady Celia. I suspect your concern is more for your preservation when it comes to facing her, rather than worry for my safety."

Nicholas swallowed a growl of amused frustration. The way her chin rose indicated she enjoyed their sparring, which incinerated any intention he possessed of keeping his distance. Their back and forth intrigued him...and only made him want her more.

"You'll need protection."

She laughed. Out loud. At him. "Protection? From whom?"

"Longleigh," he snarled, forgetting the fleeting appreciation of her sauciness. What an infuriating brat she was.

"He's not the one currently bruising my arm."

Her breathy sigh of reproach was inflammatory. A sudden need to hear it again, whispering across his bare skin, moaned in his ear, crushed Nicholas with barely restrained lust. His dominant nature reacted strongly when Grace sucked in a tiny breath of air.

She wants me...wants this. Whatever this is...

"Are you always so persistent when offering your protection?" Her head fell back, exposing the elegant line of her neck.

Nicholas wanted to latch onto that warm, soft throat with his teeth, but voices interrupted what he might have said in defense to her question. Or what he may have done in his lust.

"I left her over there. On the floor," Tristan offered, his voice carrying from beyond the bend of gravel pathway.

"Good grief, do not bellow. Why did you kiss her? She's like a sister to us. And how could you leave her like that?" Concern laced Celia's irritated words. "At the very least, you might have laid her on the bench."

An abrupt, rustling noise swallowed Tristan's indiscernible reply.

"Oh, for God's sake," Celia cried out sharply. More shuffling and muttered curses ensued. "Here...take my hand. No, no. I'll pull you up. I swear, Tristan, if I land in those bushes too, I shall never forgive you!"

Under other circumstances, Nicholas might have allowed the others to discover them, watched the young woman beside him squirm in distress. Ordinarily, not a whit would be given for her reputation and certainly not for her embarrassment. His mocking sarcasm would have left Grace bleeding as he revealed her deception. He would have shattered her with clever observations highlighting the wickedness of women.

Faced with the sudden, desperate light in Grace's eyes, he could not resist her unspoken plea. Quickly circling her wrist, he hustled her out of the gazebo and into the yawning entrance of the maze.

They moved quickly through the rows, footsteps silent on the dirt path. When they stopped, Nicholas whirled her around, finger pressing his lips, indicating she should remain silent.

Eyes wide, shocked at being handled with such familiarity, Grace nodded, the forgotten book clutched to her chest.

"I don't know what came over her," Tristan slurred. "I only kissed her. Just a kiss. But it was glorious, even if something about it wasn't quite right. Too much brandy, I suppose."

Releasing Grace's wrist, Nicholas twined their fingers together, his body caging hers against the towering hedge. He brought her hand down, holding it snug by his hip. With a small sound of protest, she attempted sidling away until his eyes flashed a warning.

A grin twitched Nicholas's lips when her movements immediately stilled. He appreciated her reluctant surrender, even though her mouth flattened into a tight line of disapproval.

"Contain yourself, Tristan." Celia's vexation carried into the maze. "Unless you possess a mane, tail, and four hooves, or you've transformed into a frightfully boring book on Greek mythology, Grace barely realizes you exist." Her sigh was heavy. "Are you certain it was this gazebo? There are so many on the estate."

"Yes, yes. I kissed Grace here. She struck me with a damn book...probably gave me a black eye. Then she fainted dead away. I could not rouse her."

"Fainted? More likely feigned it. She has an uncanny knack for outsmarting you, Tristan."

Nicholas and Grace stood so close, they would melt together if either leaned forward one scant inch. While his ears remained tuned to the conversation just feet away, every other sense Nicholas possessed fixed on his hostage pinned against the hedge. An intoxicating fragrance drifted about her, a strange mix of hay, heather and lemons. It had his mouth watering.

Does she truly taste of lemons? Or damned strawberries. Tart or sweet? God, I must find out.

"Could she have come to her senses so quickly?" Tristan asked, his voice tight in acknowledgment of how easily Grace could outsmart him.

"I doubt she ever lost them. Perhaps you did frighten her into a swoon." Celia's placating statement held a slight ring of pity. "Remarkable, not impossible. You are intoxicated and swearing like a Liverpool sailor. It is quite terrifying, actually. Her book is missing so she must have returned to the house. Dear lord, why are you so drunk?"

"Why not, is a better question. Yes, I'm good and goddamned foxed. And Celia, has anything frightened Grace in the past six months?" He muttered an unintelligible curse. "She whirled in, fearless and determined, and I'm trying my damnedest to melt the ice in her veins. Self-absorbed, spoiled girl. That's what she is. With no care for anyone's feelings, damn her."

The girl Tristan referred to with such vehemence lifted her chin. Framed with lush, sable lashes, caramel colored eyes sparkled with incriminating moisture. An inarticulate sound escaped the back of Nicholas's throat, but Grace turned away, staring out at the maze's groomed pathways. From the way her own breath hitched, she was either on the verge of sobbing or laughing hysterically.

There was something dazzling about Lady Grace, framed against the boxwood's vibrant green. She seemed lit from within, shining gold from the inside out; a chaotic little fairy flitting through the maze as she pleased. Whether she lured with beguiling smiles or melancholy stares, any man would eagerly lose himself with her in the cool, verdant shade. Nicholas abruptly realized even he welcomed the opportunity.

To follow her.

Claim her.

Take her.

Deeper. Darker. Until her secrets were laid bare and she writhed beneath him.

A shake of his head dispelled the image. God save the men of London if their eyes ever opened to what lay beneath their noses. Grace Willsdown would either rule the city or leave it in ashes.

Placing a forefinger beneath her chin, Nicholas turned her face toward his. Her eyebrows knitted in consternation, skin pinkening at his perusal. Such a velvety canvas of high cut cheekbones and softly angled lines, unmarred by freckles or blemishes, save for an intriguing scar the size of her smallest fingernail. A miniature half-moon, it curved above the outer edge of her left eyebrow. Curious of its origin, he gently traced it before his fingers drifted over her cheek and down across her mouth.

Brushing the pillowy fullness of her lower lip, the pad of his thumb dipped in exploration. The tiny indentation in its middle was bewitching. Grace's frown unfurled in an instant as he rubbed her lip. Her breath rushed across his thumb, her mouth falling open with the soft pressure.

What a pleasant diversion she could be. If he seduced innocents. And she *was* innocent, her gaze startled and curious. A shame his jaded tastes were indecently carnal—a sweet thing like her would never survive him. Maybe, after a year or two of marriage, bored with whatever husband they pushed upon her, maybe then he might pursue her. When there was no chance of entanglement. Until then, he would remain ignorant of how delicious she surely tasted. He also could not forget she was Sebastian's cousin. The relation she shared with his oldest friend and sworn enemy was enough to keep him hundreds of miles from her.

"You know that's not true, Tristan. How cruel you are, entertaining such thoughts. Grace is kinder than we deserve. Especially you, dear brother. Why you persist in vexing her, I'll never understand," Celia admonished before offering unenthusiastically, "Perhaps she ventured into the maze. Should we look?"

"It's like Satan's lair in that maze," Tristan grumbled. "I lost Grace within it yesterday, and it was two hours before I found my way out of that hellhole. When I returned to the house, hot, sweaty, and scratched from foolish attempts of cutting through hedges, there she sat in the parlor. All cozy. Sharing a pot of tea with Mother and Lady Calmont. She enjoyed more than a few giggles at my expense. No, thank you. I'll not enter this maze, nor another of its kind anytime soon."

Nicholas's hand dropped. The thought of Tristan pursuing this girl sent an uncharacteristic jolt of anger coursing through him. If it happened again, Nicholas decided he would teach the viscount a lesson he'd not soon forget.

"Oh, my darling brother." Celia's tone was soft with sadness. "Did I not warn you? Not to waste your affections? I adore Grace, we all do, but she does not regard you in the same manner. She loves Bellmar Abbey, her books and those horses. And not necessarily in that order. It's better you turn your attention to another. Lady Violet, for example. She's so sweet, and beautiful, and she—"

"Who? Lady Violet...? Oh, damnation, Celia! It's Grace, and only Grace, that I want. I can make her love me. If she would just listen to reason." Tristan's voice rang ugly with frustration and brandy. "She's run wild far too long. I don't know why Father approves of these ventures to Cornwall, wasting time with those damned nags and no supervision. Why does he allow her to go back there again and again? She must be taken in hand. And she won't be able to hold the estate without a husband anyway..."

Feet stomped with haphazard heaviness down the gazebo steps.

"What do you mean to do, Tristan? Don't you dare walk away without telling me."

"It doesn't matter. Forget I said anything. I'm going back to the party now, and I need another drink. Besides, aren't you looking for Richeforte? He arrived a while ago, I hear."

Celia's lighter footsteps followed her brother's unsteady gait. Her reply was annoyed. "He's proving very elusive, capable of disappearing at the snap of a finger. I saw him depart the house, but before I could catch up, he was gone."

"Careful what you wish for, Celia. They call him a wolf for a reason, you know. Nicholas has no interest in the virginal set or securing a wife, for that matter. Prefers livelier game—and no strings attached. While I value his friendship, he's not someone I'd choose for my own sweet sister. He would chew up a little morsel like you, then spit your bones aside without blinking an eye." Tristan chuckled, not unkindly, but in the easy manner of a man intoxicated. "He'll never marry, but if he did, I would actually pity the girl. Richeforte uses the fairer sex for one purpose, and it's not one meant for innocents like you. I wish I was present when you set your cap for him. I would have saved you the trouble."

As the voices grew fainter, the danger of discovery lessening, Nicholas eased away from Grace. She observed him silently, no doubt curious why his friend spoke with such brutal honesty.

Celia's words drifted on the warm breeze, a thread of self-deprecating humor readily apparent. "Don't be crude, Tristan. Perhaps when you abandon the pursuit of Grace, I'll do the same with Richeforte. Although, I suspect it will be far easier for me to remove my cap than you to remove yours."

CHAPTER 3

*S*ilence held before Grace trusted herself with words.

"Let me go, Richeforte."

Her voice was breathlessly high-pitched, a hand still pressed against the duke's hip, their fingers still laced together. For unfathomable reasons, his free hand cupped her jaw, and were it possible to die from pleasure, Grace thought she might expire on the spot. Something fluttery sharp, like a thousand bees set free all at once, tumbled about her stomach.

How strange it was, her willingness to remain a complacent hostage in his arms for this long. This stranger, this man, held her too close, touching her with knowing hands. Searching out secrets she usually hid with precise care. That he was known as the Winter Wolf shook her more than she cared to admit. Was the title a result of his notoriously icy nature or because he devoured women and their foolish hearts? She suspected a combination of both. There was nothing wintery about his touch. His fingers were practically burning her skin.

"Richeforte." The name slipped from her lips in a shaky plea.

Eyes the color of an angry dragon glittered down at her,

scorching and fierce. "May I impart a word of advice, Lady Willsdown?"

Grace swallowed, sensing a restrained violence inside him. It lurked below the civilized exterior. She felt it in the hand on her jaw. Advice? The infamous, immoral Duke of Richeforte offered advice?

"Endeavor not to find yourself alone with Longleigh again."

Grace's mouth tightened. "I assure you, Tristan has always..."

A feral snarl interrupted her. "I'll not repeat myself."

"He is your closest friend."

"And why I know you should not be alone with him."

"What of you?" she responded, brow arched. It was foolish, challenging him, but she couldn't help herself. "Should I be wary of you?"

"Yes. Especially me." Richeforte's grim scowl confirmed. "I am the worst of the worst. Inquire of anyone. Or perhaps you might seek counsel from your own dear cousin and heed his advice."

"Let me loose, and I'll heed yours now."

He released her hand with a mocking bow, eyes glinting with dry humor. "Uncharacteristic of me, but the advice is sincerely given. I don't usually warn my victims."

Grace was compelled to poke at this dangerous creature. And strangely excited by his potential response. What caused such a reaction within her was unknown, other than the fact that he was infuriatingly arrogant thinking he possessed any right in dictating her actions.

"It's rumored you do not possess a soul." Her heart raced as if it might burst from her chest as she mocked him. "I shall gladly spread word this is untrue. The Duke of Richeforte is surprisingly tenderhearted and eagerly assisted a lady when the need arose."

His reaction sent a giddy little tingle racing along her veins. Oh, she was foolish, tweaking his nose like this!

Eyes wide in disbelief, Richeforte growled, "Little fool. Not only will Ravenswood try snapping my bones like twigs if he learns of this encounter, you'll find your reputation in tatters should you even casually mention—"

"If you keep our secret, my honor will remain untarnished and my cousin will not kill you." Grace interrupted with a cheeky grin. While Richeforte regarded her with wary suspicion, she stood on tiptoes, placing her palms on either side of his cheeks. "As for your own wicked reputation, perhaps I'll destroy it with anonymous tales of your extraordinary kindness."

It could hardly be categorized as a kiss when her lips brushed his; it was more a soft suggestion of a whisper. For a timeless second, they both stood frozen. Then, face flaming pink, Grace fled the maze. But long after her hasty retreat, the heat of Richeforte's gaze lingered on her skin, a warmth she savored. Like time spent basking in the summer sun.

WHY DID YOU DO THAT, YOU STUPID, STUPID GIRL? THE question pounded in Grace's brain, over and over.

What occurred inside that maze should have alarmed her, and if she had an ounce of sense, the niggling thought she should have stayed would be ignored. Sebastian would be rightly horrified if he ever discovered she'd willingly kissed his old enemy. And Tristan would explode with misplaced jealousy.

Oh, what possessed her? Why did she kiss him? Although technically, it was merely a touching of skin. No more significant than a touching of fingertips. Or knees. Or even elbows brushing against another...

Blast it. I cannot ignore how I felt.

No, she could not easily dismiss the compelling urge that had dragged her forward, up onto her toes, until her lips pressed his. No explaining why her hands itched to explore the washboard structure of his abdomen, the iron bandings of muscles her fingertips felt through his shirt and waistcoat. Just after she had brushed her lips against his, Grace found herself fantasizing. Richeforte was picking her up, his large palms cradling her rump. He pinned her against a vine covered pillar. Kissed her until she forgot her name. And moaned his. More than anything else, the shocking images her mind produced sent her fleeing the maze as if fire chased her. With her brain turned to mush, she nearly tripped on the loose gravel during her hasty escape.

Now, hours later, she was still a hopeless bundle of nerves, her lips tingling as if they'd just touched his. Still plagued by wicked thoughts she had no business entertaining. She would almost certainly see him at dinner that evening; retaining her composure would be difficult after everything experienced while in his company.

She worried needlessly. Their formal introduction, as other guests entered the grand dining room, fell curiously flat. There was only a brief moment when Grace feared he might reveal their previous encounter and that was when Tristan pulled her forward, his hand set possessively on her waist. Richeforte's eyebrow rose in question before she tactfully removed the viscount's hand. A conspiratorial half-smile lifted the corner of her mouth when she laid a finger against her lips, indicating silence in the same manner he affected while they hid inside the maze.

He flashed a smirk of acknowledgment, the twin dimples in his cheeks stabbing her heart like miniature arrows before disappearing. He casually introduced the baroness hanging on his arm, and Grace was promptly ignored from that moment forward. For the rest of the evening, whenever her gaze helplessly wandered in the duke's direction, his attention was elsewhere.

He'd forgotten Grace's existence, and everywhere he sauntered, Lady Ralston and her bountiful bosom trotted behind him, determined to stay at his side. He ignored the baroness, apparently unconcerned whether she accompanied him or not.

"It's said Lord Ralston died in her bed. Trapped beneath her," Celia huffed, determined in repeating every bit of gossip concerning the cold-eyed redhead.

"Celia," Grace murmured in bemused warning. She knew of Lady Ralston's exploits even before making her acquaintance. The woman was a notorious figure, and rightly so. She switched lovers as easily as other women changed their shoes.

"It's most likely true. Just look at her. I've yet to see her smile at anyone other than Richeforte. She probably froze her poor husband to death. Like a chilly blanket," Celia pouted, tugging a curled lock of her chocolate brown hair. Dinner was over, and they stood in a drawing room where open doors led to a small terrace. "What does His Grace see in her?"

"They make the perfect couple. Ice cold, the pair of them. But, we should not dwell on their attraction for one another."

"There are at least two things *he* finds attractive." Celia took a gulp of punch, glaring with no subtlety whatsoever across the space where Lady Ralston and Richeforte stood engaged in conversation with the Earl of Stoketon. "They're in danger of popping free of her bodice. Wouldn't that be a conversation starter at breakfast tomorrow?"

Grace choked on a laugh. Her eyes touched on Lady Ralston's bosom, where it did seem the aforementioned breasts might make an appearance. Helene Ralston's reputation was well-deserved. The baroness was meaner than the last snake in Ireland, and she was glued to Richeforte's side. Occasionally, she smoothed a palm over the arm of his formal coat while the duke tolerated her attention, a hand resting occasionally in the small of her back with a cold politeness. Grace's heart twisted a little. How foolish she was, wanting the heavy heat of his hand on *her* back.

Celia sighed. "He's a complete savage, but Richeforte is far more interesting than any other man in attendance. Don't you agree?"

Grace murmured a noncommittal reply as Celia continued, almost dreamily. "They say an actress killed herself last year when he ended their affair. Anne Adamson. She was a pretty little thing; Violet and I saw her last performance at the Lyceum, just before she did herself in. You see, Richeforte decided the Earl of Banberry's wife was more to his liking, and poor Anne was dropped as if she carried the plague." Celia grimaced with sympathy. "She was heartbroken. You could see it in her overly pale features, and she sobbed during all of her scenes. The understudy was called upon so the play could finish its run. Days later, Anne was discovered sprawled in a pool of blood on the floor of her dressing room. Drank herself to death, the gossips say. Poor Violet was so distraught over the news, she wept on my shoulder when next we saw each other. She's such a tenderhearted thing," Celia said, referring to her childhood friend. Lady Violet Everstone was incredibly lovely, and very shy, with a headful of deep, auburn hair and eyes so darkly blue they were nearly amethyst in color.

"Celia. We shouldn't be discussing such things. I know your mother would not approve." Grace tried sounding disapproving, but she leaned toward her friend, desperate to hear more.

"Oh, posh. I heard Mother discussing this very subject with Lady Overton. It's how I learned of the duke's very last mistress, the one before the baroness. That would be Elizabeth, Lady Banberry. Now, that one, the brazen hussy, decided she would leave her husband for Richeforte, but no sooner than she did so, the duke spurned her. Told her she should crawl back to Lord Banberry. Beg forgiveness of the first husband rather than hunt herself a second." Celia shook her head, sipping a cup of lemonade. "Banberry, being ever so accommodating, accepted Elizabeth's apologies, then promptly shuttled her off to some remote estate. She's gone a little mad, Mother said. That she does nothing but write letters, dozens and dozens of them, all addressed to Richeforte. Begging that he reconsider their affair."

Both girls watched Richeforte across the room. The man possessed an easy, confident manner, his caustic wit adding immeasurably to his appeal. It certainly did not hurt that he resembled a Greek god. All sinewy, lean muscle and breathtakingly handsome features. His strongly cut jawline was sheer perfection, the shaggy cut of his dark blond hair providing a sharp contrast to the trimmed styles preferred by his colleagues.

Celia breathed deep, leaning against one of the pillars delineating the large room. "What do you suppose makes a man like that so irresistible? So tantalizing, a woman would kill herself in despair when he tires of her? Does he entice with money? His wicked reputation? Power? Or is it strictly in the bedchamber where he enthralls her using his expertise?"

"You shouldn't—*we* shouldn't be discussing such things," Grace said nervously, tugging the lace cuffs of her rose-hued dress until they lay in a dainty line at the bend of her elbow. She recalled the duke's nonchalant remark regarding his luck with actresses. How callous he sounded.

"Richeforte collects woman the way other men collect cravats." Ignoring Grace's admonishment, Celia wrapped an arm about her narrow waist. "They are for his amusement. And he's as careless with them as a wolf toying with a frightened rabbit. I'm afraid his horrid reputation does nothing in diminishing his appeal, however. Women trip over their own feet if he crooks a smile in their general direction, and even Baroness Ralston is completely smitten with him. There's something to be said for attempting to tame such a creature. Even a horrid thing like her will try."

"Let us talk no more about the duke. Gossip of his conquests is unnerving." Grace shuddered, turning her back on the trio. She imagined the heat of Richeforte's eyes tracing her spine, then realized how foolish that was. His Grace had no interest in her.

Celia nodded in agreement. "All right. I will instead apologize for Tristan's actions today. I know he kissed you." She smiled gently at Grace. "It doesn't help matters at all, but my brother does adore you."

Grace blinked in abrupt awareness. Had Nicholas March kissed her, she would not have resisted, despite his arrogance. "What Tristan loves most is the hunt...the chase. Not me. I care for him, Celia, in the same manner I care for you. You are like brother and sister to me, and I'll never see either of you differently."

Locating Tristan across the room, a twinge of unease tugged the pit of her stomach. As if aware of Grace's thoughts, the viscount raised a glass in salute. His dark eyes turned somber, drifting with purpose from her and landing on the duke. Wearing a slight frown, he made his way toward the small group, and Grace breathed a sigh of relief that he was not headed her way.

"I know, dearest," Celia replied sadly. "We shall all be relieved when he realizes it. His heart will be shattered though."

"No more than it would destroy mine if I lost Bellmar Abbey and my horses." Grace's chin lifted slightly. "I won't marry. Neither Longleigh nor any man. I've no intention of allowing another the rights to what is mine. I swore on my mother's grave and the memory of my father, I would keep Bellmar Abbey. And I *will*."

CHAPTER 4

Down this dark tunnel
behind a fortress of indifference
walls of pride and callous fences
my honor hides.
~Nicholas August Harris March
Ninth Duke of Richeforte

"*There, there, darling.*"

Mother's crooning held a faraway quality beyond his comprehension. "Won't you try a bit harder, my little love? To please him? Things would be easier if only you tried harder..." She stroked his tousled hair, darkly golden with perspiration and tears.

Nodding, face pressed against her hip, he sobbed with broken breaths into the cool silk of her gown. His thin legs burned. And his back. The sting of the duke's riding crop left little streams of fire trailing across his skin. He was five years of age. He should not be crying like a baby. He also should not have tumbled from his pony's broad back during that last jump.

"I will try, Mama." Leaning back, he stared into the mossy hued sadness of his mother's eyes. "I will."

The door of Her Grace's private suite flew open, his father bursting in, wild-eyed and shaking with rage. "I knew I'd find him here, sniveling into your skirts. Get out from behind your mother, boy. Damnit, what a disgrace you are! Weak, useless. Why was I cursed with such a stupid, lazy child? It's your doing, Brianna, turning him soft...encouraging those damned scribblings. By God, I'll fix him. I'll mold him into a duke if it's the last thing I do." With one hand, he snatched his son up by his narrow shoulder, ignoring the blood that seeped through the linen shirt.

Mother intervened with a sharp cry of alarm, grasping her husband's arm, but the duke half-turned, slapping her with a casual brutality across the cheek. Like a cut flower, she crumpled to the floor. The boy wailed, a sad, mournful sound. He forgot his own injury at the sight of his mother so dreadfully abused.

The duke's attention returned to the pale, trembling victim held tight in his savage grip. "Richeforte falls to you one day," he spat, one cruel hand moving to the scuff of the boy's neck, holding him as if he were a rabid gutter rat. "I won't let you destroy what I've built! Do you hear me? Do you?"

Blows fell, one after another. Like raindrops from a grey sky, melding the line between the heavens and storms that raged without mercy. The world rumbled, bright with lightning and booming thunderbolts. Blinding flashes of gunfire surrounded him. The aroma of green grass, wet with dew assailed his nostrils and the warm, sweet scent of his pony mingled with the coppery tang of blood. Men shouted, frantic calls for the physician. His mother wept into a white silk handkerchief. When he pried his eyes open, Sebastian Cain, the Earl of Ravenswood loomed over him, face twisted with hatred, hatred like his father, the Duke of Richeforte always wore.

A cloying, desperate cloak of misery covered him. Swirling faces twisting together, bits and pieces of time blurring into nothingness...and all of it cold. So damned cold and desolate.

Nicholas woke, drenched in sweat. A feminine form pinned

him to the mattress. Swiping a forearm across his damp brow, he inhaled several deep breaths to banish the remnants of the recurring dream. As was his custom since recovering from the duel with his best friend nearly six years before, he absently rubbed the puckered divot scarring his left thigh.

The Baroness of Ralston lay draped across his midsection. Nicholas frowned. He did not invite her to stay. Women were never extended an invitation, and he never actually *slept* with them. They were dismissed once they tended his needs. Prostitute or nobility, it didn't matter; all suffered the same treatment.

A hard slap across the baroness's round buttocks sent her scrambling to the other side of the bed.

"*Ouch!*" The glow of the banked fire illuminated Helene's resentful yet pleased scowl while Nicholas rolled from the bed in a smooth motion, heedless of his nudity.

"You're such a beast, Nick." Her eyes greedily traversed the length of his body.

"You should return to your own room. Before the hour grows too late and someone sees you." *Jesus. I need a robe. Or a suit of armor.*

"I'll stay until morning."

Pouring a brandy from the decanter on the dressing table, Nicholas spoke over his shoulder. "No. You won't."

The baroness should gather her things and depart his room here at Calmont Downs as quickly as when she visited his exclusive corner of Mayfair. Flicking her a glance when she expelled an irritated sigh, he watched impassively as she arranged herself in a most provocative manner; stomach flat upon the mattress, pale rump slightly lifted and exposed amongst the tangled sheets. She slowly brought one leg up, bending it at the knee, a wavy mass of red hair streaming to her waist. That hair was most recently wrapped about his fists while he thrust repeatedly into her mouth.

Nicholas's gaze dropped. While in the heat of things, he

remembered imagining Helene's hair as straight and golden, flowing over and through his hands like liquid sunshine. A pair of bronzed topaz eyes, not icy blue, gazing up at him. And the mouth encompassing him was a soft rose pink, not Helene's blood red. Damn if the earlier fantasy wasn't arousing him now.

During dinner, he could hardly tear his eyes away from Grace Willsdown. That heart-shaped face, with its stubborn chin and high cheekbones, was not the beauty set by society's rules, but it was lovely just the same. There was something about the girl that left Nicholas a little dazed. Every time she laughed, his eyes sought her out. When gentlemen swarmed around her during a lively conversation regarding Irish racers, he felt like barreling into their midst, throwing her over his shoulder, and carting her off so he'd have her full attention. He would have dragged her into some dark corner. Taken her sweet mouth. Claimed her for himself.

The unruly thoughts made him angry. With her. With Tristan. With the Earl of Ravenswood. Mostly, his own lack of control infuriated him. Control was important. It carried him through disaster, and the knowledge old friends no longer held faith in his honor. Lifting him above censure and his own self-hatred, that control was his very existence. It was quickly disintegrating, and all because of a silly, blonde chit.

When the baroness slipped into his room just after midnight, Nicholas found himself in a devil of a mood. He took his erstwhile mistress so roughly, he left bruises, his frustration soaring because her hair was not shimmery blonde, her eyes not dark honey, her skin pale white instead of Grace Willsdown's gold-dusted ivory. Helene did not mind his roughness. She never did.

Helene's blue eyes narrowed as she watched him now. The softness of her voice belied the aggravation evident in her grip of the pillow clutched between her breasts. "You seem interested in what awaits you here."

Pulled from his memories, Nicholas's gaze deliberately

dropped where his semi-erection rose between his legs. "Trust me. You have no part in this." Pulling on a pair of sleeping pants, he willed his arousal's demise.

"That cruel streak of yours is showing," Helene shot back.

"You had no complaints earlier. When you begged for more. Harder. Deeper. More vicious. You always do."

"You were...different tonight, Richeforte. I cannot explain it."

Richeforte. Would he always flinch when called by that hated name? If only the title could rot with the man from whom it was inherited. Maybe the cruelty, this coldness inside him would die too. Maybe, but doubtful.

Nicholas did not hide the sneer in his voice. "Can't explain why you love it?"

Taunting Helene brought no response. She enjoyed his savagery during sex, liked being dominated, loved the roughness. Their affair centered around it, although lately her participation had become a desperate clinging, morphing into hope for something more. She desired a connection, a permanent relationship, as impossible as that was. Women were temporary solutions to satisfy his lust, and he'd cultivated his reputation based on that fact. When gossips called him the Winter Wolf - behind his back, of course - it only steeled his resolve in remaining aloof and unattached.

There could never be anything more than a superficial arrangement with the women he encountered simply because something within him was absent. No one was allowed inside his icy world, not after the disaster with Sebastian Cain and Marilee. And because of his father. Whatever was once soft and tender inside him was beaten out with a riding crop by that hated man and destroyed by those he once called friends.

Accepting defeat, Helene sat up, the pillow falling away and exposing her naked breasts. "You'll have to help me with my gown. I can't reach the buttons in the back."

"Completely unnecessary. If you encounter anyone in the halls, mention your habit of sleepwalking."

"I don't sleepwalk," she gritted out.

"If someone comes across you, you do." Nicholas tossed a gown and a few undergarments onto the bed, ignoring her mutterings. "Hurry, my dear. Unless you enjoy dressing in the hall."

He maneuvered her into the corridor in record time, closing the door with a firm click, but seconds later the hushed, angry raps of her knuckles sounded on the oak.

"Richeforte? I don't have my bloody sho—"

The heavy portal swung open, the forgotten slippers shoved into her hands, the door slammed and locked again, all in an unhurried, brusque manner. Nicholas sighed in relief as Helene moved down the hall, cursing the entire time.

Morning was close. Dangerously so. Beyond the bedroom window drapes, shifting shades of black and charcoal grey shrouded Calmont Down's sprawling landscape. Stepping over to the desk, he withdrew a battered leather-bound journal and quickly scrawled the lines of verse he'd dreamed. It was a habit when he awoke. It helped him focus, calmed his nerves. A pitiful way of dealing with the darkness lurking inside him; putting to paper his even darker thoughts.

Many times, the lines made little sense. Often, he was inspired to write a complete stanza. He kept the "scribbles", as his father once referred to them, in a walnut chest. He'd filled dozens of journals over the years, all private, certainly not intended for anyone's eyes other than his own.

Looking over the words, Nicholas frowned. He pulled out a bottle of setting powder and sprinkled a little over the page. While it dried, he peered into the darkness from the vantage point of the fourth-floor room, idly wondering how much longer until the sun rose.

A slight movement in the pre-dawn darkness caught his

attention. Someone had just exited the manor near the kitchens and now rushed down the path toward the stables. A stable boy, based on the dark coat, breeches and cap. Returning from a secret assignment with a kitchen maid, no doubt.

A pale sliver of remaining moonlight broke through the clouds, and with it, a robust gust of wind. Snatched away by the breeze, the person's cap flew off, revealing a braided gold waterfall of hair tumbling over delicate shoulders. Hardly a stable boy after all, but a girl. Illuminated in a pool of light, she scampered after the cap as it cartwheeled end over end. When it was finally within her grasp and jammed back into place, shiny locks tucked securely beneath it, her gaze lifted. Apparently satisfied no one watched from the numerous glassy eyes of the mansion's windows, she tugged her coat closer and turned again toward the stables.

Cold, surprising fury bombarded Nicholas.

He counted.

One through ten.

Contemplation. Decision. Anticipation.

Whatever business Lady Grace Willsdown attended at this hour, or more precisely, whomever she hurried to meet, was now his concern.

"OH, YOU CLEVER CREATURE...HOW DID YOU KNOW WHAT was hiding there? Stop now...that tickles! All right. Wait a moment. I'll pull them out for you...but if you bully me, you'll get nothing and be glad for it," Grace giggled, half-turning her body. "You beast. You'll ruin it, shaking it so!"

Mildly exasperated by the gelding's playfulness, she hopped, snatching her cap from between his teeth. The thoroughbred had already ruined one hat two days before. When the horse kept his head high, just out of reach, Grace relented. Three sugar cubes were withdrawn from her coat's inner pocket.

The gelding promptly dropped the cap, stretching his neck and lipping at the treats in Grace's palm. While he crunched the cubes, she retrieved the cap, jammed it into her coat pocket, and continued tacking the sleek animal inside the dark box stall. Slipping on the bridle, she carefully avoided hitting the metal against Percy's teeth. For an animal so mouthy and curious, eagerly picking up almost anything in exploration, he'd always been touchy regarding the placement of a bit.

"I'm grateful we became reacquainted, Percy. You've made my mornings here pleasant, and I'll miss you terribly when I leave. Will you miss me, handsome boy? And our morning rides?" The steady stream of soft chatter was a habit around horses. All the foals she raised were accustomed to it, and the gelding Lord Calmont purchased two years ago still remembered her. Gathering the reins, she turned with the intention of opening the stall, when Percy pushed her forward with a nudge of his large head.

"Percy! Not so rough, mind you! Will you have me covered in bruises for your impatience?"

No sooner were the words from her mouth when the stall door flew open. Grace stifled a scream, scrambling backward.

Standing in the stable aisleway, Richeforte loomed in her path. By the flickering light of a single lantern, Grace saw a riding crop, held tight in his hand like a sword. Percy flung his head high, snorting and sidestepping until she soothed him with a quiet word.

The fury on the duke's face was frightening.

"Where is he?"

"Richeforte! You scared me half out of my wits!"

"*Where. Is. He?*"

Grace was confused by the level of emotion contained in those three words. "The stable lad? I sent him back to bed. The

41

poor boy is sick. Besides, I could saddle a horse in pitch darkness if needed—"

"Not the bloody stable boy. Whomever you were talking to. Where is he, damn it?"

"Oh, you mean Percy." Grace blushed. "Quite the one-sided conversation, wasn't it?"

"Lord Blanton's son? That Percy? Tell him to come out of that stall. If I must come in after him, things will end badly." A muscle ticked in Richeforte's jaw, his green eyes shaded black as ebony in the flickering light. Astonished by his conclusions, Grace giggled.

The heat in his eyes flared higher than the lantern's flames.

"I'm sorry. I don't mean to laugh, really. It's just there is no one else. Only myself and Percy." Grace stroked the bay's black muzzle. "Say hello, Percy. The Duke of Richeforte joins us this fine morning. You'll excuse him, my lord, if he doesn't bow. I did not have the chance to teach him before Lord Calmont took possession."

"Who are you meeting, Grace? Tell me now."

"I told you...it's only me. And Percy."

"I'm not a fool."

Grace shrugged, her amused gaze locking with his. "I did not think you were, my lord. I've no reason to lie. You may check the stall if you like." She led the gelding out, waiting in the aisle while the duke quickly examined the stall. When he turned back to her, her brow arched as she cheerfully stated, "A simple apology will suffice."

"I'm Richeforte. I never apologize," he replied calmly, although his voice seemed rougher than before. "What should I think when you sneak away and I hear what sounds like a conversation with a lover?"

"I wonder why you would think on my actions at all." Grace tilted her head. "Pardon my confusion, my lord. Were you concerned for my safety? My reputation?" Her quick intake of breath revealed her amusement. "Oh! Were you coming to my rescue?"

When her gaze pointedly touched on the crop he still held, Richeforte flung it aside with a muttered curse. "I don't give a goddamn what you do, but after my warning yesterday..."

Her laugh interrupted him. "You are wearing the same clothes you wore to dinner, shirttails untucked..." her nose wrinkled, "and you reek of Lady Ralston's perfume. How did you know I was here, I wonder? Oh, goodness...did you just come from her bed? Or were you meeting her in the stables?"

Grace swiveled, expecting to see the woman emerge from an empty stall, picking straw from her hair. Why she felt a tiny sting of jealousy with the mention of Lady Ralston's cloying perfume, she had no idea. She hated the envy evident in her words. Richeforte's head would likely swell to unmanageable proportions if he suspected she harbored the tiniest bit of interest in his choice of companion.

"There's no need for secrecy, my lord. No one gives a pauper's shilling if you two share a bed. Or a stall." *Except maybe Celia. She'd like Helene Ralston's head on a platter if possible. Perhaps I might as well.*

"*How* I knew you were here does not matter," he said coldly. "*Why* you are here does."

"It's rather obvious, I think. Lord Calmont gave permission I could ride as I wish. It's best no one sees me dressed in this manner, so here I am. Before the rest of the world wakes up."

His eyes flickered over her body. When his gaze darkened even more, Grace suppressed a shiver.

"Without a groom? Unsafe and unwise."

"Which is why I ride Percy. I bred, raised, and trained him. He's completely dependable, although very mischievous." Looping the reins over the gelding's neck, she released him. Like Llyr, her prized stallion at Bellmar Abbey, Percy would not venture far from the sugar cubes in her pocket. "You've develóped an interesting approach in maintaining my flawless reputation. This is the second time you've placed yourself in a position where it would be difficult explaining an otherwise innocent situation."

"Nothing about this is innocent," he growled.

Grace blinked. "I assure you, my lord. This is fraught with innocence. Dripping with it, actually."

CHAPTER 5

*And my demons always know
the depths of sincerity when I whisper,
Come out! Come out!*
*~Nicholas August Harris March
Ninth Duke of Richeforte*

*N*icholas clenched his teeth. *Her choice of words is intentional. She's deliberately throwing the tantalizing prize of her virginity in my lap. Damned little tease.*

"Your Grace," the reminder came out in a grow.

Amusement danced in Grace's eyes, even half-concealed as they were by that ridiculous cap. His gaze traveled over her, taking in the dark brown coat fitted to her body's trim proportions. *St. Simon's Cross, her legs go on for miles.* Encased in black breeches and knee-high leather boots dyed the same color, he'd like those legs wrapped about his waist, her heels digging into his lower back as he invaded her flesh.

Nicholas stepped back, stunned by the erotic vision in his mind's eye. It wasn't wise, getting too close, not when he teetered on the verge of turning visions into reality. He'd shove her onto a pile of fresh hay, rip the boots and breeches from those long legs, tear off her tidy coat and the dark green shirt, and when she was finally bare, fall upon her like a ravening wolf. Consume every bit of her innocence. And that shining braid of hair? He'd use it as a handle, directing her placement as he wished.

Raising a hand to his brow, Nicholas rubbed hard. A pitiful attempt at erasing his thoughts.

"You are a puzzle, my lord," Grace finally said, head cocked slightly. "You claim disinterest in my actions, yet here you are. You don't seem to care for your title, but you insist I call you by it. Why is this, I wonder?"

"Even the Devil likes to be called by name."

"That's not an explanation," she scoffed. "Perhaps if we knew one another better, you would not care to stand on formalities."

Knew each other better? He wanted to know her in every way, shape and form possible. Her innocence irritated him, goading a harsh response.

"Honeybee, you don't want to know me. I haven't a drop of honorable blood in my entire body. I'm cold. Selfish. Hollow. And I enjoy the reputation my cruelty has gained me." Her eyes widened. Was it because of his honesty or the new pet name bestowed on her? "Those are my most admirable qualities, according to the unfortunate few who call themselves my friends."

Undaunted, Grace leaned forward as if imparting a secret. "I don't believe you. That makes you sound like an ordinary monster. Your inclination of rushing to the rescue when I least expect it indicates there must be something else that redeems you."

Nicholas recognized the thread of humor in her tone, and even he couldn't explain his intentions upon picking up that riding crop. But the instant he believed Grace was in danger, he was prepared to beat the perpetrator into a bloody pulp for daring to lay a hand on her.

Now, she was grinning at him. Teasing him. Enticing him.

Nicholas gave in. Coming closer, he almost hesitantly trailed a finger over the curve of her cheek, marveling at its velvet softness. Grace's eyes drifted shut for a brief second, but she did not shy away.

"So, a tidbit of personal information will make my disappointing lack of character easier to bear," Nicholas murmured, the request pondered. After a moment, a tiny smile lifted the corner of his mouth. "Watercress."

"Beg pardon?" she whispered, swaying forward until he detected the scent of the soap she must use. It was clean and fresh. Wild heather and lemons. And rainstorms.

"Watercress. Those green leaves people insist on cramming between two slices of bread and declaring fit for consumption. A vile substance, it has no taste, gets caught in one's teeth and serves no purpose that I can determine. Watercress is banned from all my estates. Saving countless victims from gruesome, freckled smiles."

"Watercress." Grace regarded him as if he'd gone mad.

"Yes." Nicholas's eyes sparked. "Are you comforted by this? Relieved? Does this make me less a monster?"

"It should make you more so since I adore watercress sandwiches. A monster would hardly care if his victims lay drenched head to toe in it. However, you only prove the point, my lord. You can't be that terrible if you worry for the victim's dental health."

"Ah, but their appearance must please me before I devour them. Even monsters have standards." His gaze swept her, imagining her trussed and plated as the main entree on his dining room table. "A pity you like the stuff. Perhaps I'll make an exception and expand my palate."

Kissing her would help...maybe. At least he would discover the flavor of her mouth. He'd thought of little else since finding her on that gazebo floor. Abandoning all previous reasons for avoidance, Nicholas closed the distance between them.

Grace's attention shifted to a point over his shoulder. "Oh, no."

He clutched the waist of her coat in case she considered escape, then rubbed the garment between his index finger and thumb. The fabric was rough, a sturdy material often used for servants' garbs, but the coat was modified so it fit her proportions perfectly. The same went for the breeches and the shirt. Seeing her atop a horse, one would think from she was merely a stable lad.

"Not a good idea," she murmured.

"I agree." Nicholas inhaled sharply, brushing his nose alongside hers. It was electrifying. Sparks practically ignited between their bodies. "This is a terrible idea. Because once I begin, I won't stop. I'll take all of you, even the pieces you don't realize exist. I won't stop until we are both ruined."

"No, you see, oh. Goodness, he found—"

"Hush now," he ordered. Her words made little sense.

Until they did.

Nicholas felt a nudge to his back. *Bloody hell. Tristan.* He must have stumbled across them. Or he intended meeting Grace all along. What a mess of magnificent, hellish proportions this would be.

With the second bump, he swung about, eager for confrontation. Two thoughts consumed him. Dispatch Tristan Buchanan. And return to Grace's lips. Lips that beckoned him. Entranced him. Made him forget friendships and oaths and vows of avoidance; all those foolish promises he couldn't possibly keep now.

It wasn't Tristan confronting him, but Percy, the curved handle of a metal coal scuttle clenched between his teeth. Tiny grey clouds poofed in the cool air as he banged it back and forth with excessive glee, occasionally striking Nicholas in the chest.

"The scuttle," Grace squeaked, peeking around him. "Oh, please! Don't grab—!"

When Nicholas reached for his bridle, Percy flung his head

48

high, shaking the bucket as if it were a new toy. Soot exploded, coating everything in blackish grey.

An enormous cloud of ash billowed into the air when the horse released the scuttle with a snort of alarm. The clatter it created on the stone paved floor sent the gelding bolting sideways.

"—that," Grace finished lamely. Nicholas's broad back provided a shield from any soot landing on her, and she could not see the full effect of the gelding's mischievous behavior as her explanation tumbled forth. "Percy adores anything he can pick up with his mouth. If you try taking it away, he thinks it is a game. That's what you overheard earlier. You see, he had my cap, and he'd already ruined one..."

The explanation trailed off as Nicholas slowly rotated. Grace gasped, her expression morphing from amazement into amused horror. From the top of his head to his untucked shirt hem, he was covered in soot, face and neck discolored black. In the midst of it all, his eyes were stark white orbs, the irises glowing with the darkness of the devil's gaze.

He held his temper by the thinnest of threads as they stared at one another. Then, bubbling from this infernal creature came a sound that could scarcely be believed.

Laughter. Peals and roars of it. Grace laughed until she gripped her stomach, overcome by such hilarity, she couldn't catch her own breath.

Grunting in annoyance, Nicholas reached out, but with a squeal of alarm, she ducked beneath his arm, escaping down the aisleway. He couldn't chase her. Damned if he could see more than a foot in front of him, blinded as he was by soot.

"I'm sorry, my lord. So terribly sorry. Truly." Grace caught Percy's reins, the gelding nickering and bumping his head against her side while she wiped tears from her cheeks. Even the cursed horse was laughing at him. "You'd best hurry along to the kitchens and get cleaned up. Cook probably has just the thing to remove soot. And don't worry. I won't tell a soul." A giggle undermined the depths of her sincerity as she assured him, "It shall be our secret."

She swung up on the horse, a delicate, purposeful motion highlighting the delightful curve of her arse in the tight breeches, and Nicholas nearly bit his tongue in two.

Thank God for small miracles. I'm not completely blind.

On the verge of combusting from fury, but not blind. He saw her well enough as she trotted out of the stables, out of reach, her spine perfectly straight. As straight as that braid of sunshine hanging down her back.

GRACE DID NOT SEE NICHOLAS AGAIN UNTIL TEATIME, BUT she thought of him incessantly during their time apart. How he looked at her, as if he might kiss her. The husky growl of his voice. The warning he wouldn't stop until they were both ruined had the opposite effect than he probably intended.

Inside, she was screaming, *Yes, yes! Ruin me! Show me what happens beyond kisses. The same as that between a stallion and a mare? Is it accomplished in a similar manner? Are men, their... sexes... do they become as large as horse when aroused? Surely, that isn't possible. It would be entirely uncomfortable. Not to mention the difficulty concealing the proceedings...horse breeding is such a messy, ear-piercing affair. Everyone would know when a man and a woman actually...*

Thoughts of how such matters might work consumed her during her morning ride.

Now, watching the duke stride across the perfectly manicured lawn toward the table set up on the rose garden terrace, that tall, muscular form of his displayed in a dark grey afternoon jacket and tight-fitting black trousers, Grace's cheeks pinkened. If any male possessed the honor of comparison with a stallion, Nicholas March was a prime candidate.

"Good afternoon, Your Grace. Won't you join us?" Lady Calmont exclaimed, her face alight with excitement. She possessed a soft spot for the duke, catering to his every need since his arrival. Bemused, Grace watched as she instructed a footman in moving a chair beside Celia's.

Nicholas paused before seating himself, eyes momentarily narrowing when noting the close proximity between Tristan and Grace. "How kind of you. I trust I am not intruding."

"Not at all, Your Grace! Your presence could never be intrusive. There is an abundance of treats, as you can see." Lady Calmont impatiently shooed the footman away so she could pour Nicholas's tea. "Please, help yourself to whatever you desire."

Nicholas's gaze latched onto Grace at the elderly woman's invitation, and a smirk lifted his lip. "Thank you. I can scarcely restrain myself from tasting all of it."

Grace felt her cheeks grow warm.

He reached for a tiny sandwich while at the same time Grace warned, in all seriousness, "I wouldn't eat that if I were you."

The advice was ignored as Nicholas popped the entire thing into his mouth. A grimace formed, expressed as a frown between his eyebrows, followed by a choking cough. After a few moments, he finally swallowed with great difficulty and took a healthy gulp from the cup a wide-eyed Lady Calmont set before him.

"I did try warning you," Grace muttered under her breath, smoothing the stomach of her bright, lemon yellow day gown. "Watercress, you see."

"Are you all right, Your Grace? Did it go down the wrong pipe, as it were? Perhaps we should get you some lemonade." Celia's lips pursed with concern, ignoring her mother's quelling glares. If Lady Darby was not sitting right there, and she thought she could get away with it, Celia probably would have rubbed Nicholas's back to ease his distress.

"No... I'm fine, just an aversion to watercress." he choked.

"Other than the bread, everything about that was green," Grace pointed out.

"I was temporarily blinded in a freak accident this morning," Nicholas said once he regained control of his breath. "My vision has not yet returned to normal."

Grace's hands folded in her lap. *What a fibber he is! His eyesight is perfectly fine. He's having no problems glaring at me.*

"My apologies on your injury. I do hope there is no lasting damage."

"Only to my pride, Lady Willsdown."

Those tiny, elusive, heart-melting dimples flitted into view. Transfixed, the other ladies stared at Nicholas, but he ignored them. His eyes bored into Grace.

"How is it you know Richeforte despises watercress, Lady Grace?" Tristan asked in the chasm of sudden silence. Five sets of eyes turned in her direction.

Grace's gaze flitted to Nicholas as he shrugged, eyebrow raised as if wondering the same.

That's how it's to be? In retaliation for this morning? Oh, the scoundrel!

She'd have no help from him explaining their previous encounter.

"Yes," Nicholas drawled in that husky voice that softened her insides and her brain for good measure. "Enlighten us. I confess, I'm curious as well."

"Your reputation precedes you, my lord." Grace took a calm sip of tea, thinking fast. "Tales of your hatred for watercress abound in polite society. It's a safe subject...safer than how many women compete for your attention."

CHAPTER 6

A shocked gasp escaped Lady Calmont, a hand held to her wrinkled throat as if she swallowed a whole lump of sugar along with her tea.

Lady Darby muttered beneath her breath, shooting her daughter and Grace a look that could not be misconstrued. The clatter of her delicate bone china teacup on its saucer gained everyone's attention.

"Celia, I'm sure you and Grace would like a bit of rest before this evening's activities." Her tone brooked no argument as she regarded her daughter and ward. "Have you decided on your gown for tonight? Has your maid seen to its pressing?"

Grace did not wish to retire to her room; this particular conversation, and Nicholas's irritated frown, was very amusing. An unexpected thrill existed in verbally sparring with the rigidly polished duke, although she wisely chose against examining that fact too closely.

"If you will excuse us, Lady Calmont, Mother, I was hoping for a private word with Richeforte. Now seems the perfect opportunity," Tristan interjected, his jaw set in a hard line.

"Of course," Nicholas agreed calmly. Rising from the table

and with identical bows, the men excused themselves with a murmur of apology.

And with the duke no longer present to poke or gaze upon, Grace quietly finished her tea.

Within the confines of a well-appointed study, Nicholas concealed his astonishment as Tristan dropped a cannonball in his lap. The Richeforte Duchy held an encumbrance on Bellmar Abby.

"Sell it to me. It's the only way I'll convince her to marry me otherwise." Tristan shot back the contents of his glass, grimacing slightly as the liquor burned a path down his throat. "I'll pay whatever you deem a fair price."

Nicholas could not respond, not when everything inside him roared in protest. Sell Bellmar Abby to Tristan? He just learned he owned it. And Grace had no idea it was leveraged. To the Duke of Richeforte.

To him.

Her future lay cradled within his hands. The implications were astounding. Frightening.

Exhilarating.

Impossible.

It was out of the question. He could not use this as a means of driving Grace to his bed, nor would he allow Tristan to do the same.

"Rather desperate of you." Nicholas rotated his glass of brandy. The swirling amber liquid held a similar hue as Grace's eyes.

Tristan's request could not be entertained. The man could not see past his desire, and that was a dangerous thing. Nicholas witnessed the same occurrence before. Long ago, Sebastian Cain suffered the same blindness, and that man was now his enemy.

He couldn't enable the same disaster again with a different friend.

Nicholas studied his friend. Tristan's left eye was slightly swollen, a faint shadow of a bruise marring the skin beneath it. It occurred to him that Grace fended off two beasts yesterday. One, she escaped using her cleverness. The second, she eluded with the powerful force of a simple, charming whisper of a kiss.

"If Lady Willsdown does not wish to wed, bribery will not change her heart. Reconsider your position, Longleigh."

"If I don't marry her, someone else will force the issue. Once she learns of this encumbrance, she might choose anyone for a husband. Use him as a means of facilitating the release of the entailment. I won't let her slip through my fingers. The Willsdown title transferred to the Earl of Ravenswood, of course, but it seems you possess the estate and the stables. Held in some sort of secret trust by your father." Tristan's gaze landed with a calculated gleam on Nicholas. "Since you've no interest in marrying, ever, I'm relieved you are excluded from the field of competition. Besides, Sebastian would kill you if you even considered it."

"There is the fact she does not love you."

Tristan waved his hand dismissively. "That will come with time. Many marriages begin this way." He poured a second glass of brandy. "How would you know if Grace loves me? You only met her yesterday— I can't imagine she confided in you."

"The same gossips tattling of my hatred for watercress have also chattered of the lady's disdain for marriage. She's rejected your courtship thus far. I can't imagine she would suddenly change her mind." Nicholas sank further into the leather chair. "I'll consider your proposal once my barristers examine the encumbrance. I loathe surprises. Why I was not informed of this is disconcerting."

"I hoped you would know more of the details. My father is unaware of the full extent of the lien, but it involves that Irish stallion of hers. He's worth more than the entire estate. All but three of the seven animals died in that shipwreck along with her father. The ones she's bred for the past six years are prime pieces of horseflesh." Tristan's head tilted. "Do I have your word, Nick? You will sell the property only to me. Once the details are worked out?"

Nicholas swallowed past the sour lump of bile in his throat. If this was true, that he held the encumbrance, it destroyed any future opportunity of tasting Grace's sweetness. Once she became Tristan's wife, he would not seek her out or comprise her in any way. Contrary to the assertions of others, he would not ever dishonor a friendship in that manner. And Lord help him, suffering another bullet wound as a way of proving that would not occur a second time.

"I will," he heard himself say. "Although you realize, Ravenswood himself could buy it, as a means of saving his cousin from a wedding she does not want."

Tristan gave him a strange look. "True. But if done before he learns of it, then it won't pose a problem, will it?"

Nicholas did not reply. This could be a blessing in disguise, placing much-needed distance between himself and the temptation Grace presented. His cold heart agreed, even if it clenched in silent protest.

GRACE HURRIED AWAY FROM THE STUDY, CAREFUL THAT HER heels did not click on the hardwood floors. She'd sent Celia ahead without her, curious to know what business Tristan had with the duke. Hovering outside the room, her suspicions were horribly confirmed.

Anger. Shock. Despair. Emotions assailed her. Sagging against the lushly papered wall of the darkened corridor, a hand held to her tight chest, she felt faint. Truly faint. No acting required this time.

How dare they!? How dare they discuss Bellmar Abbey, her horses, *her life,* as though everything she loved was nothing more than an enticing prospect offered on the Exchange? Questions reeled in her mind, her heart breaking with the realization this was happening.

It cannot be true! Mother did not lie or mislead me. There cannot be an encumbrance. Bellmar is mine. Mine. My home! My darling horses... who will raise and care for them if not me?

Tristan was mistaken. Even if he was not, she would never marry him. He knew she did not love him in that way, and apparently, he did not care. He only wanted possession of her, something he would never have. As for Richeforte...he couldn't be trusted either, but at least he indicated he would investigate the matter before entertaining the highest bidder.

"I'll find a way," Grace vowed, fists clenched. "Bellmar won't be stolen from me." Reaching her room, the door securely locked, sobs of frustrated fury choked her. Drawing upon the same reserve of strength that pulled her through her parents' deaths, she swallowed them, dashing away tears with the back of her hand. Still, she almost crumpled under the crushing despair.

Almost.

Sometime later, Grace roused herself and left her room. She considered the duke's words that he knew nothing of the encumbrance. Of course, he could just be saying that to hold Tristan at bay. Perhaps he rather liked the idea of owning her pretty little stables and manor house.

She carried the books borrowed from Lord Calmont's library and slipping inside the dimly lit room, she pulled the drapes on a set of windows to allow more light. In the process of returning each of the five books to their appropriate spaces, she heard a slight rustle behind her.

The Duke of Richeforte rose from a leather chair situated by the fire. A decanter of brandy sat on a small table beside him, and he held a glass in his hand.

Grace jumped, so surprised at seeing him, she dropped the remaining three books.

"You startled me, my lord."

"Your Grace," he corrected smoothly, taking a sip of the brandy and gesturing toward the bookshelves. "Collecting more weapons?"

Grace smiled despite herself. "Just returning a few." She could not help thinking he was waiting there for her, anticipating she'd find her way to the library. The space went wholly unused by the majority of Lord Calmont's guests. In fact, Grace suspected she was the only one who'd visited it in some time, with the exception of Lord Calmont.

She bent down, retrieving the books from the floor, and when she stood, Nicholas was much closer. So close that all the air around her seemed to dissipate and she could only take deep, shallow breaths. Somehow, she was backed against the wall of shelves and he stood directly in front of her, crowding her space. This was extremely dangerous...to be alone with him...in such a secluded area...with his mouth so firm and kissable looking...

Grace shook her head in confusion, clutching the books tight against her chest. She must keep this man at arm's length until his intentions regarding her home and her horses were revealed. Although the heat of his eyes left her with a strange urge to lounge and stretch like a cat enjoying a puddle of sunshine.

Very slowly, Nicholas placed the glass on a shelf above her head, the movement of his arm briefly caging her in, and with a sharp intake of breath, Grace turned her face away from the firm bicep covered in broadcloth.

"What are you doing here?"

He cocked his head as if her question puzzled him. "Waiting for you, of course."

"This is highly improper," she managed to say, her tone almost normal, her heart pounding so fast, she felt dizzy.

Blast it, he smells delightful...

His mouth quirked in a ghost of a smile. "I rarely do anything proper."

She tilted her face back to his, searching his eyes because the smile on his lips did not quite reach the green depths. "Because you are wicked and dangerous and—"

"You've been crying."

How he could possibly know that was shocking. She'd scrubbed away any trace of tears, and she knew her eyes weren't swollen. She became acutely aware of his gaze scrutinizing every line of her face, peering so deep inside her, she felt...exposed. Vulnerable. Wishful.

"No, I haven't."

"Don't lie to me," Nicholas said, silky and soothing, but the underlying current in his tone made Grace's stomach clench with a twist of something unknown. The sweet excitement their exchange roused inside her was unfamiliar. She'd never felt it before with anyone. "Tell me why," he ordered, his thumb coming up and brushing the upper curve of her cheek ever so gently.

"You wouldn't understand."

"Are you so sure? I am very familiar with the tears of a woman. I'm usually the cause."

The brief flash of pain and pleasure Grace witnessed on his features startled her. And saddened her. "You should change your methods when dealing with the fairer sex."

"Why? They get me what I want most." His lashes lowered and he leaned forward until their lips nearly touched.

"Do they, really?"

"Always."

"What do you want now?" Grace closed her eyes because the duke was about to kiss her and she wanted her treacherous heart to accept that. She needed her brain to shut off all thoughts that this man possessed the means of destroying her life.

"What do I want? I want to kiss you. To touch you. Possess you." Nicholas drew away, reached for his glass of brandy and stepped aside. "But I won't. Not here. Not now."

Grace's eyes snapped open. He appeared so calm, so collected, it occurred he merely played with her for his own amusement. Confused anger bubbled inside her.

Reaching out, he removed the three books from her arms while she blinked stupidly at him. She'd forgotten she held them.

Sipping his brandy, Nicholas's eyes glittered in the low light, mocking her. "Such useless weapons, aren't they? Run along now, Lady Grace, before I give you cause for fresh tears."

Avoiding Nicholas that evening was easy.

Because he avoided her.

As if she carried the plague.

He would not look at her, nor direct any conversation toward her—but it rang false. Lady Helene Ralston was having a devil of a time distracting him. Smoothing his coat, trailing a finger down his forearm, even once across his jaw, the baroness giggled with irritating coyness at his every utterance, humorous or otherwise. But every time Tristan touched Grace, Nicholas's eyes hardened into chips of ice, fists clenching at his sides.

While the musicians tuned their instruments for the evening's entertainment, Grace slipped onto the terrace, seeking a quiet moment to consider this development. There was no reason for Nicholas's behavior. He could have no idea she had stumbled across his horrid conversation with Tristan.

She enjoyed a brief period of solitude overlooking the gardens before Tristan joined her. Taking her by the arm, he'd just begun to speak when the French doors swung open again.

They both swiveled at the intrusion, Tristan with a scowl of displeasure, Grace with a sigh of surprised relief as Nicholas stalked in their direction. Helene trailed behind him and from the expression on her pinched features, it seemed her presence was forgotten.

"I trust we are not interrupting, Longleigh," Nicholas stated coldly, but the heat in his gaze, landing where Tristan gripped Grace's arm, held enough fire to burn down that entire wing of the mansion. Was that frustration emanating from the duke directed toward Tristan, Lady Ralston, or herself?

"Of course not. Just a bit of fresh air before the dancing begins," Tristan responded, chocolate brown eyes dancing with suspicion and a bit of confusion.

"Excellent." Nicholas leaned against the low wall, arms crossed. "I found myself in need of the same."

Helene settled beside him. The same dawning awareness straining her pale face now lit Tristan's gaze.

"I was just asking Lady Grace if she might join me tomorrow afternoon for a last ride about the estate," Tristan said. "I leave for London the day after tomorrow while she travels on toward Cornwall."

Grace smiled politely, gazing over the gardens where a variety of festive paper lanterns illuminated the darkness. She had no interest in exploring Calmont Downs with Tristan. He might pull her from her horse, attempt kissing her again. Toss another offer of marriage in her lap while plotting the theft of her home. Hidden in the folds of her sage green skirts, her hands clenched.

"You should join us, my lord," she finally offered in the uncomfortable silence.

Nicholas's lips tightened. Was he angry because she extended an invitation or because she deliberately omitted his title again? It was becoming quite the habit, a guilty pleasure she couldn't resist. Her heart softened a little when his eyes met hers, the small spark of sorrow in the emerald depths surprising to see.

It was bewildering, but something about him called out to Grace's tender emotions. Even suspicions he might retain her estate if given the opportunity didn't dampen the invisible thread drawing them ever closer. Nicholas March, the Winter Wolf, a powerful, feared duke, seemed so.... well, misunderstood. And wary. As if no one could be trusted. Not his friends. Not lovers. No one. Like herself, he was alone in the world, save for his mother, with whom he reportedly shared a fond relationship. Grace wished she could sidle up beside him and knock Helene away. She wished she could warm him. Remind him a heart existed somewhere inside his rigid exterior. He needed only to find it. Maybe she could help him.

Of course, Tristan wouldn't understand her compulsion to treat Richeforte with kindness. No one would. Even she didn't understand it. Sebastian and Ivy would say she'd gone mad.

As if sensing her weakness, Tristan stiffened, the grip on Grace's arm tightening. "Yes. Join us, Richeforte," he bit out, in a tone far from welcoming.

Nicholas's eyes flared, the brief flame of sorrow extinguished. His response was blatantly dismissive. "I can't imagine anything I would enjoy less."

The baroness snickered behind an upraised hand.

"Richeforte!" Tristan hissed a warning, obviously surprised by his friend's vehemence.

Shoving his hands into his trouser pockets, Nicholas averted his gaze and Grace nearly clucked her tongue. She understood the reason for the curt ugliness of his words and the apparent shame following their utterance.

Oh, he needs me. If only I am to prove I am not his enemy.

CHAPTER 7

One day...one day I may call out
Discover its demise.
Quitely slain and buried
Elusive, shade of pale honor.
~Nicholas August Harris March
Ninth Duke of Richeforte

*N*icholas winced as the words left his mouth, but instead of becoming flustered or breaking into tears like a well-bred lady should after such a heartless insult, a smile tugged Grace's lips. The subtle restraint of her fingers left faint divots on Tristan's coat sleeve. Her gaze touched briefly on Helene's strangling hold of Nicholas's arm.

"It's all right, Tristan." Her brow arched. "I've found any wild creature will snap at others when miserably confined. Even those considered half-tamed. It's best to treat those poor souls with kindness."

Was she...*bloody hell*. Was she challenging *him?* Comparing him with some crazed animal she might heal with her sweet touch?

Before Nicholas formulated a response, Grace continued, matter of fact and breezy. Whether her next words were intentionally seductive or not, they scorched him nonetheless.

"Perhaps you'll reconsider, Richeforte. I vow, I ride better than any woman of your acquaintance. Indeed, you might learn a thing or two. Have you ever ridden bareback? I learned a long time ago." Her golden gaze flickered over the shocked baroness, whose mouth hung agape while Nicholas ground his teeth. "No saddle. No bridle. I love having my hands free, with only my knees directing the horse. Arms stretched wide as though I am flying. Have you ever done that? Surely, everyone has at some point. It can be so soothing for the soul. If you like, I can show you."

Show you. *Show you...*

Sweet Jesus.

Sweet. Holy. Jesus.

Nicholas imagined Grace slipping free of the pale green ball gown, her corset, the frothy, lace garments she wore underneath. Saw her straddling his hips, riding *him,* her hands cupping her own breasts. He saw her hands slipping down her body, fingers tangling with his as he helped her rock into oblivion. Their hands gliding in rhythmic tandem, his fingers pinching the tiny bouquet of nerves between her thighs, his cock deep inside her. And clear as day, he saw the moment he knocked her hands away, taking control of her pleasure when she began trembling. He would own her orgasm as he owned her. Every shuddering breath, every quake, every gasp. Every whimper of need. All his...

His skin was on fire, consumed by heated lust. His vivid thoughts were surely etching themselves above his head, like magical murals appearing in thin air for everyone's enjoyment. It barely registered that Tristan and Helene stared as if Grace had metamorphosed into the wild creature she mentioned moments ago. A gauzy film of sweat formed on Nicholas's brow; he couldn't swipe it away without revealing how deeply she affected him.

"Hmm. No? Very well...should you change your mind, meet us at the stables at one o'clock." Grace's smile never faded as she addressed Tristan. "Lord Longleigh, will you take me back inside? All this talk of riding has energized me, and I find myself quite restless. Perhaps the exertion of a waltz or two will help."

Tristan nodded wordlessly. Offering his arm, he led Grace away, a dazed awareness stamped across his own features.

Everything inside Nicholas struggled against snatching Grace from his friend and into his arms instead. He took a deep breath, a herculean effort at regaining control. With an audible growl, he pulled Helene along as he stalked the pair ahead of them, his eyes glued on Grace's delectable, swaying backside. She deliberately teased him. He was sure of it. And that little...*display?* A test he couldn't possibly hope to pass.

Christ, he was evolving into someone he didn't know. A man obsessed. Entranced. Beguiled by a scandalous beauty. How quickly she wormed her way into his consciousness. From the moment he laid eyes on her, curled in a heap on the floor of that gazebo, his thoughts were consumed by her. Given another opportunity, he'd kiss her so damned hard, she truly would faint. Then he'd shake her awake and kiss her again. He should have taken advantage of that moment in the library, but a sudden attack of unfamiliar scruples stopped him. He couldn't ravish her while she gazed up at him with those huge, golden eyes of hers, so innocent and trusting.

Nicholas watched as Grace slipped through the doors with Tristan, headed back into the ballroom. He jerked Helene along, irritated by her slow pace, infuriated when she suddenly tripped.

"Nick, wait...my shoe. It's broken." Helene limped beside him, her gait uneven, but Nicholas would not linger.

"Leave it," he rumbled, watching his prey disappear as the doors closed behind the couple.

"Are you mad? And hobble about on one shoe?" Helene wailed, sliding onto a convenient bench. Holding up the damaged slipper, she exclaimed, "Oh! Just look! It's ruined! I must return to my room for another pair. If you will escort—"

"I suggest you don't go through the ballroom." Nicholas executed a savagely polite bow and left the furious lady where she sat, there on the bench, the broken shoe dangling from her hand.

Tristan was leading Grace onto the ballroom floor by the time Nicholas pushed through the crowd. She favored him with a questioning smile, silently curious of Helene's absence while he considered striding into the myriad silks and satins.

And do what, precisely? Strangle her? Kiss her?

God only knew.

Pulse pounding in his veins, confused on a course of action, he didn't feel the tug on his sleeve until it became a yank.

"Good evening, Your Grace. Have you lost your dance partner?"

Damnation. Just what he needed after ridding himself of the baroness. Pretty little Celia would latch onto him for the remainder of the evening. "Actually, your dear brother has stolen Lady Grace from me."

"Truly?" Celia's head tilted. "How rude of him. I have a solution, should you be interested." At Nicholas's slow nod, she continued. "We could dance."

His scowl intensified. "I fail to see how that will help—"

Celia waved her hand. "Once we're close enough, I'll inform Tristan our mother needs him, that she's feeling ill. Mother would not wish to make a fuss so he'll believe me. And you'll continue the waltz with Grace."

Nicholas stared, a single eyebrow lifting. "And what shall you do? Stay and supervise?"

"That would not be helpful at all. I'll accompany Tristan." Celia's dark brown eyes were guileless, a resolute determination shimmering in their lovely depths. No coyness lurked there as she admitted softly, "I've seen it, Your Grace. Last night at dinner, this afternoon at tea. Tonight, even. You looking at her—I've never seen anyone gaze at another person the way you do her. As if you have a secret and only she holds the key to unlock it. I admit a bit of envy, but I'm glad as well. Because I've seen the way she looks at you too."

"Is that so?"

"It might seem contrary, but I have my reasons for doing this. You must know my brother wants to marry her. An impossible desire. And a foolish one. Grace will never marry Tristan. I hope he realizes the futility of his pursuit and understands how serious she is in her refusals. I can think of no other way of opening his eyes other than to see you courting her. He may believe he no longer stands a chance if she is interested in you and you are just as interested in her. Which you seem to be. It's most fascinating to watch."

"I've never wasted my time wooing a woman," Nicholas scoffed. "Especially an innocent."

Celia squared her shoulders, holding his gaze with a steady intensity. "I am well aware of your reputation, Your Grace. Tristan and my mother have beat it into my brain. But, I trust you will not conduct yourself in a manner that will hurt Grace in any way. As you say, she is an innocent, and very dear to our family. As well as others, such as the Earl and Countess of Ravenswood, and the Earl and Countess of Bentley. Ravenswood will be particularly incensed if she is harmed. Now, shall we dance or not?"

Nicholas could not refute the wisdom of Celia's plan, although her motivations were questionable. But if humoring this girl resulted in Grace ending up in his arms, even if only for the moment, he'd dance on hot coals. Giving a sharp nod, he whirled her onto the parquet floor.

Tristan scowled in irritated concern when Celia delivered

her news. Grace eyed them all with suspicion. She could have departed with the brother and sister, but indecision sealed her fate. Just like that, Nicholas had her. And possessing her was a little bit of heaven come to earth even as he realized this could all end badly. He would want more than one dance. Much more.

As they moved through the motions of a new waltz, Grace's eyes sparkled with caution and Nicholas realized something. She was different. As if a transformation had taken place since their encounter in the library that afternoon. She was cool, ignoring him all evening, almost as well as he ignored her. There was a reason for it, although he could not guess its basis.

"Are you truly venturing out with Longleigh tomorrow?" Nicholas finally barked, disconcerted by her unwavering silence. "Have you forgotten my warning of being alone with him?"

"I invited you along, my lord, knowing the high value you've placed on my reputation. You might have served as chaperone. Yet, you refused."

Nicholas silently groaned. Chaperone? Hell, he would more likely find a low tree branch capable of knocking Tristan from his horse if it meant having this girl all alone with himself.

"I return to Oakmont tomorrow."

"Oh?" Her manner was polite. "Then your concern hardly matters, does it?"

"It matters," Nicholas bit out, "when he wants you so much, he's willing—" He abruptly swallowed his next words as the puzzle of Grace's hostility simmered in the air. What the devil was the matter with her?

"When he's willing to do what, my lord?" Grace breathed, eyes narrowed. "Compromise me? Take what doesn't belong to him?"

"Something happened." His sharp gaze caught the slight pinkening of her cheeks with his blunt statement. "What is it?" he demanded, the roughness of his voice drawing questioning glances from nearby couples. "Tell me now."

"It is inconsequential." Grace's hand unfurled from his. "Excuse me, my lord. I've grown weary of dancing."

He recaptured possession of her fingers and, using the hand still cupped in the small of her back, jerked her back against him. Grace's tiny gasp almost destroyed him. Her breasts grazing his chest nearly dropped him to his knees.

"I'm hardly done with you, Grace. I'll have my answer."

Her internal struggle was clear. A secret lurked inside her, one she would not reveal unless he forced it. Nicholas's grip tightened unconsciously, and her eyes widened with startled awareness.

The waltz ended, other guests clapping in appreciation for the musicians. Grace took advantage of Nicholas's moment of inattention and tugged free. Dropping a curtsy hid the fact she evaded his grasp a second time. It was a mocking, pretty movement that ignited his imagination. Grace on her knees before him, head bowed, eyes flashing. Submissive, yet resistant. Dear God, the things he could do with her if given the chance.

"Good evening, my lord."

She darted out of reach in expert evasion, melting into the midst of the other chattering couples now ambling off the ballroom floor.

THE DUKE OF RICHEFORTE DEPARTED THE NEXT MORNING, much to Lady Calmont's dismay. Helene Ralston was none too pleased either. She was surly, snapping at everyone from housemaids to their hosts. Grace couldn't help a tiny smile knowing the duke left the baroness behind.

Even better, a steady rain began just before lunch, forcing the cancellation of her ride with Tristan. Grace spent that rainy, quiet afternoon considering what must be done. How she would stop the theft of her home. And her horses. The decision was made. She would not involve her dearest cousin, nor his wife. No need for Sebastian or Ivy to rescue her...this was something she could accomplish on her own.

She could save herself.

CHAPTER 8

"*Y*a haven't the full shilling, do ye?"

Grace grit her teeth. She regretted telling Hugh of the encumbrance and her plan of enticing Nicholas into releasing the estate. "I know this is crazy. It's the only way."

Scowling, the stablemaster stroked his greying beard. "Ach now, ye codding ole Hugh MacCormac, aren't ya?" His Irish accent thickened with irritation. "Ye canna be crackin' on traipsin' across Cornwall, tryna get wool from a goat."

"I hope His Grace never hears we called him a goat." She tightened the cinch on Llyr's saddle, patting the stallion's black neck when he swung his head and nudged her in the back. "I promise he would not take it well."

"A fool's journey, this is. He won't give in, milady," Hugh grumbled. "Stubborn as an ass, they say."

"How many different farm animals must you compare him to?"

Taking the reins from the grumpy stablemaster, Grace led Llyr into the bustling courtyard. Stable lads trotted to and fro, finishing up the morning feedings. A few busied themselves with rinsing the cobblestones with buckets of water. The summer morning shone bright, the brisk air sweetened by flowering camellias and buttercups. Swallows darted about, swooping low over the courtyard, calling to each other while horses nickered within stalls, impatient for their breakfast oats.

Emotion swelled inside Grace. She could not lose this beautiful place that rejuvenated her soul. Hopefully, her words would arrange themselves in a way Nicholas found intriguing. This plan must work, although showing up on his doorstep was foolhardy at best. At worst, her reputation would never survive if word leaked out.

"I must convince him to release it in trade for something else. My expertise in raising and training horses, for example. If he agrees—"

"He won't. 'Tis a bad idea," Hugh said plainly. "But here now, I see ye are determined to try, no matter my say. What lads are ye takin' for safety's sake?"

Grace grinned at the older man. "Just Robbie. You'll need extra hands when the mares from Lord Ravenswood arrive this afternoon. It's a mere three-hour ride to Oakmont. If I should encounter trouble, Llyr can outrun anything on four legs."

"Ye canna worry about four-legged creatures when keepin' watch for two-legged ones."

Grace said nothing. Hugh could not know the full extent of danger in which she willingly placed herself with the two-legged variety.

SHE KEPT TO THE MAIN ROADS. COOPED UP SINCE HER VISIT to Calmont Downs, Llyr was a bundle of excess energy. Maintaining a mile-eating steady canter, with Robbie bouncing along on a carriage horse pressed into duty, there were several times

Grace needed to slow her horse down. At this pace, they would arrive at Oakmont quicker than anticipated. Her return trip would be accomplished before nightfall if Nicholas actually heard her out. She refused to think what might occur if he did not.

Halfway into the journey, the rain started, a summer shower that quickly grew into a rare thunderstorm. Drenched, cursing the weather, Grace wondered if they should turn back.

"We can go on, milady," Robbie assured her as the roads disintegrated into a sloppy mess.

Llyr fought the bit, sidestepping nervously with the booming thunder and frequent cracks of lightning. Poor creature. Considering his past experience with storms, Grace considered herself fortunate she was still seated in the saddle.

"I think we should, considering we are now closer to Oakmont than Bellmar." Grace agreed, praying the storm ended soon.

Arriving at Oakmont, they went straight away to the stables. Not only was she drenched and muddied, Grace was now furious with herself. What a picture she must present! Straggly, hanging down her back, her hair had slipped from its pins long ago. The jaunty hat and elegant, mauve broadcloth riding habit with black rope trim and jet buttons were hopelessly ruined, although that did not completely sadden her. She despised the outfit, wearing it only in the event she came across other travelers. After all, she couldn't very well go traipsing about on public roads dressed like a hoyden.

There was little hope she would inspire anything in Nicholas other than horror, she mused, lifting sodden skirts and examining her mud-splattered boots. Young Robbie wearily sat atop his mount, spattered with muck as well. The two horses would need a warm bran mash, a rinsing of muck and a dry towel. Before Grace ventured into the duke's lair, a quick cleanup for herself certainly wouldn't hurt matters, although she considered her current state a deterrent should Nicholas entertain romantic inclinations.

The stable master greeted them as they trotted into the cavernous building. Upon learning who she was, the man reverently stroked Llyr's arched neck. A groom fetched warm towels, and Grace blotted her face and arms, ruffling the cloth through her hair. She heard the stable master dispatch a lad to alert the main house of her arrival.

The thought of Nicholas in that imposing mansion, demanding an explanation for her presence, was terrifying. Rubbing a towel over Llyr, Grace collected her nerve. *I can do this.* She leaned her forehead against the stallion's warm neck, gathering strength. *I must do this.* She could not, would not lose this horse or the others. They were hers. She would do anything to keep them.

"Where the hell is she?"

An annoyed voice echoed down the aisleway. Llyr blew out a nervous nicker, turning three times within the roomy stall and ignoring the hay set out for him.

Grace didn't think Nicholas would actually come to the stables...not in this weather. Dukes didn't go in search of people; people were delivered to them. Heart clenching, she gave the horse a quick hug. His quiet nicker steeled her resolve. She slipped out of the box stall, thinking it best to meet Nicholas halfway.

"Down there, Your Grace," the stable master said. "She's with the stallion. And a fine piece of horseflesh he is, Your Grace. And just as they say. All black, with just the one, rear white stocking. It's good luck, it is."

Quick, hard bootsteps sounded on the cobblestones, drowning out the stablemaster's lighter tread. Before Grace made her way down the end of the darkened aisle, Nicholas rounded the corner. The sight of her brought him up short.

He seemed shocked, as if the message informing him of her

arrival was surely false. Grace swallowed hard. Blast. He was just as handsome as she remembered. Dressed in black breeches, a simple linen shirt, and wearing a huge charcoal colored overcoat, there was no denying the appeal of his sculptured face. A thin line of irritation flattened his plush lips. With the breadth of his shoulders filling the aisle, he was the image of an erotic, fallen angel.

Or a wolf on the hunt.

Dark eyebrows snapped together in a savage frown. His hand lifted, rubbing over the clean lines of his jaw in amazement. The frost surrounding him could freeze a body in their tracks.

"What in the bloody hell are you doing here?" He thrust a hand through the burnished golden-brown mane of his hair.

Grace's chin jutted. She was shaking in her wet clothing. She wished she still stood beside Llyr so his body heat could strengthen and warm her. "I hoped we might discuss matters."

"What could we possibly have to discuss? The fact you've taken complete leave of your senses?" His gaze skated over her. Abruptly realizing the state she was in, those green eyes narrowed into chips of ice. "Did you goddamn ride, all the way from goddamn Bellmar Abbey? On horseback? Without a goddamn chaperone? In the goddamn rain?"

How many times, in one paragraph, would he take the Lord's name in vain? Gritting her teeth against the scathing set down, Grace was reminded neither her backbone nor her temper could be lost now. Nicholas must hear out the proposal. He owed her that much. She could not let her heart go without a fight, and a few curse words would not stop her from obtaining what she wanted most. She stood straighter.

"I'm not sure which question to answer first, but I'll begin with the most obvious. It was not storming when I left Bellmar. And I have Robbie, one of our stable boys, with me. If you'll only listen, I know you will find yourself in complete agreement with everything I'm ready to offer you."

She knew she did not look very appealing at the moment; probably more like a half-drowned cat than anything else. Still, Nicholas's gaze slid like drifting snowflakes, landing in the area of her breasts before dragging back up to her face.

Realizing the scandalous insinuation of her words, Grace almost hunched her shoulders. Her riding habit was soaked and clinging around her body in the most indecent manner. She truly held no bargaining power other than using herself. A slow comprehension overcame her. Any hope of her proposal being accepted meant everything must be utilized, including her body, which she knew Richeforte found interesting despite his attempts at resistance.

Straightening until there was no mistaking the provocative curves outlined with such clarity beneath her wet clothes, Grace confessed, "I know of the encumbrance, the title you hold against my estate. I know Tristan requested you sell Bellmar Abbey to him. A misguided attempt at forcing me into marriage. It won't work, you know."

Nicholas's brow arched. A glint of amused curiosity flitted with hot irritation in his eyes. He remained silent.

"I've come this far, my lord. The least you can do, before stealing my home, is to hear me out," Grace added without rancor.

With a fierce scowl, he again raked his rain-dampened hair, leaving it standing on end. Now it looked rumpled into disarray by her own fingers, the thought exacerbated by the fact that Grace's palms tingled. Clenching her hands into fists did not dispel the feeling.

"I can't very well leave you in the stables until the rain passes. And no way in hell will I send you home in the same manner you traveled here," Nicholas muttered. "You'll stay as my guest tonight and return home in the morning. I'll send a message at once to Bellmar. No one should needlessly worry for your safety."

A shiver of unease raced down Grace's spine at the unmistakable sting of annoyance in his tone. Her reasons for appearing on Oakmont's doorsteps went ignored.

Nicholas gripped her arm, the chill of his displeasure shooting clear through to her bones. Dragging her toward the stable entrance, he barked that an oilskin cloth be fetched.

It occurred with dizzying swiftness. He had her under his control in a matter of minutes while Grace followed his orders with uncharacteristic meekness. Robbie peeked around the corner of a stall, watching in bug-eyed amazement.

Nicholas waited while she removed her sodden hat before tenting the oilskin over her head. His movements were brisk but surprisingly gentle when tucking the fabric beneath her chin.

"I'm already soaked. A few raindrops more won't matter—" The duke's silent glare of warning cut Grace's protest short. "But if you insist," she finished weakly.

Blind intuition and his grip on her arm guided her as they raced into the rain and up a winding gravel path edged with towering English oaks. It seemed there were at least a hundred stone steps they climbed upon reaching the mansion. Grace muttered a quick prayer when she did not trip or stumble as she was dragged along.

They finally stopped on a wide terrace situated on the east side of the huge cream stone house. It was partly sheltered from the western driven rain, a large, jutting portico providing a dry spot from the storm's fury. Breathless after the mad dash, Grace held her tongue as Nicholas whipped the makeshift cloak from her shoulders. Along with his own drenched overcoat, he tossed the items onto a bench situated between two huge potted rose bushes. Then he snatched open one of the tall French doors, shoving her forward with unceremonious fanfare.

The doors slammed shut behind them with more force than necessary.

Grace glanced around the room, trembling from a mix of cold rain and apprehension. It must be Nicholas's private study. Filled with heavily carved furniture, decorated in rich shades of black and gold, it was an overtly masculine space. Above a monstrosity of a fireplace hung a massive war shield, the fierce profile of a gold, snarling wolf head against an ebony background emblazoned upon it. Red dripped from the wolf's dull white fangs.

Nicholas moved with brisk intent. Stepping into the hall, he spoke quietly with someone unseen, then clicked the door shut. He spared not a glance for Grace as he crossed over to the fireplace. Placing an additional log on the grate, he stirred until the embers glowed hot and flames licked hungrily at the wood. When it was burning to his satisfaction, he stepped to a walnut cabinet nestled in the corner, jerking it open with enough force to make the glasses within rattle. Two crystal tumblers were removed, along with something Grace suspected was a bottle of brandy. One glass received a hefty portion of liquid, splashing over the rim, while the other received less than a quarter of the same.

He handed over the smaller of the two tumblers, watching as she hesitantly sipped it, savoring the drops poised on the crystal's rim. She'd never tasted brandy before, and she licked her top lip as it burned a fiery trail down her throat and into her stomach. In a shocking instant, she was warmed from the inside out.

"All of it," Nicholas murmured.

Puzzled by the husky quality of his tone, Grace drained the tumbler in a gulp. Sputtering and coughing, she missed his fleeting smile.

His larger portion was swallowed in one pass. Taking the empty glass from her cold fingers, Nicholas set them both carefully on his desk. He moved as if having difficulty maintaining control of his temper.

"Wait here. I'll see that a room is prepared, along with some dry clothing. I'm sure there's something of my mother's you may wear in the short term. Hopefully, that riding habit isn't completely ruined, although I'm hardly an expert on such things."

He did not look at her while saying this. Grace passed a hand over her hair in an awkward sweep. *I must look worse than I thought.* Swaying from a combination of brandy, nerves and the chilling dampness, it took all her willpower not to grab his arm.

He was at the door before she found her voice.

"Wait!" Fail now, and she might never possess the nerve again. The proposal burned within her— the brandy helped overcome lingering reservations, loosening her tongue. "We haven't discussed why I came."

"I'd prefer you not catch your death from those wet clothes while in my house. Imagine the difficulty explaining that to Lord Darby. As well as your damned cousin." Nicholas's knuckles gleamed white on the doorknob. He never turned while speaking, keeping his back to her the whole time.

"I'm not leaving until I've had my say."

His head whipped around, his gaze flickering over her chest so quickly, Grace wondered if she imagined it. *At least that portion of my anatomy holds his attention.* She removed the jacket of her riding habit, feeling terribly exposed as it peeled away. Despite the lawn shirt and camisole worn beneath it, she was soaked through, down to the skin.

Emerald green eyes flared with an unholy light, Nicholas's breath sucking in as if he'd been punched in the stomach.

"Jesus, Grace," he snarled, the ferocity of his words startling her. "What do you want?"

"I have a proposition for you. A bargain, if you accept it."

"I doubt any good can come from this...what the hell are you talking about?"

The growl was accompanied by his release of the doorknob. Turning toward her, he leaned against the oak, favoring her with the same wariness he'd give an assassin bent on destroying him.

"After overhearing your conversation at Calmont, I devised a solution." She chewed her bottom lip.

"Eavesdropping, you mean," Nicholas snorted. "You did not simply *overhear* us."

Grace ignored the accusation. "Instead of selling my home to Tristan, I want an agreement with you. An exchange of sorts for Bellmar Abbey. And all of my stables and horses. Every last bit of my estate, down to the last stick of furniture and halter."

Like old iron chains, her nerves jangled together. Thank goodness for the brandy. It was fine stuff, actually. She understood its appeal. Just one glass, and she felt toasty warm and quite bold.

"I've no need of your money...I've enough of my own." He smiled that icy smile she now realized never quite reached his beautiful eyes.

"You've also no need for another estate or more horses, yet here we are," Grace accused hotly before remembering she must remain calm. An argument might cause a rejection of her plan. He must see they would both gain from an arrangement. Taking a deep breath, she willed her frustration to cool.

"I hold them because it amuses me," Nicholas taunted, arms crossed casually against his chest. Curiosity emanated from him, and something clicked in his memory. "Ah, that afternoon in the library...I was the reason for your tears after all." Again, his gaze drifted over her bosom.

He'll find me lacking there if I'm compared with Lady Ralston.

She dismissed thoughts of the baroness's plentiful breasts before plowing on. "I'm fully aware this is a man's world. And a brutal one, at that. There may be plenty of times I will weep because of a man's cruelty or mistreatment. But I will not allow someone other than myself to determine my fate. You see, I do not offer money. I wish that you employ me. To train horses and manage Bellmar until the encumbrance is paid. I can't lose my horses. And I *won't* lose Llyr."

He snorted in disbelief. "You named a horse after an Irish god?"

"Yes. The god of water and the sea—"

"I know who Llyr is, pet," he interrupted sharply, and Grace shivered. Was the worth of her labor equal that of an impoverished yet beautiful estate and a stable full of expensive horses? Would he take into consideration the cost of her pride in pleading his mercy in the first place?

"I've little need for another property manager." Coldly brutal, his words struck her. "Nor a trainer. I've no use for horses that bow, or dance, or any of the other silly things you teach them. I do, however, believe such tricks are useful within the bedchamber. If the woman is willing."

Words rehearsed dozens of times stuck in Grace's throat. For a horrifying moment, she hovered on the verge of crumpling into a sobbing heap of helpless, foolish, female weakness before yanking her careening emotions back into place. As if poured from a fountain, an alternative proposition tumbled out of her mouth.

"Very well." Her chin tilted to its highest position yet, eyes glittering with violent determination. "For one night, you shall have me. In any way you desire. Dancing, bowing, or otherwise. One night. In exchange for Bellmar Abbey and all my horses. Every last one of them. That is my proposition, Your Grace. If you are man enough to negotiate with me."

CHAPTER 9

For now, it shuffles forth
Wounded, frail creature
Assuring me it still survives.
~Nicholas August Harris March
Ninth Duke of Richeforte

*G*race's words sliced Nicholas with blistering awareness.

For one night, you shall have me.

Was she serious?

Was she *fucking* serious? Her body, her mouth, her kisses, her virginity, her soul, all offered in exchange for a few damn nags? She was bloody crazy. Insane. Daft...

His mouth watered until he nearly choked.

He wanted to cross his study and snatch her up. Kiss her senseless. Rip that damned wet blouse away and lick her cold-pebbled nipples with the heat of his tongue. He wanted to bite them—gently at first—then with increasing passion until she cried out his name. And he would thrust his cock into her so hard, so deep, she'd be unable to speak at all.

He stared at her. Like an idiot. When Grace stepped closer, he stumbled in retreat before bracing himself.

"Did you hear me?"

Her voice was high, thin. Embarrassed, as though his silence was a rejection instead of a reflection of the varied ways he would take her. He envisioned bending her over his desk while he slid into her wet heat from behind, his palms warming the cold, rain dampened skin of her buttocks until she flamed as hot as the fire in the hearth.

While he fought a molten river of lust, her bronze colored eyes searched his, waiting for an answer.

Control. He needed to regain control. Of himself. The situation.

Affecting the relaxed manner of a man humoring an irrational child, Nicholas stalked past her and leaned against his desk. He hoped his forthcoming appeasement eased the rejection of her offer, or at least erased the erotic images in his mind. The offered proposal was impossible. He could not permit it. The price she would pay was too high, even in his debauched world.

Nicholas snapped open a humidor. Selecting a cigar, he took his time lighting it, intensely aware of her nervous fidgeting in the yawning silence. Drawing on the cylinder of tobacco in a leisurely fashion, he released a puff of smoke upward. It drifted above their heads, swirling into miniature grey-white clouds.

With a smirk, he tapped the ashes into a heavy crystal bowl. "What of marriage, honeybee? A future husband, even someone other than Longleigh, will expect a virgin in his bed. How will you explain the loss of that valuable commodity? Because believe me, come your wedding night, a man will know someone else claimed the prize. And any man worth his salt will be angered by its absence." His gaze drifted over her in a lazy assessment. "Especially with you. The man you belong to will want every bloody piece of you. Pardon the expression."

At his crudeness, Grace's features hardened into steel even as her cheeks flushed scarlet. Lush, smudgy-dark eyelashes fluttered downward. "An insignificant factor, as I've no intention of ever marrying. Should you agree with the arrangement, I shall have my stables and Bellmar. With full control of my inheritance and the sale of a few foals, there won't be a need to marry. Besides, I've no desire for a husband who simply wants control of all I hold dear. I've no need for a man anyway, least of all one who thinks to buy me based on the value of my estate."

"You've no wish for children? In the future?" All silly young girls of the *ton* dreamed of advantageous marriages and children. They were raised from birth preparing for such things.

Broodmares, the lot of them. When they grew bored with being wives and mothers, they sought affairs as a pleasant, empty means of distraction. He'd slept with countless married women, all searching for an element of danger, the excitement missing from their humdrum lives. Nicholas willingly complied, for love matches were rare in their world, and everyone found pleasure where they would. His affairs were carefully conducted with women unlikely to pose any form of entanglement. From either jealous husbands or worse, romantic expectations. The moment a woman expressed anything more than an interest in being thoroughly fucked, without love, without attachment or affection, he ended the affair and selected a new lover.

The last two affairs before Helene Ralston had ended badly. Or maybe they were merely examples of bad luck. His pretty little actress drank herself into a stupor, striking her head during a fall and dying two days after being discovered. Inebriation dotted their encounters and Anne was completely uninhibited when mildly intoxicated, willing to try anything. When dealing with the aftermath of her benders became tedious, frequent, and more extreme, Nicholas moved on. He wanted a mistress he could fuck and enjoy, not a woman who'd grown too fond of cheap gin and required coddling. But still, upon learning the stage troupe was short on funds needed to give the girl a proper burial, Nicholas anonymously paid for not only a service, but a fine casket and a plot in a pretty little cemetery in the village where her sister still lived.

Following the breakup with Anne, Lady Elizabeth presented him with a charming proposition. It seemed her husband was keeping a mistress and she'd recently discovered that fact. She sought Nicholas out strictly in retaliation for her husband's wandering ways. They'd slept together twice before Elizabeth made the dreadful mistake of leaving Lord Banberry. Her express intent was to divorce her husband, marry Nicholas, and become a duchess.

He was brutal when breaking off that affair. Hearing Elizabeth's plan during their third time together at his London townhouse, Nicholas dragged the lady out the front door, clad only her chemise, with her hair unbound. Hailing a hansom cab, he gave the driver instructions and within fifteen minutes, he was tossing Lady Banberry onto the same bed as Lord Banberry and his current mistress. As squeals of indignation rose from the women and bellows of outrage sputtered from Lord Banberry, Nicholas calmly informed the man he should take his wife in hand. If Lord Banberry couldn't control the lady, he should get rid of either her or the mistress, because obviously he could not handle the demands of both. To Elizabeth, Nicholas's only words were this, "I'll never marry, madam. But if I did, it would not be to a woman who cuckolds her first husband while attempting to secure a second."

The last he'd heard, Elizabeth was in seclusion, hustled out of London and hidden somewhere in the country. Lord Banberry kept his mistress.

Nicholas considered Grace now. What sort of entanglement would he need extraction from if he accepted her offer?

"I shall have my horses and my home. That's all I want," Grace stated firmly. "All I shall ever want."

She stood determined and rigid. Nicholas supposed she'd not

had an easy time of it over the past year. Living life on her own, in her own time, she'd been abruptly reeled in by society's constricting ribbons. Her well-meaning guardian believed every girl shared the same burning desire of finding a husband in the ballrooms and parlors of London. It was natural she balked at any restrictions. She wanted the familiar life known as a girl, a world revolving around horses and her own desires. Grownup matters did not exist in that idyllic world.

Nicholas retreated to the other side of the massive desk, sinking into the leather chair.

Fear, more than anything, made Grace think she wanted nothing other than an isolated life of horses and an empty manor house. Fear left her reluctant to see outside the safe confines of Bellmar Abbey, past its pretty, broken stone fences. And for all her outward bravery, it was fear that made her seek affections from a horse's warm muzzle in the palm of her hand rather than a man's lips upon her mouth.

Nicholas knew all about empty, desolate existences. Eventually, slowly, surely, Grace Willsdown would shrivel away in that lonely world.

If he allowed himself to indulge her offer, there was no question he would drown in his lust for her. He would want more than one night, and she would not be able to give more. Bitterness made his voice intentionally cruel. It was time to end this foolishness.

"You are a reckless, feather-brained chit. Never in a million years would I allow such valuable property to slip through my fingers for such a paltry price."

Grace sucked in a breath at the barb. Frantic desperation darkened her gaze. "Are you that heartless? Holding my birthright for ransom without naming a price? If I am to be bartered, sold like livestock or a broodmare, then it should be my right to set terms. My right in deciding my worth and gaining the rewards. You wanted me before." Her voice cracked. "When Tristan...when you discovered Tristan kissing me in the gazebo. I may be innocent, but I know you wanted me."

Goddamn it to hell... She would bring that up.

"Fourteen nights," he growled, clamping his teeth around the cigar with such force, it broke in two. The lit end landed in his lap and bounced off with no damage done. Thankfully, his unfortunate reaction went unnoticed because Grace's eyes fluttered shut with his words.

Twin fists grabbing handfuls of soaked riding habit, she swayed. Dear God. Seeing her in those wet clothes had him imagining her out of them.

Her expression was both sick and relieved. "Two nights."

"Twelve." Any lingering uncertainty was pushed aside as an image flashed in his mind. Stabbing him, twisting with relentless intensity.

Tristan holding Grace by the shoulders, his mouth on hers. Grace slumping in his arms before pushing him away.

One night...or none. It suddenly did not matter. Nicholas could not, would not allow his friend the pleasure of having her.

"Six." Grace's lashes lifted, revealing burnished gold eyes, bright and hard.

He bit back a satisfied grin. *This is Grace, dealing in horseflesh, driving a bargain. Only, she's selling herself, and I'm actually buying her.*

Excitement mounted, an overwhelming elation difficult to contain. He would have her...claim her...shove himself inside her. Ravishment permission fully granted. All for the price of a few horses and an estate he didn't give a piss about.

"Eight." Setting the broken cigar aside, he leaned toward Grace until the desk shrank between them. The air turned thick with lust and the thin layer of ice he always wore.

"Five." There was a tiny hitch in her voice. Was it fear? Revulsion?

"Of my choosing," Nicholas whispered, eyes narrowed, gauging her willingness at seeing this madness through.

"If you use some manner of protection...so there is not a child...and you must not...you will not hurt me in any way or do anything unnatural."

Beneath its golden hue, her skin had paled, the magnitude of her irreversible actions seeping in. The different layers of color in her eyes was infinitely fascinating. How could anyone ever say they were just plain brown?

"The only pain will be the moment I take your virginity, and even that will be minimal. As for unnatural acts." He chuckled, appreciating the apprehension on her exquisite features. And damned if he didn't sport an erection just thinking of the moment he would claim her virginity. "I won't do anything you find unpleasant, so I cannot allow limits there. Five nights, honeybee. You in my bed, or me in yours. Five nights of my choosing. I will provide contraception, French letters, or other means, and once the terms are met, you'll have your horses, your stables, indeed the entirety of Bellmar Abbey, free of encumbrances and future claims. I've already instructed my barristers to look into the matter, but it does exist. The details are unknown, however, as the original debt seems to be missing from my father's legal papers."

Grace mutely stared at him.

"Are you bound by your word without the physical proof?" Nicholas inquired sharply. God help him if she backed out now. He could not permit that. Not when he was this close to possessing her. Not now, when he was wicked enough to accept her sacrifice. "Will you keep your oath, even if later you do not wish to do so?"

She hesitated, swallowing hard. "I will stand by it."

"Then we have an accord?"

"Yes."

Her acquiescence placed her in his control for nights of pleasure she could not begin to comprehend. Reaching out, Nicholas took her hand, intending on pressing his lips upon it, but she surprised him, grasping his hand and giving it a firm shake instead. Business-like. Matter of fact. A deal done. Irritation pricked him. He didn't like the feeling of being a business associate in Grace's world, another horse trader she somehow got the upper hand on.

"I'm sure you understand my feelings on having a contract drawn up. Something we both will sign. Should things go awry, if I'm forced to assert my claim in a legal manner," she said with a tight smile, "I'll have it to fall back upon."

Frowning, Nicholas sat down and pulled ink and foolscap from a drawer of the desk. "I shudder to think what recourse you could possibly seek if I fail to uphold this Devil's bargain. Your reputation will be destroyed if anyone learns of this."

Grace actually grinned at him. "You are unnaturally obsessed with my reputation, my lord. I would be very discreet should I ever need counsel on a violation of our agreement. But I trust you will honor our terms."

She was at ease trading herself for some horseflesh and a pile of stones, content with the consequences while Nicholas could barely wrap his brain around it.

As he jotted down the terms, Grace sidled around to his side of the desk. Scratching onto paper the extent of what he believed the estate was worth, seeing it in black and white, shamelessly scrawled in ink, had him questioning this god-awful mess. Maintaining a frosty indifference was impossible. Not when he strummed with awareness of her. Not when she smelled so damned amazing. Lemons and rain. Wild heather and hay. Sunshine and happiness. Bloody hell, he wanted to throw her on his desk and take her right there. Feel her pulsating around him. Discover the secret triangle between her legs and its flavor.

What the hell was he thinking? He could not go through with this. Could not do everything he yearned...make love to her, possess her, devour her. Have what no other man had or would ever have. Yes, he was many things. Heartless. Cold. Manipulative. But he was not a monster. Or was he?

"I do have one question, my lord." While he wrote, Grace leaned over his shoulder, her warm breath caressing his cheek.

How would she react if he turned and kissed her? Silencing a groan, Nicholas continued writing. "Oh? What is that?"

"What precisely are French letters? How do they work?"

His erection reared at her words. With a deep breath, he somehow finished the contract and signed it. Handing her the quill, he didn't realize he held that breath until she scribbled her signature alongside his, her handwriting flowing and elegant.

He was a monster. He truly was. Her name on that document proved it. Taking her virginity in exchange for an estate meant there was a special prison cell in the depths of Hades, just for him, his name stamped in gold upon the door.

Folding the document, he sealed the wax with the Richeforte Duchy stamp. "Here. Keep it in your possession for peace of mind. I'll see to your room and that bath now..."

"Won't you answer my question?" Grace followed, clutching the document as though it were a priceless treasure. She trotted on his heels as he exited the study. "Must you travel to France to obtain French letters? May I see them? How many shall we need?"

In a flash, Nicholas wheeled around, driving her against the paneled wall in the empty hallway. His body, hot and hard, pinned her in place, and a little yelp escaped her when he clutched her shoulders, fingers digging through the damp cloth of her blouse.

Her scent filled his nostrils, her flesh filling his hands. He wanted to kiss her until she moaned into his mouth. Retaining his composure was impossible when something foreign raged within him. It clawed its way up to get out. It was no use tamping it down when she was too close, too warm, too...everything.

"French letters." He breathed in unsteady gulps, Grace staring at him expectantly. "French letters are thin sheaths, condoms, in case you hear mention of such things elsewhere. They're usually constructed of sheepskin, and a man—" Nicholas closed his eyes for a brief second, then snapped them open, evaluating her reaction. "A man places one over his erection before he enters a woman. Ribbons tie the sheath at the base of the man's sex, holding it in place during intercourse. When he climaxes, his seed is captured within, prevented from entering the woman's body. Reducing the possibility of pregnancy."

His words became a low growl of arousal as he imagined doing all he just described. Or even better, having *her* place the condom on him before he did things to her long ago outlawed by church and crown.

Grace was wide-eyed, no doubt conjuring images of how it all worked. He thought she would jerk away in horror, but she did the exact opposite, relaxing in his arms.

"Oh. How very clever!" The exclamation was breathy, her eyes alight with curiosity. "I've overheard other girls whispering, but I didn't know what they spoke of. I thought it was some manner of stationery, something one could only purchase in France. How silly I am." She giggled softly.

Other girls? Who? What other girls? Who would dare speak of such things around her? Damnit, I'll have to find out...ban them from her orbit.

"D-do you have such things here? Will you use them every time we are together in that way? Do you put it on, or shall I? You will show me? I've also heard mention of sponges...are they the sort one bathes with?"

Nicholas groaned as another wave of intense lust swamped him.

He was powerless against it. He was going to kiss her. He would finally know what her mouth tasted like, what her essence consisted of. He would drink her, swallow every bit of her into himself because there was a piece of paper, currently crushed between their bodies, permitting him whatever he wanted. He could devour her, and she must let him.

"Bloody hell, Grace. I must kiss you..."

She gave him a quizzical look. "I never said you could not."

He bruised her lips with the force of his mouth, his tongue sliding down into the silken depths of hers to swirl and thrash. Plundering, taking, exploring, as if he were some type of wild beast and she his first kill. He could not get enough. His hands gripped her shoulders, preventing her from slipping away while his lower body pinned her against the wall, the heavy heat of him grinding into her. He wanted her aware of his arousal, aware of her effect on him. The first of their five nights was tonight; she'd better goddamn accustom herself to the idea.

Whatever strange emotions warred within him, the whispering warnings he could not possibly do this to an innocent girl were silenced by desire shouting a triumphant war cry in his head.

"God. You taste incredible," he groaned. "Like...like..." Grace tasted like nothing he'd ever had before. She was undefinable.

"Like what?" She whimpered when he bit her lower lip then sucked it. He rumbled, wanting more of her sweetness, wanting to dissolve into her bloodstream like a drug.

"Tell me," she whispered when he tore his mouth away and ran opened-mouth kisses down the slim column of her neck.

She was gripping his shirt, so he took her hands in one of his and raised them high above her head, trapping them to the wall and leaving her immobile. The dominant streak inside him sighed with relief as she squirmed a bit, then settled into his grasp.

Like heaven and freedom...warmth...innocence, his brain screamed in response. *Like laughter. Sunshine and lemonade, summer and light. You taste like...joy. All this, I no longer possess...*

Nicholas could not say such things aloud; that would give too much insight into his frozen soul. Instead, he clenched shut against the burning flame flaring to life inside him. That flame had no business anywhere near him; it was dangerous acknowledging its existence. He was dead inside. Nothing but icicles where a heart should beat.

"Like sin and honey," he muttered instead, because that was the truth, too.

Grace blushed, head tilting back, offering her mouth again, an invitation to kiss her even harder. His hand tangled in her damp hair, cupping the side of her face. Her hips rocked with an almost involuntarily movement against him, driving him crazy with desire. With want. With the need to be inside her, regardless who might come across them as they succumbed to reckless lust in the darkened hallway.

Her eyes were shining gold with excitement when he stopped, her mouth red from the roughness of his, her skin flushed. *Like warm cream,* Nicholas mused, running a knuckle over her jaw. If he kissed her forever, a hundred million times in a hundred different ways, it would never be the same experience twice. Grace did not know it, but she held absolute power. Could easily capture him, enslave him. Turn him blind to the wickedness a woman might accomplish with a flutter of long eyelashes or an upward curve of a sweet lip.

"I'll show you to your room now."

He released her hands, and when he quickly strode down the hall, trying to clear his head, Grace followed him with no hint of hesitation.

CHAPTER 10

For the longest time, Grace sat in the elegantly curved copper tub.

The bath was ready when she entered the room, a young maid standing there to help remove her clothing. Towels were stacked in a neat little pile, and on a shelf was an array of oils and scents and soaps to choose from. The girl, not much older than fifteen or so, chatted comfortably with Grace, explaining while the master bedchamber had its own bathing room, the duchess's suite did not. She also relayed that beneath the oldest wing of the house, down a set of stone steps and dipping deep into the earth, a series of caverns existed, complete with a tiny lake constantly fed by warm spring waters. The duke occasionally took his baths there.

Grace was fascinated that such a place existed somewhere below them. A similar spring was present at Bellmar Abbey, although it was not underground, but rather along the coast. She wondered if Nicholas would allow her to see the lake, especially as the maid exclaimed over the beautiful blue-green water that was somehow illuminated with light from deep below the surface.

Perhaps inviting interactions with the duke other than seeing through the terms of their contract was unwise. Contemplating her actions, the circumstances driving her to this point, Grace sighed, giving the girl permission to leave with a wave of her hand and a soft "thank you."

When Nicholas was not present, alone with her own thoughts, Grace found herself much more level-headed. When he wasn't kissing her like she was his last breath of air and he a drowning man, she could think clearly. What possessed her to offer herself without trying all options? This—this was a last resort, and she'd tossed it on the table at the first hint of Nicholas's resistance.

Resistance. What resistance had *she* put up? The moment he touched her, she crumpled like scrap paper in his fist. In the hallway, he overwhelmed her. With heat. Excitement. Feelings unfamiliar infecting her bloodstream and running rampant through her veins while Nicholas appeared capable of turning off his emotions at will. In the blink of an eye, there outside his study, he became the icy, hard, wicked, and unmoving Duke of Richeforte. And when he commanded her, she obeyed without question.

Lost in her thoughts, she never heard the door open, nor his approach until a sound similar to a strangled groan alerted her. Nicholas stood motionless in the middle of the enormous suite, and Grace was reminded again of how beautiful he was. A beautiful, fallen angel. Then his spine straightened with such purpose, she knew something momentous was coming.

"Get out," came the curt order. He'd changed from rain-soaked clothes into a coat of darkest black and a blinding white shirt. An equally pristine ascot was wrapped about his throat. He was dressed formally as if prepared to escort her into dinner.

She sank further into the copper tub. "I'm not done."

He ground his teeth; Grace was sure of it. She heard it clear across the room.

"Yes," he said, a strange tightness in his voice, "you are."

Dunking the sponge, she raised it level with her chin, then squeezed until warm, soapy water cascaded in rivulets over her shoulders and collarbone. Her eyes fluttered shut.

She must stand up to him, or this man would run roughshod over her during the course of the contract. If she didn't show a backbone, an ability to resist his commands, she'd never survive him.

He'll consume me...

"You are a dreadful bully, my lord. Regardless of our arrangement, you will soon discover you cannot order...oh!!!"

His footsteps fell silent on the thick Aubusson rug. One moment she lounged in the tub, the next she was hauled from it, Nicholas's hand wrapped tight on her upper arm.

"How many times must I tell you to address me properly, little bee?" The growl was a silky threat, issued as he crushed her against his chest, heedless of the soaking his clothes received. "A lesson is in order, don't you think?"

Grace's squeal of protest landed on deaf ears; her struggles at wiggling free laughable at best.

"You are pushing me beyond the limits of mortal men."

Snatching up a plush towel, he held her in place with one hand. His other dragged the cloth across her body, scrubbing her skin as if intent on removing it from bone.

"Stop it!" Grace cried.

Grabbing the towel and covering her nudity while he dried her was impossible. Either modesty or tender flesh would suffer the consequences. A silent tug of war ensued, the cloth balanced as the prize.

When the towel delved between her legs, Grace gripped his hands with a desperation never experienced before. Dry-mouthed, knees wobbling, her command was shaky.

"I'm not a child! Stop this at once!"

Incredibly, Nicholas stilled, glittering green eyes boring into hers. His breath touched her cheek, hot and quick in direct contrast to the thick, icy control draped like a cloak about his massive shoulders.

"I've no intention of treating you like a child, Grace. Far from it."

Easily yanking the towel from her fingers, he continued the task of rubbing her down, his gaze never leaving hers, his breath coming fast and shallow until it matched her own. Together they sounded like a pair of blooded horses, heaving air into starved lungs after a prize race.

Panic flooded Grace. Was this it, then? The first night he would claim? The initial pound of flesh forfeited in exchange for her beloved stables suddenly seemed very dear. The cost too high. The magnitude of it, the reality of the agreement seeped in....clanging against her rib cage, battling for space with her wildly pounding heart.

"An honorable man would allow me to bathe in solitude," Grace snapped.

For a heartbeat, Nicholas faltered. Behind dark sable, impossibly long lashes, she caught something wistful flit in his beautiful eyes. The strangeness of his unconcealed expression startled her.

My God. Have I wounded him?

Then, a slow, cruel smile drifted across his features, the twin dimples in his cheeks hypnotically charming. "If you expect honor, you'll find yourself vastly disappointed, little bee. However, it does seem, should you fail in upholding this bargain you insisted upon, you are the one without honor. I merely adhere to the terms you set."

Wrapping the towel around her body, he scooped her up. Crushed against the hard planes of his chest, his heat searing her, Grace felt something she had not expected. The frozen wasteland of his soul.

What had they done to him? Oh, how they'd hurt him.

Rejected him.

Betrayed him.

Destroyed him.

For a crazy, heart-rending moment, she felt like weeping. She wanted to pull the confused, rigid little boy she sensed lurking inside this soulless man into the cocoon of her arms. Comfort him until tears and pain were long forgotten. Heal him of wrongs inflicted long ago. She did not know his childhood, nor his years as a young man, but instinctively, she knew his life had been a painful one. Her fingers clenched into fists to keep from drawing his head down on her breast and soothing him, to stop herself from stroking his dark gold tousled mane as if he were some misunderstood, injured beast.

"You left me no choice. I had to make the bargain," Grace managed, swallowing against the strange urges within her.

"You leave me no option as well."

Nicholas stalked from the room, carrying her as though she were a small sack of treasures illicitly plundered. Crossing through the passage between two chambers, he closed the connecting door with a hard shove of his foot.

Grace had a quick impression of heavy mahogany and rich gold damask bedclothes and draperies. Everything was black, gold and the darkest of emerald greens. She was within a wolf's lair, about to become his meal.

Nicholas dumped her on the massive four-poster bed. There she sat in stunned silence while he removed his coat. Making sense of this turn of events was difficult. How he held and kissed her with such warmth, and yet such coldness at the same time mystified her.

"You will honor our bargain. Otherwise, I will strip from you all you hold dear. Not because I dislike you or hold a vendetta, but simply because I am a heartless bastard and find it an amusing pastime. And it gives me pleasure to possess someone my old friend Ravenswood holds dear." His cold smile could not dent the heated desire flaring in his eyes. "You see, you intrigue me, Grace. Despite myself, I've wanted you from the moment I saw you. You willingly placed your fate in my hands, and now, I will have you. This is probably the moment I say you should have paid heed to the warning signs I gave. Did you expect to make the Devil's own deal, then waltz away unscathed?"

Grace scrambled to the other side of the bed, clutching the towel as though it were a magical shield capable of deflecting his passions.

The rumors were true. He was the Winter Duke. A ferocious, icily controlled, injured wolf mauling anyone or anything in his path. The gentleness or humanity she glimpsed from time to time just beneath the surface was either gold waiting to be discovered or simply flashes of sunlight on water. Whatever he allowed her to see in fleeting moments may not even be real. Could she be horribly mistaken in assessing his tortured soul? Would he be so cruel? Taking everything from her with no remorse? Was his intention truly to hurt her cousin? She wasn't sure, but right now one thing was certain. She should have thought twice— her attraction to him blinded her to the fact that he probably did not care. For her or anyone else, for that matter.

"I'm ready to collect my first night." His voice was unshakeable. "It cannot be altered."

Grace's throat felt raw, tight, and scratchy. She wanted to scream. Call him every foul curse word she knew.

She wanted to go home.

"I was naive... and foolish! I regret making the bargain!"

Nicholas's eyes lit up as he tossed his coat aside, unconcerned when it landed on the floor. "I don't." He moved around the bed as she backed away until there was nowhere Grace could go. She was pinned, the wall on one side, the headboard at her back, with Nicholas surrounding her. "I don't regret it at all." Placing a firm hand beneath her chin, he exerted pressure, tilting her face up. "By the end of tonight, you won't either."

"You agreed simply because of my connection with Ravenswood. Admit that at least." Grace wished her voice didn't tremble. But it did, even as she met his eyes with a level of bravery she never realized she possessed.

He smiled as if he pitied her. "This may be the only opportunity I have of burying myself between those lovely legs of yours. Ravenswood has nothing to do with what you *gave* me. Now, I'll taste every inch of you, and you will return the favor. I'll possess you in ways you don't even realize yet. You insisted on this deal. You and I struck a bargain making you my whore, and you swore to honor it."

Shock rendered Grace speechless. Her brain stumbled when comprehending the horror, the awful truth of his words. The stupidity of her actions battered into her consciousness. The enormity of the bargain...what she gave away...

His whore.

She sucked in a terrified breath. It was all true. Her innocence was volunteered in this effort of saving her home. A moan of despair ripped from her lungs. She sagged against the grip he held on her chin and elbow. He tricked her. And she was stupid. Falling into the neat trap he set. Letting her think he was sweet, but intense. Honorable, yet misunderstood. Interesting, and only a tiny bit demanding.

It was a slow wind at first, building with blistering ferocity into a hurricane of disgust, whipping and swirling within her, an instant tempest obliterating all other emotions.

Richeforte's whore...

She flew off the bed, slapping Nicholas with all her might. She struck him again. And again. Her arms became whirling weapons of stinging blows, fingernails curving with vicious intent, aiming for his eyes, trying to rake across his face.

Snarling, Nicholas snatched her up, ripping the towel away in the process. He struggled to control her, deflecting the blows she rained upon his head and torso. One tiny fist caught his jaw with enough force that his teeth clinked together. He rocked back on his heels.

"Goddamn it, Grace," he hissed. "Stop! Now!"

Grace did not heed the absence of the towel. Her only goal was to escape. If it meant doing so as bare as the day she was born, then so be it. Self-loathing fear destroyed any embarrassment she should have experienced in being nude before him.

What difference does it make anyway? He's been with countless women. What is one more naked body to his jaded eyes? God, God, God... What have I done?

CHAPTER 11

Sometimes I wonder
Would I miss this ice
This heated fury
Would I know myself without it
~Nicholas August Harris March
Ninth Duke of Richeforte

*W*ith a muttered curse, Nicholas capture Grace's hands in one of his. When her sharp teeth raked his knuckles, he fisted a chunk of her hair, yanking hard. In an effortless motion, he tossed her back onto the bed and sank a knee beside her on the mattress.

Ripping his cravat from his throat, he worked with the quickness of an experienced sailor. In seconds, the length of silk wound about her wrists, anchoring her to the ornate headboard.

"Have you gone mad?" she choked, writhing against the tangled sheets, the knots of the restraints tightening. "Let me go!"

"I'm rather partial to this face of mine." Nicholas sat back on his heels. "And you seem intent on scratching my eyes out."

"You...you heartless monster. You can't do this!" She panted like a trapped lion cub, her hair clinging to her body in dark gold strands of wet silk.

"I just did," he taunted, breathing easier once he wrestled control of her. Damn, she fought like a hellion.

His knuckles bore teeth marks. Tiny scores crisscrossed the skin, blood seeping from the deeper cuts. A scattering of fine crimson droplets marred the crisp fabric of his shirt. As he unbuttoned it, Grace stared at his bloodied hand. "Once you calm down, I'll untie you."

For his kindness, she kicked him, a foot landing dangerously close to his groin. Snagging her ankle with one hand, he squeezed until she emitted a sharp gasp.

"Careful, little bee," he warned, eyes narrowed. Relaxing his fingers, he traced the fragile bones, aware he'd probably left bruises. She was so finely wrought, her limbs delicate but strong. "Do it again, and I'll bind your legs as well. You won't like that as much as I will."

His gaze swept her from head to foot, the leisurely consideration making her squirm. Seeing her like this, naked, wet, furious, lashed to his bed was incinerating. Blood rushed through his veins in a sizzling onslaught. "Or perhaps I should...."

"You wouldn't dare!" Her eyes glowed with disbelief and fury. Cornered and caught, she refused to yield. A glimmer of admiration swept Nicholas.

"Oh, sweetheart," he breathed. "You do tempt me. For you, I would dare many things."

"You are vile..." she sputtered, kicking at him again. "A monster..."

He smirked. "Endearments will not sway me. And that's twice you've called me a monster. I don't like it."

Kissing her at that moment was essential. Like breathing air into his lungs or food, water—all necessary for survival.

He leaned over her, his head lowering. Swallowing her

outrage, he stole possession of her mouth, molding and shaping it until it fit his own.

Grace snapped against the restraints, wiggling in vain for freedom, squealing her outrage, but Nicholas slid his arms around her waist, holding her immobile. Pressing the upper half of her body into the bed, he took what he wanted, kissing her the way he wanted.

Plunging deep with his tongue, swirling to taste her, he left no part of her mouth undiscovered. His intentions morphed into something darker than a simple desire to teach the girl a lesson she'd not soon forget. He would relish any excuse for rendering her completely at his mercy.

Bloody hell. Who was he kidding? He didn't need an excuse. He'd do just as he pleased. She made the damn bargain; he'd see it through.

It was the first of his five nights with her. She would not soon forget it.

He abruptly pulled away, leaving her gasping. Without uttering a word, he rolled from the bed and stalked to the wardrobe room. Rummaging about in the dark for a few moments, he found what he needed.

Grace lay silent, twisting against the knotted silk until Nicholas emerged from the darkness, looking like the devil himself, two additional lengths of white silk dangling from each hand. A smile twisted his lips,

Her voice quivered. "What are you doing?"

"Finding these," he replied softly. While she watched in horrified fascination, his nimble fingers fashioned slip nooses from the lengths of silk.

"Wh-what do you mean to do?" Anticipating his answer, her legs clamped together, knees locking in desperation.

"Don't worry. You will enjoy it." When he came to the end of the bed and reached for her ankle, she came alive, legs flashing with vicious intent.

"Did I say you could move?" he admonished, capturing one golden leg and looping the cravat around her ankle. Her muffled curses assailed his ears. Where had she learned such foul language? "Sshhh. Do not struggle, pet. You'll cause yourself harm." The trailing end of the fabric was lashed around the bedpost.

Her other leg was secured with unhurried ease while her breathing revealed her agitation. But she had ceased struggling when Nicholas stepped back.

There was a prickling twinge at his own barbarity; Grace in his bed, tied to it, should have horrified him instead of exciting him. No doubt, should he release her at this moment, she would avoid crossing his path ever again. That was not something easily accepted. At least not yet. Maybe at the end of this arrangement, once he had his fill of her, he'd be pleased to let her go.

When he moved toward the top of the bed, Grace sucked in a breath.

Desire tempered the ice in his voice. "This shall be pleasurable, Grace. Fortunately for you, I do very wicked things and do them very well. Now. Shall we begin?"

Working silently, he smoothed Grace's hair into a damp curtain across the pillows. He drank in her glorious beauty. God, she truly was magnificent. Concealing such perfection beneath clothing should be a crime against the Crown. Her legs were so long, supple from riding horses, and her waist nipped in before the lines swelled outward in graceful curves, forming hips made for a man's grasp. High and firm, her breasts were exquisite ...the perfect size to fill his hands, just as he imagined. Like confectionary embellishments, nipples a shade of dusky peach tempted him. They sat like perfectly formed, sweet little morsels, waiting to melt like sugar in the heat of his mouth.

Grace tapped into some manner of internal strength. Her breathing quieted, fists falling open against the silk. Relaxing her jaw, unclenching her teeth, her entire body stilled itself. A gleam of curiosity sparked in her eyes when Nicholas caught her gaze. It caused a hitch in his own breathing.

He examined the restraints on her wrists. He'd tied her in haste, with no hint of finesse, but he had no wish for the silk to cut her flesh. He did not want to hurt her; giving her pleasure, however, was a burning need inside him. And he did not wish she scratch his eyes out while he did so.

"What do you intend, Your Grace?"

She finally used his title? Now? Calmly demanding answers while tied up on his bed? He almost grinned at her fearlessness. Did she believe him capable of mercy? Or that she could manipulate him? He still wondered why he threatened her with Ravenswood's discovery of this bargain. It was more to his own benefit it remain secret, but an unfamiliar desire to hurt his old friend had seized him earlier. Surely, Grace knew he would do everything possible in keeping their arrangement private. His very life depended on it, because he had no doubt Sebastian would kill him should he ever found out.

"Be quiet now." Stripping off his shirt, Nicholas was gratified when her breath snagged at the sight of his bared chest. A slash of red etched his stomach, and Grace glanced away, disconcerted by the wound caused by her fingernails.

Smoothing a palm along the underside of her upstretched arm until he reached the curve of her hip, Nicholas marveled over the silk-like quality of her skin. For someone who preferred riding horses instead of flitting around a ballroom, she was surprisingly soft. A deceptive illusion however; beneath all that feminine softness lay a flexible strength completely different from the perfumed, plush ladies of his experience.

"It will please me if you use my given name when we spend our nights together." His unmarked knuckles brushed along her cheek.

Golden eyes narrowed as an inadvertent way of vexing him

was provided. Her lips curved with a hint of a smile. "That is not part of our bargain, Your Grace."

Nicholas cursed beneath his breath. This strange, willful little virgin was determined to disobey him. Astounding, really, considering she was at his mercy. How very like her, using his demand as a tiny weapon. But he found her defiance strangely adorable.

He resisted kissing her again because the taste of her in his mouth was too intoxicating. He wanted more. He wanted everything. He wanted to immerse himself in her, understand whatever it was about her that fascinated him. He wanted possession by her and possession of her.

"You will call me by my given name, Grace. Indeed, by the end of this night, you will scream it in pleasure."

"I hardly think so...Your Grace," she replied with great deliberateness, tensing against the silk as he caressed her hip. "Might we get on with things? I've a very busy day tomorrow and will need some sleep once we are done."

GRACE HID HER NERVOUSNESS BEHIND A PAPER-THIN curtain of nonchalance. She suspected fear, and perhaps even her anger, excited him.

Maybe calm acceptance would bore him.

Nicholas stared as if dumbfounded. If the situation were not desperate, she might have even laughed, delighted at stunning him into silence.

How she lay there, calm, bare as the day she was borne, while he roamed her body with his freezing gaze, touching her with his hot, hot hands, she did not know. If only the Earth would open up and swallow her whole. Or at the very least, open and devour him.

"You need sleep," he echoed.

"Yes. Upon my return to Bellmar Abbey tomorrow, I shall be breaking in a new colt. A strenuous undertaking, Your Grace. Dangerous. It requires all of my concentration. You understand, I'm sure."

Flexing one foot, her toes curled in a subtle testing of the knotted silk. Bloody hell. Although not tight, there was little chance of wiggling free. Why that strangely excited her, she did not understand.

"Breaking colts." His voice was sharper than splintered glass.

Grace frowned. "Yes. Breaking colts. And settling in a few mares arriving from Ravenswood. I'm sorry, is there an echo? I swear you are repeating my every word merely to irritate me."

Nicholas's mouth opened, then snapped shut. He considered his options while Grace suppressed a tremor. Perhaps overtly antagonizing him was unwise...at least while she lay in such a vulnerable position.

In a level voice, as though being lashed to a duke's bed was an everyday occurrence, she said, "Your Grace, if we may be blunt with one another, something greatly disturbs me, other than the barbarity of your actions thus far. We only struck our bargain this evening, but you vowed the use of certain devices, which prevents a pregnancy during the undertaking of our contract."

Grace's cheeks flushed scarlet, denying her affected casualness with her present situation. This breach of terms would surely result in her freedom. Even Richeforte, for all his renowned wickedness, would not be so cruel as to break his vow on this important point.

Her remarks apparently amused him rather than bringing him back to civilized behavior.

Smoothing his face into a pleasant mask, Nicholas trailed his fingertips up, skimming the indentation of her waist. As he stroked, Grace didn't know whether she should melt or jerk away.

"I asked before if you were in possession of these devices. You did not answer." It was difficult keeping her wits in place when he caressed her like that. His touch burned like fire. "Do you carry them with you?"

"I do not keep French letters here, nor sponges. I shall obtain them in London." Nicholas's head tilted, lips quirking with a smile. Those twin dimples flitted into view and disappeared just as quick. "We shall manage without them."

She squirmed. "Your Grace. Y-you promised. You gave your word. When I presented the bargain to you, it was my greatest concern, and you assured me...you cannot mean to—you can't..."

Nicholas laughed softly. "Not having such things immediately at hand has no bearing on our beginning. I have every intention of adhering to my promises if you do the same. Now, shall we get on with it, as you insisted with such eloquence? I should hate keeping you from your rest."

He sat on the bed next to her hip, facing her, and Grace's reaction was instant. She shrank away, as far as the restraints would allow. However, her eyes refused to unglue themselves from the golden expanse of Nicholas's chest, sliding down in an unconscious caress of the rippling slabs of powerful muscles defining his abdomen. The vast breadth of skin sprinkled with lightly burnished hair narrowed into a vee where it reached the top of his breeches. He was hard, unyielding and satiny all at the same time. She felt tiny and weak and helpless beside him.

Nicholas placed one arm on the other side of her body so he was braced against the mattress. Biceps bulging, he loomed over her, his face inches from her own, a wolf guarding his prey. Green fire glittered in his eyes.

"I'll not hurt you. As long as you do not struggle, there will be no pain. This night is for you. My pleasure exists in giving you pleasure." He paused. "If you will stay where you are, in my bed, at my mercy, I'll remove the restraints."

Grace hesitated, opening her mouth, then shut it. A tiny frown crinkled his brow, and she hated his little laugh of sudden understanding as something inside her unraveled.

He knew she did not want the cravats removed. The same sensation that gripped her when riding at breakneck speeds across open fields or deserted beaches seized her now. It was a wildness that sometimes caused a yearning to break into a frenzy of whirling limbs in the midst of London's boring ballrooms.

She'd stumbled once upon a gypsy camp in her woods. Unable to tear her eyes away from the sensual display of the women dancing, she watched as they used their bodies in beguiling fashion, as though telling a story. For a fleeting moment, Grace yearned to join them—dancing for the drumbeat in her own head. The same drumbeat echoing now beneath her veins. She needed something she'd not experienced in a long time, a lack of power over her situation. A moment of letting herself free, allowing someone else the opportunity to decide matters. She'd taken care of things for so very long now. Taking over the responsibility for the stables after her father died. Caring for her mother. Selling horses and worrying over the estate and how she'd keep it running.

She was suddenly so very tired of being in control. What would it feel relinquishing that control? To *him*?

Restless for something beyond her understanding, she quivered. The very idea of his dominance excited her beyond comprehension.

"Do you want the restraints removed, Grace?" Nicholas asked softly, a note of curiosity in his voice. His gaze burned a hole through her, straight into her soul. "Do you want them removed?" he repeated when she did not answer right away.

"Yes! Wait—no." They stared at one another for a long moment as Grace worked it out in her mind. What she wanted. What she felt. *How* she felt. Slowly, she shook her head. "No. Just...my legs. Untie my legs."

With just a simple command, she felt infinitely lighter. And powerful. Control was wrested from the duke in that instant. He would release her if she wished. He would restrain her if she wished. He would do whatever she wished. At least in this matter. His eyes, glowing bright green, told her he knew exactly where the balance of power lay. In Grace's tiny, inexperienced hands. And Nicholas would guide her if she allowed this to continue. If she let him, he would help her make sense of it all.

"Can I touch you? While you are lashed to my bed, unable to escape?" His voice turned raspy, a dangerous edge seeping through that made Grace shiver even while she nodded consent. But her nod wasn't good enough. He pushed for more. "I'll have your words, pet, telling me you want what I'm about to do."

"I don't know what you are about to do," she replied honestly.

"You have some inkling. Words, Grace. Now."

"Yes," Grace stuttered, turning pink with helpless embarrassment and a strange heat warming her. "I want... this. Like this. I don't know why, but I do and—"

"Shhh." He cut her confused explanation short.

For a long moment, Nicholas merely stared at her, as if she were a vexing puzzle in need of solving. When Grace thought she might scream from the unbearable tension, he made his decision. Reaching down, he loosened the silk around her ankles and pulled it free.

Then, as she watched, Nicholas put a finger to his mouth, wet it, and slid his hand between her legs. Every nerve in her body migrated, rushing down, down to where he touched her.

He sucked in a shaky breath—his gaze colliding with hers.

A flash of understanding passed between them, wonderment and desire. In a portion of her brain, Grace knew she should be repulsed by his actions, by the way he twisted their bargain, how he used her innocent, bewildered need for his own sexual pleasure. Another portion, a tiny part she never knew existed until now, loved the absolute power he held, how he forced acknowledgment that she wanted him. Indeed, she would allow him anything he wanted.

Now he knew it as well.

"Sweet hell," Nicholas whispered, gliding deeper into her depths, wringing a helpless moan from her. "You are already wet for me." He regarded her as if she were a dangerous creature, newly captured and caged. Her hands twisted in the silk of the cravats. "How you astound me, Grace."

Then she could not contemplate matters of free will or escape. Of control and power. His mouth sweetly searched hers while his hand slid up, cupping the fullness of one breast. Grace whimpered, confused when he no longer touched the center of her body, confused why she hated that his hand was no longer between her legs.

This kiss he gave her was different. This one beseeched as if asking permission. It flitted and danced and teased, and Nicholas was a master at using it. Tracing the corner of her mouth, he pressed kisses along the seam where her lips met, an indiscriminate pattern, coaxing and cajoling, the tip of his tongue darting here and there as he tore her defenses down. A kiss had never moved her so powerfully before. Never had she felt this breathless excitement or gnawing hunger deep in her belly. More. She needed more.

With an unsteady breath, her lips parted, and it was the opening Nicholas sought. His tongue plunged deep, twisting, swirling with hers, meshing together in a heated tangle. A cry caught and held in her lungs as the taste of him, brandy and spice, invaded her. His hand never stopped molding her breast to the shape of his palm. Squeezing, lifting, stroking the fullness, his touch was magical and her body gloried in the manipulations, her flesh swelling into his hands.

With her arms stretched above her head, she could not wiggle away. But she did not wish to. The kissing, the kneading pressure of his fingers, it all created a pleasurable ache. When he encircled the tip of her breast, pinching the nipple between thumb and forefinger, Grace's back bowed off the bed in startled surprise.

Exquisite sensations carrying the white heat of lightning bolts shot through her. How she accepted his caresses while bound to his bed went beyond comprehension. Somehow, her helplessness intensified the pleasure a hundredfold. Maybe she was equally wicked. Maybe she wanted this all along, this magnetic pull tugging her every time he was near. Maybe she'd longed for his touch from the moment he found her in the gazebo.

Nicholas smiled, his mouth nibbling at the fullness of her bottom lip as he broke the kiss. His gaze held hers as his fingers rolled and tugged her nipple until she shook.

"You are so damned beautiful." Shifting his body, he lavished the same wonderful treatment on her other breast. "Your skin is like honeyed cream. So soft, so smooth. Do you know your nipples are perfect berries? God, I've dreamed of tasting them..."

His head bent, taking her in his mouth while pinching the peak of her other breast with wicked fingers.

Grace nearly shrieked from the heat of his mouth. The sensations were too overwhelming, too erotic. Being unable to move made it worse. Or maybe better. She couldn't decide. By the time his head lifted, she was a trembling mess.

"You like that, don't you?" Nicholas murmured, tormenting her. "Tell me, Grace, tell me you like it. It's all right if you admit it. It will be our secret, as will everything else we do."

She shook her head, keeping the words from spilling out how much she *did* like it. Good Lord, she prayed he wouldn't ever stop.

"Bloody hell, you are stubborn." His head lowered with a ragged sigh. "Our time together will be very interesting."

He drew her nipple into the heat of his mouth once more, catching the hardened bud between his teeth, flicking mercilessly with his tongue until Grace writhed against the silk restraints. The fire was countered by his hands, smoothing the underside of her breasts, stroking the soft skin there like it was the belly of a kitten. Over and over, he moved between the two peaks, never letting up, staying with her, his fingers at first gentle, then twisting with a dark intensity that turned her blood into a molten river.

The difference between the two sensations drove her mad.

"Stop..." Her plea escaped as a gasp.

The cravat burned her wrists as she tugged against them, but the single word was directed at herself. Her treacherous body and the way it responded with glee, to his mouth, his touch, his fingers. Every time Nicholas paused, even for the briefest second, she wanted to scream that he continue.

"Do you really want me to stop, Grace?" His gaze burned her everywhere it drifted. "I am very aware of what women dislike, and I particularly know what pleases them. You enjoy this. Your body quivers for me, shaking in anticipation, little sparks of electricity shooting from here..." he licked her nipple, one long, slow lap of his tongue wringing another desperate whimper from her, "...down to your core."

Grace's eyes fluttered shut. She could not watch as he expertly teased her body into a state of arousal unlike anything she'd ever experienced. "Your Grace..."

"What shall I do, honeybee? Stop? Or continue?"

She whimpered, stricken by the thought he might cease such delicious torture. "Don't stop."

"Each time I touch you, when I lick or bite you, you feel it... here, between your legs. Eventually, your desire will become overwhelming. You will want me there, where no man has ever been before. You will plead that I slide into you. Claim you, possess you. Oh, Grace. I will kiss you until you never get the taste of me out of your mouth. I will plunge myself into you so deep, you won't know where I end and you begin. You will need me. Inside you. Filling you. And you will beg me for it."

Grace's eyes snapped open at that, staring at Nicholas in dazed wonderment. He might know her body already; with his wealth of female conquests, he easily recognized her responses. He asked for her consent, and she willingly gave it, but he did not know her mind. Even if her body arched for him, even if her skin shuddered in delight every time his fingers or lips dragged across her flesh, she would not plead with him.

She would see this bargain through, she would honor the nights promised in exchange for Bellmar Abbey and her beloved horses, but never, *never* would she beseech him for anything. God help her, she'd made a pact with the Devil himself and she would not beg for a glass of water while in this hellish paradise.

"Hell will ice over before I beg anything of you, Your Grace."

Nicholas smiled in pity, as if he knew something she did not. "Ah, there she is. My little honeybee, all sweetness and stingers." His lips brushed hers. "It will be such a pleasure breaking you."

"I won't break," she gritted between clenched teeth. "I won't. You'll break first."

He grinned, confident and so handsome it made her heart hurt. "We'll see about that."

CHAPTER 12

*G*race watched in fascination as his head lowered once more.

Time ceased to exist as Nicholas tormented her flesh, drawing the peaks of her breasts into the heat of his mouth. Biting, licking, suckling. Until a heaviness pooled between her legs and her body no longer seemed her own.

It could have been an eternity or only a minute. It might have been years or the blink of an eye. Grace only knew all of her world centered on him.

When he finally climbed fully onto the bed, settling between her legs and in a looming manner, moved over her, the excruciating sensation of hot skin, the crisp hair of his chest sliding against the sensitive tips of her nipples, ignited her. When he kissed her, his tongue deep in her mouth, her moans overflowed with greedy eagerness. Feeling the rigid proof of his erection between her thighs, she writhed, agitated and burning. Her hips struggled against the limitations set by the restraints. Not to escape, but to get closer. Closer to something she did not understand. Closer to something she craved, something she needed.

Closer to him.

"Will you beg me now?" Nicholas breathed against her lips.

"Never!" But she sounded unsure, even to her own ears.

He chuckled, kissing the tip of her nose in an oddly affectionate gesture. "We've all night."

He slid further down her body, trailing kisses along the flat plane of her stomach. Reaching her navel, his tongue swirled in lazy exploration around its rim. When her muscles contracted, he did it again.

"You're ticklish."

Dear God. She wasn't strong enough to withstand him. He knew it, too.

"Are you ticklish here?" His mouth pressed against her hip. He did not seem to expect an answer, his lips dragging in a train of fire. The raking of his teeth made her jump.

Every nerve strained toward the heat of his mouth, his lips' firmness, the sting when he nipped the thin skin covering her hipbones. Blood thumped slow in her veins, then fast, then slow again, the erratic tattoo leaving her dizzy.

Nicholas's hands rested with a light possessiveness on her waist as he crouched between her legs. His chest pressing against the open vulnerability of her body was electrifying. She fought against arching toward him, seeking a relief of the heaviness she felt there. It was a strange, overwhelming ache.

"And what about here?"

Slowly spreading her open, Nicholas found her wetter and hotter than before. He was so still, Grace looked down to discover him staring at the womanly flesh usually concealed by soft, golden curls.

His gaze was riveted on her, and he wore an expression that could only be described as rapt fascination. He regarded her as if she were art, or a priceless possession finally within his hands. When she squirmed in embarrassment, his eyes lifted to meet hers watching him and his groan of approval reverberated through her bones.

"You are so beautiful. Perfect. What am I to do with you, little bee?"

With slow intent, he dragged a finger through the plump folds of her sex. Grace cried out with inaudible despair. His touch was heaven and hell. Heat and lust and sin. It was nothing she should want and everything she desired.

Skimming his fingers along the tender flesh, Nicholas gathered her arousal as if collecting honey from a hive. His own breathing grew harsh, one hand resting on her lower belly, holding her still if she dared move. The heaviness of his hand intensified the flames he coaxed between her legs.

His thumb slyly brushed a hidden button of nerves. "You are soaking wet for me. Do you even understand what that means? You are ready for me."

Grace jerked against the restraints. The words were meaningless, but something in his tone sent a warm flush suffusing her entire body.

When she tried skittering away, he strummed her again. "You cannot hide from me, Grace. I feel you. Growing hotter, wetter. When I stroke a bit faster, do you know what will happen, my little stubborn pet? Your breathing will increase. Your blood will thicken, pulsing harder, your body quickening for my touch. All nerve endings will concentrate here, where my fingers touch you now. Pleasure will build, slowly at first, or perhaps quickly, because, God, you are incredibly responsive for a virgin. When it builds into an unbearable crescendo, you'll fly. Over the edge of the sun, where you will explode in a shower of a million stars. Do you know what you will do then? You will thank me for showing them to you. You will plead to see them again. And you will. Again, and again. Until you beg me to cease."

Nicholas steadily increased the motion of his hand as he spoke, dipping his fingers in a shallow exploration, his eyes glittering as he watched her reaction. He swirled the wetness around her body's opening, never going any deeper than the tip of his index finger, just enough to gather the moisture. As if denying himself something he wanted very badly, his teeth clenched, his jaw hard as stone.

Grace's eyes squeezed shut against the sprinting pleasure. She was spiraling. Nothing could catch her from going over the edge. Sparks illuminated her from the inside out, igniting with the brilliance of a thousand lightning storms until she could not hide...not from him. Or herself.

Over and over his fingers stroked. If only her hands were free. She would shamelessly press his palm against her and this maddening pressure. Would it ease whatever flitted inside her? Was this something only he could give her?

Slowly, with wicked intent, Nicholas pushed a finger deeper into her depths, stretching her, filling her, while his free hand pinched one of her nipples.

"That's all I dare right now," he said regretfully, his whisper a silky promise of more. "Just one, yet you grip me so tightly I shudder, wondering how I will fit. Eventually, I will. All of me. Deep. Then deeper still. Until I can go no further. And you will hold my cock just as snugly as you do my finger."

A harsh breath hissed between his teeth as he withdrew his hand, only to return in a gliding motion a little further inside her. Shifting quickly, his mouth fastened on the peak of her unattended breast while his fingers still tweaked the other.

A cord of sensation linked the three areas of her body, where his hands and mouth mercilessly pleasured her. It was too much. She exploded with a cry, arching against the silken ties.

Nicholas was wrong. She did not see plain, ordinary stars, but an entire universe, glittery with whirling shards of piercing, multicolored lights. Never had she experienced anything so marvelous, so utterly soul-shattering. She was soaring and sinking. Drifting and flying. Whiplash sharp pleasure surged and ebbed inside her veins, a river of nerves and tingling peaks and valleys hidden before now. Biting her lip, containing the sob of fulfillment bubbling in her throat, she floated until the tide finished with her.

Flung back ashore, harsh reality returned.

Sweat dampened her body, mingling with her hair still wet from the bath. She wished she could melt away. Avoid the truth of her response. Avoid the duke and his smug smile as her insides clenched and pulsed around his invading finger.

Dear God, my own body betrays me.

It betrayed her still.

Nicholas lazily kissed his way down until he reached her inner thighs, trailing his tongue in random patterns over her skin, stirring up sparks that refused dousing.

It was over. He was done tormenting her, for surely, this was the end of things... the end of the first night. Grace honestly wasn't sure what a full night entailed—damn her thoughtlessness for failing to set terms for that particular detail—but Nicholas said this was for her pleasure. She experienced that beyond expectation. Beyond the limits of what she believed possible when he'd lashed her to the headboard. What occurred between them just now changed everything. Could he see? Did he realize? That things were different now?

She was different now.

And if he would remove his long, blunt finger from inside her, untie that blasted silk cravat, she could gather the scattered, shattered pieces of her soul, sleep a dreamless sleep and find her way home on the morrow. Because deciding who she'd become, who she was now, required deep reflection.

"You can let me go now, Your Grace." Sharp and high, her voice echoed in the room's stillness. She did not sound like herself. Lord only knew who or what she sounded like.

His chuckle was alarming.

"Oh no, Grace. I'm hardly through with you."

CHAPTER 13

It is selfish
Wanting more than is plenty
More than my share
More than she will give me
I always take more than I deserve
~Nicholas August Harris March
Ninth Duke of Richeforte

*N*icholas was so aroused, he actually hurt. Trapped inside his breeches, his erection throbbed with indignation.

Never did he think himself capable of resisting her lush warmth. By some virtue of a deal made with the Devil, he kept his promise. Somehow, he did not enter her, did not take her virginity. Somehow, he stopped short of screwing her until they both saw stars.

But now, oh now he wanted more. He wanted the taste of Grace on his tongue, the essence of her in his mouth. Wanted her scent filling his nostrils as he devoured her, her demanding cries filling his ears.

He wanted everything.

She stiffened, subtly pulling away from him, and with a wicked smile, Nicholas hooked his finger, pressing a hidden, secret spot deep inside her.

Her quiver was immediate, her body's softening almost frightening. Searching for more, her hips jerked upwards. Greedy. Needy. It was an involuntary movement; Nicholas knew she could not help herself. Find that particular spot, and a woman would fall apart. Come undone.

How he loved seeing Grace come undone.

"That is something few men know anything about. Fortunately, I learned this delightful trick during my travels. It never fails to impress the women I've entertained in my bed. No doubt, it contributed to my somewhat less than saintly reputation."

His chuckle was humorless, his voice dry, as if giving a lesson. Would she stop him if he removed his finger and pressed that spot inside her with his body? He'd seen women's eyes glaze over when such mysteries were revealed. And never had one stopped him when he showed her what her body was capable of achieving.

Why had he hinged everything on obtaining the damned French letters? He would obtain sponges instead, although they were less reliable. Because what he wanted was best done with his body buried inside her, bare, with nothing between them. Rocking against her, thrusting and searching until he found the key and unlocked heaven for them both.

Assailed by mental images of the different positions he'd place her, Nicholas sucked in a breath.

He pressed his finger deep inside Grace again, just so he could watch her tremble. While he pulsated a steady drumbeat against her inner walls, she gave him a second climax. The melting against his fingertips was unmistakable, a nearly silent moan of gratification bouncing around within her.

God, what a responsive little creature she is.

Her reactions were slightly alarming. Those little cries of pleasure held the power of becoming addicting if he wasn't careful.

The rippling quakes were endless, and throughout them she resolutely retained her silence. Nicholas admired her perseverance, her resistance. With a frown, he realized he might not succeed in breaking her after all, at least not this first night. He'd made a promise she would beg him, and by God, he would have that from her. Affirmation she wanted everything he'd done so far.

He still possessed one weapon, however, and it never failed him. He reached up, pulling the cravat free with one hand so her hands were suddenly free although the opposing end remained tied to the fretwork.

"Don't let go of that, honeybee, or this all comes to a halt." He settled back between her thighs, and her knees bent reflexively.

"Amazing, isn't it?" His whisper against the flat plane of her stomach was soothing as her shudders eased. The sweet, pale skin just above her pubic bone entranced him. He licked it with a slow sweep of his tongue. "I can show you something else even more astounding..."

Using his free hand, he spread her folds wider, his mouth nuzzling into the soft heat. Grace stiffened in shock when, flattening his tongue, Nicholas covered every part of her sex.

Licking with slow purpose, he took all of her sweetness into the inferno. His tongue flicked at the button of nerves, and when she panted on a low, gasping breath, she was sucked into his mouth, hard, without mercy, his curved finger keeping a steady, driving beat until at last, she surrendered.

"Oh god! Please, Nicholas. Please...please...please."

Her hips rolled with the pace he set, meeting his lips with greedy abandonment, her words a litany of surrender. Ruthlessly following her every movement, Nicholas did not cease, even when he knew she was mindless with need and would willingly allow him whatever he wanted. She gripped the silk cravat as if it were a lifeline in a stormy sea.

Her high, quavering scream excited him, more than anything he'd ever encountered as another intense climax slammed her. She quivered beneath the onslaught, her legs coming up and over until the space behind her thighs rested on his shoulders. With her heels digging into his lower back, Nicholas kept her spread. He filled himself with her, every tremble of her flesh swallowed into his soul, her pleasure complimenting his satisfaction. His growl shuddered through her as his tongue claimed her, drinking her in until she sagged into the downy mattress.

When the pulsating against his mouth died away, he brushed one more kiss on her soft heat before reluctantly withdrawing.

She did not seem aware when he rose from the bed. He massaged her shoulders and her forearms with gentle hands, frowning at the dark pink lines marking her wrists.

Her skin is far too delicate for such depravity.

Like a sleepy kitten, Grace folded against him when he lifted her slightly to pull the coverlet back.

No, a lioness. All golden heat and flashing temper.

Every fiber of his being ached, wanting to ease into the passage made slippery hot by his efforts. Laying her back against the pillows, he pulled the covers over her as she rolled away. Sleepy and complacent, she did not struggle when Nicholas swept a hand from her shoulders down along the small of her back.

It was as perfect as the rest of her. A smooth expanse of light gold and creamy skin. Seeing her rounded rear, his erection surged. Before he could stop himself, his hand glided over the curve of one cheek.

Grace sighed, arching toward him.

Goddamnit.

Stripping his breeches before he could second guess his own actions, he crawled beside her.

She nestled into his arms when he encased her, her bottom cupped by his lap. Every time she shifted, her silky skin brushed against him until his cock throbbed with such violence, Nicholas feared it might spring free from his body.

Pushing his erection into the tight space between her thighs sent stars exploding behind his eyes.

He wasn't even inside her, and the sensation was so damn perfect, he couldn't catch his breath. If he lifted her leg the tiniest bit, he could ease into her wet heat.

Just a little taste. A brief glimpse of heaven.

Didn't he deserve it after the goddamn control he exhibited while giving her orgasm after orgasm? Three, if anyone was counting. He'd never experienced such overwhelming desire as when Grace clenched about his fingers and came on his tongue. And he never exhibited such control before. He deserved this. A reward...

Rocking into the narrow crevice, the foreign sensation of his erection wedged between her thighs, the feel of his muscular thighs pressing against the back of her own dragged Grace from a semi-conscious state.

"Your Grace?" It was a sleepy, horrified whisper. "What are you doing?"

"What I should have done at the start," Nicholas muttered, frustrated. "I want to feel the inside of you clenching about me. I need to feel your heat burning me as I take what is mine."

She shifted, although her limbs did not fully cooperate. "But...you promised."

Her voice was weak, hovering on the brink of complete surrender. Finally, she was at his mercy. What he wanted all along. Begging as he vowed she would...only he wasn't sure he wanted that now. Her supplication felt wrong. The guilt he felt made worse as the words assailed him in a rushed sob. Shaky. Pleading.

"Please don't. You promised. You promised...please, Your Grace..."

Nicholas's gut roiled even as desire reached unimaginable heights. With a choked breath, he rested his forehead against the back of her skull. Breathed in her clean fragrance.

He'd tamed her after all. Broke her down. A hollow, useless victory.

"Jesus, Grace. You don't understand, you have no goddamn idea how badly I want you. I can't just...turn it off. I don't have the control I should have around you. You must let me..."

Her voice, small and accusing, curled around him. It ripped at his cold, hard heart, leaving a minuscule tear just large enough for a tiny, fragile heartbeat of warmth. Of compassion. Concern and hope that she would forgive him.

And shame.

"You promised me. And I trusted you. I *still* trust you..."

Nicholas was motionless, lust shredding his willpower. He wanted her. Badly.

Knowing he shouldn't take her was enraging.

Remnants of a tattered conscience still existed somewhere deep within his soul. Those ragged pieces had never kept him from taking anything he wanted for the last five years. Would they stop him now?

"Don't you goddam move."

Growling, his hand gripped the top curve of her hip, the other holding his erection as he withdrew from between her legs. With impatient movements, he positioned himself until he lay heavy and hungry atop her perfectly round bottom cheeks rather than between them, the broad head of his penis throbbing.

"Bloody hell, I'll see to my own satisfaction, but you will be a participant. You shall be still and quiet because, God help me, if you move, our bargain be damned. I'll take you without benefit of bloody French letters." His words were an icy command. "Do you understand?"

126

Grace nodded consent. "Yes." Worry threaded her relieved whisper. "You won't hurt me, will you?"

A frustrated curse escaped him. "Bloody hell, Grace! This is more painful for me than..." Breaking off with a deep breath, he regained his misplaced control, swallowed hard, then rasped, "No, I will not hurt you. I won't ever willingly hurt you."

She relaxed immediately, softening against him, warm and liquidly compliant when there was every reason in the world she shouldn't be. "All right."

Nicholas's insides twisted painfully as she placed herself in his hands. She trusted him. For some goddamn reason, she trusted him.

With trembling fingers, he dipped between Grace's legs, wringing a startled gasp from her.

"That was for me, to do...what I must," he groaned against the curve of her neck. With her silky moisture on his fingertips, a fresh wave of intense need washed over him.

"I won't do anything more than that. Just let me touch you...yes, a little more, my sweet pet..."

Sweet Jesus, how the hell would he survive four more nights of this torture?

Anointing himself with her essence, he gripped his erection, sliding against the curve of her rear, up to the enticing dip of her lower back. Pushing hard against her, he moved. Thrusting his hips, his hand wet with her moisture, the motions combined into a parody of making love.

"Fuck..." His broken breaths melted into her tangled hair while she remained limp, obedient and boneless. "This...this is insanity..."

It wasn't long before his explosion occurred, and when it did, it was an empty, frustrated release entwined with faint resentment.

His body found satisfaction. His mind did not. He wanted inside her. He wanted Grace clenching around him. He wanted her moving, her legs wrapped about his waist, moaning his name as he soared with her, high above the Earth and into the heavens. He did not want her still as a piece of driftwood because of his threats. Restraining her now seemed an abomination. He wanted her willing and eager for all he could show her, all he could teach her...all they could experience together.

Crushing her, he kissed her slender neck, breathing deep of her perfume. *Heather, thunderstorms and lemons. She fits within my arms as though crafted for me.*

He'd not pleasured himself like that since he was a boy of sixteen. Not long following that birthday, he, Ravenswood, and Bentley all had a go at a lass in a London tavern. The barmaid was comically willing, eagerly teaching three fine young lords what the equipment in their breeches could do. From that day on, whatever sexual desires Nicholas had, a woman tended to it.

Now, as his seed joined their flesh, warm and sticky, his lust pacified for the moment, he felt cheated. This was not how he envisioned their first time. Not pressed against her sleek backside, his own hand providing the pressure and friction needed for release.

With a ragged sigh, he moved from the bed, and when he returned with a damp cloth, Grace lay in the same position. As he silently wiped away the evidence of his passion, she remained motionless, barely breathing.

Slipping beneath the covers beside her, he gathered her close, her back against his chest. She relaxed, apparently undisturbed they were both naked. She seemed quite content, cradled in his arms. Nicholas overlooked his habit of not sleeping with the women he used, and moments of silence dripped by, the air heavy with drowsy warmth.

It surprised him. He never held a woman afterward. Usually he was on his back and his companion sprawled across him, perhaps attempting to insert herself into his life by pressing onto his skin. That behavior was allowed for a few moments before he hustled the woman from his bed, unwilling for the intimacy to proceed any further than the sexual act itself.

"Your Grace?" Her whisper was lethargic.

"Yes?" His hands migrated between her breasts. Grace clasped them, holding them tight as their bodies spooned together. Like lovers. It felt right, holding her like this. He almost felt content.

"Thank you."

Her quiet gratitude stunned Nicholas. *After what I just did? The graphic things I said?* He'd spread her, tasted her, bound her to his bed. Using his damned cravats, for Christ's sake. Violated her with his fingers, in places only a husband should be allowed to touch, then masturbated to an orgasm against the silky curve of her buttocks. And she thanked him.

"Why the hell would you say that, Grace?"

"You kept your promise." With a shy softness, her lips dragged over his knuckles, kissing the small wounds she'd inflicted.

Nicholas's lips twisted. He was a monster. A cold, heartless devil. He had no right touching such purity.

It wouldn't stop him. The remaining four nights may damn his soul for all eternity, and he would probably go stark, raving mad before they were through, but he would have his nights with her.

And the devil take him, he would enjoy every goddamn moment.

CHAPTER 14

*T*angled in the sheets, Grace rolled until she faced the fireplace. For a moment, she was disoriented. Before ruthless memories flooded her brain.

She was in Nicholas's bed. Naked. She willingly placed herself there for his pleasure. And her own.

Pushing herself up on one arm, she scanned the room. Rain still pounded outside the windows. It lashed against the floor-to-ceiling glass behind closed drapes. Two lamps were lit, one by the bed, the other on a table near a door, illuminating the room in a golden glow. Searching the shadows where the light did not reach, she realized she was alone.

Where was he? Running a hand through her tangled hair, she wondered if she should retreat into the connecting room or stay where she was. Had he moved to another bedchamber? His bed surrendered so she might sleep with no fear of further sexual encounters? That seemed unlikely and out of character for such a man.

Propping herself against the headboard, she winced at the ache lingering between her legs caused by his finger stretching her. The remembrance of his tongue sliding over the secret triangle there sent a tremble racing through her limbs. How had she survived that? Even worse, how could she want more? Dear lord, how could she have lain with such complacency while he expended himself across against her lower back?

Images bombarded her without mercy until she groaned, dropping her head into her hands. Nicholas March was a gilded, tousled archangel, twisting their bargain to his own liking while somehow ensuring she longed for the remaining nights in his bed.

I truly am as wicked as he is.

"I hope your despair is not on my account."

Grace clutched the covers. She'd not heard the door open and silently close, nor his approach from the far end of the room.

Carrying a silver tray and wearing a black silk robe, which thankfully covered his magnificent form, Nicholas's brow arched when she slumped against the mound of pillows.

"We missed supper. I, for one, am starving." He set the tray down on a mahogany table in front of the fireplace. Two chairs were pulled up, forming a makeshift dining table. "It's not much, just what I could find in the kitchens without making too much of a clatter. It'll tide us over until breakfast, I think."

He spoke nonchalantly, as though this were an everyday occurrence for him. A peer of the realm, a duke, rummaging about in the darkened kitchens gathering his own meal. Since her recent immersion into society, Grace knew there were members of the peerage unable to bumble their way out of their own homes without a map and assistance, much less find the pathway to the kitchens. Constructing a sandwich from two slices of bread required even more cleverness.

"Are you shocked by my resourcefulness, or the fact I can focus on something other than sex?" Nicholas asked as he poured two glasses of wine.

Grace blushed at the casual mention of lovemaking.

"Is it very late?" Her voice was a husky murmur. Strange even to her ears, it did not escape her notice when Nicholas's grin faltered.

Staring as if mesmerized by the very sight of her, he finally shrugged and took a sip of wine. "Just before twelve. The witching hour." He gestured toward her with the wine goblet. "Come, come. Surely, you must be hungry. I promise I shall not bite you." His grin was a quick flash of blinding sunlight. "Or kiss you."

She clutched the covers tighter. His smile made her pulse leap in crazy spikes. She did not recall seeing him smile so easily at Calmont Downs. He'd been quite stone-faced there.

"I've nothing to wear, Your Grace. Unless I use the bedsheets..."

"I've no objections seeing you dine au naturel at my table. Indeed, I prefer it."

Grace's chin tilted. "I'm not your plaything." Only four hours ago, Nicholas pulled her from the tub. A lifetime ago. She became a different creature during that interlude. Now, she wasn't sure what she was, but she was positive she would not be a toy for his amusement.

His eyes glittered with the fire of rare emeralds as he considered her calm assertion. Then his shoulders lifted in casual shrug. "Very well."

Setting his glass down, Nicholas stalked to the dressing room and Grace stiffened. When he disappeared into that room before, he'd emerged with silken ties and the ability to steal her soul.

This time, he merely tossed her a black robe similar to his own.

"I apologize for its size, but it will suffice for the occasion." He turned his back, a subtle gift of privacy. "It may surprise you that my legion of female conquests do not keep articles of clothing here."

"I would think at least one would have left something

behind." Grace despised the tiny thread of jealousy coloring her voice.

"You are the first woman to sleep in this bed—that is, the first since I became Duke and began sleeping here myself. I've never allowed a woman above the first floor of this godforsaken place." A smile colored his words. "Does that please you?"

When she was sufficiently enclosed in black silk, Grace threw back the covers and padded to the table, pulling the sash of the robe as tight as possible. The sleeves flopped well past the end of her fingertips and the garment's length meant she must gather it up in one hand so she wouldn't trip.

Nicholas swiveled, watching her approach. The corner of his firm lips twitched. "You look quite sumptuous in black silk, honeybee."

Grace frowned. "I fail to see the basis for this nickname you have given me."

He laughed softly, reaching for her hand. "I've my reasons and explained them before. There's all that sweetness, along with a possibility of finding a stinger in my hand when I touch you. But because I like honey, I'll keep returning to the hive for more." He rolled one sleeve up past her wrist. "I wonder, Grace, have you always been single-minded in your determination to get what you want? Even if it is to your detriment?"

"Have you?" she countered, already knowing the answer. He'd go to any lengths necessary in gaining what he wanted.

Nicholas did not reply as the robe's cuff revealed red stripes encircling her flesh.

Tracing the welt with a gentle finger, his brows drew together in a pensive frown.

"Christ, I'm sorry for these..." The moment the hushed whisper escaped his lips, his gaze snapped to Grace's startled one.

The apology slipped out without conscious thought and his face darkened. Even with her limited social polish, Grace knew that this man never, ever apologized. For anything. He lived with no regrets. His actions never met repercussions.

His mouth flattened. "I'm sure you understand the damage to my reputation if it's bandied about I've uttered an apology of any kind. I am Richeforte. I never apologize."

Grace pulled her hand back and finished rolling up the sleeve. "You made that perfectly clear once before. Besides, I can't imagine how I would explain the circumstances of this monumental event. Relax. Your secret is safe." She sat at the table, waiting for him to join her.

Nicholas's usual indifference slipped into place. "Regardless, I shall refrain from leaving such marks in the future." He took his seat, handing her the other glass. "Such drastic measures are no longer needed at this juncture anyway."

She blushed at his observation and the reference to the pleasure found at his hands. Taking a quick gulp of her wine, she murmured, "No, I don't suppose I will fight you on the remaining nights."

Lifting her clear, direct gaze, she found Nicholas staring as if he found her quite fascinating.

"A pity," he murmured. "I enjoy having you at my mercy. An intriguing situation. As were your responses."

Grace nearly bit her bottom lip in two, her thighs clenching together at the blaze of heat his words induced. She lifted the serving platter lid, revealing paper-thin slices of tender roast beef, flaky croissants and a bowl of fruit compote.

"Perhaps next time I'll tie you up, Your Grace."

A flush of hot pink colored every inch of her skin left visible by the robe, and Nicholas's eyes gleamed with surprise at her reckless statement.

"Careful, I may accept your offer. Although the idea of giving up control in any situation unnerves me more than you can possibly comprehend."

He prepared their plates, refilled the wine glasses, and

companionable silence fell between them as they shared the meal. When it was done, he leaned back in his chair, studying her features as though solving a vexing puzzle.

"You intrigue me, Grace," he finally admitted. "There are few women willing to sacrifice what you let go for the sake of a few horses and a house needing refurbishment."

She shrugged, a comfortable sleepiness creeping along her veins. It was the wine. And the cozy warmth of the large room. It explained why she felt at ease with him.

"It's my home. My fondest memories are wrapped in its walls, and I will love it until the day I die. The horses? They are a part of me. I am devoted to their care, creating something I'll be proud of...that my parents would also be proud of, if they were still alive. Surely, you love Oakmont just as deeply."

Nicholas's brow furrowed. "It is foolish attaching sentimentality to such things. And you are wrong. I despise this house and everything it represents. The only pleasure I've gained owning it is knowing how it vexed my father that it would be mine." A hardness overcame his features. "You should know, if I retain ownership of your Bellmar Abbey, I will sell it for as much profit as possible and do the same with your damned horses."

When he spoke of his father and inherited title, it was like being immersed in an Arctic chill. And beneath his cruel words, Grace caught an undercurrent.

It was difficult placing a finger on it. She sensed he merely repeated a mantra, one he'd told himself for years. An unaccountable sadness flooded her. This cold, cynical man was quite possibly the loneliest person she'd ever known. Why she was drawn to him would bedevil her for many days to come. Why she wanted to help him, she didn't understand. He would destroy her. She knew this without a doubt.

Still, she couldn't help herself, wishing she might heal him in some way. *Foolish of me...wanting to show him kindness and understanding. Eventually, he'll use that weakness against me.*

When she refused acknowledgment of his plans, Nicholas pushed away from the table.

"You should return to your room now."

"Must I go?" She could not leave him just yet. There was no wisdom in her decision, but she wanted to stay.

He reached down, fingers on her elbow, hauling her against him. She was held prisoner with just that light touch.

"Should I lie and protect your delicate sensibilities? Or simply explain why you shouldn't be here?" His gaze turned dark and secretive. "I think the latter will do. You are a naive, innocent little thing. You think since I've had an orgasm, I'll keep my hands off you. However, nothing could be further from the truth." His gaze lighted on her mouth with unconcealed hunger.

"You will not find slumber in my bed, Grace. I will give you more pleasure than you can possibly bear. You think what happened before was intense? This would be much more...far beyond your virginal comprehension. My hands and lips will be on your nipples, our tongues mating as I kiss you as I like and wherever I please. I shall enjoy kissing you between your thighs the most, my tongue in your core until you come so hard, you can't breathe. I will lick you, suck you into my mouth until you have several climaxes, one after the other. That way, when I kiss you again, you'll know your own flavor from my lips."

His voice became rougher, his fingers unconsciously caressing her elbow in soft circles. "And when you are weak with satisfaction, mindless with pleasure, I'll slide inside you, my cock driving deep until you quiver around me and I shatter inside you. And then? I'll begin again by flipping you onto your stomach, gripping your buttocks hard enough that bruises in the shapes of my fingers form on your flesh. Deny me, and I'll spank you until your skin glows red from the weight of my hand. I'll lift your hips. Slide into your tight, wet channel from behind and fuck you until we are both senseless. Over and over until dawn arrives and this first of my five nights is well and truly done."

Grace's head tilted, a stubborn, speculative light entering her eyes. Her body was on fire with his descriptive words, a shameful wetness seeping between her legs. Nicholas, his breathing quick, stood rigid and tense, as though he might bolt if a hand extended toward him. She was reminded of a young stallion allowed free will for too long. They were the hardest to gentle, but once accomplished turned into the best of horses. Llyr was a prime example.

What would happen if she gentled Nicholas to her hand, her touch? She could bear the remaining nights if she controlled a small portion of their time together. There was the distinct impression the duke spouted such shocking things in hopes of frightening her. It was his way of keeping others from settling too close and peering too deeply into the depths of his soul. That caustic wit and surface cruelty hid a surprisingly gentle nature, she was sure of it. It just needed uncovering. Nurturing. Did she possess the courage required for such a task? Or was she mad even considering the possibilities?

Did she dare tame the Winter Wolf?

"The night is not over, Your Grace." Her chin rose. "I prefer spending the remainder of it in your bed. There will be no question I've upheld my end of the bargain."

With a deep, shaky breath, she brushed past him, dropping her robe before climbing into the middle of the huge mattress.

Nicholas wrestled with confusion. His hands clenched into fists and with the available light, Grace saw a muscle working in his jaw. Would he stalk over, snatch her from his bed as quickly as he'd thrown her into it? The thick air shimmered while he stood immobile with indecision.

Finally, with a muttered curse, he turned down the lamps until only firelight illuminated the room. From the corner of her eye, she watched as he discarded the robe, his lean, muscular frame shrouded in the darkness. Like the marble Greek statues in the Countess of Bath's formal gardens, his firm buttocks gleamed white. He disappeared from view, then the mattress protested with a slight creak as he slid behind her.

Letting out the breath she held, Grace waited for his arms to wrap around her. Nicholas did not move. His stiff, unyielding demeanor confounded her.

Rolling over, she found him on his side, facing her, one arm folded under his head with a jaw clenched tight enough to crack teeth. He wore an expression of furious puzzlement.

"Won't you hold me as you did before?" Her hesitant question was a tickle of a whisper. She didn't dare speak louder, suspecting Nicholas might leap from the bed if she made too much of a fuss.

"No."

"Why not?"

"Goddamnit, I already explained why you should not be here."

Grace chewed her bottom lip then, then her decision made, scooted closer, slipping one arm around his narrow waist. She tucked her head beneath his chin, using his hard, wide chest as a pillow. Unsure where her legs should go, she kept them straight and just slightly away from his. Her breasts, however, lightly grazed the wiry hair on his pectoral muscles. In response, her nipples drew into tight, aching buds. Between their bodies, his shaft, hard, thick, heavy, swelled in massive proportions.

Nicholas sucked in a breath.

"What the fuck do you think you're doing?"

His body heat was an addictive drug, and although the hostile snarl unnerved her, Grace snuggled closer. "You won't hold me, so I'm holding you, Your Grace. If anyone needs this, it's you. Please don't curse at me, not after all I allowed you tonight. Just...be still...let me have this."

Her arm tightened in anticipation of him pulling away, fingers splaying across his back. *How odd. Are those welts criss-crossing there?* The raised scars were numerous, each no bigger in diameter than say, a bow shaft. Or a riding crop. Before she could inquire of their nature, Nicholas found his voice.

"After all you allowed..." he hissed incredulously, body strumming with tension. A moment later, one golden arm snaked up, resting in the crook of her waist. He inhaled, slowly letting the breath out as if calming himself.

Grace almost sighed with relieved pleasure. This was no different from slipping a halter onto an untried colt— gentle persuasion and a firm hand usually did the trick. That and a bit of oats. A giggle rose in her throat at the notion of offering Nicholas a handful of feed as an enticement. Bourbon, or maybe a fine cigar, would prove better choices.

His heart thumped against her ear, a succession of beats quicker than normal. He still hadn't completely relaxed, but bit by bit, the stiffness eased from his body, his heartbeat slowing into a steady cadence. Silence pooled between them, his warmth making her drowsy even as his erection nudged her bare stomach.

"Grace?"

She felt the reluctant smile in his voice as his lips moved against her temple.

"Yes?" she whispered.

"What if, ah...something comes up during the night?"

He sounded amused, a vast improvement over his typical, cynical coldness. Yawning, feeling safer than she should after that ear-blistering description of everything he could do with her, she edged closer, one knee hitching up against his. A second of hesitation passed, then his ankle slid between her legs in lazy response, tangling their lower limbs together.

"We'll address it, I suppose, although I'm not terribly worried." For all the ice encasing him, Nicholas was warm and extremely comfortable. Quite surprising, really. Grace never expected finding such ease in his arms, not after the way their evening began. Already drifting asleep, she mumbled, "Besides, I'm sure you will think of something very clever."

CHAPTER 15

hen Grace woke sometime later, the drapes covering the massive floor-to-ceiling windows were pulled open. The rain had subsided. It was now a steady downpour, with just a few low rumbles of thunder and distant flashes of lightning. Watching the rain while snuggled in bed was one of her favorite things in the world. She savored the cozy feeling, knowing a cold, miserable world waited out there while she was safe and warm, tucked inside.

She faced the bank of windows, Nicholas lying behind her, her position echoed by his. A muscled arm dipped heavily in the curve of her waist, his hand against the flat plane of her belly, iron-banded thighs pressed against the backs of her own. The coarse hair dusting his legs almost, but not quite, caused a tickle along her tired limbs. The swell of her buttocks grazed the lines of his lap. With her shoulder blades touching his chest, his shallow breathing stirred her hair and she knew he was awake.

"I love watching the rain," she admitted softly.

Nicholas was silent so long, she wondered if he might not answer.

With a small sigh, he surrendered. "Why?"

"You'll think me strange."

"Too late for that, I'm afraid." Humor laced his words.

Grace smiled. "Then I have nothing to lose. Nights like this, thunderstorms outside, me inside, remind me how fortunate I am. There's a roof over my head. I'm warm and dry. I've food, clean clothes, my friends."

Nicholas's arm tightened around her waist. He was silent for several moments, considering her statement, then said, "Such gratitude puzzles me. The roof you speak of? In danger of being forfeited. Your friends? The children of your guardians, necessary because your parents are deceased and you are alone in this world. As for being warm and dry, you lay in a scoundrel's bed, your virginity bargained against that dubious comfort. Oh, and let's not forget, your clothes are currently being laundered. At this moment, you technically have not a stitch to wear."

Grace's shoulders shrugged away the sardonic cataloging. "You don't enjoy the rain?"

"No. I do not."

"Do you suppose you might grow to like it?" For some reason, it seemed important he say yes.

"I rather doubt it," he rumbled, lips brushing against her temple. "It occurs to me, should this god-awful weather continue, you will be unable to travel home. The roads will be far too dangerous."

Two unchaperoned days in the Duke of Richeforte's company was akin to a death sentence. "I've no choice, Your Grace. I dare not stay another night without a chaperone."

"Don't you know? My housekeeper, Martha, has not left your side from the moment you arrived," Nicholas replied with silky resoluteness. "Her reputation is beyond reproach. And she's a bit terrifying as well. No one would dare question you staying here as long as she guards your innocence. It carries the same weight as if the dowager duchess herself guards you."

Grace swallowed. He decreed it, and it would be so. "Tell me,

Your Grace. Are you so powerful, you always succeed in bending others until they believe a twisting of truth? Even if it is so far removed from reality as to be fantastical?"

"I am Richeforte," he said as if that was answer enough.

Grace realized now it was the standard answer when his motives were questioned. The all-powerful Duke of Richeforte did not explain himself or allow others to question his actions.

Holding such power did not please him, however. On the contrary, he was wary of everyone. Grace considered again her half-formed intentions. Taming Nicholas would not be easy, but beneath his caustic, snarling exterior something else lurked. Something wounded and tender and trembling for the slightest breath of kindness. She could give him that if he would only allow her in. She suspected much of the problem could be found in his upbringing, but there was little doubt that whatever occurred between Nicholas and her cousin was equally traumatic. And very bitter and very deep.

"Should Sebastian discover I'm here, regardless of whether I'm chaperoned or not, there will be the devil to pay," Grace breathed. "And Tristan to contend with as well."

"I shall deal with them." Nicholas's arm tightened. "Do not concern yourself over it."

"How can I not? I've no wish for discord, nor to be the cause of it." She waited a heartbeat, then hesitantly asked, "What is behind this bitter blood between you and Sebastian? You, Lord Bentley, and my cousin were once very close. Childhood friends before a deadly rift opened between the three of you. Won't you tell me? Why you dueled?"

Grace felt the frost forming around Nicholas. Although he did not move a muscle, he retreated inside his iceberg, where she could not touch him.

"You ask too many goddamn questions about things which do not concern you."

She pressed on, undaunted. "I am a part of it now."

"They are two different issues. Do not combine them. Now, go back to sleep," he said against her hair, pressing surprisingly gentle kisses to the tangled, blonde mass. "Unless you care for engagement in matters I find more interesting. After all, the night has not truly ended. Not yet."

Grace grew still. Something within her reared its head in response to the soft challenge. Something dangerously wild, seeking pleasure from his hands, from his touch and his lips. From his tongue. A thousand blissful memories flushed her in a river of heat. She almost turned in the circle of his arms, almost reached for him.

If he does not like seeing the rain, why open the drapes? Why deny something so innocuous? Is he afraid of a connection with me? Why does he hold me like this, kiss me so softly? As if he is content in this moment? The sudden rush of excitement, the thought of sharing something so simple and perfect with him left Grace a little dizzy. *Would a wolf allow me to hold him?*

With a rueful stammer, she tamped down all the questions and hope bubbling inside her. "I will sleep, Your Grace."

"A wise choice." His soft chuckle tickled her ear as his arousal pressed her buttocks. "Although you challenge every ounce of willpower I possess, I will honor your choice."

JUST BEFORE DAWN, NICHOLAS CARRIED GRACE INTO THE adjoining room, settling her beneath the bed's coverlet. Rain still lashed the house, darkening the sky, but morning was fast approaching. With it came reality and all its terrible harshness.

"Don't go..." she murmured in sleepy protest.

"It's better this way, little bee." His fingers slid through her hair as she burrowed into the pillows, and before drawing away, he skimmed her furrowed brow with the barest of kisses.

I may be a bastard, but I'll not have you discovered in my bed come morning.

He eased the room's chill by rekindling the fire. When it was once again blazing, he found himself back at Grace's side, drawn there by something unnamed. He couldn't help himself. A perverse need to be near her swamped every intention of leaving. For a long time, he watched while she slept. When she sighed once, reaching a hand toward him, it galvanized him. Made him painfully aware of what he was doing.

He hastily made his retreat and did not look back.

CHAPTER 16

Lust overcomes my madness
She has become my moon
Howled for and to
Worshipped
Adored
I am consumed
An insanity happily suffered.
~Nicholas August Harris March
Ninth Duke of Richeforte

*S*tanding on the brick steps of the bachelor's residence, he wondered why this time felt so different.

"You bastard! You bloody bastard! Why did you do it?" Sebastian Cain shouted, tumbling from the coach.

Hot on his heels, Alan, Earl of Bentley, leaped from the same conveyance, grabbing at his friend. But Sebastian was far quicker, and there was no preparation for the large fist that connected with Nicholas's chin. Stumbling beneath the onslaught, he did not go down, nor did his arms raise in defense.

"Why? Why her? You took what didn't belong to you. Something pure and innocent, something you could destroy," Sebastian grunted, fists slamming one after the other into Nicholas's stomach.

The pain was sobering, but when Nicholas opened his mouth, Sebastian landed a savage right cross. Staggering, jaw throbbing, he committed a grave error by grabbing on to Sebastian for support just as Alan reached them.

"How long ago? When did you take her?" Roars of thunder billowed from Sebastian, his face contorted with the pain of treachery.

"She wanted—"

Another punch cut off Nicholas's words. Groaning, he felt his left eye swelling shut. Alan shot him a wild glare filled with panicked concern as he grabbed Sebastian from behind. He held the man's arms just long enough to prevent any further blows.

But Nicholas braced himself, accepting the inevitability of a serious beating. He could not defend himself, not when every word was true. He had taken what did not belong to him. Infected her with his wickedness, stripped away her beautiful innocence. Sebastian would never believe or understand her sweet surrender was as necessary to his soul as the air he breathed.

"Marilee was mine. My fiancée and bastard that you are, you stole her from me. Betrayed me...our friendship." Sebastian wrenched from Alan's grip and tackled Nicholas. They tumbled down the steps of the townhouse, landing in a heap with Sebastian on top. While his friend pummeled away, Nicholas took the punishment with a dazed bewilderment.

Who the devil was Sebastian talking about? Marilee? He never wanted her. Never even touched her. Marilee was nothing more than a treacherous, sweet-faced bitch who had somehow buried her claws in his best friend. But Grace, oh God, Grace was everything. The sun and all the stars in heaven. The moon and tides. The sweet breezes of spring and the sticky warmth of summer. She was everything Nicholas ever wanted. Everything *worth living for. Worth suffering for. Sebastian would kill him for ruining her...that was certain. And she was worth dying for.*

Nicholas tried explaining he never wanted Marilee, but Sebastian's features were morphing into something different. Someone different. Slowly melting, fading like dust on a windowpane, washed clean by raindrops until Tristan Buchanan stood there instead, his handsome face twisted with terrible sadness.

"Damn you, Richeforte." Tristan struck Nicholas, splitting his lip. He tasted his own blood. "Why Grace? She's not yours. Not yours—"

Nicholas screwed his eyes tight. Instead of agony, a wave of shame swept him. It left him dizzy and breathless, panting at the enormity of his actions.

"She's mine. Mine. Mine..." he mumbled over and over.

"Nicholas."

At first, he ignored the soft, sweet voice. But when his name was repeated, his lashes slowly lifted.

He no longer lay prone on the ground. Instead, he now stood over Grace. She was on her knees, her honey-colored gaze riveted on him. He blinked, confused, gliding his fingers over her head, through her silky hair. Across her jaw. She was gold. Fire. Chaos in the palm of his hand.

She whispered something, and he bent down, his lips brushing her tiny, shell-like ear.

"Won't you let me hold you?" She asked, her cheek pressing against his. "Won't you let me in?"

Nicholas bolted upright.

He was alone. In his bed. His heart pounding. His room was so bright and it wasn't usually. Sunlight streamed through the windows. He remembered now. He'd opened the drapes during the night. Fell asleep watching the lightning and the whipping, raging storm, his arms wrapped about sunshine. Wrapped around Grace

She was not there, of course. He'd deposited her in the

bedroom adjacent to this chamber. The level of regret he felt for that surprised him. He rubbed the scar on his leg and pushed back the covers. Slipping into a robe brought memories of rolling the sleeves on hers. Jesus. What was he thinking? The things he'd done...and said. She'd probably fled at first light, back to Bellmar Abbey on her fine, Irish thoroughbred.

Strawn, his valet, had already come and gone in his silent way. A pot of steaming coffee waited on the table by the fireplace, the dishes from the midnight meal removed. If he ventured into the dressing room, Nicholas knew he would find his clothes for the day laid out. He still resented the valet's services, having decided long ago another man's assistance was not required in dressing himself, however, fresh coffee first thing in the morning was worth tolerating the servant's discreet attendance.

Nicholas jotted down a few lines of the thoughts floating in his head in the journal on his desk then poured himself a cup of the dark brew. He wondered if Strawn was shocked at seeing the expensive cravats adorning the bed's posts and fretwork. The silk pieces were missing now, but they were stretched anyway, ruined for future use. Well, he owned dozens of cravats and couldn't imagine a better way of suffering the loss of a few.

Tying the robe's sash into a loose knot, Nicholas entered the antechamber. He stood with a hand resting on the doorknob leading into the duchess suite, wondering why he hesitated.

These were previously his mother's rooms. When his father died and Nicholas claimed possession of Oakmont, she took up residence in a different wing of the house. She insisted her old rooms were for the new Duchess of Richeforte, whomever that might be. Nicholas didn't have the heart to remind his mother he had no intention of ever marrying. She was pleased when he redecorated the space in shades of soft creams and light sage green. A far cry from the severe black and gold his father insisted upon in all the private living spaces.

Nicholas listened for a moment, hearing voices coming from

within the room, followed by the click of a door as someone exited out into the hall. With a deep breath, he pushed the antechamber door open and entered as if braving a lion's den.

"Good morning, Your Grace," Grace trilled.

She sat perched beside the fireplace in a lovely chair upholstered in cream and gold damask. A small fruitwood table held a tea tray, and she cradled a delicate cup as if warming her hands. Swamped by black silk, her bare feet were curled in the seat under the excess fabric, all but hidden beneath the robe. Her freshly brushed hair was a cascade of sunlight streaming over her shoulders.

"You just missed Miss Martha. What a delightful woman...you are certainly fortunate having her as your housekeeper. She's promised my clothes shall be clean and dry by tomorrow morning."

Grace smiled at him. As if he'd not ruined her the night before. As if he'd not thrust his fingers inside her. As if he never ravaged her mouth with his. As if he wasn't intimately acquainted with the curves of her lush, golden backside.

Nothing could be lovelier than seeing her features light up at the mere sight of him. Nicholas's heart skipped. Yes, skipped. And then clenched when he heartlessly crushed his own reaction. She was so bright and shiny. The silk wrapped about her like a thundercloud trying to encompass the sun. And he was the frantic storm, roaring in, destroying everything.

Tilting her head, her eyes traveled his form. Then she blushed, remembrances of the night staining her cheeks a pretty pink.

Nicholas's cock twitched. He remembered too. It infuriated him.

"You must go." His words were a guttural rasp.

Grace's eyes snapped up, meeting his, and her wide smile almost broke him.

"I must? Miss Martha said the bridge at Riverbend Road is

underwater. How do you propose I go home?" She took a sip of tea, watching him over the cup's gilt rim. "I could take the long way about. It would mean a four-day journey and two nights at an inn. And, of course, there's no way of knowing the conditions of the roads so far from here."

Damn. His luck could not be any worse. No way in hell could he allow Grace to undertake the trip alone, even with a couple of his footmen and her groom accompanying her. And should word leak he traveled with her...the repercussions could bury them both.

"It appears I'll be here for a couple of days, at least. I suppose I shall need something other than this robe to wear." Grace plucked at the hem of the garment, shooting a glance at Nicholas from beneath a fringe of sable dark lashes when he did not respond. "May I beg a favor, Your Grace? I'd like to check on Llyr's welfare. As well as my groom, Robbie. Will you accompany me? I realize you are very busy being a duke, but I welcome your company. And if you will show me the library after that, I'll occupy myself there and keep out from underfoot."

Underfoot? All Nicholas could envision was Grace *under* him. That was dangerous. He should stay as far away from her as possible until she departed Oakmont. "There are matters I must attend—"

"Oh, please. Won't you come with me?" she interrupted. "I'd rather not go alone. It shall be less awkward if you are with me..."

Soundlessly touching down amidst his orderly life, destroying his walls with a sweet smile and sparkling eyes, Grace Willsdown was truly the little storm others called her.

If Nicholas could manage it, he would see that she quickly whirled out of his life.

CHAPTER 17

$\mathcal{T}$he duke was as jumpy as a scalded cat, maneuvering around Grace as if she were made of glass.

After obtaining the necessary items, Grace pulled Llyr from his stall and set about currying the horse. Robbie, devouring a bowl of porridge from a nearby bench, offered his help, but Grace shook her head to the contrary. Brushing the horse out with brisk, efficient strokes, she laughed softly whenever he nudged her with his large head. It was only when she pulled out the tool to clean Llyr's hooves did Nicholas intervene.

"Let me do that," he ordered. Realizing her borrowed dress might be ruined, Grace silently handed over the instrument. He began with one of the stallion's rear hooves.

Llyr stood immobile, sleek and hewn of ebony stone. When the first hoof was done, Nicholas released it from his grip, then grunted in pain. That same hoof, the size of a small village, currently sat atop Nicholas's boot, stomped there with the willful nature of a bully eager to prove his mettle.

Nicholas shoved the horse's flank, finally moving the beast off his foot. He bent over with a sigh of relief when Llyr let out a nicker that sounded curiously like a chuckle. Swishing his thick tail into Nicholas's face, the horse peered over his shoulder as if checking on how the duke was taking things.

"Grace," Nicholas bit out. "I highly recommend this horse be gelded."

"Oh, my goodness!" Grace exclaimed. "Llyr! What a naughty boy you are! I'm sorry, Your Grace. He's likely a bit out of sorts because of the storm and unfamiliar surroundings. He's not done that in a long time."

Catching Robbie's incredulous squint, Grace shook her head, encouraging the lad's silence. The stallion did this sort of thing on a regular basis. Never with his full weight, but enough so a person understood the necessity of hoof cleaning was not a favorite procedure.

"Gelding will temper bad behavior." Nicholas quickly finished the other three hooves, carefully stepping aside before letting the hoof fall from his hand.

"Then I would have no stables to speak of. Llyr is the heart of Bellmar Abbey. He is the very reason Bellmar still exists," Grace commented cheerfully, smoothing a hand down the stallion's thick neck. Llyr leaned into his mistress, dozing like a sleepy cat in the sun. "Besides, gelding is an extreme measure and completely unsuited for a horse of his caliber. One must allow concessions for such a magnificent creature. Don't you agree?"

Nicholas merely grunted. When Llyr was groomed to Grace's satisfaction, the duke led the horse back to his stall. He stood silent as she kissed and whispered in the stallion's ear. Grace did not care it was silly or that Nicholas probably believed her foolish in forming an attachment to an animal. Showering the beast with love, she found herself thinking Nicholas would benefit immensely from such affection.

They silently returned to the mansion for their own breakfast, avoiding numerous rain puddles and downed tree limbs scattered about the pathway. Grace watched the groundskeepers haul away a large branch that had fallen from an oak tree. She was so overwhelmed by the tornado of Nicholas's attentions, she'd not realized the intensity of the night's storms.

Oakmont's butler, imposing and of an indeterminate age, opened the mansion's doors as she and Nicholas ascended the last half of the numerous stone steps.

"Thank you, Teaks," Nicholas said, guiding Grace inside with a hand in the middle of her back. She could barely breathe with the weight of it, and she smiled nervously at the stoic butler.

"Your Grace. Milady."

Teaks's grey head nodded, closing the front door quietly behind them. In the massive center hall, decorated in rich tones of emerald and gold, boasting an impossibly high barrel ceiling encrusted with medallions and ornate trim, a pair of young maids paused in their dusting duties. In wide-eyed wonderment, they stared at Grace before dipping matching curtsies.

Nicholas's lack of concern with the household staff seeing her, when she should not even be there, eased Grace's apprehension. Her impulsive smile at the girls sent them into even more curtsies and a chorus of "Good Morning, milady! Good morning, Your Grace!"

Upon viewing the seating arrangements in the huge dining room, a frown of consternation furrowed Grace's brow. Nicholas purposefully placed her at one end of the impossibly long table, giving her a formal bow before taking a seat at the end. A space wider than the English Channel stretched between them. Conversation was impossible. A hundred people could easily fit between them, and Grace's fingers lightly drummed on the pristine, white tablecloth as she considered methods of erasing the distance.

One of eight footmen leaped into action when her empty teacup clinked on its saucer. In a matter of seconds, the cup was refilled while Grace squirmed. Why two people required so many servants for one meal was mystifying. She was never comfortable having servants hovering about, anticipating her every move. And these footmen were so impassive. Not even the tiniest of smiles cracked their expressionless facades. But their eyes were kind, each man nodding respectively whenever she glanced their way.

Still, they unnerved her.

She leaned over, peeking around three magnificent porcelain centerpieces overflowing with a profusion of lilies, roses, snapdragons and greenery. Nicholas could barely be seen. Six towering candelabras with no less than twenty candles each also adorned the dining table. A breakfast service for the duke and one for her, complete with domed platters, pots of tea, coffee and hot chocolate, occupied each respective end of the table as well. Grace decided a map might be necessary if she wanted to locate her host.

She fidgeted with the neckline of her lovely borrowed dress as egg soufflé, strips of bacon and a fluffy scone were placed on her plate. When a footman delicately smeared currant jam and clotted cream on the scone, Grace couldn't help tsking beneath her breath.

"Would milady prefer a different flavor?" The servant politely inquired with a raised eyebrow. He appeared both differential and genuinely puzzled by Grace's show of faint exasperation.

She smiled, nodding at the scone he held in one hand and the small knife in the other. "No, thank you. Currant is my favorite. Only, I prefer doing such things myself."

"Of course, milady."

Silence filled the room again, and as the seconds passed, Grace became certain Nicholas was intentionally avoiding her. Were their moments of shared intimacy so disturbing? Did he wish to be rid of her as quickly as the other women warming his bed? Her jaw tightened. Motioning the footman closer, she murmured her request and rose from her chair.

At the other end of the table, Nicholas tilted sideways until

Grace filled his line of sight. A scowl darkened his features. "Is the food not to your liking? The kitchen will prepare anything—"

"It's not that, Your Grace." With purposeful strides, she stalked the length of the room. Juggling plates, silverware, teacup and saucer, three nervous footmen trailed in her wake.

Letting out a heavy sigh, Grace plopped into the chair on Nicholas's right. "There. Much better, don't you think? I wondered if I should send a message from my end of the table, requiring permission to join you. But in the time it would take sending an answer, breakfast would be over," she teased while her meal was reassembled.

"This is not how it's done," Nicholas growled.

"No doubt that's true." Grace took a bite of eggs, chewed and swallowed before continuing. "I've not yet learned how it's done. Lady Darby has done a terrible job instructing how one should properly take breakfast at a duke's table."

He snorted. "A paltry excuse, and you know it."

"Perhaps, but Your Grace, you honestly could not prefer I remain a world away while within the same room. Besides, I was lonely down there."

"Lonely," Nicholas repeated, taking a sip of coffee, gaze narrowed as he examined her. "You don't understand the danger you are in."

Her eyes collided with his. "Yes, I do."

"Should you value even an inch of your tantalizing hide, you will return to your former seat." Emerald green eyes flashing, he said, dangerously soft, "Now."

"I'd rather not," Grace replied just as softly, determination lacing her words.

"Stay, and I won't be responsible for my actions."

Grace flicked a glance at the impassive servants, hesitant in light of the quietly heated statement. Hopefully, the duke's words were difficult to understand in the cavernous room.

Catching the path of her concern, Nicholas gave the slightest wave of his hand. Precisely five seconds later, the footmen exited, and they were now alone.

"Who will prepare my scones now?" Grace murmured, biting back a nervous laughter. "They haven't enough cream, and in such a short time, I've become accustomed to being coddled." She licked the clotted cream from the top of the little biscuit.

Nicholas groaned, eyes closing as if in pain. "How do you do that?"

"What, Your Grace?"

"Something so innocent and yet so extremely wicked, I wonder if you had lessons from the most practiced of courtesans." Head tilting, he studied her as if she were a fascinating curio stolen from a museum.

"I do that?" Her eyes widened. "Are you sure?"

"Yes. It's driving me mad if you must know."

Grace practically preened with satisfaction. "How wonderful! I thought perhaps you were immune to me."

"Impossible. And obviously, you enjoy this effect you have on men." Nicholas's tone turned a little harder, even while a smile tugged at his mouth.

"Not men, as in plural," she admitted shyly. "Only Tristan has complained thus far. And now you, Your Grace."

"Won't you call me by my given name?"

"Shall I call you 'Nicholas' when we are not in bed?"

"I suspect you will call me a great many things before this is over."

Grace's gaze landed on his mouth, her cheeks blooming an even brighter pink than the centerpiece lilies.

"Hmm," Nicholas mused when Grace said nothing. "I'd give my entire dukedom to know the thoughts going around your pretty head."

Grace laughed and refilled her teacup. "Your riches would remain intact, for I am thinking of nothing in particular." She could not tell him she was remembering how she nearly moaned his name aloud when he placed his beautiful mouth between her thighs the night before.

"I think you are up to mischief." The dimples in Nicholas's cheeks made a quick appearance, then were gone, like fireflies confronted with the first rays of sunrise.

Grace dreamily thought the little divots were extremely appealing on the duke and in a moment of weakness, she said, "I confess I'm surprised you do not eat small children and innocents for breakfast. Your reputation has labeled you an ogre."

"I despise children. As for innocents, I'd say I'm just getting started this morning."

The flush in her cheeks spread to her chest. "You do not care for children?"

"No." Taking a sip of rich, dark coffee, he eyed her over the rim of the cup and said, "It won't work."

"It won't?" Her head tilted. "And what is that, pray tell, Your Grace?"

"This attempt at distracting me. You should know every time you use my title, I'm reminded of our contract."

Nicholas leaned back in his chair, and Grace couldn't help admiring the regalness of his pose. He truly was a magnificent duke. All dark gold and leanly muscled man. He played idly with a knife beside his plate, fingertips testing the blade's sharpness. It drew attention to the bite marks she'd given him. How she kissed them as if she could heal them. Her face flushed with thoughts of all they'd done.

How fine he tasted on my lips. So warm and strong. Like brandy and mint and woodsmoke.

"All right," Grace conceded, hoping she might shock him a little. "I was remembering how you kissed me last night. How much I liked it - once I became used to it, that is. How very different it was compared to Longleigh's kisses. And how glad I am the bridge at Riverbend Road is under water."

Nicholas's exasperated sigh was barely audible. "Do not

speak of Longleigh's kisses and mine in the same breath. Why aren't you using my name as I requested?"

"Because you insisted I use your title, Your Grace."

"You are intentionally vexing me," he drawled.

Now Grace was the one who was shocked, seeing Nicholas's pupils dilate, the beautiful green color of his irises almost swallowed in black. "I swear I'm not," she stuttered.

He merely raised a brow in response. Silence stretched, growing taut between them. Grace fancied she heard everything in that silence. The tall clock tick-tocking away in measured beats, the soft, muffled voices of Richeforte's army of staff waiting outside the dining room doors. She even heard the birds outside the windows, chirping in a language no one else understood. And her own blood, thumping slow in her veins, keeping precise time with her heart.

Will he kiss me again? Will he do those wicked things that make me feel I've grown wings and can fly?

"Come here."

At the husky roughness of his voice, Grace closed her eyes and squeezed her legs tight against a wave of sudden lust. "Your Grace—"

"I won't ask twice."

She stood from her chair as his scraped back on the hardwood floor. Taking one of her hands in his, he drew her into the small space between the table and his lap. With his legs stretched out, she found herself caged by his body, their fingers tangled together and his free hand resting lightly on her hip.

Nervous, Grace shifted her feet. Their position and the height of his chair meant his eyes were now level with her chest. The dowager duchess's dress was a wee bit tiny in that particular area; Grace's breasts strained prominently against the tight bodice.

For Heaven's sake. They might have found something with a

bit more fabric to it! If he leans forward, his lips will touch bare skin and...

"Have you any idea what happens when I'm deliberately provoked?" Nicholas murmured, rubbing his hand in a sweeping motion down her hip and along the perimeter of her thigh.

She noticeably swallowed. "I don't know, Your Grace. I wasn't..."

His eyes drifted up, capturing hers. He was suddenly unapproachable. Cold and rigid, and Grace nearly shivered.

"I think you do know." His lips thinned. "Or at least, you wish to. And how clever you are, thinking the use of my title will sway me from my purpose."

"What is your purpose?" she asked cheekily, her breath ratcheting until it felt she was gulping for air.

There was no avoiding Nicholas's gaze, the hot, silky darkness of it. When his free hand slid north from her hip until it brushed the bottom of one breast, Grace jerked back in surprise. Where their fingers tangled together, his tightened just enough so she was kept in place.

"Shall I show you, little bee? How unwise you are to sting me and expect to fly away? Nothing will give me greater pleasure than ripping your tiny wings off. One by one, until you lay helpless and trembling in my palm."

His words sent a tendril of both fear and desire streaking through her veins.

"But it isn't night, Your Grace."

"Night?" His brow rose again. "Do you think I care the sun is up?"

"N-no." Grace bit back a moan when his thumb flicked over a satin and lace encased nipple. It was like the flame of a candle whispering over her skin. "But it should matter—"

"It doesn't." His thumb never stopped rubbing, and she swayed with the motion, a mixture of desire and dismay flooding her senses.

Damn the man. How easily he ensnared her in a web of lust. She'd do just about anything if it meant experiencing those sensations again. To have him do those magical, wonderous things to her body with his amazing hands and lips and his beautiful mouth. She stared at him as if in a trance, captivated by the darkening of his green eyes and the way his smile curved as if he knew her every thought.

"Besides," Nicholas smiled. "This isn't about our contract. Not really."

"What is it about, Your Grace?"

"Consequences. Satisfying your curiosity. And mine, I suppose."

"I don't understand." Her head tilted in confusion.

"You will."

Nicholas abruptly tugged her closer, down across his lap, her bottom in the air. Grace was so startled she didn't resist until it registered what he intended. Then it was too late.

"Your Grace, you mustn't." She gaped at him over her shoulder. "I'm begging you…"

His eyes pinned her. "Hearing you beg arouses the goddamn beast in me."

Taking the braided rope of her hair, he pulled it away from her neck so that it tumbled over one of her shoulders.

One large hand pressed into the small of her back. "Place your hands on the floor, palms flat."

Grace wiggled in horrified outrage. "You can't mean to go about in this manner!"

"Of course I do. Perhaps you will find enjoyment in surrendering. As you did last evening. Shall we see if this is so?"

The rough timber of his voice was shocking. The willingness seeping into her bones even more so. Where her stomach pressed his thighs, Grace felt heat and hardness. Her upper body hung off the edge of Nicholas's knees, her breasts swelling against the too-tiny bodice and threatening to breach the boundaries. Her bottom tingled. As if in anticipation. Or denial of the situation.

She tensed. Waiting for the heavy weight of his hand to strike her backside. But, Nicholas did nothing for what seemed like forever. And, hanging there, waiting, a strange calm overcame Grace, a heady, hedonistic swirl of lust and acceptance. Would his hand striking her arse sting? Burn? Ache? Would it be excruciating? Or bearable? Would she like it? She couldn't imagine she would. A secret, inner voice of insanity whispered otherwise. She silently screamed at it.

Shut up...shut up!

Bending close, Nicholas's soft murmur caressed her ear when she tried lifting herself from his lap. "Do not struggle, pet. Now, will you be still for me?"

She was probably selling her soul to the very devil, but Grace slowly placed her palms on the floor as instructed. Hearing Nicholas's sharp intake of breath was incredibly gratifying. It surprised her how much she liked it.

"The servants..."

Her whisper was strangled. How mortifying it would be should anyone find her thus. Why did she agree to this? His hand casually circled and caressed her flesh through the layers of fabric.

"Will not dare enter unless I command it." A few more circles, then, his voice rasped, "Your gown. It's in my way."

"Your mother's gown," Grace corrected, confused at why he chuckled.

"Ah, yes. How could I forget? If you think it will dissuade me, you'll be disappointed."

With a quick motion, he flipped the skirts up, leaving her exposed. Thank God her flimsy undergarments had dried much quicker than the heavy wool riding habit. Face flaming hot with embarrassment, Grace wondered what her backside looked like and, Heaven help her, if he found it pleasing.

"Tsk, tsk." Nicholas's palm smoothed over the thin silk covering her. "I'm disappointed by this discovery; however, I'll allow your undergarments to remain this time. Now, let's begin."

CRACK!

That first strike jolted Grace forward. She processed the sensation with a dazed sort of awareness. Numbness at first, then heat. Blooming and spreading. As if Nicholas struck her with a hand containing fire. Surprise was surely etched over her own features when, biting her lower lip, she looked back at him over her shoulder. His eyes were heavy-lidded, inscrutable, a tawny gold chunk of hair partially obscuring his face. The abrupt desire to brush away from his brow assailed her. Her fingers itched to trace that slight stubble on his hardened jaw, to feel the scratchy abrasion against her palm.

Greedy lust bloomed in Nicholas's eyes, and Grace moaned at the anticipation billowing around them. They stared at one another until she lowered her head, bracing for the next swat. A tendril of hair, straying loose from the braid, hung before her eyes. She blew at it with pursed lips, the slight puff of air moving the fringe of bangs off her forehead.

"Do not tense your muscles," he commanded in that low, husky voice that did strange things to her stomach. Grace trembled, finely wrought waves chasing each other, like riptides on the beach, each frothy curl of water pulled and pushed along by invisible undercurrents. From the tips of her fingers pressed to the hardwood floor to the soles of her stocking feet, everything within her undulated and swayed as if she were at sea.

A muffled giggle escaped her. She only wore stockings because the dowager duchess wore shoes a size larger, and her riding boots, while perfectly fine for visiting the stables, were not appropriate for her borrowed, sky blue silk gown and breakfast in this grand dining room.

"If you find this amusing," his voice roughened, "I'm not doing a proper job of it."

Before she could muster an explanation, he struck again. This time, a little squeak of protest slipped past Grace's lips. Nicholas paused, hand hovering, then slowly, oh, so slowly, he smoothed away the sting. His palm, almost as large as one cheek of her bottom, was incredibly warm, the rubbing circles mesmerizing, almost hypnotic. It was rather pleasant how he ministered until she relaxed against his thighs. They were bunched beneath her stomach, the muscles hard as iron, and Grace sighed, lulled into complacency.

A strange sensation formed between her legs. An achy, needy feeling was melding into the sting. How confusing to discover her breath coming a bit faster, Nicholas's matching it. Confined within the gown, her breasts tingled, nipples blazing. Pressing her legs together, she became aware of a growing wetness in the triangle there. She felt...hollow...and only Nicholas could fill the emptiness. For unfathomable reasons, her bottom lifted, seeking the heaviness of his palm.

What the devil is wrong with me? I should not like this...I should not! Even if it doesn't truly hurt, I cannot allow this madness...

Deciding enough was enough, Grace gathered herself, intent on rising from his lap, and found herself pushed back into place, one hard hand spanning the entire width of her lower back.

A broad finger suddenly thrust through the small opening in her drawers. Finding her softness. Impaling her.

"*Nicholas.*"

His name on her lips was a wicked little moan. Hearing it, Nicholas stilled for a brief moment, then remembering his purpose, he leisurely resumed the exquisite torture. Pushing beyond the dull ache present from the night before, he explored her, one finger, then two, dipping and curling inside her, massaging a secret, sensitive bit of flesh until Grace helplessly bucked against his hand.

Melting. Burning. Wanting.

"How wet you are, little bee. Like honey dripping all over my hand." His growl tickled her ear just before he nipped her earlobe, the sharp bite wringing a soft squeal from deep in her throat. "Will you come for me?"

"Come where?"

Grace gasped as the same tidal wave from last night rose inside her, hurtling her toward a universe where she had no cares other than this extraordinary pleasure. She felt drunk. On the cusp of exploding. Dizzy and lightheaded.

From your head hanging upside down, silly goose.

Dear God, the tight circles he was making with his hand, the way his finger rubbed inside her...she was about to twitch free of her skin with delight. Riding high on a wave that tossed her along...

"You make me forget your innocence. And that this was not intended to be pleasurable." Nicholas's own frustrations bled into the words.

With abrupt cruelty, his fingers withdrew, although he kept the one hand riding the small of her back. The pleasure from the impending orgasm receded into the sting on her rear, although it lingered along the edges in a very curious way. He struck her again, harder this time, sharp and stinging. After a few moments of allowing it to sink in, Nicholas silently stroked the fiery burn imprinted on her flesh.

When it eased into little more than a banked glow, Grace blew out a shuddering sigh. A strange, vague release drifted over her. Euphoric and heady.

The instant she slumped, boneless and soft, Nicholas lifted her, rising from his chair so she was pinned against the table's edge. The dizzying swiftness of his actions surprised her. She was now on her feet, head swimming as the blood rushed away.

Nicholas claimed her mouth with a savage, hungry greediness, iron-banded arms wrapping about her. Lips, a contradiction of hard and pillowy soft, crushed her mouth. Taking what he wanted, his tongue invaded and tangled with hers with such ferocity, a tiny thread of fear snaked through Grace.

Tender and still hot from the three swats of his hand, her bottom almost landed in a silver platter of bacon just before Nicholas heaved it away. It tumbled to the floor with an ear-splintering crash as he deposited her on table's edge. Grace curled her arms around his neck, holding on as he plundered and stole and gave back every sensation he'd just wrung from her while she lay across his lap. Her hair was still somewhat captured in a simple braid and he twisted his fingers in the loose strands, wrapping its length around his fist.

He began kissing her neck and throat, the tops of the breasts she wished were bare. There was a thunderstorm roaring inside her, drowning out everything except his hands, his mouth. The rasp of his stubbled jaw abraded hers when he cradled her chin in one large hand, tilting it up and to the side so he could feast on the slender column of her throat. His body, braced against hers so she wouldn't collapse backward while her world spun out of control. His teeth latching onto the tender crook between her neck and shoulder, his tongue tracing over the sting and across her collarbone.

He surely left a mark, she thought dazedly.

And she slowly became aware of Nicholas's words.

"You've bewitched me. I should rip this gown off you. I want you naked. I want you bent over this goddamn table so I can fuck you. Until you bleed your damned virgin's blood on me and I can wash you away and forget you. You'd let me, wouldn't you? Let me use you and hurt you until I've had my fill and no longer want you. Let me have you...give me your sweetness...wrap it around me, around my cock. Until I tire of you."

It was a rambling litany, lust spoken aloud, spewing as though he'd lost control. Most of it wasn't even English, but a bewildering mix of French and Italian, love words and curses. It should have shocked Grace, but when his hand closed and tightened around her wrist, she did not recoil. Her fingers gripped the ascot at his throat as though she might strangle him with the depths of her own desire.

"Nicholas...please..."

Grace's choked sigh broke through the haze wrapped about them. Nicholas tore away as if she'd scorched him. Staring at her in horror, he moved until the chair toppled in the wake of his retreat. The clatter it made was abnormally loud in the stillness.

With the quickness of a cobra strike, he jerked her off the table, uncaring when she stumbled. His grip on her wrist released just as fast.

"Get out of my sight..." The harsh command was ripped from the depths of his soul. "Go now."

CHAPTER 18

I fight
Like wolves
Trapped
Snarling
I wait
I quiver
A pathetic beast needing her touch
~Nicholas August Harris March
Ninth Duke of Richeforte

Grace reached a hand toward him, a beseeching gesture.
"But the library—"

Her bewildered expression had Nicholas closing his eyes. "Ask a footman, Martha, anyone...but get the hell out of here, and do not seek me out today."

Wheeling, he presented his back, ears pricking at her soft exhale of breath. *God help me, if I turn around, I'll take her. On this very table.*

There was a rustling noise as Grace gathered herself, then, incredibly, her slender arms wrapped about his waist. While he stood, trembling like a blooded stallion presented with a mare in heat, she embraced him, her hands moving up and spanning the breadth of his shoulders. Standing on tiptoes, her mouth pressed the middle of his back, the heat of her lips burning through the linen shirt. Nicholas's eyes snapped open, realizing her actions. Her quiet offering. He swore her tiny hands traced every single lash mark scarring his back. As if she were memorizing them.

"I don't know why you've lost your temper, but I shall do as you ask. Even if under protest."

Her mouth was surely branding him, searing his flesh with secret symbols proclaiming to the world he belonged to her and she to him. Nicholas shuddered, his response intentionally harsh. "I haven't yet lost my temper. I am keeping it locked tight, but if you are still within reach within the next ten seconds, you'll witness it for yourself. Now, do as I say."

"Very well, Your Grace." Grace's lips touched him a second time, a whisper escaping her, then she was gone.

Only her sweet perfume lingered in the air when Nicholas turned. Righting the upended chair, he sank into it, leveling both elbows on the table, head buried in his hands.

Grace was fast becoming an addiction. A craving. Something he could not slake. No matter how many times he tasted her, it wasn't enough. He wanted more. And when he had more, he wanted more still. He wanted her until he possessed everything that was her. *All* of her. She was a definite threat to his sanity. Dangerous. Not just because he found himself counting the different shades of gold in that mass of hair or because her skin was creamy silk. Or because she was so warm and soft. Nicholas marveled over the difference between them. He was a chunk of ice attempting to embrace the sun.

Her eyes were entrancing, the color of caramel. Or honey or whiskey, or whatever it was that made them something other than plain brown. But he didn't like the way she looked at him, as though she could see straight through him. No. That wasn't quite accurate. He *hated* the way she looked *into* him, into his very soul, terrifyingly deep and unblinking, searching out his secrets.

A grimace of disgust slipped over his face. Yes, everything about Grace was wrong. And yet, when he kissed her, it felt right, her mouth full and always smiling. When he held her, it was as though all the pieces of a puzzle had slipped into place, his hands curving into the spaces of her body as if she was custom made to fit his fingers. And she smelled perfectly right, all sunshine and lemons and wild heather. God, she tasted even better, like honey wine on his lips.

But she was wrong. He was wrong. And they were wrong together.

It was only a matter of time before it all crashed down.

GRACE TOOK HIS ADVICE TO HEART. NICHOLAS DID NOT SEE her for the rest of the day, although he inquired of her whereabouts sometime in the afternoon.

"The sweet dear is curled up in the library, Your Grace," Martha informed him with a tsking sound. "Surrounded by books, she is. Milady has a hundred of them stacked up. I took in a spot of tea and a pair of slippers one of the upstairs maids lent her just now, and she seemed quite surprised by the watercress sandwiches. Naturally, I explained you sent a lad sent into the village to procure some, seeing how she likes it so much."

Martha ignored Nicholas's scowl and continued. "Your collection of books has left quite the impression on the miss. She said she intends reading all the ones pulled from the shelves, and the next time she comes for a visit, she will choose just as many, and so on, until she's gone through every single book you have."

"Humph." Was all Nicholas offered in light of the housekeeper's report. There would not be a "next time." Not if he could help it.

"May the lady take a few books when she leaves, Your Grace? She says there's nothing left to read at Bellmar Abbey. Seemed quite disheartened about it."

Nicholas only stared at the elderly woman until she favored him with a frown, muttering something about stubborn dukes beneath her breath. She left him standing outside the door of his study.

That was hours ago. He'd spent that time pushing around a pile of papers, unable to focus on them. It was only when Teaks announced supper that he realized evening had approached.

During the long, solitary, boring day of avoiding Grace, one stark fact became clear. As distracting as it was being around her, it was far worse knowing she was only a few hallways away, and he was the sole reason the pleasure of her company was denied. Several times, he actually jerked open the door with the intent of invading his own library. Each time, he drew up short.

Seeking Grace out would only result in a repeat of that morning's incident. He would kiss her. Or worse. It was a fine mess he could not allow right now. Best he kept his distance, but still, a groan escaped him, remembering how he pinned her against the dining table. He wasn't sure of all he'd said, so overcome with lust and heat and want that the words flowed from him like lava from a volcano - none of it anything a gentleman should say to a well-bred young lady.

Grace needed to go home. She *was* going home, bad roads or otherwise. Surely, the bridge was passable by now. Arrangements were already made for a rider to investigate the conditions the next morning, and upon the man's report, she'd be bundled into one of his carriages and sent on her way.

Thoughts of her leaving sent a shiver through him. They shared a dangerous attraction. Grace seemed as fascinated by him as he was by her. Nicholas was having a hard time making sense of his emotions. It was a struggle, controlling them and himself. It was frightening, how easily he lost control with her.

Stay to the bargain, he admonished himself. *See it through, satiate my hunger, consume her innocence and fire. I govern this situation, not her. Damn everything else, and take my pleasure*

Then let her go.

GRACE PEEKED INTO THE DINING ROOM. SHE COULD NOT tear her eyes away from the table where she'd found herself and her entire world upended over the duke's knee. She still could not believe he'd done that. Her brain could not fully comprehend it, and every time the memory flashed, she felt as if she were consumed by an invisible fire. It was insidious. Exciting. Disturbing.

"Milady?"

Grace whirled, hearing Martha's courteous voice coming behind her. The elderly housekeeper wore a sweet smile as she reached out and closed the dining room door.

"I tried catching you before you left your rooms, but you'd already come downstairs. His Grace requested dinner on the west terrace. With the clearing of the weather, he thought you might enjoy it more..." Martha's words trailed off, and Grace swallowed, imagining the woman's embarrassment. Did everyone know what transpired that morning in the dining room? God, she hoped not.

"Oh," Grace managed. "That sounds nice."

"I'll show you the way, milady. His Grace is waiting there for you."

They passed by several rooms and through myriad corridors until a salon decorated in shades of blue and gold was reached. A pair of floor-to-ceiling glass-paned doors were flung open and a warm breeze swirled into the room, carrying the scent of the night, the sounds of chirping crickets and rustling leaves.

Just beyond those doors, staring out over the moonlit grounds, stood Nicholas, his hands braced against the waist-high brick wall. At first glance he seemed unaware of her arrival, but as Grace softly thanked the housekeeper, his broad shoulders hunched forward, as though accepting the heaviest of burdens. Slowly approaching him, her recently borrowed slippers falling silent on the Turkish carpet, Grace tucked her bottom lip between her teeth as she debated what to say.

The salon doors closed with Martha's exit. Nicholas straightened, then turned toward her, and any words Grace thought of uttering died a quick death.

His eyes burned her as they traced her form, displayed so temptingly in another of the dowager duchess's gowns. The peachy rose silk complemented Grace's complexion and blonde hair, the material clinging to her curves. And like that morning, the bodice on this gown was just as snug. There was a constant urge to tug it upward and Grace did so now without thinking.

"Don't."

Snapped in icy command, the single word was startling enough that her hands instantly fell to her sides. For a long moment they stared at one another, until Nicholas pushed off from the wall.

A tremble shook Grace. She was prey, and he a wolf, circling his victim.

His kill.

As he approached, bringing the dark scent of the night and the faint aroma of pine mingled with sandalwood and bay leaves, she stood frozen at the terrace entrance. He smelled so delicious, her mouth watered.

Reaching out, Nicholas took her hand. She went willingly, a small sigh escaping as she was pressed against his hard body. He was a solid mass of muscle, with nothing soft in his form or manner, and yet, she was not afraid. Not really.

"You have no idea how exquisite you are," he murmured against her hair.

"Some might find me attractive, but beautiful? Such compliments are reserved for women like Lady Ravenswood...she's so lovely."

"You are infinitely more so, Grace. I cannot place my finger upon it, but your beauty is different. It comes from your very soul, and I am entranced by it. By you. I find myself pondering how I can get more. How I can take everything there is to take from you. I want it to be enough, but I think perhaps it will never be enough."

Grace stood silent while digesting his assertion and puzzling words. No one had ever called her beautiful before. Or wanted all of her. She couldn't help wondering how much of the compliment was driven by lust. Hearing her name on his lips was addictive. She basked in the glow of it, savoring the pleasure of how it eased past his lips and into the air. She wanted it whispered in the curve of her neck while he held her tight and slid deep into her body.

When he realized she had no answer, Nicholas leaned back, brushing her fringe of bangs with a forefinger before trailing down, tracing her mouth.

The slight smile on his face seemed genuine. Again, the matching dimples in his cheeks, barely hidden beneath the scruffy stubble roughening his features, were mesmerizing. Even with the rugged shadow cast on his jawline, he was almost too gorgeous to gaze at. It was a sinful, breathtaking beauty, and Grace was dazzled by it, as every woman in London surely was.

"It's a pity I can't do what I would like right now." His gaze flitted over her features, and Grace flushed as liquid heat filled her.

"Why can't you?"

"Now is not the time. Are you that impatient, pet?"

She subtly pulled away and glanced past him. The table was set but no servants were present. Only the two of them occupied the terrace. She licked her lips, thinking of the last time they were alone.

"What would you wish to do, Your Grace?"

His smile turned even more predatory. "I would first order you down on your knees."

"Why would I do that?"

"Because I would like you to."

Grace frowned. "I don't think I like that...at least not when you say it so harshly."

Nicholas stepped aside when she brushed past him. "Please get on your knees, honeybee, does not have the same effect."

Looking at him over her shoulder, her chin tilted. "I don't like that either."

"Of course you don't. But I'm a cruel bastard, and you'll do as I say when the time comes."

"When will that be, Your Grace?" The question was breathless and nervously flippant. "During dinner? Or after?"

"Sweet with a sting," Nicholas chuckled, helping her into a chair. "Relax. While last night was for your pleasure, tonight is for mine. Anticipation is a heady, delicious thing, and right now it pleases me to wait."

CHAPTER 19

Softness
Wetness
Silkiness
These parts of her do not belong to me
Or any man
~Nicholas August Harris March
Ninth Earl of Richefort

Nicholas held her elbow, his fingers gentle and firm and somehow caressing even though they were motionless upon her skin. There was so much he felt with this girl, so many sensations capable of knocking the breath from his lungs. The silk of her skin, the softness of her hair. The gold of her eyes. Nicholas wanted possession of all of it.

She was a strange little creature, his sweet, practical Grace. All soft edges and hard determination, wrapped in a beautiful package that made the blood in his veins sing. She liked being mastered, but it must be a delicate undertaking on his part. Grace would never be completely tamed, and that in itself held tremendous appeal.

He dished out the meal onto the ducal, gold-edged dinner plates emblazoned with the Richeforte crest and trimmed in flourishes resembling pearls. Neither spoke as they enjoyed the roasted capon served over creamed spinach. A side dish of braised carrots rounded out the simple meal. They shared a bottle of the finest wine from his cellars, and after her second glass, Grace twirled the stem of the glass between her fingers.

"May I ask a question, Your Grace?" Her eyes were bright with ill-concealed curiosity.

"Do I stand a chance of stopping you?"

She had the decency to blush before shaking her head.

"Do your worst," he invited with a slight frown. His displeasure didn't deter her in the least.

"It's rather impertinent," Grace warned.

"I expect nothing less."

She regarded him for a long moment, as if the words were having difficulty forming in her mouth. Nicholas thought she'd ask about his former lovers. The baroness who'd only recently shared his bed. Hell, even questions regarding his blood feud with Ravenswood would not have surprised him. Her quiet inquiry shocked him.

"It's said, on the night your father died, the duchess took all of the duke's one hundred-year-old brandy, started a fire with it, and she, along with every servant in this house, feasted on oysters and champagne until dawn in celebration."

"Who told you that?" He couldn't keep the fury from his voice. *Goddamn gossips.*

Grace dropped her gaze, almost guiltily. "Sara, Lord Bentley's wife."

Nicholas didn't know whether he should be stunned or incensed. First, news of that night would not have escaped Oakmont's confines unless his own mother was the culprit. The servants would keep such secrets until death in order to please her. And to avoid his wrath.

A hint of a smile broke across Nicholas's face. He remembered the time he and Alan helped themselves to a cask of that same brandy when they were merely thirteen years old. He recalled the liquor's sweet bitterness. How it slid down his throat, smooth, like a ribbon of silk. Just one bottle gifted the opportunity of forgetting the emptiness inside him—if only for a short time.

He also remembered the brutal thrashing his father administered upon discovering the transgression.

"I've heard that rumor as well. Only, my mother did not throw all the brandy into the fire."

Grace's jaw dropped at the confirmation. Nicholas continued. "She gifted several bottles to the staff. As well as gold in compensation for the duke's miserly tendencies and petty cruelty over the years. And the oysters were gone within an hour, so no, they did not dine on those all night. But it is true the sun had rose before many of them fell into their beds."

"Your father must have been a difficult man," Grace said quietly, taking another sip of her wine.

"That is a kind way of saying it." Nicholas knew his growl was harsh. Speaking of his father in any capacity brought out the worst in him.

"Were you sad at all when he died?"

"I was devastated it didn't occur sooner. He was a miserable bastard."

Grace did not immediately respond. Nicholas knew she compared the affection for her own parents with the hatred he carried for the man who sired him.

In a little exercise of courage, she cleared her throat. "Is he the cause for the marks on your back?"

The question was asked so tenderly, Nicholas almost discounted it. His eyes narrowed slightly in warning. "What did you say?"

Grace traced the pattern on the tablecloth with a forefinger.

"It's just...I felt them. I cannot understand what they are. Or why they are there. But, I think I know and only a monster would—"

"Enough!" Nicholas's hand slammed down on the table, shaking the cutlery and causing the glasses to teeter precariously. He trembled with emotion. Anger; at Grace or himself, he wasn't sure. Despair. Because his father really was a monster. Hatred. For his father. Always for his father.

"It is none of your concern," he finally managed, biting the words out because they tasted bitter on his tongue.

Grace tilted her head as if attempting to solve a puzzle or perplexing riddle. "When my father's ship sank five years ago, Llyr was one of three living creatures that survived. He was trapped in a cove for more than a week before anyone located the wreckage, and since he was but a two-year-old and only trained to a halter, he was quite wild. I can't imagine what he endured. Trapped on the ship, then breaking free and swimming to shore during a horrible storm. It's why I named him after a god of water. He conquered the sea. Survived. I chose the perfect name for him."

Her sweet, soft voice drifted over Nicholas. Soothing. Calming. Entrancing. "A pitiful thing he was. Starving. Frightened. Savage. He's a magnificent horse, but that wreck nearly destroyed him. Hugh MacCormac, our stablemaster, thought we should put him down. Llyr suffered numerous gashes on his flanks from debris and rocks, but the worst injury was to his mind. Hugh said Llyr would never recover from the trauma. And even if he did, he would always be dangerous and unstable."

Nicholas glared at Grace. She was sucking him in, lulling him with her gentleness. She miraculously struck him silent when he wanted more than anything to rail and curse.

"Every day for a year, I cared for Llyr, putting special poultices on his wounds so they would fade away. Gaining his trust, accustoming him to my touch until the dear thing was restored to health and I could train him. But do you know what I discovered,

Your Grace? Even when wounds heal, they leave a trace on the flesh and on the mind. Although the marks faded, something as simple as a rainshower would refresh the scars in his memory. It was quite dangerous, for one never knew if he would lash out. However, I was persistent and stubborn. It took nearly three years before he realized the sound of thunder or the crack of lightning did not mean the end of him. Or maybe he simply forgot the cruelty of the shipwreck. He began greeting me at the gate, looking for an apple or scratch under his forelock. Nickering when I entered the stables. Letting me ride him bareback, with nothing but a grip on his mane. Trusting me..."

The blazing heat surely evident in his gaze finally provided results. Grace's words trailed off in awkward silence while Nicholas nearly bit his lower lip in half, fearing the release of his own savagery. But it couldn't be helped.

"Are you goddamn serious?" he breathed in furious wonderment. "Do you think it is such a straightforward matter as treats and a caress? Or affection? Are you so simple-minded, you believe it's possible I can be cured of my past? Make no mistake, Grace. Sharing a bed does not change anything. Fucking you will not magically erase my darkness. You hope it does, don't you? You hope our time together is so astounding and breathtaking, I'll realize how I've hurt and used you and take steps at rectifying the situation."

Nicholas reached across the table, grabbing her wrist, holding tight even when Grace cried out, twisting in a useless bid for freedom. "Foolish girl. You see, I enjoy using you," he hissed. "I enjoy hurting you even more. Because, *that* is my true nature, honeybee. Do not seek anything deeper than what you see on the surface. And understand this. When our time is done, I will forget you and find the same pleasures between another woman's legs. And another after her. And another."

Tears welled in Grace's honey colored eyes, her lower lip quivering. She looked at him as though he truly were a monster come to life. Nicholas's lips curved. He *was* a monster. His father's son. A man without honor or friends. It was best she learned that lesson now.

"Go," he ordered suddenly, in a voice deep and raw. He released her wrist. "Wait for me in your bedchamber. I can see you need proof of my cruelty to understand it. I'll show you. I'll *enjoy* it more than you can possibly fathom...bloody hell, how I will enjoy breaking you."

A mocking laugh escaped him when she sprang from the table, toppling over her wine glass in her haste. Nicholas thought she would run from him as fast as she could, but at the terrace doors Grace came to a halt. She slowly turned back to face him. Crickets chirped faintly in the distance, the sounds of the night gliding about them. Her voice drifted over him, soft as a doe's hoofprints in the forest.

"You won't forget me, Nicholas. I won't allow it. You've more in common with Llyr than you can possibly understand. A lost, dark, frightened creature deserving of kindness and understanding, and patience, no matter how dreadfully you kick and bite anyone who comes near. You delude yourself if you believe you will ever be able to forget me. And you won't break me. No matter how hard you try."

In response, Nicholas drained the wine in his glass, then reached for the nearly empty bottle. His jaw set in a tight clench when the salon doors clicked shut behind her.

CHAPTER 20

*G*race stalked from the salon, fury and despair combining in a dizzying cocktail of emotions. She was trembling and there was no doubt if she stayed on the terrace a moment longer, she would have slapped Nicholas with all her might. For the hateful, disrespectful way he spoke. For making her care. For making her hope he would ever possibly care.

His attentiveness during dinner surprised her, as well as his willingness in discussing his mother. And his father. Grace appreciated his dry wit, how he seemed relaxed but wary. A state of being she related to, having now spent time amongst society. One could never truly let down your guard, but Nicholas had opened up, even if it was just a little.

Then without warning, he lashed out, hating either the truth of her words or the emptiness he carried inside himself. Perhaps both. Regardless, his cutting words hurt her terribly. He truly had the power to draw blood, and although the effort of staying her hand tested her willpower, the incident also steadied her resolve.

I will succeed! I will! He needs me, even if he is not yet aware of it.

More than an hour passed before the faint sounds of movement came from the adjoining room. She heard low, masculine voices and assumed Strawn, Nicholas's valet, was there assisting him. It was still early in the evening, and Grace wondered if he might indulge in a brandy or cigar before retiring.

She'd already disrobed with the help of the same sweet maid who assisted her that morning. Now Grace stood at the door of the antechamber wearing nothing more than a flimsy chemise. Indecision froze her limbs. Was she supposed to go to him? Or would he come to her?

The door to the duke's chambers clicked shut, and the valet's footsteps echoed in the hall. Grace shifted from one foot to another for what seemed an eternity. Waiting. Wondering. God help her—hoping.

Her temper, successfully stifled until now, grew like a summer weed watered with Nicholas's neglect.

She entered the antechamber, a hand on the doorknob to the master chamber. One twist of her wrist, and she would stand before him.

And what then?

NICHOLAS HEARD THE DOOR OPEN. HE'D ALREADY DECIDED on leaving Grace be. To keep himself from her. She was consuming him, and each attempt at placing a distance between them failed. He could not allow himself the pleasure of drowning in her again so soon. This last night together and the exercise of his restraint was more for his sanity than her safety.

One long braid of hair tumbled over her shoulder. He'd be damned if she wasn't clad in anything more than a thin, ivory-hued chemise. The lace-trimmed garment barely edged the upper part of her thighs, dipping in the bodice to skim the tips of her breasts. Lust flared inside him, and every intention of keeping himself from her disintegrated like paper tossed into fire.

"Come here, Grace."

His voice was hoarse, scratchy with need, his hand stretching toward her.

Grace obeyed, and when she was standing before him, eyes blazing with temper and tears, she reared back, striking him across the cheek with such force, Nicholas rocked on his heels.

His eyes closed, quelling the instantaneous response of snatching her up and kissing her with a matching fury. God knew he deserved that slap, and so much more. He'd hurt her earlier. With his words. His animosity. The inability to reconcile these bewildering feelings for her. Something was happening inside him, unraveling him, unfreezing him, and he didn't know what to do other than lash out.

When he finally opened his eyes, meeting her gaze, the silence stretched, the air snapping taut with electricity. Nicholas did not move. Not even to rub the sting of her handprint from his cheek.

As it had earlier, Grace's chin trembled. She drew her bottom lip between her teeth, biting until he thought it might bleed. With a low sigh, Nicholas cautiously opened his arms, and after a second of hesitation, she flew into them, burrowing against his chest as if she'd always belonged there.

Holding her, something inside him cracked. Scary and over-whelming enough that he was breathless from it. He embraced her tighter, frightened by what swirled inside him. In two days' time she'd swept through his defenses and destroyed his icy fortress. It would be madness acknowledging it aloud or giving any indication of the power she held over him, but it was there.

He scooped her up and carried her to the bed. Surely, she thought he would descend upon her, ravaging her as before. Taking liberties, using his mouth, lips, and hands, those dangerous methods causing far more dangerous consequences. Instead, he merely held her, lying on his side with his front to her back, one arm encircling her midriff, the other placed beneath her head. She seemed content, wrapped in his embrace, a hard bicep partially serving as her pillow.

When Grace attempted to speak, Nicholas squeezed her waist in gentle warning.

"Sshhh," was all he said, and she relaxed against him, her breath exhaling in a tiny rush of relief.

She appeared just as reluctant in addressing matters between them. Yes, it all needed working out, but it was best such things were undertaken in the sober light of morning. When heartache could be managed more efficiently and with an absence of emotion.

Nicholas drifted asleep imagining the bleakness of an existence without Grace Willsdown, breathing in the clean heather and lemon sunshine scent of her hair, tracing intricate patterns on her skin with a forefinger. Invisible evidence of his need for her. A secret branding as permanent as one laid by hot iron.

His name.

His name and hers. Together.

She is mine...

Mine.

Nicholas woke the next morning with sunlight streaming through a wide crack in the drapes, instantly aware of three separate facts.

One, he'd not dreamed during the night. No nightmares, no bloody recollections of horrors suffered or friends betrayed. For the first time in five years he slept deeply, without conscious or unconscious thoughts of anything. Just deep, black, numbing slumber.

Second, he was alone in his bed.

And third...his heart stuttered with panic and regret. With loss.

Third...

Grace was gone.

CHAPTER 21

*T*wo weeks passed since the morning Grace hastily dressed and departed Oakmont.

Fourteen days of wondering. Would Nicholas suddenly appear on her doorstep, demanding an explanation for why she fled? She almost hoped he would, the letter she left behind an indication of her feelings. She'd taken five books from his extensive library. The note essentially instructed Nicholas to come get them. If he dared.

Her own boldness shocked her. Now, Grace wished she'd been a bit more subtle.

"Llyr dinna suffer durin' the stay at Oakmont," Hugh commented, coming to stand beside her.

Yesterday, the last of the breeding with the mares Sebastian sent was completed. Now, together they watched the stallion in his turnout. Llyr's ebony coat shone like onyx in the sun as he pranced, shaking his head until the thick mane tumbled over his thickly muscled neck. Grace was reminded of his arrival nearly five years before and the difference from then and now.

She also thought of Nicholas and her comparisons between him and the horse. *He probably believes I am the most eccentric of females, even if what I said was the truth. He is like Llyr. Proud. Wounded. Resilient.*

"They took excellent care of him while we were there," Grace answered the stable master honestly.

"Ye dinna say if your offer was taken."

She could not look at Hugh, afraid he'd see the truth on her face. Afraid he'd recognize the sacrifice she made for Bellmar Abbey. Numerous times the man brought the subject up, and Grace avoided it every time. Now was no exception. "I told you before. It's complicated, but for the moment Bellmar is safe."

Hugh tilted his head, disappointment darkening his weathered features. He pulled his grey mustache in agitation. "I dinna think ye would do it. What I knew ye was plannin'. But still, ye did, aye? Och, lassie..."

"You needn't worry. Things will work out."

"But ye—"

Hugh was abruptly cut short. Rounding the tree-lined drive, a four-in-hand team approached, mud-splattered horses high trotting. The coach bore a familiar dark blue color, the Ravenswood shield emblazoned upon the door. Grace inwardly groaned. She expected someone from her cousin's stables to arrive any day to collect the Ravenswood mares. She did not think it would be the earl himself.

"Not another word on the subject, Hugh. His Lordship must not know I ventured anywhere near Oakmont. Or the duke," Grace warned, leaning away from the paddock fence. She waved at the approaching vehicle. "Promise me."

The Scotsman tucked his chin and grumbled beneath his breath.

"I'll take that as your vow." Grace patted his arm.

"Grace! Hello! Grace!" Lady Ivy Ravenswood hung

out the open window of the coach, laughing, waving frantically with one hand, the other holding her hat atop chestnut hued curls. Obviously, Sebastian did not care to see his wife draped through a window, shouting like a washwoman on Sunday. A masculine arm wrapped about her waist and tugged her back inside.

But Ivy was difficult to keep contained. As the coach rolled to a stop, the young countess appeared once again in the narrow opening.

"My darling Grace! I've not seen you in forever! Hurry, Sebastian. I must get out of this coach at once."

"And I must insist you wait at least until the vehicle is no longer moving, my dear," Sebastian drawled from the shadowy interior, the request clear above the sound of horse's hooves.

His tone exhibited the highest affection for his wife, and a shot of envy zinged Grace. The love these two shared was deep and unequivocal. They cared not a whit that it was unfashionable for spouses to be so deeply infatuated with one another.

"Wretched man." Ivy laughed, leaning back into the coach.

Grace was fairly certain her beautiful cousin-in-law was at that very moment pressing a warm kiss upon the earl's lips. Her own lips suddenly tingled as she recalled the feel of Nicholas's mouth on hers. And other places.

Hoping it might dispel the images flashing in her mind, Grace wiped her mouth with a shaky hand.

When Ivy finally tumbled from the coach, she immediately wrapped her arms about Grace, squeezing tight. "Sweet little cousin! How happy I am seeing you again! It's far too long since you've visited Beaumont. You left us no alternative other than braving the wilds of Cornwall just so we might see your beautiful face."

"I've missed you both terribly. What a pleasant surprise you've come for a visit." Extracting herself from Ivy's arms, Grace returned Sebastian's affectionate embrace, accepting his kiss on her cheek.

"I know we've surprised you; however, Ivy would not be deterred. Although, I suspect her true motive for coming along was simply that she'd have me alone in a coach for an extended period of time," Sebastian said, flashing a grin at his blushing wife.

"You reprobate." Ivy wagged her finger at the handsome, dashing earl. "Behave yourself, my lord."

"I always try, madam." Sebastian executed a slight bow, lips turning upward with amusement.

Two servants sitting topside with the coachman jumped down and began removing the couple's baggage. While that was undertaken, Ivy linked her arm with Grace's.

"I'm assuming all has gone well with the mares?" Sebastian asked, watching the men handle the bags. Once assured all was taken care, he turned his attention back to the women as Grace ushered them all into the house.

"No problems at all. We finished yesterday...the storm set us back a couple of days."

"The innkeeper at the Red Stag mentioned it when we stopped last evening. He said the bridge at Riverbend Road washed away," Ivy commented.

"Not completely. It was underwater for a while, though. It has since receded to its usual depths." Grace cast about for a way of changing the subject. The last thing she wanted was a discussion of the bridge and storm. "I planned on visiting Beaumont now that the mares have been bred. Lady Celia Buchanan would like to attend the ball you have planned for Alan and Sara when they return from Paris. I said you would not mind if she accompanied me. I've missed Sara dreadfully and can't wait to hear all the news of the honeymoon."

Ivy laughed as she affectionately embraced Grace. "You are always welcome at Beaumont, and you don't need a ball as an excuse to visit. I'm hoping I'll convince you in returning with us when we leave here. It seems our time together is always far too short."

It was later in the afternoon that Grace found herself in the parlor with Ivy. Sharing a cup of tea while Sebastian checked on his broodmares, the two women discussed Alan and Sara's adventures. The earl and his wife were on honeymoon in Paris. For the past two months Sara had sent regular letters expounding on the social scene and beautiful scenery. Grace missed the new Countess of Bentley a great deal, the three women having become the closest of friends over the past six months.

"I can think of no subtle way of asking you this, Grace, but Lady Celia indicated you met the Duke of Richeforte at Calmont Downs." Ivy set her teacup down.

Grace's composure slipped a little. Was her interaction with Nicholas now fodder for gossips? Not that Celia was a gossip, but if she mentioned it, others probably had as well. "Oh? When did you see Celia? How is she?"

"She's well. We attended a series of plays performed at the Marquis Blackthorne's estate. Dreadfully boring; the plays, not the Marquis. I vow, had Sebastian gone with me, I would have expired from sheer boredom. Anyway, Celia said you and Richeforte shared quite the exchange." Ivy's expressive turquoise eyes studied Grace. "More than once. It seems her brother was quite disturbed by that and grumbled of it."

Grace thought surely every illicit act she and Nicholas had committed was etched on her face at that very moment. Answering nonchalantly was a struggle.

"The duke and I did meet. He's quite arrogant."

Ivy smiled. "And dark-natured. And sarcastic. And terribly

wicked." She gazed at Grace as if determining something quite vital. "He's like a dangerous, wild creature. Fascinating when admired from afar, but one wouldn't dare keep him as a pet."

Grace took a deep breath and sipped her tea. Ivy could not possibly know just how wicked the duke truly was. Nor how dangerous. "Is he? I thought him quite clever once his arrogance eased."

"You are aware of the background between Sebastian and the duke. Needless to say, your cousin would prefer you have no contact with him at all, but you are an adult woman. You have the right in making your own decisions. But you must be careful of certain gentlemen and their courtship, darling. Richeforte's reputation is quite scandalous. Perhaps not deserving of every rumor, but scandalous nonetheless."

Grace could not meet Ivy's gaze. Not while uttering the most blatant of lies. "You've no cause for concern. I'm certain the duke's interests lay elsewhere." *This is not completely untrue. Nicholas's interests do not include courtship of any fashion.* "Do you believe the rumors? Is he really that terrible?"

Ivy bit her lip and slowly stirred her tea. She thoughtfully tapped the spoon against the teacup's rim before answering. "No. I do not believe all of it. He was Sebastian's closest confidant for many years, and I honestly cannot fathom the level of betrayal that caused the rift between them. How a friend could be so cruel. Richeforte, by all accounts, considered Sebastian his brother, and Sebastian did the same. They were friends from such a young age. Alan Bentley as well. The three of them always together. As children, and as men."

"What happened?" Guilt pinged Grace. It felt underhanded obtaining the story from someone other than Nicholas. Especially when he declined to provide an explanation when prodded. "Why would Richeforte cause Sebastian harm?"

"Over a woman." Ivy reached forward and took Grace's hand. "Never repeat any of this. To anyone, darling. I only relate this now because Celia said Richeforte's interest in you went beyond mere politeness. You should know the truth so you can protect yourself."

"Go on." Grace steeled herself. It could not be that awful. Could it?

"Six years ago, Richeforte—he was the Earl of Landon then— conducted an affair with Lady Marilee." Seeing Grace's blank expression, Ivy elaborated. "She was Sebastian's fiancée at the time. When she became pregnant as a result of the affair with Richeforte, he refused to marry her. With that rejection, she attempted to convince Sebastian they should wed earlier than their scheduled wedding date. Understandably suspicious for the sudden haste, Sebastian would not agree. It was then that Marilee, in a fit of anger, confessed she carried Richeforte's child."

Grace's breath caught in her chest. Nicholas refused his child? Coming from a man whose own childhood was rife with heartache, it did not ring true. She hoped Nicholas was incapable of such cruelty toward an innocent. And one of his own flesh and blood. She desperately needed to believe that.

"Sebastian challenged Nicholas to a duel, but not before they came to blows on the steps of Richeforte's townhouse. Then, at the duel, Richeforte fired into the air, and Sebastian's shot, deliberately altered at the last moment, hit the duke's thigh instead of his heart. It's believed during the confusion, Lady Marilee mistakenly received word it was Sebastian who was shot. Fatally." Ivy's voice dropped to a whisper. "She hanged herself in her bedroom. Unable to face the shame and gossip. So tragic, although I do despise her actions and the heartache she caused my husband. Sebastian left England immediately after. After Nicholas recovered from his wound, he left England as well, sailing off in a yacht only six months later. An escape, I suppose, from the damage he caused. Or maybe he was snubbing his father. They were at cross-purposes at the time. Well, the two of them were always at cross-purposes. Regardless, Sebastian had no intention of murdering his best friend, but it didn't really matter. He and Richeforte have not exchanged a civil word since the duel."

Grace was stunned. This was much worse than she imagined. There was no ignoring how her stomach twisted with thoughts of Nicholas suffering a gunshot wound. And then shunned by those who were once his friends. She looked Ivy straight in the eye.

"Do you believe the duke would jeopardize so cherished a friendship? All for a woman who willingly betrayed one man for another? Or that he would reject his unborn child and heir? Did Richeforte love Marilee enough to steal her, but not enough to marry her?"

Ivy smiled sadly. "Men do terrible things when in love. Or lust. I've long thought there is more behind it all, some elusive, hidden detail, but Sebastian is convinced of these facts as he knows them. I tried once...to heal the rift, after the duke extended a kindness to me, one for his own benefit, but a kindness all the same. Sebastian would not even listen to me. But I know he suffers the loss of their friendship. To this day, he suffers."

CHAPTER 22

*E*arly the next morning, Grace made her way to the stables. She quickly saddled and bridled Llyr and within a half hour was riding along Bellmar Abbey's western boundaries, where the terrain slipped into cliffs and catapulted into the dark green sea far below.

Grace pushed the stallion, reaching greater speeds, hopeful the pace might free the nagging thoughts roaming around her brain. Sleep proved elusive the previous evening, dreams of the duel between Sebastian and Nicholas overtaking slumber, her active imagination filling in details Ivy did not provide. And Grace always woke during a moment she crouched at Nicholas's side, cradling his head while blood streamed in dark, lacy-like ribbons.

She'd tossed and turned; worried Sebastian would learn of her contact with his enemy. Worried Tristan would challenge the duke when Bellmar's lien was released in her favor. The viscount would surely feel betrayed. He might even seek to redeem her honor if he suspected a relationship between her and Nicholas. Between her cousin and the son of her guardian, Grace should have felt protected, instead, irritation pricked her. The two men were obstacles. Standing between her and Bellmar Abbey. Between her and what she feared she wanted far more.

Nicholas.

It was all so dreadfully complicated. And anxiety-producing. After the death of both of her parents, her life had devolved into something relatively simple, survival forced squarely on her own shoulders. For years, she'd handled things in her own manner with only her mother, then the distant, relaxed oversight of her guardian guiding her. Now, Grace was embroiled in a dangerous situation of her own making. And it all revolved around the Duke of Richeforte in some fashion or another. He had become the sun, and she was a tiny planet, rotating aimlessly until his rays caressed her once more.

Leaning low over Llyr's neck, Grace reveled in the stallion's strength, his uncanny intelligence. She trusted him in finding his way, flying over the uneven ground, navigating the massive boulders dotting the cliff edges. The sweet scent of heather mixed with the sea air creating a heady fragrance, and the crisp breeze swirled as if urging a faster, dangerous pace. Bursting between cracks in the rocks, star-like clusters of white and pink stonecrop flowers provided patches of color while kestrels circled overhead in a blush pink and blue cloud-streaked sky. Grace squeezed her eyes shut, shaking disturbing thoughts away while racing across the terrain to her destination.

Upon reaching the Bellmar Abbey ruins, she sat for a long time on a pile of upturned rough rocks. The ancient abbey consisted only of half walls and tumbled entryways. There was no roof—that disappeared at least four centuries ago—just ghostly rooms filled with wildflowers and rocks sprawling across at least an acre she'd explored many times over the years. Her house was built of the same cream-colored stones that were stacked and scattered about. And like the ones of the ruined abbey, those stones became a warm pink with the sun's rays at dusk and with the early morning light.

While Llyr grazed, Grace stared out over the sea, absorbing the sunshine and salty air. The breeze tossed her hair about, pulling strands free from the braid it was twisted into. Sometimes, when the wind blew just right, she tasted the brine borne on the currents, and Llyr did as well. He lifted his head every so often, nickered in obvious enjoyment, then continued munching the thick grass and wildflowers scattered everywhere in a carpet of dark, emerald green.

How should she act the next time in Nicholas's company? It would be difficult pretending ignorance of his rift with Sebastian; indeed, Grace wondered if she should even try. Perhaps he might be convinced of the benefit of sharing his side of things, but it was doubtful. Nicholas was extremely reticent in sharing anything of his past or feelings. Grace dejectedly wondered how an issue from so long ago, one she had no part in, could affect them now. It was disheartening. How could one ever hope for anything more than a superficial relationship when the man was so damaged and distant?

Neither the faint crashing of waves nor the swirling sea winds provided answers today. And that was confusing. She'd sorted her thoughts in this place more times than she could count. That it failed her now both angered and saddened her. And steeled her resolve. Bellmar Abbey, the quaint, cottage-like manor, with its drafty hallways, two cozy parlors, and rambling library, was the most valued component in this devil's bargain. She must ignore the pounding in her heart each time she thought of Nicholas and focus solely on gaining full control of her estate.

Whistling for Llyr, Grace took up his reins and gave his neck a swift hug. He smelled of the sea and of the sweet grass he'd eaten. Warm and solid beneath her cheek. Llyr allowed the embrace, turning his fine head ever so gently to snuffle her hair and lip at the fabric of her shirt. It was a sign of affection, in the manner horses cleaned each other's withers. It meant she was his...that a bond existed far beyond that of horse and owner.

Grace's eyes pricked with tears. "I won't lose you, Llyr. Even if I have fallen for that man, I won't lose you."

The horse nickered softly in reply. As if he understood his mistress's distress. He stood perfectly still while she clambered atop a pile of rocks and swung into the saddle.

Cantering up the wide drive of Bellmar Abbey, Grace noted with sharpened eyes the need for the east pasture fence repair. And the crumbling rocks surrounding the small fountain in the courtyard, the two uneven, broken steps at the front door. The paint there on the threshold was peeling as well. A fresh coat would be needed soon. Should a sale of one of the newly broke colts occur, those funds would be of great use. New dresses or ball gowns would gladly be forgone in exchange for the estate's repairs. It was one of the reasons a stay with Sebastian and Ivy at Beaumont would be advantageous. It was easier finding buyers from the many guests enjoying the earl's hospitality. From there, she would visit her guardian's estate in Hampshire and do the same, although she dreaded facing Tristan and his renewed courtship.

After unsaddling Llyr, she released him into his stall with an affectionate pat on the rump. Cutting through the east wing of the stables, which formed the shape of a 't', an unfamiliar nicker came from what should have been an empty box stall.

What the devil? Who else has decided to visit?

A beautiful blue roan stallion, larger than Llyr by at least a hand but fine-boned and clean of line, poked his head over the stall door. A thick, ash black mane tumbled on either side of his neck.

Grace looked about. The stable lads were busy with their chores, and Hugh was absent. Rifling through the tack stacked neatly atop a bench beside the stall, her heart stopped, then beat double time upon seeing the crest embroidered on the saddle pad.

Richeforte.

He was here. At Bellmar Abbey.

Her pulse raced with joy.

He'd come for her.

And he's under the same roof as Sebastian.

Bloody hell.

∾

Bellmar's ancient housekeeper, Mrs. Cooper, met Grace in the center foyer. Leaning heavily on her cane, she shuffled determinedly, having experienced a bout of rheumatism just the day before that necessitated twenty-four-hour bedrest. Being a small household, the elderly woman's assistance was not missed. She was a dear, sweet thing, part of the Bellmar staff for many years, and Grace saw no need to replace her.

"Lass, a gentleman awaits you in the large parlor. Name of Bickels. Or maybe it was Freckles..."

Grace sighed. Mrs. Cooper's hearing was as feeble as her knees and back. "It's Nicholas, actually, Mrs. Cooper. The Duke of Richeforte," she half-shouted in the woman's ear.

"You don't say?" Mrs. Cooper exclaimed, looking suitably impressed before scowling. "Then why didn't the blasted man say so to start with? I'm old, but I know the proper way of welcoming a duke. And this may be Cornwall, but we aren't savages."

"It's all right, Mrs. Cooper. I'm sure His Grace does not doubt our civility." Grace headed toward the parlor, tossing over her shoulder, "Will you have tea brought in? And some scones? I haven't had breakfast and feel a bit at odds."

She dared not admit that the thought of Nicholas, here in her *parlor,* for God's sake, had her stomach rolling in knots. A quick prayer was sent heavenward that hopefully Sebastian and Ivy had recently developed the habit of rising late. With any luck,

Nicholas would be gone before the pair of them ever discovered this impromptu visit.

Entering the bright, cheery parlor, Grace's heart fluttered with such ferocity, she believed it might fly up her throat and out of her mouth. Nicholas stood at the fireplace, casually inspecting various items displayed on the mantle. The sight of his shoulders attired casually in white linen muddled her thoughts. Dark tobacco brown colored breeches accentuated every muscle in his long legs and backside. Knee-high black Hessians completed the ensemble. Seeing his black broadcloth riding coat tossed over the back of a Sheraton chair, Grace considered how they were dressed in similar fashions, her own breeches a shade of fawn, her boots matching the black of his.

He reached for an item, and the shirt stretched even tighter across that muscular back of his. Grace wobbled a little, growing lightheaded. She'd traced those muscles with her fingertips, smoothing over the welts crisscrossing the broad expanse as if she could heal them.

Oh, she was in trouble. Trouble, indeed. Because seeing the duke reaffirmed everything she'd convinced herself was untrue.

Besotted. Infatuated. Entranced. Oh, blast. Every poetic word one might normally use for love described her current state with perfect, horrifying precision.

She'd fallen in love with the Winter Wolf. Cold, imposing, wicked Nicholas. An untamed duke she wanted to tame and keep forever.

"Your housekeeper struck me with her cane and called me a vagabond," he said, never turning around.

Grace did not answer. Because, really, what could she say to that accusation?

Nicholas picked up a block of metal upon which a preserved horse hoof was mounted. It was one of a pair, serving as bookends. Seeing it in the duke's hands reminded Grace how bizarre the object was. Her father had received them as a gift long ago.

She'd always wondered what poor horse was sacrificed for so strange an item. It invariably saddened her, although as a child she'd held one in each hand, clip-clopping up and down the foyer on her hands and knees. Her mother would laugh, say Grace was being silly, and the bookends would be replaced so they could sit in grandeur once more upon the mantle. Father would offer her a sugar cube, saying with an affectionate wink, that she was his favorite, loveliest, little pony.

When Grace remained silent, lost in her memories, Nicholas glanced over his shoulder, brow lifting. "She's quite intimidating, but I understand her confusion. I'm not precisely dressed as a peer of the realm."

When she finally found her voice, Grace was horrified that it squeaked like rusty hinges on an ancient door.

"Why are you here?"

His gaze sharpened. Darkened. Filled with secrets Grace doubted she'd ever learn the truth of.

"You know why." Setting the hoof down, he turned fully toward her. A frown immediately pulled his brows together. "Why are you dressed like that?"

Grace swept a hand down the front of the breeches. She never wore a riding habit unless absolutely necessary, and since fleeing the duke's home in the last one, she doubted ever wearing one again. There was no forgetting how it felt, the fabric scratchy, abrading her skin, reminding her the entire trek home how Nicholas looked at her that first afternoon. Drenched from the storm, her body displayed for his pleasure. How overwhelmed she was when he first took her in his arms, the wet material clinging to her body and his, the heat of him seeping through and scorching her. No, she would never wear that garment again. The memories, how she'd suddenly found herself turned inside out by desire, were too much to bear. She ignored his question.

"You must leave."

"Why is that, pet? I just arrived."

Grace folded her hands. They were trembling. "My cousin and Lady Ravenswood are here."

"I know."

"Then you realize why you must go," Grace hissed, disconcerted by his calm response. "My God, have you gone completely mad?"

"Perhaps. Would it be madness if I bent you over that desk as a demonstration of how much I missed you?"

She was saved from a response by the arrival of the tea tray, carried with exact care by one of the downstairs maids. "Thank you, Darma." Grace sighed as the girl set it on a low table, then exited with a giggling curtsy.

Mrs. Cooper had relayed the importance of their guest to the kitchen staff. Not only did the tray contain tea and two cups, but a pot of coffee, a variety of scones, four flavors of jam, and a plateful of fat sausage.

Grace desperately tried ignoring the slight smile lifting Nicholas's lips, those blasted dimples flitting into view. He needed a haircut, the tawny locks tumbling past his collar. It was long enough, he could gather it into a queue if desired. Her fingers twitched with the desire of attending that task for him. She remembered well how the dark gold strands shifted through her fingers. Oh, why must the man be so achingly beautiful? And why did she consider his last words as if hopeful such a scenario would occur? Her blood nearly scorched the inside of her veins with the thought.

What *would* it feel like if he folded her over the delicate walnut desk? Was it even possible it could hold her weight and his? The dark night when the duke spent himself across the flesh of her back stabbed her memory. Would he do that again, or something different?

Grace's hands were clammy as she marched across the room and gratefully sank on the dark blue upholstery of the settee. Too overwrought to even consider eating a scone, or a sausage for

God's sake, she poured a cup of tea, all the while hoping it didn't spill. If she had her wits about her, she would have offered Nicholas a cup. But witless she was. At least momentarily.

Nicholas took up his coat, his hand going into one of the deep pockets.

"You cannot stay," she mumbled around an unsteady sip of tea.

"So you've said. Five nights of my choosing, remember, honeybee? As I made my way with all haste to London and back again for you, forgive me if I have no intention of leaving just yet. Besides, you dared me to come after you, and you are holding my books hostage, after all."

London. He'd gone to London. Which only meant one thing. He had the necessary items to complete...to... to...her brain couldn't comprehend the reality of this moment. The duke had come. Prepared to take what she freely negotiated. The thought revitalized her.

"And how does Baroness Ralston fare?" Grace asked pertly. Maybe a bit more than was wise.

Nicholas frowned, vexed by the question. "I wouldn't know. I'll not lie to you, Grace. She came to me while I was in London, and I turned her away. I've not been with her, nor any other woman, since Calmont Downs, and I've no wish to change that. My interest is in you, Grace Willsdown, and only you. Until our arrangement is complete, there will be no one else in my bed. With my reputation, this is a significant development. A change of pace, as it were."

"Will you blame me for your abstinence?" Grace's heart pounded with joy at the thought no other woman had entertained him since Calmont Downs.

"No. I blame myself. The smile of a little storm has captured me. Now, you are all I can think about. Day and night."

"I'm flattered." Grace grinned at him. "Will you pursue me

like a proper beau? And attempt kissing me in darkened alcoves and deserted hallways?"

"I prefer such things in my bedchamber. Or in yours," Nicholas growled. "But I'll settle for wherever a kiss is most convenient. And necessary. It would be wise you limit such engagements to the two of us. Should I hear of another placing his hands on you, I won't be responsible for my actions. I've become very possessive in a month's time. Another new development, it seems."

"Duly noted, Your Grace. You should know I've no interest in kissing anyone other than you. I quite enjoy your kisses," she admitted, her cheeks turning scarlet.

"I hope you like the other things as well," Nicholas drawled.

"I've thought of little else since leaving Oakmont."

"If we don't change the subject, I may reenact a few right here in your parlor. Besides, I come bearing a gift," he said, so slyly, Grace wondered if he would pull the instruments for her complete ruination from his coat pocket.

He handed her a gaily wrapped box, no bigger than her palm and tied with a gold ribbon. Grace couldn't help but think how strange that he would go through the trouble of wrapping something as scandalous as French letters.

Her horrified curiosity must have shown plainly because Nicholas chuckled softly, shaking his head. "How delightful you are. Had I known such a gift would intrigue you, I might have wrapped that as well. Do go on and open it."

At his encouragement, Grace untied the ribbon and removed the box's lid. Nestled on the velvet lining was an exquisitely thin gold band decorated with delicate flowers. Petals of gold made up each tiny blossom with creamy pearls adorning the centers. They twined about the circumference of the bracelet, little flowers shaped like blooms of heather. Tiny gold bees, glittering with diamonds, filled the spaces between each blossom.

Her eyes filled with tears. "I cannot accept this, Your Grace. It is too costly."

"Nonsense." Removing the bracelet from the box, Nicholas slipped it onto her wrist. "I had it crafted specifically for you."

"Young ladies are not allowed to accept expensive gifts. Or jewelry."

"They are also not allowed bargaining with the Devil, but here we are. No one other than the two of us shall know I gave it to you."

Grace bit her lip. Nicholas watched her closely, and she had the feeling if she kept the bracelet, it would be an invisible shackle. Something binding her to him, even after they parted ways.

"Why would you give me a present?" she asked softly. Did he always buy his mistresses such lovely gifts? Did he buy them anything at all? And why was she thinking of herself as a mistress?

You are a business partner. No more, no less. A binding contract says so.

His answer wasn't really an answer, his deep frown indicating he was just as puzzled as she by his actions. "Because you always smell of heather, and your hair is..." He paused, then said in a more temperate tone, "It would please me seeing you wear it."

Grace swallowed a gulp of the scalding tea, never feeling the burn in her throat. The bracelet, so light and airy, felt heavy nonetheless. She would treasure it. More so because it came from Nicholas. And he had thought of her...

"Thank you," she surrendered. "I adore it. But you still must go. Ravenswood...and you...."

"I'll worry about that," Nicholas murmured, sitting beside her and capturing her free hand. His thumb rubbed across her knuckles. It was soothing. And mesmerizing. As though he were settling a frightened creature. "I truly have missed you, pet.

Which is astonishing. No woman has ever occupied my thoughts quite like you these past weeks. Your audacity in leaving me put my temper in league with the devil's very own."

"I could not stay. It was too...risky."

"Hmm," was all he said, tugging her close and covering her mouth with his.

Heat and lightning lit Grace up from the inside, her heart bursting with the fire. Her helpless little moan was more encouragement than despair. She leaned into him, teacup and saucer balanced precariously between their bodies while he devoured her mouth. She made no attempt at withdrawing, although it would have been wise. One kiss, the slightest caress from his hand, and she readily gave him anything he desired.

Nicholas drew back, his eyes glowing with something unknown. They were hot. Bright. Shades of green dancing with lights that dazzled and beguiled. Perhaps he really had missed her...

"I will be staying the night." His hand cupped her chin, preventing her from looking away.

"You cannot. You *must* not."

"Oh, honeybee. You don't realize it yet, do you? That you are mine...and I shall play with you as I please."

Grace thought she must resemble a gasping fish, plucked from the water and thrown upon the ground. She stared at him. "I'm not your plaything—"

Nicholas's hand tightened. "Aren't you? Your eyes say otherwise. Your kiss tells me you are. And when you are screaming my name, I know the truth of your soul. You are mine. Until I decide I can let you go."

"But our contract...at its end, you must end us..." Grace babbled desperately.

"Damn the contract," he said so soothingly, she hardly noticed the expletive. "I'll have you, regardless of that bit of paper."

CHAPTER 23

I fling her amongst the stars
Watch as she commands adoration
From angels
From devils
And monsters like myself
~Nicholas August Harris March
Ninth Duke of Richeforte

Taking the teacup from Grace's hand, Nicholas placed it on the table. The motion afforded a bit of space between their bodies, a kindness he could afford extending. It allowed breathing room so she might fully comprehend his words. He meant what he said. He was staying the night.

His eyes strayed, touching on her long legs, encased so deliciously in those blasted breeches. He wanted to snatch her up and peel them away from her body. Rediscover the soft flesh behind her knees and the tender expanse of her inner thighs. He wanted her sighing his name, then sobbing it aloud as his mouth reacquainted itself with the sweet, hidden fruit tucked away between her legs. Seeing the bracelet on her tiny wrist affected him more than he thought possible. He liked the idea of encircling her. With jewelry and delicate bands of gold. His hands. His body.

He'd missed her. More than he should admit aloud.

Taking a deep breath, he settled back beside her, and God help him if his cock didn't immediately jump. She smelled heavenly. Like the wild sea and heather, the earthiness of horses.

This was how Sebastian and Ivy found them. Nicholas wondered if his old friend's hostile reaction would have been any different had he entered the parlor just a few moments earlier. When he nearly had Grace in his lap, lips planted firmly on hers.

"You goddamn bastard," Sebastian spoke from the doorway. Ivy's tight grip on the earl's shirtsleeve restrained him from storming into the room. "Move away from her this instant."

Nicholas's grin was cold. He felt Grace shiver. She shoved the box and ribbon deep into the seat cushion behind her. The bracelet was hidden under the cuff of her shirt sleeve. She was worried they'd been discovered, but Nicholas suspected her involuntary shudder was caused more by the icy shift of his demeanor.

"Good morning, Sebastian. Lady Ravenswood." Nicholas moved not an inch from Grace's side. Instead, he slid closer, inclining his head as if imparting a secret. "Your cousin does not care much for me, my dear. You must forgive his surliness. In fact, it's best he is ignored altogether."

Sebastian's features darkened, straddling a dangerous precipice: murder or restraint. Somehow, he made it past the threshold with Ivy clinging to his arm like a tiny wildflower attempting to ensnare an enormous oak tree.

"Why are you here?"

"He's interested in breeding mares—" Grace blurted out.

"I'm looking at buying a colt—" Nicholas drawled at the same time.

Sebastian's eyes narrowed at the conflicting statements. The heated tension in the room rose by at least another hundred degrees.

Nicholas was not deterred. With a smile certain to incense the other man, his arm came up and draped casually across the back of the settee, dangerously close to Grace's shoulders. His ankle crossed over the opposite knee as if he intended on staying for a long time. Of course, that was the plan, but Sebastian did not know that. Yet.

"Which is it?" Sebastian snarled. "Breeding or buying?"

"Depends." Nicholas smirked. "I'll consider the better offer. Although I'm more interested in breeding now that Lady Grace has made the option available."

Sebastian shook free of Ivy, crossed the space, and gripped the front of Nicholas's shirt tight in his fists. The table tipped, spilling scones, tea, and sausages onto the carpet.

"You bloody degenerate," Sebastian growled. "Do you think I'll stand idly by while she becomes one of your whores? I'll finish the task I started and kill you

myself—"

Before Sebastian could finish the sentence, Nicholas reversed their position. Standing behind the earl, a forearm pressed along the back of the man's neck, Nicholas wrenched Sebastian's arms high into an unnatural position, locked in the middle of his back. Nicholas held them there in a relentless, one-handed grip.

Ivy cried out a warning, reminding them all of the gunshot wound Sebastian had only recently recovered from. His own aunt, in a state of unfortunate madness, had shot him only months before. Grace sat as if struck by a sudden ice storm, frozen in place.

"First and foremost," Nicholas said in a low, amicable manner, loosening his grip only slightly in deference to Ivy's plea. "Do not *ever* refer to her in such a manner again, or I shall rip out your heart with my bare hands. Second, like you, I also learned rather unorthodox methods of combat while abroad. As you can clearly see. And third," his voice dropped even further until it was a dark murmur, "do you think I'll complacently allow you another attempt on my life? You had your one chance at that, friend."

Nicholas released Sebastian with a tiny shove, turning his back so he could right the table. Picking up various items, he glanced at Grace. She stared back, and damned if there wasn't the faintest glimmer of sympathy in the honey-colored depths of her eyes.

Sympathy, of all things.

For him.

"I want you out of this house," Sebastian demanded as Ivy glided up beside him. It wasn't lost on either man that more words were being exchanged between them in this cozy parlor than during the entire six years since the duel.

"Darling?" Ivy interjected softly, patting his shoulder in assurance he was unharmed. "Isn't that Grace's decision? After all, this is her house. And we are guests."

Nicholas stood quickly, teapot in hand. He could scarcely believe the countess was on his side of things. There must be a reason for it, one unknown unless you were a woman yourself and understood the machinations of the female brain. He didn't miss how Ivy's gaze darted back and forth between himself and Grace, as though the two of them were a puzzle in need of solving.

Grace knelt at Nicholas's feet, and he nearly snatched her back up before realizing she was retrieving the sausage links that had rolled beneath the settee.

"His Grace can stay as long as he wishes. I have several yearlings he may be interested in purchasing." Grace's manner was quietly determined. She wouldn't be commanded by Sebastian, nor would she back away from the secret contract. The realization made every ounce of blood in Nicholas's body pound with arousal. He felt euphoric, ready to burst from his own skin. *She wants me to stay.*

"My mount pulled up lame on the ride over, so I rely on your goodwill, Lady Grace." Nicholas ignored Sebastian's snort of disbelief. He picked up a couple of scones that had escaped being smashed into the floral rug by their bootheels.

"Of course. If you will follow me to the stables, Hugh, our stable master can take a look at your horse. He concocts a rather magical poultice. It does wonders." The eagerness of her response suggested Grace was ready to escape the charged atmosphere of the parlor. Nicholas extended a hand, helping her up from the floor. She pinkened, embarrassed by his assistance, then briskly brushed her palms on her breeches.

"Sebastian, Ivy, if you haven't eaten this morning, Miss Nancy will prepare something and serve it in the breakfast room."

Her cousin glared at her, a look of furious disbelief crossing his features. "Do you think I trust *him* anywhere alone with you? I'll accompany you..."

"My lord, shouldn't we have breakfast before you undertake the role of guardian?" Ivy asked Sebastian with a small smile. "Grace is perfectly fine in her own stables. There are plenty who will aid her if needed. Besides, I'm sure His Grace will be on his best behavior."

Nicholas raised an eyebrow at Sebastian, gratified he was so handily managed by his spitfire of a countess. Once again, an unwelcome wave of nostalgia rose inside his gut, a tide of happiness for his former friend that could not be stemmed. He covered it with a gruff clearing of his throat while Sebastian shot daggers at him, grey eyes blazing with anger and distrust.

"Have no fear," Nicholas said, addressing Ivy. Shockingly enough, the countess gave him a tiny, encouraging grin. "I've witnessed the damage Lady Grace can wield with a mere book on an unwanted suitor. That she'll be surrounded by pitchforks and various sharp objects all but guarantees her safety."

"Is your horse really injured?" Grace questioned as they took the path to the stables.

"I would not invent such a thing," Nicholas replied. "He began limping about a mile from Bellmar Abbey, and I walked the rest of the way on foot."

"I saw him. They placed him at the opposite end of the stables, far from Llyr's stall. He's beautiful. What is his name?"

"Skye. He's Scottish bred, named for one of the islands."

Grace nodded. "He's a bit bigger than Llyr. And his coloring does look like the sky, maybe during a spring storm. Bluish grey and dark, all mixed together. Have you had him very long?"

"I won him in a card game shortly after returning to England. That was almost three years ago."

"I did not realize you were abroad the same time as my cousin. Did your paths ever cross?"

"Fortunately, no." A hint of a smile lifted his lips. "It would have been a scene straight out of your parlor if we had."

"I'm sorry you quarreled. If I'd known you were coming, I could have warned you to stay away." Grace cast him a glance. "Or had I known Ravenswood intended a visit, I would have requested he delay his trip by a few days."

"It's a matter we shall discuss later. I'm still vexed over your actions."

Grace tilted her head. "Are you angry I took the books from your library without your permission? I thought..."

"I have been forced to chase you," Nicholas interrupted, eyes heavy-lidded, mouth tightening into a hard line with the reminder of her flight from his bed. "The books are inconsequential. I did not notice their absence. But you, my dear little bee.

You, I missed a great deal." A pink flush spread across her exposed throat at his choice of words.

He remembered, as she likely did, the last time he was 'vexed'. Something in his groin tightened at the memory of Grace prone across his lap. His hands smoothing over those perfectly round, golden-hued buttocks hidden beneath a flouncy layer of lace.

He abruptly changed the subject. "Your suggestion of breeding is an excellent idea."

Allowing Grace entry into the stables ahead of him, he saw her shoulders stiffen. He meant something completely different in the parlor, but she misunderstood him now. Nicholas almost grinned, knowing the path of her thoughts.

He still couldn't explain why he'd antagonized Sebastian so ruthlessly. The man should be commended for defending Grace's reputation, even if she cared not a whit for it herself. And there was no understanding his visceral reaction when Sebastian unintentionally insulted her. His own anger surprised him. Frightened him. He'd wanted to snatch Grace up, tuck her safely under his arm, and shield her from the wretched ugliness commonplace between men.

Nicholas clarified his statement now. "Horse breeding, pet. I believe we would both gain from such an arrangement. And I fully intend on buying a colt, or even a filly. Perhaps two of each, provided you have no other buyers."

Grace slanted golden eyes at him. "I suppose you would rather keep them all within your grasp."

Nicholas somberly took her elbow. "Actually, I am within my rights if I demand all sales cease until this is over. You are selling something you do not fully own."

"Are you sure of this?" Her cheeks flushed with temper. "Have your barristers provided any answers?"

"No," he admitted. "Although they are digging deep into the matter. My father's death, welcomed though it was, left behind quite a tangle. Many others are indebted to the estate, and naturally, my father's own team was reluctant in handing over documents when I discharged them of their services. I've been assured the encumbrance does exist. It is mentioned in the duke's will as a separate provision. But a provision no one can locate. The lead man on the matter is certain it's buried in the mountain of other debts owed. It's only a matter of time before it is uncovered."

Grace tugged her arm from his grasp, turning down the aisle where his stallion was stalled. "On her deathbed, Mother assured me Bellmar was mine. I made this bargain as a means of being certain...covering all scenarios."

"Whether it's found or not, I will still dissolve it at the end of our arrangement. In the meantime, I'll take a look at your herd, select a few yearlings and arrange a breeding between Skye and any mares of your choosing. Llyr is a magnificent animal, but diversification with a new stud will be advantageous to your stables."

"You are very kind, Your Grace," she grit between pursed lips, her tone shouting distrust.

"Ulterior motives, pet," Nicholas nodded. "I always have them. And this provides a convenient excuse for our contact. I'll have my remaining nights with you. You at my mercy has consumed my thoughts."

Grace did not respond, and Nicholas frowned. *Is she remembering our last night together?* That night should not count against the talley, but it was he who chose spending it that way.

"Sebastian will object. He won't believe you're merely interested in buying horses," she said glumly. "He's suspicious and will watch me like a hawk from here out."

Nicholas was amused by the way she bit at her bottom lip in her worry.

Brushing a loose tendril of hair behind her ear, Nicholas was gratified when she sucked in a quick breath, her eyes heated when they clashed with his. Grace was definitely intrigued by the thought of completing their contract. He couldn't disappoint her, even if he lacked the necessary items for taking her as he wished. Those things waited at Oakmont—and he would use them there. Dear God, not here, where Sebastian might be lying in wait, ready to burst through her bedroom door, eager for a reason to destroy him.

"Do not fret, little bee. There are ways around Sebastian's scrutiny. Trust me."

CHAPTER 24

"Stop pacing, Sebastian." Ivy refilled her cup, watching her husband stalk in front of the windows facing the stables.

"I can't help it. Why the devil are they taking so long?" he growled back. "I'm going out there. You can't trust that man around someone as sweet and innocent as Grace. I know him. I know how he thinks, what he's capable of—"

"You'll do no such thing." Ivy calmly bit into a biscuit and did not flinch when the earl spun around.

"Someone must be concerned for her safety. I don't understand why you aren't."

"She likes him." Ivy's shoulders lifted in a shrug. "You were so busy barking threats, you did not see what I did."

"What are you talking about?"

"Grace does not find the duke's attention objectionable. You know him well. Has he ever chased a woman? I'd say probably not."

"There was Marilee," Sebastian said in a low voice. "Although I admit, she most likely pursued him, knowing he would be Richeforte one day."

"I had the opportunity of viewing the man over the past three seasons. He is hunted by women. He ignores them, remaining aloof, detached. Society's expectations do not concern him. Now, Grace has captured his attention. Entranced him, I think."

Sebastian scowled. "If that is true, all the more reason we should be concerned. And diligent in safeguarding Grace."

Ivy's head tilted when he finally plopped into the chair beside her. She pushed a teacup his way; however, he was too agitated to drink. "He rode here from Oakmont. Just to see her, Sebastian. Not to discuss breeding mares or buying horses. He helped her up from the floor, cleaned up scones, for goodness sake. Most telling though was his anger over a perceived insult. He is not pursuing to conquer. In fact, he seems perplexed by the attraction between them. Did you honestly not notice? The sparks?"

"He's dangerous, Ivy. Dangerous."

"Grace does not seem alarmed. She's not shown the slightest interest in any of her suitors, not even Longleigh, and she is so very fond of him, although in a platonic sense. She could not take her eyes off His Grace just now."

A look of absolute horror crossed Sebastian's features. "Damnation. Could something have happened between them at Calmont Downs?"

Ivy shrugged again. "I don't know. From what Lady Celia said, they had limited contact and Richeforte was only there three days."

"Three days is enough. Especially for *him*. You are right, though. They appear well-acquainted now. Bloody hell. What should we do?"

"It will be difficult, but we will not meddle." Ivy reached over, clasping their hands together, and wound her fingers through her husband's until Sebastian's grey eyes met hers. "Do not worry, my love. Grace is very level-headed and intelligent. She's taken care of herself for many years, without our assistance and interference. She knows what she's doing. I'm sure of it."

"The man is an unprincipled libertine. The things he's capable of..."

Ivy rose from her chair and perched herself in Sebastian's lap. His eyebrows lifted in surprise, but he folded her close against his chest, nuzzling into her neck. Her orange and lily perfume tickled his nose, and he sighed in contentment.

"Had he not been so wicked, then perhaps another lady would occupy your lap, snuggling with you now. I'm glad the duke is unscrupulous. He played an important role in our happiness." Ivy kissed Sebastian's cheek. "I'm not asking that you forgive him, but please, for Grace's sake and mine, be civil and refrain from murdering him over dinner."

Sebastian considered her words, slowly nodding. "I do hold a measure of gratitude for his betrayal. His debauchery led me to you. And you, sweet wife, you are the love of my life. Very well. Because you asked so sweetly, I promise I shall not murder him during dinner."

"Thank you, darling. Now, allow me the opportunity of properly demonstrating my appreciation."

Ivy's fingers slid through Sebastian's dark hair, and just before her lips touched his, the earl murmured wryly, "I cannot guarantee such restraint tomorrow morning, however."

The countess giggled and nipped his lower lip. "Then it's up to me to save the Duke's life, and possibly Grace's future happiness. I must ensure you are too exhausted to even consider leaving our bed to share breakfast with them."

DINNER, OF COURSE, WAS A DISASTER. NO MATTER THE succulent rib roast. And neither the roasted green beans served with a creamy champagne sauce nor the leek soufflé could save matters. And the clover, tiny tartlets with dollops of fresh cream mounded atop raspberries served for dessert? Those went unappreciated.

It was difficult concentrating on such things when the dinner guests might use their knives for something other than carving the beef on their plates. Grace, always a virtual chatterbox, hesitated in speaking at all when faced with the abundance of unbearable tension.

Ivy, however, was unaffected. She questioned Nicholas, prying really, on matters ranging from his time abroad to his views on the last session of Parliament and the passing of the Chimney Sweepers and Chimneys Regulation Act. Sebastian sat stoically throughout the entire meal and the discussions his wife instigated. Several times, an unmistakable scowl darkened his features whenever Ivy laughed at some remark by the duke. If not for the countess, the entire meal might have passed in utter silence.

"Are you well, Lady Grace?" Nicholas inquired, concern evident in his tone.

Grace startled, abruptly aware of rubbing her forehead in an attempt at staving off the memories of the last time she and Nicholas sat at a formal dining table. How she ended topsy-turvy across his lap, the hot palms of his hand striking her lace covered bottom, the fiery cracks echoing in the room. She closed her eyes against a swirl of dizzying lust.

Opening her eyes, she knew Nicholas was fully aware of her thoughts. His gaze drifted to her wrist, a tiny, knowing spark lighting the green depths as she fingered the piece of jewelry adorning her wrist. The bracelet paired beautifully with the deep bronze gown she wore, the crystal beading adorning the square bodice sparkled in the light when she took a deep breath.

"Grace?" His voice dropped an octave.

"I'm fine, Your Grace," she stammered, taking a fortifying gulp of wine. "Just a slight headache."

Nicholas's dimples flitted to the surface of his cheeks. "I hope my presence has not proven tedious."

Sebastian grunted, then grunted again when Ivy's elbow dug into his rib cage.

"Far from it," Grace replied somewhat unsteadily before Ivy could comment. Her dear cousin-in-law would rue her friendliness with the duke. The baleful glares Sebastian kept leveling upon her indicated her husband was far from pleased with her.

Grace wondered how Ivy managed convincing the earl into lending a few articles of clothing for Nicholas's use. Luckily, the two men were similar in size, although Sebastian was a bit broader across the shoulders. His suit jacket conformed was only a bit large on Nicholas, the superfine black cloth highlighting his tawny hair and green eyes. Grace's dress complimented Nicholas's borrowed clothing so well, it seemed they'd planned it.

A shame such beautiful finery and excellent food was ruined by the acrimonious edge between former friends who despised one another. And Grace's own delirious recollections of the Nicholas's hands caressing her body ruined her appetite.

Hoping her contribution to the conversation would prompt a more amiable atmosphere, Grace said, "I'm fascinated by the many places you've visited, Your Grace. Did you miss England while abroad?"

"No." Leaning back in his chair, Nicholas's heavy-lidded gaze never strayed from Grace's features. She squirmed in her chair at the head of the table.

"I imagine things were very different when you came home."

"I found them the same as when I departed." His gaze flickered over Sebastian and back to her. "A monster for a father and other unavoidable disappointments. I've only recently discovered a few advantages in returning, one being the delight of having you as my neighbor."

Grace stared at Nicholas. What did he hope to gain with this turn of the conversation? Something about it eluded her, but while Sebastian stiffened even more, his fists clenching, her foolish heart leaped at being called a "delight". More often, she was labeled a stubborn menace or bluestocking. Many times within the same sentence.

"How kind of you, Your Grace," she murmured as the dessert plates were cleared away. "Do you think Skye will be well enough that you can ride tomorrow?"

"I hope so. He was much improved when I checked before dinner. Hugh is a magician with his secret poultice."

"If he hasn't recovered by morning, you may borrow any horse in my stable. In fact, you may take Llyr back to Oakmont and breed the mares we discussed before. We'll be leaving for Beaumont later this week, and I'll happily loan him. Besides, he could use the exercise as no one rides him when I'm away."

The quirk of Nicholas's full lips said the intentions of her impulsive offer were very clear. The eventual swap of the horses, at Belmar Abbey or Oakmont, provided an excellent opportunity for continuing their relationship in a legitimate context.

"A generous offer, Lady Grace, and an excellent idea, regardless of Skye's recovery from the stone bruise. With this venture, you may become a frequent visitor at Oakmont. Given our close proximity," Nicholas said with a tiny smile, "we should discuss arrangements for an extended stay..."

He wore that smile Grace witnessed many times before. The one that did not quite reach his eyes. Oh, blast it. He intentionally poked Sebastian, hoping for a reaction.

As expected, her cousin shot to his feet, despite Ivy's warning grip on his arm. "A word, Richeforte. Now."

Nicholas merely tilted his head, gazing at the other man as though he'd taken leave of his senses. Sipping his wine, he tsked. "I'm loathe to abandon the ladies, but should you insist."

"Sebastian..." Ivy implored.

Sebastian vibrated with anger, his mouth tight, but he spared her a glance. "I won't break my promise, butterfly. But an understanding must be reached."

"My lord," Grace interjected quietly. "Please sit." When the earl remained standing, she stood as well. "You are abusing my hospitality and intimidating my guest. Please. Sit down."

Sebastian's jaw clenched with such force, it should have cracked. Nicholas watched serenely as the earl slowly sank back into his chair and tossed his napkin beside his plate. It was akin to throwing down the gauntlet. Tension increased a hundredfold in a matter of seconds.

"I appreciate your defense, Lady Grace; I've no issue speaking with the earl privately." Nicholas stood, draining his wine goblet. "He'll not want blood splatters on the clothes he lent me, so I'm probably safe."

"I already made a vow that I wouldn't harm you," Sebastian bit out.

"How solicitous," Nicholas drawled. "However, it's the spilling of your own blood that should concern you."

CHAPTER 25

Eyes of gold and morning dew
They see everything I cannot conceal
Few secrets remain once she looks her fill.
∼Nicholas August Harris March
Ninth Duke of Richeforte

The earl entered the drawing room and wordlessly poured two brandies from the assortment of liquors on the sideboard, handing one over as Nicholas nodded his thanks.

For a long moment, neither man spoke. Sebastian had apparently reined in his temper while making their way down the hall, but he was a dangerous opponent.

"What are you about, Nicholas?" Sebastian finally sighed in exasperation. His silver gaze caught and held the duke's. "What game are you playing with Grace?"

"No games, Seb." Nicholas grimaced at how easily the nickname slipped off his tongue. A gulp of brandy hid his discomfort. "She is in full control, whether I remain or leave Bellmar Abbey. I await her pleasure."

"Bollocks. Must you pursue and ruin yet another innocent

female?" Sebastian's features held true concern for his cousin, banked anger glittering in his stare. "Was Marilee not enough?"

Nicholas rotated the brandy snifter in the cradle of his palm. His voice came low, almost in a growl. "Marilee was neither pursued nor innocent. Do not make the mistake of comparing Grace to her."

"Are you saying Marilee lied to me?" Sebastian demanded.

"No. She was pregnant. That much is true."

Silence fell between the men, hanging in a fog of animosity and mistrust until Sebastian said in a whiplash-like voice, "How you must have hated me to do such a thing."

Nicholas poured himself a second brandy. Quite suddenly, he was tired. Tired of holding his silence. Tired of the blame. Disappointment seeped in, coloring his words.

"So, we are back at your insistence that Marilee and I were lovers."

"Weren't you?" Sebastian sneered. "Although, as Ivy pointed out, she and I gained with your actions. I would not have fallen in love with the most wonderful woman in the world if not for you. Your selfishness worked in my favor ...and Ivy believes you should deserve forgiveness because of it."

"The countess gives excellent counsel. Perhaps you should heed her advice."

"I don't give a damn about Marilee. That relationship was doomed long before everything went wrong. I knew it, but was too stubborn to admit it," Sebastian said. "That was never the crux of the matter, Nick. You were once my best friend. And you betrayed me. I can't understand it. I probably never will."

Nicholas lowered his head, staring into the depths of the brandy. *Now.* He should let go of everything inside him now. Everything that was bursting to escape. All the truths which were ready to spill. Now was when he should reveal everything.

Anger hobbled his tongue. Fury crippled him that Sebastian believed him capable of dishonor. Rage fueled his vindictiveness that wanted his friends suffering because they turned their backs without question. So, like that night on his townhouse steps when Sebastian attacked him, Nicholas remained stoically silent.

Instead, he bowed with lanky elegance in his borrowed coat and shirt. "I was always your friend, Sebastian." *Perhaps you'll realize it one day.*

"Stay away from Grace."

"I cannot."

"If you harm her, I swear by all that is holy, I will destroy you." Sebastian's eyes were a stormy grey, his chin set at a hard angle.

"If I want her, nothing you do or say will keep me from her." Nicholas swirled his brandy. "And we both know that."

GRACE RESTED HER HEAD AGAINST THE COOL WOOD OF the door.

It was just after midnight, and she stood outside Nicholas's room. One she purposefully gave him, far from Sebastian and Ivy's quarters and her own. A flash of lightning briefly lit the dim hallway. Thunder rumbled, low and restless. Off in the distance, rolling in from the sea, was one of the summer thunderstorms Cornwall rarely experienced. Like the one that sank her father's ship, this storm would be loud, violent, and messy.

It seemed as if the storm itself emanated from inside her, a manifestation of her own internal agitation. When it swept through, it would carry her past a point of no return. If she allowed that, words that should never be uttered aloud would rain from her lips. And she would be forced to deal with the aftermath. She trembled, thinking how Nicholas would react if she revealed her secret. That she had fallen in love with him.

She hadn't knocked yet on the door. She couldn't make herself do it. *I'll say I'm only making sure he has everything he needs. Or that Miss Nancy wondered if he had any special requests for breakfast. Or...maybe...maybe I should be honest. Tell him I've thought of nothing but him since the day I left Oakmont, that I could not forget how he kissed me. That I've missed him so terribly, I hurt because of it. I should tell him I need him...to hold me. So, I'll understand why I feel this way.*

"Blast it, Grace," she muttered. "Either knock on the door or go back to bed. You cannot stand here all night."

Gathering her courage, taking a deep breath, she exhaled with eyes closed, palms flat against the wood as she leaned against it for support. Silently rehearsing what she would say. The worst that could happen was a rejection of her advances. The bracelet on her wrist glittered as if confirming that possibility.

The door swung open.

Grace tumbled forward, landing in a heap of white cambric.

Nicholas uttered a strangled curse, then scooped her up from the carpet.

"Jesus, Grace. Must I forever be picking you up from the floor?" Standing her upright, he twitched her nightclothes back into place. "You stood out there so long, I thought you changed your mind."

"Changed my mind about what?" Grace stuttered as his hands traveled her curves. Her wrist hurt the tiniest bit, but she forgot the slight pain as his fingers seared it all away.

"Coming in, of course. That is why you are here, isn't it?" She was a bit wobbly, so he leaned her against the wall as he shut the door. "Are you hurt, pet?" His voice was rough, but his hands were surprisingly gentle as he took her by the forearms.

"N-No."

She actually gulped, realizing he wore no shirt; just breeches. Taut and smooth, his chest gleamed like expensive satin in the lamplight, muscles bunching as he caged her in. His hands came up on either side of her head, palms flat on the wall. Surprisingly, his expression was somewhat less than friendly.

"Are you...are you angry with me, Your Grace?"

"Hmmm. What do you think?" Leaning closer, his mouth brushed her temple. *He doesn't sound angry, but his expression...it's so fierce.*

"I don't know. I never know what you are thinking."

Grace could not breathe. Desire swamped her senses. His lips were lightning bolts, streaking across her skin and igniting her from the inside out.

Those blasted dimples of his abruptly peeked out. "I think I'm going to kiss you right now."

"Is that all?" Grace squeaked.

"For starters."

His mouth covered hers, blazing hot and sweet, like cinnamon melted in sugar. When he requested entry, sliding his tongue along the seam of her lips, she opened with a gasp, welcoming him inside. Nicholas kissed her with such thoroughness, Grace lost track of seconds and minutes. The earth revolved in a slow whirl, existing only in the space between their bodies. He gave her kisses so hungry, it felt he was devouring her, and kisses so tender and full of promise, she could only loop her arms around his neck and hang on.

"Such a clever girl," he murmured along her jawline. "Giving me a room so far from the others. Your cries of pleasure will scarcely be heard."

Grace drifted high in a blissful state. "I won't make much of a racket, Your Grace."

Nicholas bit her lower lip until she moaned. "Challenge accepted, pet. And do recall our agreement, if you please. I've no wish hearing the words 'Your Grace' when we are together this way."

"Yes, Your Grace." Her soft voice carried a teasing lilt.

"You court trouble with that smart mouth of yours." His mouth traveled to the crook of her neck and shoulder. When he nipped her, licking the spot immediately so the sting was soothed,

Grace nearly swooned. "Especially when I'm still vexed with you."

"Why?" The single word was barely audible. She was drowning in sensations, and speech was difficult. Somehow, she opened her eyes, meeting his stare. "Why would you be vexed?"

"You ran from me, remember?" Settling his hands in the curve of her waist, he pressed forward until their bodies finally touched. "Don't ever run from me again," he warned. "I will go to the ends of hell and back to catch you."

The heat of him was scorching, enough so Grace could not catch her breath. "Please, I can't breathe."

"Good." Nicholas pushed her flush with the wall, looming over her. "I want you unable to breathe, unable to think, unable to do anything other than feel what I'm about to do to you."

Grace's stomach flip-flopped with a heady sense of anticipation. "What...what will you do?"

"Nothing too terrible. You may even survive. If you're lucky." His finger traced along the curve of her jaw until he reached the underside of her chin. Lifting it with just enough force until she had no choice but to gaze into his glittering emerald eyes, Nicholas's face remained hard as stone. "Shall we begin?"

"It seems I have little choice."

The corners of his eyes crinkled at her rebellious response. "I doubt the need to force my attentions on you." He kissed the tip of her nose, that oddly affectionate gesture he'd done twice before. "I've missed you. Will you stay?" His brow furrowed slightly and Grace knew it was because he was unaccustomed to asking for anything. If he wanted something, he took it.

It melted her. She'd do anything for him, regardless of the token resistance she put forth.

"You missed me?" Her words were hesitant.

Nicholas swore beneath his breath. "You know I did, little bee. I've not had a moment's rest since you left. Nightmares, you see..."

Grace's head tilted, bewildered by his casual admission. Nightmares...what were they about? How did she unwittingly help with those? Questions assailed her; however, a more pressing matter needed addressing. "There is no remedy for it, Nicholas. After this, only two nights will remain."

"Truthfully, it is three. That last night at Oakmont, we only slept."

"That was your choice." Grace shrugged.

"Bloody hell, I should have drove a better bargain."

"It would all still come to an end," she murmured, suddenly conscious how that truth made her heart ache.

"Give me more," Nicholas demanded, dark and silky. His eyes shone like a wolf on the hunt, closing in on unsuspecting prey.

Grace shook her head with a sorrowful smile. "I can give you tonight."

He regarded her for a long moment, perhaps considering how he might bend her resolve. "Will you give me everything else?"

"What will you want?"

"Whatever I ask for."

"I've given you that as part of the five nights." Grace frowned. "You want something more?"

"I will limit my demands to three." His features darkened in the lamplight. Mysterious. Wicked. "First, do not go to Beaumont. Stay here or come to Oakmont. Either way, I want you close."

"Sebastian will suspect..."

"I don't care. You want me as much as I want you." His next request made the blood boil in her veins. "Second, kiss me. Kiss me as if you are mine."

"I am yours, Nicholas. For three more nights." Her voice quavered with the thought of being completely his. And with the very notion of Nicholas at her mercy. Even if for a brief moment. "And your third request?"

"I cannot ask for the third yet. But when I do, you will grant it without question."

Grace nodded, then, slowly leaned forward and embraced him, her fingers tracing the scars and welts crisscrossing his muscular back. Nicholas barely breathed as she did this, but she felt his heart hammering against her own as their chests touched. How she wished she could heal every single one of those awful marks. Erase every hurt he'd suffered, replace pain for pleasure. Change the past, change *him* before he became wicked and dangerous.

And sinfully damaged.

With gentle hands she soothed him, standing on tiptoes and nuzzling his throat. She scattered soft, butterfly light kisses along the corded column of his neck and the space under his chin. The rasp of his unshaven jaw was a rough contrast against the plushness of her lips. Rubbing against him as an affectionate cat would, a small purr-like sound tickled the back of her throat.

When she licked his ear, her tongue darting hot and quick in discovery, Nicholas's hands tightened on her waist, the white cambric of her robe squeezed by his fists until it was in danger of ripping.

Sliding a hand around the back of his neck, Grace urged his head down, tangling her fingers in the tawny silk of his hair. She sighed with pleasure as the waves sifted with her touch. When their mouths finally met, her moan was captured by Nicholas's rumble of approval.

Grace kissed him as if her life depended on it. Like he was her reason for living, the air in her lungs and the blood in her veins. She kissed him with all the fire, passion, and confusion rioting inside her. Until this moment, she'd thought it was enough...having her horses and the estate. Her stables. All of it hers and hers alone. But now she wasn't so sure. Now, she wondered if perhaps, she wanted...no, needed, more than that. She wondered if having Nicholas, forever, was her heart's desire.

She couldn't imagine never kissing him again. Couldn't fathom how she would exist if she never again felt his hands on her body.

"You may ruin me, if you like." Her offer was brashly given when he drew back for a moment. "That is, should you wish..."

"All in good time, pet," Nicholas chuckled darkly.

He released her waist, wrapping one arm around the small of her back. His other hand swept the neckline of her wrapper out of his way, then the lace-edged bodice of the nightdress was tugged down, exposing her collarbone and the tops of her shoulders. He kissed her again, although Grace was becoming light-headed from the increasing ferocity of Nicholas's mouth on hers. It was as though he expected a ceasing of their activity at any moment and was determined he'd get as much of her as possible.

Slipping a hand between their bodies was more difficult than it should have been. Nicholas had her anchored tight, but she was able to trail her fingers along the hardness between his legs. When she palmed the fabric covered heat of him, he responded with such a feral growl, Grace's knees almost buckled.

The next instant, Nicholas scooped her up, carrying her to the sitting area before the fireplace. He sank into a large, over-stuffed chair, cradling her in his lap. With both her legs dangling over his thighs, she felt the iron-like length of his erection pressing her hip. She kicked her slippers from her feet and continued kissing him, or more precisely, he began devouring her. Deep, soul-searching kisses that left Grace dizzy with need. She twisted and squirmed in his lap, arms looped about his neck, agitated and searching for a closeness that could occur only one way.

"Be still," he murmured against her lips.

Grace swore she *tasted* his slight smile. It intoxicated her, enveloped her, made her wish for things she shouldn't.

"I—I cannot," she replied honestly, almost plaintively. "I want to be closer..."

Nicholas hesitated, then abruptly yanked her nightgown high

over her bottom, while at the same time rotating her body until she straddled him. Now, her legs rested on either side of his hips, knees cushioned by the plush chair, her gown fluttering down and covering the upper portion of her bare buttocks and the base of her spine.

Beneath the lacy hem, Nicholas palmed her bare cheeks, the sudden heat of his hands on her naked flesh startling Grace. She was infused with such desire, she couldn't help kissing him even more fiercely, his touch causing a reaction so visceral and overwhelming, she didn't feel in control of her own body.

She ground herself on the hardness rearing up between Nicholas's muscular thighs, sobbing against his lips as the resulting lightning strike sizzled her bones. In some sane portion of her mind, she knew her actions were dangerous, but it didn't matter.

I want him...here. Now. I don't care how...or that it's sinful. I want him. Inside me...inside me.

With clumsy fingers, Grace unfastened the top row of buttons holding his breeches closed. She unfastened the second. Then a third, all the while kissing his neck and shoulders with sweet, scalding brushes of her mouth. Nicholas trembled beneath her, tiny earthquakes rippling across the flat expanse of his belly. She pulled the last button holding his breeches together, pushing aside the fabric. His erection sprang free. Hard, throbbing insistently for relief.

I can heal him and hope he loves me as I love him.

Her fingers coasted over hot flesh, tracing the ridges of his abdomen, tugging slightly at the dark gold hair just below his navel. She could not give up Bellmar Abbey, and she could not give him up. Which was just as well. Nicholas would never wed her, but he might decide he'd keep her as a mistress once their contract was done. Grace reconciled herself to that fact. It was possible to have both him and her estate. Could she live with that? Having only a portion of his affection? Yes, Yes, she could live with and she reached for him, her mind made up.

Nicholas tore his mouth away, sucking in a breath of intense lust.

"Goddamn, Grace..." Her hand, so incredibly tiny compared to his body, tried wrapping about his cock, and he hissed in fiery response, *"Fucking hell..."*

"I want you to show me, Nicholas. Show me everything that comes with being yours. Show me what it's like to be possessed. To be loved. To be claimed and conquered. Tame me, if you dare try," she breathed, pressing lightning hot kisses along his neck. It was corded tight with the effort of keeping himself from her. "Or perhaps I should tame you."

Every muscle in his body snapped taut with her husky words. "Please," he said, the words escaping on a jagged exhale of air, "stop."

Grace smiled a secret smile. Victory was inevitable. He could not resist her, no matter his legendary self-control. With silken intent, her hand closed even more firmly about his flesh, her fingers gentle as a bluebird's wings.

A strangled curse escaped Nicholas as he abruptly folded in surrender. He pulled her head to his, deepening the kiss, pouring his heart into hers, filling all the empty spaces of their souls until they both overflowed with desire and the need for more and more and more. His body shifted impatiently, demandingly, between her fingers. One rough hand held her head steady for the blooming arrows of his kiss, buried in the silk of her hair while the other dug into the tender flesh of her bottom, his fingers surely marking her with bruises. He yanked her into a position that flattened both his erection and her hand against the softness of her belly.

"You don't know what you are asking of me, Grace," he said in a final effort of resisting her.

The scars he carried inside him were not visible, but Grace

saw them as clearly as the ones crisscrossing his back. Those internal wounds were thick and tender. They made him shy away from the slightest hint of true intimacy. Once, he'd been broken, and he put himself back together the best way he knew how...with an iron will and caustic wit. Holding the frayed edges of his soul together was a level of control preventing anyone from getting close. Until now.

Sadness overwhelmed Grace. She wanted to soothe him. Embrace him. Kiss away all his pain until the dark wings shrouding him were forced into recession. Forever.

"Come out of the shadows, Nicholas," she said softly. "Come to me."

In a husky voice, he replied, "You'd be wise to fear those shadows, honeybee. Should we continue, you will become one of them."

His hand gripped the back of her neck. It was far from gentle, but Grace pressed closer, terrified she was losing him.

"Your shadows do not frighten me." Her eyes welled with tears. "You have become all my thoughts. The ones I cannot erase in the hours before dawn, and those that brighten my days. I want you, Nicholas. All of you. Even...even the shadows."

"There is a darkness inside me you cannot comprehend," he grunted.

Grace nodded her head. She knew. She loved him anyway.

She kissed him then, tasting brandy and hope in his mouth, and Nicholas drank her in like a drowning man on the edge of a vast whirlpool of nothingness. She was the only thing keeping him from being sucked into the dark oblivion of a lonely existence.

When he pushed her back, Grace had the impression he both savored and hated the feel of her skin on his. His eyes closed, long, sooty eyelashes concealing the emerald lights in his eyes. She leaned into him, tracing the scratchy, stubbled jutt of his chin with her lips. God, he tasted of divine things. Mint and darkness, starlight and warm linen. Spiced brandy and the slightly crisp tang of evergreens.

"I would give up everything to be with you," she whispered. "You draw me in so easily. Without effort. I scarcely know myself when I'm with you, as if you turn me into a stranger. I do and say things I never thought possible, and yet it feels right. We feel right. You make me whole, Nicholas. I've found a piece of myself I never knew was missing." Grace shrugged, shoulders lifting with her own bewilderment. "I'm yours."

With an audible grinding of his jaw, Nicholas jerked her off his lap.

Dislodged so quickly, Grace slipped between his legs. Down onto her knees, shoulder level with the juncture of his legs. Down where she still gripped the massive hardened steel of his body within trembling fingers.

Nicholas's eyes narrowed. "Do you believe there's been a moment since I met you when you were not mine? All the devils in hell are surely here now, torturing me with the thought of having you. It is madness for us to be together outside this infernal contract."

Grace stared at him, her heart in her eyes.

"Let go." The command was brutal in its harshness, but his eyes, burning a fiery path over her body where she crouched, left no doubt what he wanted. What he would do if she allowed it.

He would bury that impressive weapon between her legs. Make her cry out in a heady mix of pleasure and pain. Love her until she could not breathe without feeling him inside her, filling her. Possess her until there was nothing left in the world but the two of them. God, how she wanted that. She would love him enough for the both of them.

"Let go," he repeated.

Grace slowly shook her head. "Tell me how to please you."

"I won't be able to keep myself from taking you...get up now." His voice was a low growl of need. Grace's insides clenched.

Silvery tremors raked her body until she was ravenous for him. She wanted him. So much that she was becoming reckless.

"No."

Leaning forward, she covered him with her mouth, sliding her hands along his thighs. Whether she braced herself or it was a feeble attempt at keeping him in place, even she was unsure.

He tasted warm. Salty. Clean. Something undefinable. Maybe a spice. Experimentally, in the interest of gaining a better enlightenment, her tongue swirled around the broad head before she raked her teeth slightly down part of his length.

Desire flooded her, surprising in its intensity. Her legs clamped together in an attempt at suppressing it.

Nicholas nearly shot out of the chair, his entire body stiff with shock. He buried his hands in her hair, almost painfully, gripping the sides of her head. Large and calloused, his palms nearly covered her entire scalp.

"Jesus Christ!" he groaned, slowly sinking back into the cushion.

Grace's hair brushed her cheeks and tickled the tops of his thighs. She took more of his massive erection in her mouth, as much as she could manage. Nicholas cursed again. This time beneath his breath. He may have thought of stopping her, but that died a quick death. She'd won the battle, but Nicholas took the field and the day.

Meshed in her hair, fingers tugging the silky strands, his touch morphed into something almost caressing. Holding her with a gentle strength, Grace abruptly realized the balance of power had shifted back into his hands. When next he spoke, his voice was lush and guttural.

"Eyes on me, Grace," Nicholas commanded. "Eyes on me. Now."

CHAPTER 26

I hate her, although it is impossible
When she keeps my heart hostage
It beats in rapid thumps hoping to escape
Or avoid notice
I curse it
Because it beats for her
~Nicholas August Harris March
Ninth Duke of Richeforte

*W*hen Grace slowly glanced up at him, eyes sparkling gold behind a fringe of lush, black lashes, Nicholas felt something inside him crack apart.

Ice. His heart. His soul. He wasn't sure, but it was profoundly affecting. Even as he reveled in the return of his control, the trust in her gaze humbled him. Made him question every wicked thing he'd ever done in his life. And he realized a very important fact. Grace was special. Not just because she willingly sought ways of pleasing him. No. It went far beyond this momentary pleasure.

She soothed the wildness inside him. Tamed his demons and the monsters living within his nightmares. A touch of her hand, a sweet word from her lips, and he was entranced. Destroyed. Redeemed. He could become a better person. Because of her.

For her.

His little Cornwall storm. His sweet honeybee.

Every male atom in his body tightened with desire, seeing her plush, warm pink lips wrapped so prettily about his cock. Desire and nervous anticipation danced in the depths of her eyes. Nicholas knew he should end this madness. Yes, end it, even though his hands gripped her head, pulling her down as his body thrust up.

Sweet hell... just a few moments more. I've dreamed of this since I laid eyes on her. Envisioned her just like this. Taking me deeper...deeper...

A moan emanated from deep inside him. It was plaintive. Mournful. With a jerk of his hips, Nicholas pushed further. It would take but a few seconds to finish him off. Somehow, he buried the domineering streak demanding he take her mouth as he pleased. His hands lowered to Grace's shoulders, pulling her away.

She snarled. Like a fierce she-wolf guarding her kill.

"Did you just growl at me?" Nicholas breathed incredulously.

Grace's eyes locked on his, and she hummed a confirmation. Her fingers tightened on his thighs, fingernails digging into the muscles as if she could keep him there with that tiny bit of strength. Her defiance amused him. And inflamed him. A sigh of pure lust hissed between his teeth.

"Grace...stop. You must stop. Before I am overcome and unable to stop."

She made that intoxicating sound again and nestled closer between his legs. If he really wished it, he could remove her. Could hook his hands beneath her arms, roughly lift her and that decadent mouth away from his body.

Her eyes never left his during the struggle with his

conscience. Like the golden stare of a predator, they ensnared him. Hypnotized him. Drawing him into fire and swirling lights. A place where right and wrong mingled until there was no clear answer other than he must have her.

Lazily, Grace licked the underside of his erection, her tongue tracing a vein that tracked the length. "Bloody hell," he moaned, his hands tightening again in her hair.

Lightning ignited and blazed through his blood, turning him inside out. God above, she still wore her virginal white nightgown. It screamed her innocence. Nicholas shut off his senses to anything other than her mouth pleasuring him. A curse indicated the unraveling of his willpower. With a shuddering breath, he surrendered it.

Reaching down, his fingers laced with hers, bringing them up along the base of his shaft. Without words, he showed her how her hand could almost encase the flesh, while her mouth attended elsewhere. She caught on quickly, mouth and hand moving simultaneously; up, down, twisting and undulating until Nicholas thought he would shout aloud from the hedonistic thrill.

Just when he thought he'd surely reached a pinnacle of debauchery by allowing her to do this in the first place, he heard himself snarl in a tone he'd never used before, "All of it, love. Every drop."

Grace could not possibly understand that dissolute command. A portion of his brain registered that fact and processed it as truth. But she whimpered in approval, her tongue swirling around the molten steel of his cock. With her golden gaze upon him, he exploded in her mouth, a heated frenzy of sensations leaving him disoriented.

And goddamn.

Reality exceeded all his wildest fantasies.

∾

He must have blacked out. When he came to, eyes fluttering, his gaze immediately went to the space between his knees.

Grace still knelt there, leaning back slightly, watching him with a quizzical expression. Her mouth was flushed red, her lips plump from use. But her eyes held his attention. They glowed, a slightly wild, almost smug look about them.

Letting out an unsteady breath, she licked her bottom lip and asked softly, "Are you all right?"

Nicholas couldn't speak; he could only stare, dumbfounded by their encounter and the stunning visage she presented. A temptress he'd never seen coming. One he never expected. A girl...young and innocent. And she wrapped him about her finger as easily as an experienced courtesan would a green lad in the throes of his first sexual experience.

"Nicholas?" Grace leaned forward, sliding her hands along his thighs. Nicholas actually trembled. The first hint of uncertainty glinted in the topaz depths of her eyes. "Did I do it wrong? Are you angry with me?"

"God, no." Still woozy, his fingers sifted through her hair, an indolent caress that allowed the strands to filter and fall like sheaves of thick, liquid gold. "No, you were perfect. Amazing. Have I ever told you how beautiful your hair is?"

Grace smiled at the arbitrary compliment, appearing amused by his sudden turn toward the abstract. "It is wretchedly straight." She rested her chin on his knee, watching him as if she found his mood quite curious.

"Like rays of sunshine. I've wanted to do this since I laid eyes on you." Nicholas ruffled the fringe of bangs feathering her forehead, pleased by how easily it all fell back into place.

"You may thank Lady Celia Darby when next you see her. She is responsible for my hairstyle."

"Why is that?"

"She was so excited when I first arrived in London, she

insisted on making me presentable. She forgot the wrapping papers when winding my hair about the curling tongs. It singed it off until little more than a half inch remained." Grace gave him an irrepressible grin at the memory. "It smelled hideous and looked even worse. Once it began growing back, Annabelle, our upstairs maid, took me in hand and did what she could. Now she cuts it like this because I ask her. She's quite good at hairdressing —for that matter, dressing me in general. She's my lady's maid when I've need of one."

Nicholas's jaw tightened. The women of his acquaintance would have delighted in that sort of cruelty toward a rival. That Grace might be the victim of such subterfuge angered him.

"I trust Lady Celia was punished. Her father— "

"Oh, no!" Grace interrupted. "She was far more upset than I. She cried over the incident for days and days. Until she was ill with remorse." They stared at one another, and then she said softly, "I'm glad you like it."

The quiet statement rattled Nicholas. She was so pleased by the compliment. He suspected she received very few of them, which seemed impossible, for she was stunningly beautiful, if not conventionally so. She was especially lovely at this very moment.

He abruptly became aware she still crouched between his legs. Her knees were surely sore by now.

With a slight curse, he tucked himself back into his breeches then hauled her up so she straddled his lap, her upper body resting against his, legs spread wide again on the bulge in his breeches. Of course, that's where the trouble started before, but Nicholas loved having her nestled within his arms. She was warm and tiny, and the protective streak burning through his soul was not unwelcomed. A man could get used to such delights as this. Holding a woman. Gaining pleasure in her warmth and sweetness, in the perfumed softness of her flesh. But not just any woman. He only wanted Grace. And that was problematic.

Nicholas hooked two fingers in the bracelet, holding Grace

prisoner with the slightest of effort. The pearls in the intricate gold setting paled in comparison with her skin. Her eyes widened as he brought her wrist to his mouth. He kissed the pulsating beat beneath the surface of her flesh, then bit down softly.

Her pulse jumped in response, and he recognized the dreamy look on her face. He'd seen it before in women who became attached to him, despite their insistence to the contrary. A virtual battlefield existed in his wake. He'd ravaged and abandoned so many of them without even a backward glance. Without concern or thought. Or regret.

Now, he had ruined his Grace. And she had ruined him.

"Oh, little bee. What have you done?" His groan was borne of weakness and desire. It was becoming increasingly difficult denying what he felt because of her. The emotions careening around inside him were confusing.

In answer, she kissed him, pulling the fullness of his lower lip between her teeth, nipping softly as he'd taught her. He smelled her arousal. Tasted the lust in her kiss. Tasted himself on her lips. Knew she wanted him as desperately as he wanted her. But a brutal reality existed. It demanded a distance must be maintained between them. For both their sakes.

"Do not fall in love with me, Grace," he warned. "I'll destroy you."

"Take me to bed and destroy me now," she murmured agreeably. "We will not speak of love."

"You cannot sleep here."

"I have no desire for sleep," Grace replied, pulling his head down so she could give him a melting kiss. "I want you. Your hands. Your mouth. I know we cannot make love, but I need you, Nicholas. If you wish me to beg, I shall..."

He couldn't resist her silken pleas, nor her soft body pressed so intimately against his. Pushing her back slightly, he stripped away her nightdress and recaptured her mouth. When he rose from the chair, her legs automatically wrapped about his waist, her arms looped with languid possessiveness around his neck. With his palms cradling her bottom, Nicholas carried Grace to the bed, where he deposited her, never once breaking their kiss.

Lying beside her, his hand dipped between her legs, finding all the hot, achy parts, kissing the tender places that made her whimper and sigh. As he began working her body, coaxing moans of passion from her, he whispered with a twinge of regret, "I can give you this, Grace, but do not expect love. I am incapable of it."

CHAPTER 27

*G*race was aware of two things as sleep receded and consciousness fluttered in.

First, an uneasy sense of doom washed over her. As if everything wrong in the world had suddenly descended upon Bellmar Abbey. It was surprising, really. Because Nicholas loved her so well with his magical hands and clever mouth, she'd slipped into a deep state of satisfaction. They fell asleep in each other's arms, the thunder and lightning outside the windows a faint lullaby.

Second, she heard shouts and....*dear god.*

Terrified whinnies, the sounds animals make when in pain. Agonized, horrifying screams.

Her horses.

Leaping from the bed, Grace grabbed her nightgown from the floor, throwing it on as she ran toward the windows. Beyond the glass was the stuff of nightmares.

The stables were on fire, flames shooting from the beamed rafters, billowing out in in sheets of orange and red from the long portion of the T-shaped building.

"What is it?" Nicholas asked, propping himself up against the pillows.

The dim light of the banked fire in the grate provided enough of a glow that Grace saw him rub his face, wiping away the sleep. He looked disoriented at seeing her still in his room. That stood to reason. She'd promised after that last climax, she would rouse herself and seek her own bedchamber. Nicholas agreed, then promptly folded his arms around her, stroking her hair until they drifted off asleep together.

"My horses..." Grace choked out. She could barely breathe. Fear momentarily paralyzed her limbs. "My horses. The stables...it's on fire."

Panicked, she whirled and stumbled toward the door, reaching for handle with numb hands as Nicholas flung back the sheets and grabbed his breeches.

"Grace! Wait.... Grace!"

She paid him no heed. Racing down the hall, she took the stairs in such haste, it was a wonder she didn't tumble down them. Although she didn't remember, she'd picked up her robe, belting a clumsy knot about her waist with shaky fingers.

Doors slammed open in the corridors below and above the second-floor landing where she'd stood just moments before. Nicholas shouted something. A moment later, Sebastian answered. Before anyone could catch up with her, Grace raced out the front door and down the gravel drive.

Reaching the cobblestoned area of the stables, she gaped in open-mouth horror. Stable boys raced in and out, like insects from a disturbed anthill, sometimes with horses in hand, sometimes with panicked animals bolting loose and disappearing into the darkness. A line of water buckets had formed, six grooms and three groundskeepers passing the pails while two men alternated at turns pumping water from the well. Hugh was at the front of the line, grabbing buckets, sloshing water on the flames, then tossing the buckets behind him for a return journey to the well.

With a wail of despair, Grace clapped her hands over her ears. The screams from the stables were terrifying. They made her physically sick, until she thought she would vomit. And the smell. Dear God... the smell of burning hair. Flesh. Of leather and wood and straw. It rolled through the pretty courtyard like fog from Satan's own hell, permeating everything.

There were thirty-eight horses at Bellmar Abbey. Twelve feisty yearlings in box stalls. Numerous broodmares, her carriage horses, and Sebastian's matched greys. There were also the five Ravenswood mares. Nicholas's stallion, Skye. And deep within the longest part of the building...her precious Llyr.

"Get back, milady!" Hugh spotted Grace's ashen face in the swirl of rain and black smoke. "It's too dangerous! Get back!"

Grace shook her head. Tears streaked down her cheeks, mixing with the drizzling rain and soot. Glancing down, she realized she'd forgotten her slippers. Would she be able to bear the heat inside the stables without the protection of shoes? At least her clothing might not immediately catch fire, drenched as she was now.

"Where's Llyr?" she screamed at the stable master, knowing from his sorrowful expression the stallion was still inside the building.

Grace removed her robe. She would cover the horse's eyes with the garment. It would enable easier handling if he couldn't see. Knowing how Llyr responded to storms and fire in general, it was the only way he could be led out safely.

Starting toward the stables, Grace made note of the horses that had escaped. They were ones kept in the uppermost portion of the 'T'. Horses easily reached. Llyr was kept down the longest section of the structure, in one of the roomiest stalls. It was the part currently aflame, the same section housing the upcoming yearlings. Sebastian's carriage horses were in that portion as well.

She was grabbed after only a few steps. Nicholas held her impossibly tight, arms like iron bands contracting around her waist, dragging her away from the blazing heat. Despite her struggle, he spun her around, shouting above the horrible racket.

"No, Grace. No!" His eyes were dark, frantic, and yet, at the same time there was a deadly calm in the green depths "Stay here...Sebastian, don't let her go. By all that is holy, if you value your life, do not let her go."

Before Grace could process what was happening, she was thrust into another pair of masculine arms. There was the fleeting impression of dark gold hair shining richly in the firelight, a set of broad shoulders clad in white then Nicholas rushed past, disappearing into billowing black smoke.

"The goddamn fool..." Sebastian swore against her hair. "He's gone in.

Fear unlike anything she'd ever experienced overtook Grace. Like a leaf caught up in a tornado, she trembled, fighting against Sebastian's chest. "I must go after him...he won't know where Skye is stalled...he'll be lost. Please, let me go...let me go!"

"Darling.... his horse is safe," Ivy cried, rushing up and wrapping her arms around Grace too. The three of them stood in a tight circle, husband and wife restraining their cousin. "He's gone for Lly."

Grace twisted to get free, her clothing clinging indecently until Ivy snatched a carriage blanket from a terrified stable boy and threw it around the both of them.

"He won't reach him," Grace screamed in near hysterics. "And if he does, Llyr won't follow him out! Oh god. Oh, god!"

"Darling.... darling," Ivy murmured, stroking Grace's wet hair, unsure how else to console her.

Forcing her heart rate to slow, Grace focused on Sebastian's stony features, eerily lit by flames and flashes of lightning. "Let me go, Sebastian. I must help him. I cannot allow Nicholas to do this. He could die while rescuing my horse." She sobbed, uncontrollable gulps of despair, despite her efforts at calming herself. "Please...please. He's in there...let me go after him."

"*Goddamnit.* Goddamnit!" Sebastian thrust Grace fully into Ivy's arms, shaking a finger at his wife. "Keep her here. No matter what."

"Sebastian, you can't...don't you dare leave me!" Ivy cried, holding Grace so hard, she was leaving bruises on her arms.

"I'll be right back, butterfly. You know I cannot allow that man the opportunity of throwing his honorable sacrifice in my face."

He flashed a grim smile and landed a fierce kiss on Ivy's lips. As he sprinted for the stables, he snatched Grace's robe up, using it as a covering for his mouth.

"*Sebastian!*"

Ivy screamed for him, but her grip on her cousin did not ease, not until some moments later when Grace took a deep breath, swiping at her tears. For some inexplicable reason, a strange sense of calm overcame her, knowing Sebastian was going after Nicholas. With a good understanding of the stable layout, he knew exactly where Llyr's stall was located.

"We are of no help just standing here." Grace tugged herself from Ivy's arms, then the two women watched, wide-eyed, as three of the five Ravenswood broodmares suddenly burst from the stable entrance. They were quickly followed by a handful of yearlings...not all of them, but at least half. Grace sent a prayer heavenward. It might not mean what she hoped, but the yearlings were stalled closer to Llyr. Perhaps the fire hadn't ravaged that far. Perhaps someone, Nicholas or Sebastian, unlatched their stall doors.

Their hands entwined, Grace pulled Ivy toward the line of men and procession of buckets. All the house servants were now assembled, including Mrs. Cooper, grey hair concealed under an old-fashioned white mop cap. Her plump form wrapped in a stunning, richly brocaded robe of scarlet red, she waved her cane, shouting instructions like a contentious brigadier general. If Grace wasn't frightened half out of her wife, she would have stared in absolute wonder at the housekeeper.

She dedicated herself to the task of passing buckets until her shoulders ached and her arms grew numb. The rough handles cut into her fingers, little rivulets of pink seeping onto her palms. Blood mingling with rain.

Beside her, Ivy toiled just as hard, mouth set in a grim line, her beautiful chestnut hair trailing down her back in wet, curling waves. She was so astoundingly beautiful, even disheveled and soot smudged. Grace felt a surge of love for the countess and utter sadness. The men they loved were inside that building, and they shared a fear for their safety.

It seemed the combination of well water and drizzling rain which morphed into a steady downpour was finally diminishing the flames. As their efforts slowed, so did the screams of the horses still trapped inside the stables. Grace did not know how much time had passed. Half an hour...perhaps more. With no sign of Nicholas, Sebastian or Llyr.

Nicholas. Oh, God, Nicholas...have I lost you?

"There!" Ivy shouted in relief, dropping a bucket and running toward the side of the stables. "There they are!"

Grace could not move as Sebastian stumbled toward them, half-carrying, half-dragging Nicholas. Both men were almost unrecognizable, their clothing and skin covered with black soot and char marks. Racking coughs filling the air as they came closer. Several men rushed forward, reaching for Nicholas, easing Sebastian's burden as Ivy launched herself into her husband's arms.

Nicholas appeared dead. Half-dead, at least. In the dim light cast by the dying flames, Grace saw dark streaks on his face. She shook her head in silent denial. It couldn't be what it looked like. It couldn't be blood. She refused to believe it was blood. Why wasn't he coughing like Sebastian? Why wasn't he fighting off the hands holding him? Why wasn't he coming to her and assuring her everything was all right? Why was Llyr not galloping free from the stables?

She finally forced her feet from their frozen state. Advancing on the group huddled around Nicholas, now lying prone on the ground, she pushed through everyone until she was kneeling beside him. Someone wiped his face with a wet cloth, forcing water between his lips

There was a gash on his left temple. Vivid red stains mingled with black. The same discolorations marred the previously white shirt, now a filthy shade of dark grey. He held a halter, clenched so tight between his fingers, the imprint of the buckles was surely etched into his flesh. It was Llyr's halter.

Cradling Nicholas's head in her lap, Grace lifted her eyes and found Sebastian. His own shirt was similarly marked with blood and soot. He forced himself to meet her gaze over Ivy's head, his voice breaking when he spoke.

"He made it to Llyr's stall, but the ceiling had already started to collapse. There was so much debris scattered about, I'm not sure what struck him. A rafter beam, perhaps. It's blocking the entrance to the stall. Nicholas almost had him, Grace. Almost..."

A wave of despair rolled over Grace. The pain was almost unbearable, deep and stabbing. She began shaking.

"Is my horse dead?" Her voice was chillingly tranquil. It became stronger, bolder. "Is my horse dead? *Is my horse dead?*"

Sebastian shuddered, and Ivy let him go so she could sink down beside Grace, wrapping an arm about her shoulders. She was crying; Grace realized she was crying too. Silently. Screaming on the inside like the insane must.

"Yes," Sebastian finally replied. "The beam landed partially on Llyr. He was pinned beneath it, sweetheart. It broke one of his forelegs, maybe both...he was suffering. I had to put him out of his misery."

"And how did you do that?" Grace asked woodenly. *My dear, sweet, funny Llyr is gone. Gone...gone...*

Sebastian closed his eyes at the horrible memory. "In the quickest, least painful way possible. I—I slit his throat. It was over, almost instantly, exhausted and broken as he was. I barely got Nicholas out of there before the beam crashed down the rest of the way. The entire aisle was engulfed in flames and thick smoke, but I remembered an old side door Hugh showed me once leading to the back paddocks. I busted it open and got us out of there." He choked, eyes welling with tears. "I couldn't save all of the yearlings...they were too frightened and wouldn't leave their stalls no matter how I yelled and cursed at them. My greys, they are gone as well. I believe your carriage horses made it out. And maybe all the broodmares, mine too. I assume Nicholas opened their stalls as he passed, hoping they would bolt for the outside."

"My Llyr is dead," Grace said with no emotion. Her hand trembled as she passed it over Nicholas's brow, brushing back his blood-soaked hair. Tears landed on his chest and were absorbed by his shirt. "Nicholas risked his life for my sake, and you risked your life for his. Thank you, Sebastian, for saving him. Thank you for easing Llyr's suffering. For doing what needed to be done."

"I wish—I wish I had gone in sooner. Perhaps, between the two of us, we might have saved him. And the others."

"It is done now. I'm grateful you are both alive."

Grace ducked her head, bowing closer to Nicholas's lips. He muttered something, stirring with her touch. Then he coughed, a wretched sound that made her wince.

"We must get His Grace into a bed. Robbie," Grace addressed the stable lad crouched down nearest her. "Ride for the village and fetch the doctor. The rest of you, follow Hugh's directions in capturing the horses." She swallowed hard, forcing herself to continue, "We'll deal with everything else in the morning."

CHAPTER 28

She seeks me out despite the cold
The infection of my darkness
The cruelty of my soul's endless winter
She has decided she needs me
~Nicholas August Harris March
Ninth Duke of Richeforte

K nives. Jammed into his skull. Relentless and cruel. Why it was happening, he did not know. Every time he tried rubbing his head, it was with hands too clumsy and thick to ease the pain. At one point, he howled with frustration, reaching up and finding the movement arrested.

"Do not fret so, Your Grace." A soothing voice admonished gently. "You must calm yourself, else we shall restrain you. Shhh..."

Restrain him? Who would dare such a thing? Nicholas reached for his head again, desperate for relief. Someone gripped his arms in an infuriating manner. Opening his eyes, he couldn't understand the vision before him.

An angel. With soft blonde hair and eyes the color of Heaven's Golden Gates. They were ringed in dark shadows, the tracks of tears on her pale cheeks. She wore a pastel lavender gown, with ropes of ivory braids edging the neckline.

Do angels wear colors other than white?

Befuddled, his gaze shifted. A dark-headed devil with a sad, crooked grin held down his arms.

"Am I dead, then?" Nicholas croaked, wondering at the dry, raspy quality of his voice. His throat ached like hell. It felt as though he was on fire from the inside out. "Has Sebastian finished me off? He was always a good enough shot with a pistol. I haven't told him the truth though. I must tell him..."

"Shhh, Nicholas. Drink this," the angel said, as iridescent as if made of sunbeams.

Something cool and sweet passed between his lips. Grateful when the stabbing pain in his head eased after a few moments, Nicholas melted beneath her touch. He reached up, intent on touching the beautiful face above him, but the angel gently took his hand. She pressed a kiss on the inside of his wrist with a barely audible sob. There was a throbbing within his palm, stacked in agonizing layers, and keeping his eyes open was increasingly difficult.

"It's all right," the angel whispered, her tears landing in silky drops on his skin. "I'm here, I'm with you. Sleep now."

He drifted. Like a feather released into a high wind. Light shifted and shimmered all around him, glittering and beautiful. Floating. In the sea. On a cloud. On a ship made of diamonds and pearls and gossamer wings. The angel never let go of his hand, smiling at him with those eyes made of amber and gold.

I know her...

Grace. This angel, *his* angel was Grace. He could never forget her. How could he when his soul was bound with hers?

~

In and out Nicholas drifted. Sometimes the screams of horses invaded his mind, other times the sound of gunshots. Or the crack of wood splitting and crashing above his head. He saw faces...Grace's lovely one, bending over him, eyes dark with worry and fear. Sometimes, she sobbed. Her pale face hidden in her hands. She would look up, and those haunted, pain-filled eyes of hers would bore into him, as if she could see all his dark secrets, as if she knew every wish and longing he carried in his tortured heart.

An army of invisible foes persisted on attacking him. Some unknown while others were once close friends. He saw Sebastian, that handsome face of his streaked with black soot. Sometimes with blood. And Alan Bentley's charming, striking smile turned toward him, laughing as if sharing a jest. Once, Nicholas saw his own father standing with Marilee Godwin, Sebastian's former fiancée. They stood in the center of a blazing fire, scowling one minute, laughing maniacally the next. Tristan was with them, but when Nicholas called out his name, he turned his back.

At one point, he heard Sebastian command that he must "pull through." Whatever that meant. Nicholas closed his eyes against the insistent pounding in his head, shutting out everything for a long while.

Nicholas squinted against the glow of the bedside lamp. It was dark in the room other than that little bit of light. He wondered if it was dusk or dawn behind the closed window drapes.

"Are you awake, Your Grace?"

Startled, he turned his head and discovered Lady Ivy reclining in a high-backed wing chair pulled alongside the bed.

Her foot were tucked beneath her and a book lay in her lap. She regarded Nicholas curiously, patiently waiting for a response.

When he only stared at her, she set the book aside, fussing with some items arranged on the table. A cup of cool water pressed his lips. Nicholas grabbed the cup without success as one hand was bandaged in thick layers of surgical cloth. Ivy tsked and transferred the cup into his other hand. When he'd quenched his thirst, she returned the cup to the table.

"You gave us all a fright, Your Grace."

"Where is Lady Willsdown?" Nicholas barked, wincing because the sound of his voice made his own head spin. Reaching up, he found his head wrapped with bandages. It was tender alongside his temple; he probed the spot carefully.

"We finally convinced her she must lay down and rest. She's kept constant watch over you for three days and has exhausted herself."

Nicholas's throat convulsed. "Is she all right?"

"As much as can be expected," Ivy replied, her sharp eyes noting the clenching of his jaw.

He looked away, unable to face the truth but desperate to know what he already suspected. "I failed, didn't I?"

Ivy nodded. "What do you remember?" Ivy Cain was the toast of London, both before and after her love match with Sebastian. And now, Nicholas feared the wife of his enemy knew more of his secrets than she had a right to.

"Going into the stables. Locating Llyr's stall and grabbing his halter from a hook. He was standing there, patiently. As though he were waiting for me. I decided I could lead him out because the fire did not appear so terrible in that section. Then, a crash... and nothing more until now."

"Something hit you in the head and gave you a rather nasty injury. You were running a fever that first day so the doctor gave you laudanum to keep you calm. You thrashed about so violently..." Ivy gave a sad shake of her head. "A beam landed full on

Llyr. Sebastian found him pinned beneath it and you unconscious. Most of the building was destroyed, but thank God no human lives were lost, just scrapes and burns. Sebastian's greys died and half of the yearlings. And two mares. But the worst blow is the loss of Llyr."

Sorrow overwhelmed Nicholas, blotting out details of the fire and the knowledge that Sebastian was responsible for his rescue. He failed Grace. Failed in saving her most loved and prized possession. Tears pricked his eyes until he rubbed them away with his uninjured hand. His poor, sweet Grace. How devastated she must be.

Realizing that Ivy was regarding him strangely, he cast about for a topic that did not involve Grace.

"Has Sebastian come often to gloat over saving me? I'm sure he would have preferred leaving me to my fate."

"There was no keeping him from the building, Your Grace. Whatever you might think, that he hates you or wishes you dead, is just not true. Although he won't yet admit it," Ivy replied. "Sebastian left for London this afternoon. To begin the process of rebuilding the stables, hiring carpenters and skilled mason workers. He intends on hiring Sir Cedric Barrymore, but I doubt he'll be able to drag him from his work at Westminster Palace."

"I can help Grace..." The words were out of his mouth before they could be stopped.

"And why would you do that?" the countess asked. Nicholas couldn't decide if she was amused or just curious.

"She will need aid. I would do the same for anyone in this situation." The excuse was a paltry one. It proclaimed for all the world his concern for Grace's welfare. He, the Winter Wolf, interested in someone other than himself.

The corner of Ivy's mouth lifted with a tiny smile.

"May I ask a question, Your Grace?" She spoke so calmly, Nicholas felt physically soothed by her voice and he nodded she continue. "How long have you cared for her? Did it start at

Calmont Downs? Or even before that? We were absent from London with that unfortunate incident involving Sebastian's Aunt Rachel, so perhaps the two of you met during that time and we were unaware of your association with one another."

Nicholas's head throbbed as the path of the countess's questioning became clear. "What the devil are you saying?"

"You are the Duke of Richeforte. You risked your life for a horse. A *horse*. One you don't even own. Why? You have a reputation as a wretchedly cold-hearted, dispassionate man. Your selfishness is legendary, your disregard for women well-documented. Forgive me if I wonder at your motives when it comes to my cousin."

"I did what any other rational man would have done."

Ivy laughed, her head tilting. "Is that so?"

"Yes...that's so." Nicholas ground out. "My motives have little to do with Lady Grace. We barely know each— "

"You barely know each other," Ivy interrupted incredulously. "Why were her slippers in this room, *your room,* the night lightning struck the stables? I picked them up myself, there by the fireplace, while they laid you out on the bed. No one else noticed, so I hid them in my robe pockets and later returned them to Grace's room. She has no idea I did that." Ivy smiled sadly. "Do you know she would have followed you into that fire if Sebastian had not? And when he dragged you out, bloody and burnt, she dropped to her knees at your side. She cried over you, Richeforte. She has cried so much the last three days and not always for the loss of Llyr. For her sake, do not diminish whatever is between you."

Nicholas was speechless. *His* Grace? Weeping? For him? God, he couldn't imagine the depths of her pain. Didn't think he had it in him to even try, but for a wild, breathless moment, he wished she was in his arms. So he could comfort and console her. Take care of her as she'd cared for him.

"You won't answer me, will you?" At his continued silence, Ivy stood, stretching her back. "Very well. The doctor indicated your bandages could be removed today, and as your valet arrived this morning, I'll let him know you are awake. You should make yourself a bit more presentable before Grace returns."

Nicholas understood Ivy was on his side where Grace was involved. For whatever reason, she'd decided the pair of them should continue on, so he chose his words carefully. "I cannot explain this arrangement between myself and Grace, Lady Ravenswood, only that it is for her benefit and at her insistence."

Ivy laughed, murmuring mischievously, "Your Grace, you may call me by my Christian name. I assisted Sebastian with you after the fire, so I regard you now as one might a brother. You and my husband share many similarities." She winked at him. "There's no need for such formalities and I've a feeling you'll be part of our family soon enough." Cocking her head, she regarded him for a long moment, then said thoughtfully, "Come to Beaumont, should you feel well enough. Alan and Sara return from their honeymoon in three weeks and we are hosting a ball in their honor. Your mother is attending, if she arrives in time from Ireland. I think you should be there, too."

CHAPTER 29

I become envious of little things
The sun kissing her face
The breeze caressing her hair
The silk embracing her body
I am a man possessed
Wanting to become these things
~Nicholas August Harris March
Ninth Duke of Richeforte

*H*is valet was as efficient as ever, although slightly
frazzled seeing the duke so terribly incapacitated.
Within the hour, Strawn had assisted him with a bath, despite
Nicholas's persistent, dizzying headache, a much-needed shave,
definitely difficult to accomplish one-handed, and carefully
removed the bandages wrapping his head and hand. He'd also
ordered a messenger travel immediately to London, with specific
instructions on what to do.

The last task was helping Nicholas into a pair of sleeping
pants designed specifically for him in London, based on garments
he'd discovered in the Far East. Comfortable and loose, riding low

on his hips and tied with a drawstring, the silk pants were an article of clothing he rarely wore but one Strawn now insisted upon.

"You are not well, Your Grace, a guest in this house, and with many people coming and going from this room." Strawn's thin, elegant face pulled tight with propriety. "These *are* a necessity. At least until you are back at Oakmont."

Nicholas grumbled and agreed.

His bed sheets were changed out by a sympathetic and genial Mrs. Cooper and now, Nicholas examined the palm of his right hand. There was no mistaking the scarlet-red, square imprint of the halter buckle. The burn mark was already turning brown around the edges as it began healing. He closed his hand slowly, testing the level of pain. It twinged sharply in protest, but he would gain its full use within a day or two. The gash on his head was healing nicely as well. In a few days, the stitches would come out and he'd have only a thin white scar, trailing off into his hairline.

Strawn had brought along the travel chest containing his writing materials and journal. It sat on a bureau a few feet away, and Nicholas found it a more welcome sight than his own clothes. He anxiously awaited the moment he could put his feelings to paper once more.

The house grew quiet, at least in the corridor where his room was located. Nicholas sighed, tilting his head against the mound of pillows. As always, his thoughts were of Grace, the ache within him difficult to comprehend. He had never wanted a woman with such desperation. Her soothing touch. Her small capable hands and sweet voice. He needed all of her. Even if she only sat at his bedside. At least she would be near him.

It was foolish, hoping Grace would come this night. She was exhausted, after all...would likely sleep until morning, as long as no one disturbed her. Disappointment flooded Nicholas. He was a selfish, wicked man; no one knew better than he did. But he craved her with such intensity, he would settle for the cool touch of her hand on his forehead and nothing more.

When he finally fell asleep, he dreamed of rainstorms and wild heather and how those things had thrown his life into utter chaos.

~

GRACE GENTLY CLOSED THE DOOR BEHIND HER. FOR A LONG moment, she merely stood there, looking at the man asleep in her guest bedroom, wondering if this was a dreadful mistake.

Nicholas's eyes opened, pinning her in place and Grace choked back a sob. *I almost lost you...*

"Grace..."

He reached a hand out for her. She wondered how he knew it was her...the light didn't reach that far, pooling around the bed and going no further.

"Come here to me, little bee."

She approached slowly, tears welling in her eyes. "I had a nightmare."

"I know. Come here,..."

Reaching the side of the bed, she stood in nervous uncertainty. "You were inside the stables...at first I didn't know where you were. You were lost in there...in the blackness. There was smoke and screaming. So much smoke. But, somehow, I found you. Helped you to the entrance, and we were almost safe. I turned for a moment, and you were gone. Then I was running through the smoke and everything was happening again. As if it were the beginning of the same nightmare. Over and over."

Nicholas took her hand and pulled her closer.

"I'm so sorry, Grace..." he choked, her pain obviously affecting him. "So very sorry."

It was as though his words unleashed a torrent inside her. She became vaguely aware of tears streaming down her cheeks as she hurtled into the circle of his arms.

Nicholas quickly arranged the bedcovers so their bodies were covered. Then he reclined on his side, facing her. "Let me hold you. Nothing else."

Grace nodded, sobbing against his chest, breathing in the wonderful sandalwood, linen, and mint scent that was uniquely Nicholas. His skin was warm, the swirl of tawny gold hair on his chest tickling her nose. She was too upset to appreciate being held like this, her heart turned inside out and shattered, but his embrace was comforting. Safe. For a long time, she wept in his arms while he quietly consoled her.

The entire household lay draped in sorrow. The day following the fire, Hugh sought her out, catching her in the hallway outside Nicholas's door. He blamed himself, although Grace reassured the stable master no one could be blamed for an act of God. The poor man sobbed like a child against her shoulder, as dazed and heartbroken as she was over the loss of the stallion.

"We buried him, we did," Hugh had said, wiping his eyes with a small handkerchief he always kept on his person. "In the corner 'neath that auld tree. Got his halter 'anging from the marker there." It was Llyr's favorite pasture, the apple tree at least a century old and profuse with leaves. It was a beautiful resting place. Later, she would retrieve the halter and place it somewhere in the stables as a tribute.

Nicholas's heart thumped steadily in her ear as she thought of what her loyal employees endured the morning after the event. They cleared away as much debris as possible, removing deceased horses and ruined tack. She could not bear watching as they removed the charred remains, aware her tenuous hold on sanity may have snapped at the sight. She'd not yet ventured to the grave, and her heart tightened with the thought of seeing the marker. Knowing her brave, beautiful Llyr was buried just below it broke her heart.

Never again would she ride her horse along the cliffs. Feel his warm breath as he quietly snuffled her hair, seeking her scent. Watch him mischievously stomp a massive hoof on the toes of an unsuspecting stable lad. Hear his eager whinny as Grace approached his paddock with an apple she'd selected just for him. Or the delighted nicker when he found the sugar cubes she'd hidden in her coat pockets.

Her grief poured out against Nicholas's sculptured chest until she felt cleansed and somewhat sane again. The sadness lingered, it would be there in her heart for a long time, but Grace was pragmatic. Crying would not bring her dear stallion back. Now, she must focus on plans of recovering from the devastation.

Taking a deep breath, she thought of matters now at hand. Lurking in the back of her mind was the niggling worry Nicholas would abandon their agreement. He might consider her stables unworthy of the contract and withdraw or feel pity for her situation and refuse taking advantage of her. She wasn't sure what she would do if that happened. When had the thought of losing him become more devastating than losing her home? Or her horses? Was it the time spent with him that night in this very room? Or did the fire and his heroic efforts force the realization she couldn't let him go? Afraid of a future without him in it.

Nicholas's hands smoothed up and down her back. The injured hand must surely pain him, but he gave no indication of it as he murmured in her ear, pressing soft kisses in her hair and on her forehead. "I've got you, little bee. I've got you."

For a long time, they lay in this manner until Grace was calmer. When she tried pulling away, Nicholas's arms locked about her waist. His hands resting low in the small of her back, he traced small circles that burned her flesh through the pale-yellow silk of her nightgown.

"Don't go. Stay with me. Stay all night. I'll hold you in case your nightmares come back. I'll keep them away."

Grace relaxed. "What of your own nightmares, Nicholas?" She brushed a tawny lock of hair off his brow, careful of the wound snaking into his hairline.

Nicholas brought a hand around and grasped her wrist, dragging his mouth ever so lightly across the skin above the bracelet. She'd not removed it since the morning he gave it. Watching over him while he was unconscious and feverish, she'd rubbed the piece of jewelry with her index finger, counting the diamond bees and pearl flowers as if they were rosary beads.

"You'll keep my nightmares at bay, Grace. Now, sleep. I've got you."

"What if someone comes in? Sees us like this?" Drowsiness drifted through her bones. Her eyes were suddenly so heavy. It was warm in Nicholas's embrace. Someday he would break her heart, but right now she was safe.

"Should anyone dare intrude, I'll run them through myself. No one will begrudge you this, not after everything you've gone through." A kiss brushed her forehead. "And I can't let you go, so you may as well rest. I'll wake you when it's time to be Lady Grace Willsdown again. Right now, you're my honeybee, and you need me holding you as much as I need to hold you."

GRACE CAME AWAKE MUCH LATER IN VARYING DEGREES OF awareness. The soft touch of lips feathered against her temple. His breath stirred her hair. The hard planes of his muscled chest warmed her back. She'd shifted onto her side, facing away from him during the night, and now Nicholas curled around her. The curve of her waist cradled his arm, one of her hands nestled in his. He was awake, lightly tracing the fine, superficial cuts on her palms.

"What are these?" His thumb gently rubbed over a tiny blister. "Were you injured?"

"From the bucket handles. When Ivy and I helped the others in putting out the fire."

Nicholas raised her hand to his lips, tenderly kissing the injuries. "Are you hurt anywhere else? Damn, I told Sebastian to hold on to you. To keep you safe."

"No, I'm not hurt. Nicholas, you should know, Sebastian was beside himself when you were trapped," Grace said, eyes closing at the sweetness of his actions. "Even more so while you've been ill. He'll say it's because his heroic act was wasted on you, but I know different."

Nicholas did not respond, and Grace plunged forward. "You were quite talkative while sedated." His entire body stiffened. He literally held his breath as she spoke. "A great deal of it was bits and pieces, phrases and nightmares come to life. Scenes lived again as if occurring anew. I watched over you, took care of you...and now I've become one of your secrets. Do you understand, Nicholas?"

He muttered low. "Apparently, I spoke of us. Did anyone else overhear?"

"I don't believe so. If they did, I'm not sure they would even understand. But there's more, Nicholas. So much more. Do you wish to know? Everything I know?" Her fingers threaded with his, and she kissed his knuckles. "If you don't, I promise I will keep your secrets as well as you do." Her head twisted until she could look at him.

"Tell me."

His face turned hard as granite, the emerald eyes shuttering all emotions. Grace couldn't read him. It frightened her.

"You must tell Sebastian you did not betray the friendship you share. He should know it was your own father and he betrayed you both."

CHAPTER 30

I am easily wrecked
Shattered on her shores
Sails tattered
By the hurricane in her eyes
~Nicholas August Harris March
Ninth Duke of Richeforte

"How do you know that?" Nicholas growled.

He sat up, pulling Grace so she faced him, the position placing her on her knees. She was so pale. And thin. Shadows darkened the delicate skin beneath her eyes, eyes still red and slightly swollen from days of weeping. During her grief, she'd taken care of him. To the detriment of her own health.

She shivered at the harshness of his tone. Christ, he was scaring her, but the emotions rolling through him were dangerous. And heartless.

"You lived through that duel and everything associated with it. Several times, Nicholas." Grace slid her hand along his jaw. "The details were filled in, piece by piece. I know the old duke was Lady Marilee's lover and the father of her baby. He ordered that you marry her because you once said you would die before taking a wife and ensuring the March bloodline with a legitimate heir. You told your father you would see the dukedom pass into oblivion rather than do what he wanted. Marilee was furious when you refused her and your father's plan. She intentionally told Sebastian her lies as a way of hurting you. And Sebastian, because he had rejected her as too."

Bile rose in his throat. Grace watched him with the most tender of expressions until Nicholas feared he might throw up.

"What else?" he managed to croak.

Her golden eyes dropped. "Your father was terrifying and cruel. He hurt your mother many times and the scars on your back are from his hand. He abused you physically. Mentally. Damaged your soul. You hated him so much, you often goaded him into violence, hoping his own anger would cause his demise. What I don't know is the reason for your silence since the duel with Sebastian. Why, Nicholas? It was your father's shame, not yours. Your friends would have understood, surely they would have."

"Would they?" Nicholas snarled, lip curling. "My *friends*, the ones I've known from childhood, knew the type of man my father was. And those two same friends quickly decided I was more than capable of betrayal."

"If you would have explained—" Grace cried out.

"Explain that my bastard of a father seduced my best friend's fiancée? Then demanded I pass the child off as my own? No, Grace. It wasn't just Richeforte's shame. It was mine, too. And when Sebastian and Alan branded me a dissolute monster, it only proved they were never my friends after all."

"You were all so young. And hotheaded. Had you told them, they would have stood beside you. Protected you."

"Hotheaded, indeed," Nicholas hissed. The wickedness of his father's actions made him sick. And he was just as wicked. Just as monstrous, even if Grace refused to acknowledge it. "This wasn't a simple misunderstanding we could discuss rationally over a few brandies at Whites. Sebastian nearly killed me. I'm fortunate his aim was not true as usual that morning."

"He missed on purpose," Grace whispered. "Ivy told me. Sebastian couldn't bring himself to kill you. He has no desire to see you dead. Just three days ago, he entered a burning building and pulled you to safety. Oh, Nicholas...you must tell him...you must. I'll help you."

"I don't want or need your help, pet."

Nicholas's tone was a chill winter breeze. How dare she learn his secrets?! How dare she try repairing the damage facilitated by his own silence all these years. Hatred for his father burned him from the inside out. And damned if the lashes on his back weren't suddenly aflame as well, as if newly administered by the old duke's hand. All the hurt, the rage and hatred swelled inside him; his father the root of it. Nicholas directed that toxicity at Sebastian. At himself.

And at Grace.

"Oh, Nicholas..." Grace choked on a sob, her fingers tentatively touching Nicholas's thigh where a bullet had gouged out the flesh. The old scar lay hidden beneath his sleeping pants and the covers, but he felt her touch as though she caressed his skin with a blazing hot poker. "Please, after all this, let me help you put things right. You need this...you just do not realize how much."

"The only thing I need right now is for you to remove your gown. Climb atop me. Now."

Grace froze at the frigid, brutal command. "Nicholas, don't..."

"Don't what, honeybee?" His cruel smile taunted her. "Demand one of my nights with you?"

"Dawn approaches. You've only one night left."

When she edged away freezing rain immediately surged

through Nicholas's veins. She was so warm. Like sunlight. He could not control his emotions with her as he did with everyone else. She pulled forth all the anger and pain and sorrow from deep inside him until everything floated on the surface. Like curdled milk waiting to be skimmed away. He suddenly wanted to curl around her and sob into her neck like a weak child, hoping she could fix things.

My sweet, capable Grace. She'll try and rescue me even if I don't deserve saving. Even if she's the one who winds up needing rescue.

"I'm not counting this one. Not under these circumstances."

She frowned, trembling a little more. "It counts, Your Grace. And you only avoid the true problem at hand. You must tell Sebastian what your father did."

Nicholas pushed her from him, eyes blazing at hearing that vaunted and hated title fall from her lips. "Run along to your bedroom, Grace. Our interlude is over."

Grace fell back against the mattress, elbows catching her from landing flat. Her mouth twisted as if she might begin weeping again. It took everything savage remaining inside Nicholas to keep from dragging her back into his arms and begging forgiveness.

"Don't do this, Nicholas," she whispered, rising upon her knees before him, searching his stony features. Her fingernails dug into his forearm, leaving half-moon marks. "Please...please let me help you."

"Your negotiation skills leave much to be desired, but it's an excellent start that you are on your knees. In fact, I find I like you best there," he sneered.

He could no more stem the poison flowing from his mouth than he could quit breathing. That she'd discovered his secrets only increased the venom. His rage was misplaced. She didn't deserve such treatment, but he couldn't stop.

"Two more nights, Grace. Burned down stables or no. The

loss of your prized stallion? Insignificant. We have an agreement. A bloody contract, set down on paper, at your insistence. Your body for Bellmar Abbey and your horses, no matter their number or the condition of your stables. I intend on collecting all of it. And you. Soon."

CHAPTER 31

He's leaving.

A sob caught in Grace's throat, one she quickly covered with a small cough. Ivy's gaze touched on her as both women stood on Bellmar's steps, watching the duke climb into his expensive, well-sprung coach.

Other than polite goodbyes and a request to leave his stallion behind, he'd not said a word. Although the horse had recovered from his minor stone bruise, he was still flighty from the aftermath of the fire. Nicholas would pay for his keep while in Grace's care until the beast was returned to Oakmont.

There were no kind words for Grace herself. Nicholas was cool, distant, as if what passed between them the night of the fire meant nothing. When his eyes touched on her bracelet, his beautiful mouth lifting in a half-smirk, it nearly broke her heart.

Grace yanked the cuff of her striped apple green and cream color gown down in an effort of concealing her wrist. Of course, Nicholas noticed the gesture, and their gazes clashed for the briefest of moments. Could he see the longing in her features? The anguish in her eyes? Or did he not care? When he executed a curt bow and turned away, she had her answer.

A wolf masquerading as a gentleman. My wolf.

She very nearly chased the coach as it rumbled down the gravel lane. She wanted to scream after him that she would never mention his secrets again, would give him his two nights, as many as he wanted, if only he would hold her and whisper endearments in her ear.

"Come, dear," Ivy said softly as the Richeforte coach and its matching white geldings disappeared from sight. Her arm wrapped around Grace's waist, keeping her from making a fool of herself. "Perhaps a cup of tea will help."

"It won't," Grace's reply was dull and lackluster. *I cannot think of tea when my heart is breaking. First Llyr, and now Nicholas...it's too much to bear.*

"I think it will. We'll have a nice chat."

Ivy tugged her into the house, calling for Mrs. Cooper to serve tea on the back terrace. The sunshine was warm, the day pretty and bright, but all Grace could see was thunderstorms and despair. Nicholas only wanted her because of their agreement. He did not want *her*. Did not want to even attempt a reconciliation with Sebastian, a reconciliation that might have meant he could freely court her.

And marry me. Take me for his own, for his wife. But he doesn't want that. How many times did he tell me he would never marry? How many times did I say the same? And now that I want him, he doesn't care. He will go on, hating Sebastian. Sebastian hating him. And all of society will believe the Duke of Richeforte is a wicked, dishonest devil.

They settled into iron chairs set around a small table, Ivy waiting until the tea was delivered and two cups poured before gently broaching the subject of Grace's unhappiness.

"You can go to him, you know. Take Skye, ride to the duke and tell him how you feel."

Grace, staring out over the garden just beyond the edge of the terrace, shifted her gaze to her cousin, "What—what did you say?"

"You know what I said." Ivy laughed softly. "Oh, my dear Grace, you are in love with the man. It's as clear as a sunny day."

Grace shook her head. "No. I'm not. Where did you get such an insane idea?"

"I've eyes in my head. And I know how a man looks when he is fighting what is in his heart. Richeforte has fallen in love with you. It's quite obvious."

"You're wrong, Ivy. His Grace does not even like me, much less love me. I haven't the faintest idea what you are talking about." Grace sipped her tea, hoping it would hide the trembling of her hands.

"He loves you. I'd bet my life on it. And you love him. Oh, Grace. What a tangle love can create. Believe me, I know the troubles it can cause very well. I nearly lost Sebastian because I could not admit I loved him more than my own life. Darling, do not repeat my mistakes."

"He will never marry me, you know," Grace said bitterly. "He uses women and tosses them aside. Although I admit an attraction between us, his reputation...and other factors...leave no hope for marriage."

"Yes, he is wicked. And hard. And God knows, he has hurt people in the past, including my own husband. But he can change. If Sebastian could change, I know Richeforte can. Some manner of connection exists between the two of you. He admitted as much when he first awoke after the fire. I did not tell you before, you were so distraught over everything, but I found your slippers in his room and confronted him. No one other than myself knows you were with him that night. But my darling, I hold out hope you have not completely ruined yourself for him." Ivy's face was a study of trepidation and sympathy. "You haven't, have you?"

My slippers. I never even thought twice about them. I did leave them behind. God, I'm so foolish. So very foolish.

"Our arrangement is not complete, so at the moment I remain somewhat unruined."

Ivy sighed in relief. "What is your arrangement? And what does that mean? Somewhat unruined?"

Grace hesitated, unwilling to divulge everything between her and Nicholas. "A business one. And confidential on both sides, I'm afraid."

"I can think of only one arrangement that would eventually leave you in a state of ruin," Ivy murmured sadly.

Grace did not answer, sipping her tea instead. It tasted like dry paper in her equally dry mouth. Flavorless.

Ivy frowned. "Grace. I cannot pretend knowledge of what makes a man's heart work. Or, for that matter, how love might manifest itself. I can only advise doing what you think best, in your heart of hearts. If you love Richeforte, and I believe you do, and he loves you, as I believe he does, then you must do something. Grab it with both hands, my dear. If this business between Sebastian and Nicholas is the reason for your hesitation, it will work itself out. I won't allow Sebastian to hate someone who will marry his own dear cousin." She winked at Grace. "It would make for difficult and awkward family gatherings, don't you think?"

Grace choked on a horrified laugh, wishing she could relate the details of Nicholas's supposed betrayal. But that was not for her to reveal. Nicholas must do that. She only hoped he would accept her help when he did.

"I will consider your advice, Ivy. And hopefully make the right choice."

Five days later, Tristan arrived at Bellmar Abbey. He

came by horseback, complaining his coach traveled at a snail's pace. A servant sat perched atop another horse packed with bags containing the viscount's clothing and other necessary items.

Leaping from his gelding, Tristan swept Grace into his arms, hugging her tight.

"I'm so thankful you are well. I was beside myself with worry upon hearing of the fire and came as quickly as I could. Mother, Father, and Celia are currently at the Countess of Shelton's summer fete. I convinced them I could travel faster without them or they would have come as well. Are you sure you are all right? You are so pale. And you've lost weight."

For a moment, Grace closed her eyes, allowing the viscount's embrace. For a moment, a brief, awful moment, she pretended it was Nicholas holding her as if she were the most precious thing on Earth.

"I'm fine. Really." Subtly pulling away, she smoothed her gown and gave Tristan a weak smile. "Your mother will be glad for my paleness. She always says I've too much sun and should soak my face in lemon juice and buttermilk. I've not been outdoors nor ridden since before..."

The words broke off in a strangled cough of despair. She'd barely roused herself from bed that morning, much less mustered the energy required for venturing outside. And at no point in the past week had she stepped foot anywhere near the stables.

"When the earl related the news, I immediately rode for Cornwall. Lady Ravenswood," Tristan turned with a smile for Ivy. "I've a letter from your husband. He asked that I escort the two of you to Beaumont. Business detains him in London. As I was coming here regardless, I gladly offered my service." He retrieved a small, folded envelope from his coat pocket and handed it over.

"I'm staying here until the men repairing the stables arrive. Only then will I leave for Beaumont," Grace asserted. She did not miss the quiet glance Tristan and Ivy shared over her head. It made her fists clench with frustration.

Taking Grace by the hands, Tristan tugged her a few steps away, gazing at her longingly. "Darling, I'm so sorry for the loss you've suffered. Ravenswood said you were not injured, but I know losing Llyr is a devastating blow."

Grace replied without emotion. "I suppose Sebastian told you Richeforte risked his life to save my horse?"

Tristan's jaw tightened at the mention of Nicholas. "Yes. I heard he took a nasty bump on the head and suffered from fever for a few days."

"He was very heroic. And Sebastian, in turn. He saved the duke's life."

Tristan's beautifully dark brown eyes sparked with surprise. "Ravenswood failed in mentioning that. Only that Nicholas was pulled from the burning stables. With the animosity between them, I would hardly expect Ravenswood would do something so surprising as the rescue of a man he hates."

Grace stiffened. "You sound almost sorry he did." The words popped out of her mouth.

Tilting his head, the viscount stared at Grace. "Why do you say that? I'm one of Richeforte's only friends. I would not wish him harm. Although, I do wonder why he was here in the first place."

"To purchase a few of my yearlings, if you must know."

"How odd of him. He snapped up half a dozen Scottish yearlings at Newmarket only a month ago." Tristan's hand moved up, intending on grasping Grace's elbow, but she sidled out of reach. "Why would he be in the market for more?"

"I'm sure I don't know." Grace turned toward Ivy, who'd finished her letter and was folding it with a little frown. "Is everything all right?"

Ivy waved her hand, almost distractedly. "Oh yes. Sebastian says all the arrangements for the repairs are made, although the note doesn't indicate whether he retained the architect he hoped for. Shall we all go inside, Grace?" Ivy prodded gently. "The parlor is far more comfortable than the courtyard."

"I told the earl his assistance was unnecessary," Tristan inserted, voice low with agitation as they entered the manor and made their way down the center hall. Sinking onto the settee beside Grace when they reached the parlor, the viscount announced, "As Grace and I will marry soon, it is my responsibility to take care of the estate's needs."

Grace stared at the handsome young man for a moment, searching for words. Several things swelled inside her. An urge to take charge of her own life. Anger. Frustration. An unwillingness of allowing anyone or anything to stop her from obtaining what *she* wanted.

"Tristan." Her voice was strong. Steady. Resolute. "I will never, *never* marry you."

Tristan frowned. "Of course you will. How else will you survive otherwise? I know you, my dear. You would not wish to be a burden on your cousin. The only other option is marriage. You know how much I care for you, Grace. I love you."

She regarded him, then softly asked, "Tell me something, Tristan. Would you have gone into my stables to rescue my horses?"

His hesitation was answer enough although he tried covering it. "Not immediately. I would assess the situation, of course, but, after all, a horse can be replaced and..."

"Someday, Tristan, you will love someone so much you will do anything for her. Even if it places you in grave danger. Nicholas did not hesitate. He ran into those stables without thought. It is how I know he loves me, even if he doesn't yet realize it." Grace bounced up from the settee, desperate to place some distance between them. "I cannot marry you because, you see, I love Nicholas too. With all my heart, I love him."

Ivy's eyes widened. A smile of relief and gladness lit her face while Tristan scowled as if swallowing something very bitter.

"You are overwrought, Grace," he said, watching as she went to stand by the window and fingered the curtains. "Admiration for Richeforte's heroic effort has clouded your judgment. You can't possibly love him. You barely know him. And even if you do care for him, he'll never love you in return. It's not his way." A hand raked through his chocolate brown hair in frustration. "Hell, do you know Celia is in love with him, too? As tempted as I am in helping my sister obtain what she wants, I've steered her away. Do you know why? Because Nicholas doesn't care for innocence in any form or shy glances from blushing maidens. He uses women, tosses them aside the moment they no longer amuse him or when they demand too much of him. Don't you understand, Grace? He is not a man you should want, unless you are as wicked as he is."

Turning from the window, Grace leveled a steady glare on Tristan. "But you see, I am as wicked."

Tristan was momentarily confused. As her words sunk in, his jaw clenched with understanding and sudden anger. "Grace. I am pleading with you. Do not do this. You must marry me to retain ownership of Bellmar Abbey. Richeforte holds the encumbrance. He agreed he will sell only to me. When you are my wife, I will gift it to you."

"I overheard the two of you that day at Calmont Downs, Tristan," Grace replied calmly. "When you devised your plot in Lord Calmont's library. I know everything you demanded of him. I made my own arrangement with the duke."

Ivy was silent until this point. Now, she gaped at Grace. "What have you done?"

"The details are inconsequential, but soon I will have all of Bellmar Abbey."

"This is madness!" Tristan growled. "Nicholas won't marry

you, Grace. It's the only way you can hold Bellmar, and he'll never— "

"I've no delusions of marriage. I know full well what he is. I knew when I proposed our arrangement."

"I'll kill him for this," Tristan vowed. "I'll kill the bastard. If Ravenswood doesn't do it first."

"And you'll destroy any affection I hold for you if you interfere, Tristan." Grace fixed the viscount with a calm stare. "No matter the right or wrong of it, the impossibility of it. The scandal of it. The hopelessness of it. Nicholas is my choice. I won't have any other, nor will I change my mind. No matter what happens."

TRISTAN ATTEMPTED TALKING GRACE INTO MARRIAGE FOR the better part of that afternoon and evening. At dinner, he pleaded. During dessert and tea on the terrace, he raged. And before she escaped to her bedroom for the night, he played on her sympathies. Grace remained unswayed. When he disappeared into the library with a bottle of brandy, muttering curses beneath his breath, she sighed in relief. For three days, she endured much of the same, even with Ivy's interference on her behalf. And finally, Tristan caved in reluctant defeat. Sullen and angry. Heartbroken.

Knocking on Ivy's bedroom door late the evening before their departure, Grace questioned the intelligence of her plans. Before riding into Oakmont, carrying his borrowed books and riding his horse, she needed guidance on the planned assault of Nicholas's heart. She would tell Ivy how the evilness of the old Duke of Richeforte's actions affected them all. And reveal the extent of the bargain with Nicholas and what she'd wagered against her home.

Omitting the intimate details, Grace told Ivy everything.

Her cousin sat back against the bed pillows with a frown.

"Their quarrel was so bitter. No one suspected the old duke was involved in the sordid affair. I always believed Lady Marilee was pregnant by an unknown man, one she could not name. She was rumored to be quite promiscuous, and Sebastian was blind with infatuation for her. How terrible that Richeforte's own father could be so cruel toward him. Sebastian was far more upset over Nicholas's betrayal than Marilee's unfaithfulness. Which doesn't speak well for the lady." Ivy gently enfolded Grace's hand in hers. "I hope the damage between them is erased when the truth comes to light."

"There must be some manner of reconciliation, regardless of what happens between Nicholas and myself. Promise you'll say nothing. Nicholas should be the one to tell Sebastian." Grace rubbed her eyes, yawning. She'd had little sleep over the past few nights, mourning both the loss of Llyr and Nicholas's leaving Bellmar Abbey. "And say nothing of my arrangement with Nicholas. I must sort this out myself. Without fear that Sebastian will challenge Nicholas to a second duel."

"If he learns you've gone to Oakmont, Sebastian will come for you there. Are you sure of this, Grace? If Richeforte will not marry you, you are risking your reputation. You'll never be able to show your face in polite society again without being known as one of his mistresses. You are far too innocent and sweet to be one of their numbers."

"I've weighed the risks. I cannot spend the rest of my life wishing that I tried winning his heart. I hope Sebastian allows me the honor of fighting my own battles." Grace gave Ivy a quick embrace of gratitude along with a sad smile. "And I pray Nicholas realizes he loves me as I love him."

CHAPTER 32

Heartache is for fools
And love a sickness
Romantics do enjoy
But a wolf takes what he wills
Love be damned
~Nicholas August Harris March
Ninth Duke of Richeforte

*N*icholas scribbled his signature on the document, rubbing a hand over his eyes. His head ached again. But no more than his heart. He rubbed that, too, hoping it would assuage the dreadful pain there.

"Too much activity, Your Grace," His efficient housekeeper grumbled, placing a second pot of coffee and a fresh cup on his desk. She patted his hand. "You are overdoing things. It's too soon for you to be up and about like you are. Why, the doctor said you should..."

"Never mind the doctor, Martha." Another lecture revolving around his abysmal role as a patient was dismissed with a wave of his hand. "Do you have today's post?"

"Of course." Martha withdrew a stack of envelopes from the deep pocket of her apron. She loaded the tea tray with used dishes, then exited the study, muttering how stubborn men were.

Nicholas tossed aside each piece of mail until he saw the one he wanted. *Sir Cedric Barrymore.* Tearing the heavy vellum open and scanning the contents, he allowed himself a smile of satisfaction. Being a duke carried some benefit. At the very least, it proved useful in luring England's favorite architect away from official duties in Her Majesty's employ.

He picked up the document he was working on. It was a transfer of ownership, releasing all rights and benefits of his Scottish stallion. Not into the estate of Bellmar Abbey, or even Lord Darby, her guardian, but directly to Lady Grace Willsdown. She alone would own Skye, and no one would be able to say otherwise. There was another document too. One dissolving the encumbrance against Bellmar Abbey. Now she could marry anyone she wished, if she chose to, not because she had to.

Just the thought of her marrying *anyone* made Nicholas's head pound with even greater ferocity. Eventually, she would marry. If not Tristan, then some other man.

He remembered how bravely she stood on the steps of Bellmar Abbey days before. Her lips trembling, heart-shaped chin raised with determination while he rode away. She didn't know it, but he'd gripped the handle of the coach door, ready to fling it open. Wild thoughts of leaping from the vehicle, racing back and showering her face with kisses had assailed him. He almost stopped the coach, demanding she leave with him. He would have kissed her without mercy all the way to Oakmont. Would have told her he couldn't live without her. Would have made sure she understood his survival wasn't possible without her.

Instead, he reclined against the creamy leather. Instructed himself not to look back. Willed his heart not to love her.

Which was ridiculous. His heart beat for Grace with strange, erratic thumps he knew would persist for eternity. He would stand silent while she married another, dream of her at night, and curse his wicked life that made being with her impossible.

Nicholas reached for the coffee pot, then abruptly reconsidered. *Brandy, instead. Bourbon would be better.* Something stronger, which might erase this damnable heartache. A bottle of the finest whiskey from his cellars was in his grasp sometime later. After a while, he almost believed he could forget her.

Almost.

"NICHOLAS."

He shook his head. Dreaming again. Sometimes, in the middle of the night, he woke, hearing Grace's sweet voice. The demons inside him would rage until he put thoughts down on paper. But even that wasn't working in his favor anymore.

Mumbling, he reached for the whiskey bottle, positive he'd placed it within reach of his bed. He groped about, then half-remembered he was in his study. He'd fallen asleep, exhausted from restless nights and hours engaged in frantic scribblings in his journal. God, he thought he was actually going crazy. Could one go insane from heartbreak?

"Nicholas. Wake up."

Her voice again. *Wonderful.* Now she'd come to haunt him in truth, her lilting voice tumbling about in his head. Driving him mad.

A gentle hand stroked his hair, brushing back a lock where it fell into his eyes. He groaned in actual pain. This dream was so real. He smelled the heather and lemons that always drifted around Grace. Felt the light, drifting brush of her fingers on the nape of his neck. He trembled.

"Would you rather I go? I won't venture very far. Just outside the door. I'll wait for you to wake up..."

What an odd thing for dream Grace to say.

Nicholas slowly opened his eyes, staring into golden ones. She stood beside him, bent over and peering into his face. Lines of worry etched the corners of her mouth; she looked tired and pale. Hanging in a golden waterfall, her hair tumbled mostly free of its pins.

It's always doing that, Nicholas thought with a smile.

"Hello," Grace whispered when his mouth lifted at the corners. "Are you awake? Nicholas...?"

She shook his shoulder, a bit more forcefully than a dream should.

She was here. Standing beside him. Grace had come back to him. Well, not back to him since he left her. But she was *here!*

"There you are," she said with a grin as he peered at her in dazed wonderment.

"What are you doing here?" He was groggy, mentally shaking the stupor of alcohol away. *God, how much did I drink?* A glance at the bottle, full the last time he recalled, shouted he'd drank nearly all of it.

"I'm bringing you those things you left behind." Grace chewed her bottom lip, and Nicholas wanted his own teeth raking across that plump bit of flesh. "Your horse, your books, and my heart."

Now fully awake, he snorted in derision at her declaration, sitting upright in his chair. She retreated at his abrupt movement, a hand still resting on his shoulder, and it seemed her fingers were burning a hole straight through him. He rifled around his desk for Skye's papers.

"All of those items are yours," he said, handing her the sheaf of paper. He held on to the encumbrance release, however. Purely selfish reasons.

Scanning the document, her head tilted. "Why would you give Skye to me? I don't want him. I only want you."

The wounded bewilderment evident in her features made Nicholas's heart twist painfully.

"Gluttony is surely among your vices, little bee. Do you enjoy it that much? Being used by me?" He brusquely pushed her hand away, raking his fingers through his hair. God, he needed another drink. "Go home, Grace. Rebuild your stables. Breed Skye with your remaining mares and build your fortune. Unless you are here in the spirit of finishing things between us. Will you give me my last two nights all at once? Complete this damnable contract?"

He must make her see this was impossible. Make her understand there was no hope for them. Sebastian would never allow it. *He* could never allow it. His darkness would destroy her, and Nicholas realized he adored her too much to see that happen at his hands. Tearing into tiny pieces whatever emotion they felt for each other must be done. Before he catapulted any deeper in love.

Love. Yes, I love her. And I will save her from me. From us. Whatever it takes. Even if it means destroying the light I see in her eyes. I will kill that love so she can be free of me.

"It's one night. Not two." Grace's breath hitched.

Nicholas gave her a sharp glance. Would she weep? Jesus, he hoped not. He was doomed if she did.

"I've come for you." Her eyes were soft as she regarded him. "Don't you understand, Nicholas? I love you. I've always loved you. And I've decided I will be yours forever."

"How unfortunate. Did I not tell you to avoid falling in love with me? Now, remove that riding habit and make yourself comfortable on the settee. Or my desk. I'd prefer that, actually. Bent over it, waiting for me to take you." He wouldn't see her eyes that way. Those accusing golden sparks swirling in a sea of topaz. Love eventually mingling with hate.... overtaking everything until only contempt existed between them. When she despised him, it would make it easier to see her married to another man. "Great sport, taking a woman in that manner. Pinning her down with my body so I can feel every wiggle and squirm she makes. You will enjoy it as much as I."

"You are being unnecessarily cruel." Grace's chin lifted in that stubborn way he adored. "Intentionally debasing what we share."

"We share nothing other than a common lust, Grace. And a bloody contract. You've obviously come to further its end. Now, I told you...remove your clothes. Or I'll do it for you."

HIS DEMAND WAS SPOKEN CALMLY ENOUGH, BUT BENEATH the smoothness ran a current of such iciness, Grace was chilled. His demons prowled, and it wasn't safe, standing so close.

"I don't believe I shall do that," Grace said quietly. She would not let him bully her into submission.

Silence hung heavy with all the threatening violence of a lightning storm. Nicholas's gaze, bright green with frustrated desire, pinned her in place. With his hair tousled from sleep and glowing, hypnotic eyes, he truly deserved the Winter Wolf moniker society labeled him. Her eyes lifted to the shield above the fireplace, the wolf there snarling at her, mocking her trembling determination. Grace's spine stiffened. A wolf, yes. But her wolf.

"Are you denying me?"

"I'm saying I won't remove my clothes, nor will I bend over your desk."

His expression darkened, containing such ferocity, Grace nearly lost her resolve. She stood poised to obligingly scamper over to the imposingly wide desk and spread herself across it exactly as he commanded.

"I hardly require your willing participation." One eyebrow lifted slightly, his gaze raking her. "Need I remind you of our bargain?"

Grace's laugh was slightly bitter. "Oh, Nicholas. How can I possibly forget this devil's arrangement we've made?"

"Then get your ass over here, if you'll pardon my eagerness. This moment has been a long time coming." Nicholas gave his cravat a vicious jerk, and the ivory silk fluttered to the floor. Shrugging off his coat, he gave her a questioning glare when she remained motionless.

Grace stared at the cravat, remembering the first night of their bargain. Her eyes, hard and bright as chips of fossilized amber, lifted to his. A bubble of resentment rose in her chest, but she forced it down. His friends believed him capable of betrayal. She would not do the same. Even lashing out as he did now, he would not be so cruel as to take her innocence without admitting his feelings.

I believe in him. That he loves me. He won't betray me.

"Consider this your payment for the blooded stallion I've given you, as we were rather uneven before that. I have your required French letters in the drawer here. Or the sponges, if you prefer those. I'll have to show you how to insert them...Now, across my desk, Grace. This instant."

"I cannot."

"It will be the settee, then? I would offer the use of my bed, but I don't bring my whores above stairs, you see."

Grace clenched her teeth. "I *will* not, Your Grace."

An unholy light flared in Nicholas's eyes. His jaw tightened. Retrieving the cravat, he advanced toward her, working the buttons of his shirt free with slow, deliberate intent. The movement of his nimble fingers was memorizing. Grace sucked in a breath at the thought of them dancing across her skin.

"For Christ's sake, don't call me that. Not here. Not now." His face hardened as he stalked her. "Why must everything be a goddamn struggle with you, Grace? You've twisted and turned me inside out until I am no longer sure I'm doing your will or my own."

His words dissolved into a ragged snarl, directed more at himself than her. Grace trembled when he snagged her elbow in a less than gentle grip. His free hand, still marred from the fire, tilted her chin, and all she could think was how hot his touch was. As if he'd captured those flames within his hands.

"Don't you want this? To be destroyed by me?" His fingers tightened for a brief second as if questioning himself, then slid with surprising tenderness over the curve of her cheek. "Ruined for any man who may follow me in your bed?"

Grace thought he would kiss her, but he did not. He stared down at her. Anger. Confusion. Terror. Longing. Everything lay bare in his emerald gaze until his lashes dropped and all emotion was shuttered.

Grace's heart soared. He was trying to push her away, and she could not let that happen. "Why do you fight me, Nicholas? Why won't you let me in? Why do you keep yourself walled off from me? From the world? This mask of cruel indifference, this heartlessness, it isn't truly you. I know it isn't." Her hand rose, covering his, holding it against her jawline. When he met her eyes again, she reached as deep as he would allow. "Let me in. Please."

Nicholas yanked his hand away. "I cannot," he echoed her words, mocking them. The cravat was twisted until it resembled a garrote of sorts, the material stretching between his large hands as if testing its strength. It frightened Grace a bit. How he held that scrap of silk as if he intended evil things.

"If you will not let me into your heart, then I cannot stay." Grace glided away, but he gripped her elbow tighter, the cravat dangling from his fingers.

"No. You will stay," Nicholas muttered, his breath hitching in an unsteady rhythm laced with cruelty. "Five nights of my choosing, remember, pet? If I accept your flawed count, we've had four. You will give me this last before I let you go. After all, your estate depends on it."

"You don't mean that, Nicholas."

"Don't I?" His chuckle sounded almost tremulous. Did he think he could bury his feelings under a blanket of ugliness, hoping it would repulse her?

"Do you recall your vow you would never harm me? That our time together would only be pleasurable?" Grace asked softly. "You would break both those vows. Admit what is in your heart—and I will give you everything you desire."

"I have no heart, little bee." The curve of Nicholas's mouth was a confident, cruel smirk. "And a lack of pleasure is not possible when we are together. This time will be no different. Even if you are unwilling now, you soon won't be. If past experience holds any weight, I'll have your legs shaking within seconds. You'll be hoarse from screaming my name."

Grace regarded him with such solemnness, Nicholas's smile lessened. Her barely audible words drove it away entirely.

"And I would hate you for it." *Don't do this to us. To me. Love me, Nicholas, and let me love you.*

Nicholas released her so quickly, she stumbled, banging her hip against the corner of a marble inlaid table.

"Go, then!" he hissed between clenched teeth, throwing up an arm in a dismissive gesture. "I find myself weary of your company, after all. You're too much goddamn trouble as it is."

Grace sucked in a deep breath as Nicholas whirled away, hurling the cravat onto the desk. He splashed a generous portion of whiskey into a tumbler, downing it in one swallow. Then, foregoing the civility of the glass, he tilted the bottle, drinking the remainder of it until it was empty. The long, noisy event ended with a swipe of an arm across his mouth and a sneer of contempt.

"I prefer my whores less demanding. Even highborn ones like Lady Ralston know their place and what pleases me. If you cannot do the same, my use of you is at its end."

The angry, wounded beast within him was roaring, crazed with internal pain and confusion. There would be no soothing of him. No soft words, no gentle caresses calming his soul. Whatever tortured him was stronger than desire. But that hold was weakening. Nicholas wanted her. He was trying his damnedest to save her from his darkness. Somehow, she'd wiggled into his heart; the realization filled her with both joy and dread.

It enraged Nicholas.

Seeing Grace's eyes lit with an ill-concealed sorrow, his temper abruptly exploded. He slammed the empty tumbler down, splintering glass echoing like a gunshot. His growl was something wrenched from the depths of his own personal hell, the deepest, blackest cavern of his soul.

"Goddamit. If you won't spread your legs for me, use them to get the fuck out of my sight."

As Grace stared in dazed silence, Nicholas hissed another muttered curse, snatching up the discarded cravat. Blood ran in tiny rivulets down his wrist, trailing along the underside of his forearm in bright red ribbons. He plucked out the shard of glass piercing his burned palm, then wrapped the silk about his hand.

"Nicholas...the contract...I—"

"Get out of here, Grace," he snarled. "Get out, and don't come back. I cede the last night of that goddamn contract. I'll give you everything. All of it. Just go. The night of the fire, I said I would request a favor of you one day. This is it." He enunciated each word so she had no difficulty understanding his meaning. "Get out of my life. Before I destroy everything kind and good inside you. Before I turn you as black as my own soul. You don't need me to be happy. Or successful. You can do it all on your own...you and I both know you can." He rummaged about the desk, found what he was searching for, and thrust another piece of paper into her hand before presenting his back.

The vehemence in his tone was stunning. It took Grace's breath away. Exhibiting a calm she did not feel, with an inborn dignity she never knew she possessed, she turned very slowly, very carefully. Knees trembling, eyes blinded by scalding hot tears, she sought escape even as her heart pounded with dizzying defeat.

His low curses poisoned the air as the study door closed behind her with a soft click.

Leaning against the wood, Grace waited until her wobbly legs regained their strength, choking back sobs of anguish, still clutching that bit of paper in her hand. *He let me go. Even though he loves me, he let me go.*

The fierce roar erupting from the room was not surprising, neither was the crack of glass shattering against the wood behind her.

Maybe it was another tumbler or perhaps the heavier bottle he hurled. Grace wasn't sure, but the solid oak door rocked on its very hinges. The punctuation of his rage penetrated her stupor. Glancing at the paper in her hand, every cell and nerve ending within her abruptly awakened. Heart clenching, pulse racing madly, she reached a decision. Fatal perhaps, but a decision nonetheless.

He is mine, and I am his. He needs me.

Grace straightened. Clenched her fist even tighter. With methodical movements, she tore Skye's ownership paper to shreds. Reaching into her pocket, she withdrew the contract they'd both signed and ripped it up in the same fashion. And slowly, ever so slowly, she destroyed the release of Bellmar's encumbrance. She'd come this far, and Nicholas display of resistance wouldn't stop her. It was time she tamed His Grace.

Nicholas loved her. She knew it. He knew it.

She would make him see by throwing down her gauntlet.

CHAPTER 33

How blind I am
Heedless of her worth
She is gold
Jewels
Treasure
And I am but a thief
Stealing her breath and she has stolen mine
~Nicholas August Harris March
Ninth Duke of Richeforte

*N*icholas did not care that an expensive silk ascot was being used as a bandage. All he could see was the overwhelming hurt in Grace's eyes when he threw her love away as if it were worthless. His heart throbbed as painfully as his hand.

He needed another drink, and he would venture down into the cellars himself to fetch a new bottle. He had no fear of encountering Grace. He was positive she'd hurried away as fast as her legs could manage, at this very moment on her way back home. Back to the estate, now free and clear of any debt. Riding the horse he'd given her.

The door swung open, Grace blocking the entrance. She resembled an avenging angel in her pretty, light blue riding habit, all that hair spilling from its proper bun, the sunshine hued tendrils flowing over her shoulders. Burning with amber gold fire, her eyes held his. She clenched the shredded remnants of Skye's papers and something else. He saw his own handwriting scrawled across a scrap of paper fluttering onto the carpet.

The contract and encumbrance release he'd signed. All of it ripped to shreds.

It was just as well she destroyed it and he would have destroyed the original encumbrance if he had it before him. A written document stating his intention had already been sent to his barristers. The one he'd given her was merely a copy. He wanted her to have everything. The house, the stables, the horses. He should have given it all to her at the very beginning. Before he fell in love with her. Before she fell in love with him.

"I told you to go." His voice was more subdued, the previous bout of agonizing temper leaching the piss right out of him. "Live your life as you see fit. Now, there is no need for you to marry anyone. There is no contract, nothing binding us together. I forfeited the encumbrance. I sent the original document stating so to my barristers already. Your stables will be rebuilt at my expense and I've granted the Queen's own architect carte blanche. Whatever is necessary for the improvement of the structure, he will see to it. It will be outfitted as grand as any stables in England. That is all I can give you, Grace. There is nothing else."

In answer, Grace leaned against the door. She reached behind with one hand and deliberately turned the key. Pulled it from the lock and dropped it into the pocket of her riding habit.

"Grace." His heavy sigh carried all the pain coursing through his body. "What are you doing? This changes nothing."

Grace advanced until her soft warmth surrounded him. Hands braced against his chest, her fingers splayed across the broad, muscled expanse. Nicholas hoped she could not feel how furiously his heart was beating.

"I've no desire for a life without you," she said with quiet desperation. "If you keep pushing me away, I will only continue coming back." Her hands moved up, clinging to his shoulders, keeping him from sinking into some deep, dark vortex from which there was no return. She was a lifeline, an anchor he must cut loose. When his jaw tightened, something wild and sweet flared in Grace's eyes, a spark twisted from honeyed hope. "I don't care about our arrangement, or that you might change your mind and keep my home. None of that matters as much to me as you do. However you want me is how I will come to you. I love you, Nicholas. I love you."

"Well, you shouldn't. There's no point to it, is there? You'd do well if you forgot you ever knew me. Don't you understand, Grace? I have kissed you with such deception, you will never have another man's lips on yours without tasting mine. I've taken everything from you with no intention of giving anything in return." He brushed the fringe of hair from her forehead, tucking a long strand of gold silk behind a delicate ear.

"I've enjoyed ruining you in the most exquisite ways imaginable. Yet, still you beg me, frantic for more. I told you, do not love me. You did not heed my warning. We are through. It's over."

"You've not taken all of me. Not yet." Huge tears dotted her cheeks, each glistening drop a knife stabbing his heart. Grabbing his hand, she held it tight against her breast. She was calm despite the tears. Her eyes would not let go of his. "Nicholas, tell me you love me."

Nicholas clenched his teeth as the lie, bitter and foul, came surprisingly easily to his lips. "I don't love you, Grace."

"And I don't believe you."

His smile was brutal. Any other woman would have recoiled in horror. "Oh, pet. The pain you feel at this moment is the very reason I do not allow myself to feel anything at all."

Grace abruptly wrapped herself around him, embracing him with a strength born of restraining blooded stallions, from riding bareback against the wind along the shores of Cornwall, without benefit of bridle or saddle, from a lifetime of knowing what she wanted and persevering until she obtained it. She held tight. For whatever reason, and only God knew why, she held tight.

She wouldn't let him go. She would fight for him until her last breath. The knowledge took his own away.

Nicholas craved her with such aching, sweet tenderness, he almost sobbed aloud with overwhelming relief. Like centuries-old bricks constructed of the most fragile straw, his willpower crumbled.

A light glowed inside Grace. A thousand blazing candles. Starlight and the full moon. Fireflies dancing at twilight. The illumination of fairies and calm ocean waves sparkling. It all called to his darkness, dragging him into brightness. She was the sun, and he could not resist her warmth.

"Christ, Grace. I cannot fight you," he muttered in despair. "I can't. I can't."

"Don't." Came her simple response. "Don't fight me, Nicholas. Please, it will be all right. You must believe that."

Taking what she offered was like capturing lightning with his bare hands. Impossible and dangerous. But dear God, he wanted her. Her. Grace Willsdown. Fierce. Stubborn. Passionate. Kind.

All wrapped up...a beautiful gift.

A tiny package he would devour until there was nothing left of her. All of her light swallowed in his darkness.

"Grace, bloody hell. You don't understand what you're asking of me— "

"I do know. I'm asking you to love me. I need you...to stop this anguish, this terrible slicing of my insides that leaves me in bloody ribbons of ache and want."

"I released you from the contract. I ceded the encumbrance." Nicholas made one last futile attempt. "There can be no more nights together. I would be a monster if I allowed myself... Go. Please... please. Before I hurt you."

"Take me into your arms, Nicholas. Hold me and *never* let me go. Not just tonight. Every night."

"Oh God, Grace."

Before he knew what was happening, his hands buried in her hair, hauling her tighter against him. Their mouths crashed together and the groan escaping him spoke volumes. Her lips were lush and sweet and perfect. He would never tire of tasting them, of tasting her. Touching her, feeling her warmth.

"Take me, Nicholas," she breathed. "In my heart, I'm yours. Make me yours in truth. Make love to me without the damned contract deciding for us. I'm not leaving until you do."

In a sudden fluid movement, Nicholas hoisted her high against his body, spinning so he could deposit her upon his desk. Right where he commanded she place herself earlier. There was none of his previous animosity present now. He kissed her as though he was a doomed man and she his only salvation. Over and over, he plundered her mouth. Nipped at her lips, then soothed them with a flick of his tongue. A thousand hot, needy kisses down the column of her throat.

Somehow, even with his arms wrapped around her, Grace tugged her jacket off. Pulling open the thin cambric shirt, Nicholas swallowed at the sight of her creamy flesh caged within the sparse lace trimmings of a simple corset. With a sigh of reverence, he traced the curves and outlines of her breasts with first a forefinger, then his lips. Without uttering a single word, he worshipped her, silently begging her forgiveness for all the ugly, hurtful things said in his desperation.

"Nicholas, I'm yours. Yours..." Grace whispered, again and

again, clutching his head against her, arching into the heat of his mouth.

He loosened the corset's strings, pushing the contraption down just enough so the tips of her breasts were exposed. In turn, he drew each nipple into a tight, sucking vortex, raking the sweet, little buds with the sharpness of his teeth until she shuddered. He would devour her. Take every inch of her. Hope she survived so he could do it again.

"I've made you wet, haven't I? Do you want me to take you here?" he murmured against her skin, glancing up to see her reaction. "Squirming and off balance on my desk?"

Grace's eyes registered shock. "No, I—"

The corners of Nicholas's mouth lifted. "You are such a liar." He bit her nipple again until she moaned in response, giving him his answer. He could take her anywhere he pleased.

It was impossible to get closer to the welcoming heat between her thighs, the design of her riding habit preventing it. The tighter skirt would only spread so far, and Grace was trapped within its confines. She whimpered, as frustrated as Nicholas by this development, until his hands snaked beneath her skirt, brushing past the delicate fabric of her undergarments.

Then his fingers were gliding over aroused, silky skin and Grace's eyes fluttered shut. Her hands clenched his shoulders, her knuckles turning white.

"Hold tight, little bee. Hold tight to me while I make you fly."

Within seconds, he brought her to such a quivering climax, she buckled against him, panting cries of satisfaction escaping even as she tried muffling them against his chest. Nicholas felt the sensations of her orgasm rippling through the sensitive nerves of the flesh he stroked with soft, languid sweeps of his forefinger. He waited until the tremors subsided the tiniest bit, then for good measure, and because he loved how she came on the tips of his fingers, he drove her over the edge a second time.

Then a third.

Grace was sucking in frantic gulps of air when he finally removed his hand. She was so lush and hot., he considered ripping her clothes to shreds and burying his cock inside her at that very moment.

But this was not the place for that. This was not where he wanted to make love to Grace for the very first time. A deep breath did much in bringing his raging desire under control.

"I'm taking you upstairs. To my bedroom. So I can strip you bare and lavish every silky, soft part of your body with my tongue. My lips. My mouth..."

"Yes...yes..." Grace moaned in lethargic agreement. Coming undone numerous times in such rapid succession left her a delicate heap of womanhood in his arms.

"But we must," he kissed and nipped her neck, her mouth, the delicate line of her collarbone, her softly rounded shoulders, between each word, "be careful. It's the middle of the day, and I've no wish to alarm the servants..."

"Do you think I care the sun is up?" She laughed softly, echoing his own words from their first morning in his dining room when she willingly lay across his lap.

"Little minx. You'll pay for that bit of cheekiness."

"How will you manage that?" Her lips pressed his throat, and she licked the corded muscles there until he ground his teeth.

"I've my ways..."

"Do they involve me lashed to your bed for your pleasure, Your Grace?"

Nicholas chuckled at the relaxed, husky desire in her tone. God, the images she conjured with that simple question nearly unmanned him.

"If you are exceptionally insolent, I may do just that. Or I may take all the sweetness between your legs into my mouth, use my tongue to memorize every fold and crevice there."

Grace choked on a moan of pure lust, her voice weak when she answered him. "Then I shall try my best in reaching a level of appalling impudence. And, I'll give you anything you desire."

"Ah, hell." Nicholas folded her close, breathing in the sweet, lemony-heather scent of her hair. "I suddenly don't give a damn what the servants think."

CHAPTER 34

She is lightning in my palm
Rainwater innocence
For my parched soul
I drown in it
In her
~Nicholas August Harris March
Ninth Duke of Richeforte

*A*fter haphazardly tugging Grace's riding jacket back into place and setting her on her feet, Nicholas ushered her from the study. His arm wrapped protectively around her shoulders to shield her from any curious eyes.

He needn't have bothered. It seemed every servant he employed had mysteriously disappeared, the hallways and corridors empty and eerily quiet. He momentarily considered why everyone was absent but chose not to question it too closely.

Shutting the bedroom door behind him and turning the key in the lock, he gathered Grace against him, his hands cradling her head as he kissed her with such dark, fathomless passion, she was soon breathless. The momentum of his body pushing hers resulted in her retreating a few steps.

Nicholas wouldn't allow that. Spinning her around, he backed her against the door, capturing both her hands in one of his and holding her immobile there. This was much better. This allowed him better access to her neck, her collarbone, the spot below her ear, the tender underside of her chin. And he nipped and nibbled and kissed every available inch until they both panted with desire.

"I've no wish to tear this garment from you...you'll have nothing to wear again other than a borrowed dress from my mother's wardrobe," Nicholas muttered between kisses.

"I'd rather you not destroy it too. Fortunately, I brought my own clothing this time." Grace giggled, landing a kiss on his jaw and reacquainting herself with the shape of his ear using her tongue.

"What do you mean?"

"Robbie, my stable lad, accompanied me again. He drove our pony cart containing a few of my things. Martha placed them in the room adjoining yours before I awoke you."

"You were so sure I would let you stay?" Nicholas leaned back, his eyes dark.

"I had great hopes of convincing you it was a grand idea."

Nicholas thought about that for a moment. Should he be angry? That she knew him so well and he wouldn't resist her? He quickly dismissed that thought. If she manipulated him, it was because he wished it. He wanted her here. With him. He wanted her.

"Clever girl," he murmured. "Are you always so clever?"

"No. Oftentimes, I am very foolish. For example, I confess my love with no promise it will be returned."

"Patience, little bee," Nicholas replied softly. "I've never been in love before. It is my nature to be cautious of such things."

Grace looked as though she wished to say something, then

changed her mind. Nodding, she gave him a sweet smile instead. "Kiss me again, Nicholas. I need to feel your mouth on mine."

He obliged her, lowering her arms so he could peel her jacket off, then her blouse, and finally her skirt. Kneeling for a moment, he quickly unlaced her riding boots so she could kick them aside, then he was undoing the laces of her corset, the tapes of her drawers, removing each article of clothing until finally, she stood before him in a flimsy ivory chemise. Her nipples were visible beneath the sheer fabric, peachy colored flesh that tasted so sweet on his tongue.

"God, Grace, you are so damned beautiful. So beautiful."

Struck by a bolt of shyness, she crossed an arm over her chest, but Nicholas stopped her, taking her wrist and kissing the tender skin hiding the fragile veins. She was wearing the bracelet, and the sight of it sent a possessive leap of desire through his blood.

"Don't ever hide from me, Grace. Ever. I want every inch of you. Do you understand? Every inch."

"Yes," the word was barely a breath of a whisper.

Holding her hand, Nicholas pulled her toward the massive bed, remembering the last time they were here. When he'd simply held her all night, then woke in the morning to find her gone.

Wrapping his hands about her waist, he swung her up onto the middle of it and stepped back to remove his own clothing. Grace watched with wide eyes, drinking in his body as it was revealed, and when he was finally nude, he crawled beside her. His heart raced so fast, it felt it might burst from his chest. Reaching out, he lifted one of the straps of her chemise with a finger and eased it off her shoulder. She did not move as he did the same with the other side. The silk garment slid down until it was held in place only by the tips of her breasts.

"Grace," he said.

She whispered. "Nicholas."

"I'm a hair's breadth from losing control. Remove this before I rip it to shreds."

Reaching for the hem, she fingered it for a moment, then slowly raised it over her head, shaking her hair free and tossing the garment to the side. Nicholas closed his eyes at the sheer beauty of her, and when he looked again, he was sure everything in his soul was bare to her.

Leaning forward, he pressed his mouth softly to hers, drinking her in, easing her nervousness. Grace kissed him back, without hesitation, with her whole heart as she did everything. He moved her back until she lay against the pillows, the coverlet shoved aside so he could see her body in the shafts of daylight filtering through the half-closed drapes. She was a sunbeam in his bed. Gold and warm and shining. Something otherworldly, something made of fairies perhaps. Positioning himself over her, Nicholas held that way for a long moment, wondering if he would be able to control himself when he took her.

"Don't be afraid, Nicholas," she whispered. "I won't break."

He choked on a laugh. "Grace, you have no idea what I want to do to you. How badly I wish to—it should be you who is afraid, honeybee. This will hurt..."

"I know you won't hurt me if you can help it." Her eyes were huge. Like shining pools of sunlight. "But I expect a little pain. It's all right."

"I don't think I can be gentle."

"You don't have to be."

I'll be inside her...claiming her.... just a heartbeat away from making her mine and... fuck. The condoms. The sponges. They were tucked away in the drawer of his desk. In the study. Where they'd sat for more than a month, waiting for this exact moment.

"Goddamnit. The French letters.... we forgot them."

Grace stared at him, arousal turning her skin a gorgeous shade of rose-tinted gold. Her arms clutched about his waist, keeping him with her. "Don't leave me."

Nicholas groaned. "We cannot take the chance, love."

"I don't care. Don't go. Take me without them. I trust you." She lifted her hips to his, pulling his head down to kiss him at the same time, her lips warm and soft, eagerly parting for his.

The feel of her sex against his cock made his entire body go rigid. "Jesus, Grace."

He returned her kiss fiercely, bruising her mouth and dipping his hand between their bodies to stroke her. She was wet and velvety. Pushing a finger inside her, she pulsed about him and cried out, gripping his shoulders so hard, her fingernails left marks. Knowing he was moments away from claiming her made this different from the times he'd touched her before. An intense wave of possessiveness swamped him. He shuddered with the force of it. She was his. She would always be his.

Before she could protest, he slid down her body, nestling between her thighs and hooking his arms under her knees so she was open to him. The sight of her, glistening and damp with arousal, her folds pink and swollen, was the most erotic vision he'd ever encountered. More so than the dozens of experienced women in his lifetime who practiced enticing men and knew what pleased them. Grace pleased him by simply being Grace.

"Nicholas," she whispered desperately, reaching for his shoulders and trying to pull him up. "I want you inside me...please..."

"Shhh, pet."

He kissed the inside of her thighs, one at a time. She trembled but said nothing more as his mouth moved higher to the damp patch of curls. When he lapped her gently, a sigh escaped her, then a moan when he used his tongue to probe with greater purpose. Her hands moved from his shoulders to clutch his head, fingers threading through his hair so gently, it felt as though she were petting him.

With skill and languid determination, he brought her to the brink of climax. The tensing of her thighs, the shaking of her muscles, the soft panting breaths all evidence of the impending storm she faced. Nicholas knew her body well, knew the precise moment she hovered on the precipice, and when she was there, he slid up so they were face to face. Grace wore a dazed expression, eyes glazed with passion. Her breath came in gasps, perspiration shimmering on her cheeks and brow. She'd bitten her bottom lip so hard, it was almost raw.

"I'm going to come inside you, Grace...there will be no barriers between us..." he muttered against her neck, nipping her with such force, she'd wear the evidence of it for days.

She sighed in agreement and shifted her legs wider. He positioned the crown of his shaft against the folds of her center, wetting himself with her moisture, then carefully slid into honeyed soft heat, a slow, delicious glide that made his head swim. He'd done such a fine job of arousing her, of kindling her nerves to such a sensitive point, a fever pitch, just that little bit of him inside her set off her climax. She shuddered, her body going rigid. A flood of moisture surrounded him as she cried out her pleasure, gripping his biceps, her nails digging into them. While she was in the throes of her orgasm, Nicholas drove in a bit more until she tensed. He stopped immediately.

When she was accustomed to his body in the depths of hers, the tremors receding to a pleasant lull, he eased in a bit more, always stopping to let her adjust, making silent vows he would be gentle, despite his body demanding he plunge forth. He was so large, and she so tiny. He could hurt her if he didn't move slowly this first time. But damned if his cock wasn't demanding he pound into her until he spilled himself with all the force and fury raging through his veins. That legendary self-control of his was evidenced by the fine sheen of sweat covering his skin, his jaw clenched so tight, it hurt.

And it was all glorious torture. Grace's body both rejected and welcomed him, internal muscles pushing and pulling until Nicholas thought he would roar from the intensity of sensations.

She was silk and heat and everything sinful, all wrapped about him as tight as a golden ribbon. Grace Willsdown was made for him. She was his. And he would destroy anyone who tried taking her from him.

Nicholas continued this slow, inevitable invasion until he reached the resistance of her virginity. Pausing, he kissed her, loving how she writhed beneath him, whimpering for him. For more. He'd worked her into a delirious frenzy. She arched and lifted against him, pulling him in tighter, closer, desperate for another orgasm. One only he could give her.

"How you please me. How soft you are, how sweet. I'll never tire of hearing your little moans of pleasure. I love how you ache for me. How you burn for me. Are you ready to become mine now, pet?"

He nuzzled her breasts, sucking one of her nipples into the heat of his mouth. She melted like sugar on his tongue, moaning his name. He bit down while surging forward, the unexpected sharpness of his teeth overriding the pain between her legs. Grace yelped, pushing him in startled surprise while Nicholas suckled the nipple he rolled between his teeth. Holding her hips tight, he lazily moved onto the other breast, lavishing the same attention upon it. As she slowly relaxed beneath him, dissolving beneath the onslaught of too many sensations all at once, he allowed himself the first full measure of being buried deep inside her, so damned deep, he couldn't tell where she started and he ended.

Raising his head, he stared down at her, half-witted with drunken pleasure, blinking, hoping it would clear his brain. Hazy arousal wrapped about him. He was floating while at the same time drowning. All because of her. This beautiful, determined woman who held his heart in her delicate hands.

Grace shifted, seeking a position that would ease the stinging possession of his body where it fused with hers. The tiny wiggle of her hips sent stars exploding in his head. Gently, she stroked the lash marks on his back, her touch so soothing and sweet, it leached through his very bones. He paled, body trembling.

"For God's sake, Grace. Be still..."

"I can't," she whispered back, unaware the innocent words fueled the flames of his passion even higher. "You are so big, and it feels so...strange. I'm filled with you, and although it hurts, it feels a little wonderful at the same time. I think if I just move this way, it will be much better—"

She shifted again, a movement flinging Nicholas forward until he hung off the edge of a deep, dark whirlpool. He was being sucked in, down, down.

"*Grace.* Stop talking. Stop moving. Stop. *Stop.*" His command was a desperate mix of exasperation and amusement. "Just...be still. Please."

"I just explained to you I cannot," Grace murmured, her hips lifting tentatively. Tremors of excitement vibrated through her and into him, her body finally accepting his invasion. "I suddenly find myself unable to be still at all. Isn't that odd? I had no idea it would be like this. Did you know, Nicholas? Did you know it would feel so strange and beautiful and terrifying?"

Nicholas stared at her. She described their relationship perfectly without realizing it. His heart swelled with adoration.

She reached up, caressing his jaw with her fingertips. "Is there more? I'm not disappointed, mind you. I just thought, after all the build-up and the talk, there would be more..."

Nicholas gave a helpless laugh. "Oh, Grace. What am I to do with you?"

"Surely, you know." She smiled up at him, eyes shining. "Whatever you like, Nicholas."

His eyes darkened. "There's more, pet. More than you can imagine..."

There was a bewitching softening of her body with his words, her previous tension melting away. His unnatural ability to rein in his emotions, no matter the situation, the vaunted self-control that always ruled his life, at least until this moment, fractured and splintered into a billion pieces when she arched up and kissed him. Reaching for him. Holding him. Loving him despite his flaws. Despite his terrible darkness.

It was the last straw for Nicholas. With a muffled groan, he surged and withdrew, plunging into her like the tide receding and returning to the shore, forgetting his silent promise of going slow, to be gentle and tender. She overwhelmed him with her little gasps of hunger, her moans spiking his lust even higher, cracking him apart until little bits of her sunshine brightness filtered in. The emotions overtaking his senses were things he'd never felt with any woman. The need to protect what was his. The desire to see to her pleasure before his own. And it was so confusing, so surprising, so overwhelming, he could not defend himself against it, his walls crumbling as Grace easily tiptoed inside his heart and nestled there within it.

Before he could stop it, Nicholas was spiraling down into her heat as Grace tightened her embrace around him. She accepted the frenzy of his possession as though he'd always been hers, holding tight when white-hot satisfaction rolled over him in huge waves. During the torrent of conquest, her legs came up, wrapping about his waist. Her limbs trembled, her body arching as she peaked with him, crying out against his shoulder as the world faded away for them both.

CHAPTER 35

*G*race watched shafts of sunlight move inch by inch across the floor, shadows chasing them as the afternoon drew closer to twilight.

She lay enfolded in Nicholas's arms, her head resting on his chest. A lock of her hair was twisted between his fingers as he idly twirled its length. They did not speak, but it was an easy silence, soft and replete, with no lingering twinges of shame or regret. Grace couldn't bring herself to feel either emotion and she swore she would not. Indeed, even earlier when Nicholas fetched a towel and warm water from his bathing room, washing her blood and his seed from her thighs, she was not embarrassed.

He'd whispered apologies for the roughness of his lovemaking, murmured how entrancing he found her, how well she pleased him. How brave and beautiful she was. How he adored her, her body. Her softness and the sweetness of her mouth and skin. With surprising complacency, Grace allowed him to do as he wished, her heart nearly bursting with love upon hearing his every word, trembling when his fingers gently coasted over the faint bruises he'd left on her skin.

But he'd not said he loved her.

I am too greedy. Has he not given me everything else? My estate? My horses? For God's sake, even his own horse? He did not demand, nor trick me into sleeping with him. He tried turning me away and I would not let him. This is all he can give me of himself. These superficial things, and his body in bed. It must be enough. It has to be enough.

She pressed a kiss to the space above his heart, and he issued a low chuckle.

"What was that for?"

"Nothing in particular. Just a thank you, I suppose."

She snuggled closer, breathing deep, the light fleece of his chest hair tickling her nose. He smelled so.... manly. Mint and sandalwood and sex. Did his other women love it too? Did he allow them the opportunity of being with him like this? Or were they immediately dismissed? She pondered her role in being a mistress and how much leeway Nicholas would give as she learned what he expected of her. She did not want him to send her away now that she'd given him all of herself.

"I've a hundred different ways you may show your gratitude."

"Is that so?" Grace grinned, tilting her head to look at him, pushing thoughts of leaving aside.

"You'll soon discover I am insatiable when it comes to you." He ruffled the fringe of hair on her forehead, pausing to trace the tiny, half-moon scar at the edge of her eyebrow. "You've never told me how you came to have this."

"You've never asked," Grace teased before sobering. "Llyr gave me that little memento. About a year after he came to us. I thought I was doing a fine job, gaining his trust. One day, I was working on lifting his feet for grooming and he swung his head at me." She laughed softly. "Knocked me completely over and into a bench, of which the corner sliced my eyebrow open. Hurt like the devil and looked much worse than it actually was. But do you know what I did? I took a bit of the blood and rubbed it in his muzzle. For hours, it was all he could smell. Me. He never so much as attempted hurting me again." The thought occurred perhaps she'd done the same with Nicholas...imprinted herself on him using the proof of her virginity so he would not harm her in the future.

"And this?" His forefinger traced her nose and the slight bump that marred its fine, straight line.

She grinned. "A tumble from a pile of stones at the Abbey ruins. I was attempting a leap onto Llyr's back as he galloped past. I missed, well, I hit his rump at least and broke my nose. Mother was most upset. Said I'd forever ruined my profile for portraiture. But I didn't care. I tried it again and again until Llyr and I had the timing down perfectly."

"It suits you perfectly. And your profile is beautiful, regardless. All of you is so damned beautiful." Nicholas squeezed her tight. "Llyr was a fine animal, Grace. I know it will be difficult replacing him."

She sighed. "He was very special. I will always love him. And miss him."

"Please consider taking Skye. I want you to have him. Truly. Not for any reason other than because I want to give him to you."

"I cannot do that, Nicholas. He's too valuable, and I cannot allow you to pay for the rebuilding of my stables either."

For a flash of a second, his face hardened. "There is no discussion on that. I've made arrangements and it is done. The matter of Skye can be negotiated, but your stables will be rebuilt at my expense."

"It will create a terrible scandal. People will talk about what is between us if you do such a thing." Grace frowned.

"Once, you said you did not care about your reputation as long as you had Bellmar and your horses. It was all you wanted in this world, and nothing else. Have you changed your mind, then?"

Grace rested her face back against his chest so he could not see her eyes and the tears that sprang so easily. Of course, she wanted more now. She wanted him. His heart. His love. His life shared with hers. "I want the parts of you that you won't give, Nicholas. That's all I want. It's all that matters now."

He stroked her hair, and Grace closed her eyes at his silence, her heart twisting painfully. He gave her no answer, and she really did not expect one.

~

THEY FELL ASLEEP WRAPPED IN ONE ANOTHER'S ARMS, AND when they awoke a short time later, Nicholas rang for a light supper. It was delivered by a stoic-faced servant, who set the meal up without a word and disappeared just as silently with a quiet "thank-you" from Nicholas.

"Are all your servants so grim in nature?" Grace asked as they sat before the fire and feasted on roasted capon and creamed potatoes.

"Many of them are, I'm afraid," Nicholas admitted. He poured more wine into her glass. "Most are holdovers from when my father was alive. This wasn't the most pleasant of households, as you can imagine."

"No, I'm sure it wasn't."

Grace did not say anything else for a moment, afraid of bringing up the rather touchy subject of his father and Sebastian. The last time she'd dared resulted in Nicholas leaving Bellmar Abbey, enraged by her meddling.

Nicholas cocked his head. "I know full well what you are thinking, pet."

Grace flushed, sipping her wine in an effort of hiding her discomfort. He read her so easily. "I pray you can resolve your differences in time. Sebastian has a right to know the truth, as much as you have a right for him to know it."

Nicholas's eyes shuttered themselves, but his tone remained calm, even, with no hint of anger. "Perhaps."

Grace hesitated to take the matter any further. Absently, she pushed potatoes around the plate with her fork, aware of Nicholas's intense scrutiny.

"What shall you do next, Grace?"

"What do you mean?"

"Now that this—" he waved a hand between them— "has occurred. What shall you do next?"

Grace frowned. She'd not thought past this night. Past being possessed by Nicholas. What did happen next? Did she return to Bellmar and await his summons for their next interlude? Did she stay for a few days at his leisure? Did she travel on to Beaumont and pretend the most incredible thing that had ever happened in her life never occurred? Pretend her love for the man sitting across from her didn't exist? Deny that her heart didn't beat for him?

She honestly did not know what she should do next.

"I suppose I will go to Beaumont for Lord and Lady Bentley's ball," she said slowly. "Tristan escorted Ivy there from Belmar, but I came here instead of going with them. Only Ivy has knowledge of my whereabouts."

Nicholas gave her a sharp glance.

"Tristan was there?"

"Yes, just yesterday. He confessed he asked you to sell Bellmar to him and begged again that I marry him. I told him I already knew of his plans and had made my own bargain with you. He was not pleased."

"Fuck," Nicholas blew out in a hiss.

"He's as careful of my reputation as you are, Nicholas. He will not want anyone to know."

"Perhaps, but he will probably be of a mind to challenge me on it."

"That would be foolish and accomplish nothing."

Grace realized she may have been hasty revealing her love for Nicholas. Tristan could react unpredictably, although he was usually very level in nature. She frowned and appeared so worried, Nicholas took pity on her. Reaching across the small table, his fingers tangled with hers. The twin dimples in his cheeks popped out when he gave her one of his rare grins.

"Tristan is a sensible sort, for all that he is momentarily infatuated with you. Perhaps we'll simply stay abed...the man cannot challenge me to a duel here."

"Truly?"

Nicholas's green eyes softened. "Truly." He considered her for a long moment, then said, "Are you up for an adventure?"

Grace nodded. "Of course. I'll do anything you ask of me, Nicholas. You know that."

A spark lit the depths of his eyes. Something dark and mysterious that sent the blood rushing along the inside of Grace's veins like the wind and waves of a typhoon. Out of control. Wild.

"A dangerous bit of knowledge," he murmured.

A short time later, Nicholas led Grace down darkened corridors, through the modernized sections of the huge castle and into the more ancient portions in an area she'd never seen.

The steps were steep, the halls dark and quiet, lit every so often with huge, iron lanterns that were medieval in appearance. Nicholas had instructed Grace on what to wear, and she giggled while following him, holding tight to his hand in the shadowy corridors. She wore her knee-high riding boots and one of his linen shirts, the hem reaching mid-thigh. She was sure she made a comical picture, but before they'd left the bedroom, venturing into the hall after a quick glance to make sure it was empty, Nicholas gave her such a heated look, she'd drawn the collar tighter at her throat.

"What amuses you, little bee?" he asked now over his shoulder, holding the lamp higher to illuminate the stone steps.

"Dressed as I am, I feared coming across someone. But unless you've a prisoner hidden away in the dungeons, I'm safe. No one other than you will see this ridiculous outfit."

"Ridiculous?" he scoffed, turning suddenly so she was against the wall. He set the lamp down and leaned into her. Grace felt the damp stone pressing through the shirt fabric. It was cold and hard in direct contrast to Nicholas's searing heat. "You are a goddamn fantasy in my shirt and those damned boots, don't you know that? With your hair all wild and your mouth bruised from my kisses. I want to make love to you.... with you wearing this..." He kissed her, tempering his roughness, his hand searching out her softness beneath the shirt's fluttering hem. "I want you on your knees, with my cock in your mouth, you wearing this..." His fingers spread her folds, tangling in the patch of curls and tugging lightly. "I want to lick you here and then kiss you so you taste yourself on my lips while I make you come on my fingers. With you wearing this."

He stroked her until Grace was gasping, clutching at him. When she tried writhing against his hand, he laughed, a sound so wicked, she groaned in frustration.

Nicholas abruptly stepped away. "You're becoming insatiable, but I've honestly little complaint. Come now, I've a more pleasant surprise in store for you. And do not pout. I promise the wait will be worth it."

Tugging her by the hand again, they continued until the corridor ended at an old iron gate. Nicholas removed a set of rusted keys from a hook and inserted one into the ancient lock. It opened as if by magic, with no groaning or protest of rusty, unused hinges. After passing through, Nicholas used the same key to lock it behind them.

"Why do you keep it locked?" Grace asked.

He slanted her a glance. "I'm a selfish man. What is down here is for my own personal enjoyment. And now ours together. Believe me, you will not want anyone stumbling across us when we are here."

Grace raised a brow. "It's the dead of the night. I daresay we are the only two people at Oakmont traipsing about at this hour."

"You will be grateful for this gate and lock when I bring you here before afternoon tea and Martha sends a search party for us. Even if your cries of pleasure are richocetching off the walls, no one will venture any further than the gate."

Eyes widening with his words and the picture they created in her mind, Grace followed him silently as he picked up the lamp and continued down the darkened corridor.

The long passage opened up into a large underground area the size of a small meadow. A clear, blue-green shimmering lake spread out before them, taking up most of the space. The same lanterns from the corridors also lined walls ringing the miniature, sandy beach. Somehow, and it seemed impossible, but the water glowed with a glimmering, turquoise sparkle, as if a thousand diamonds lined its shallow bottom and floated in the water. Big stones dotted the small lake, shaped like steps made for giants. They were an odd sight, rising above the surface in various depths. Dark and sleek, they glittered as if sprinkled with moon dust.

"Oh, it's so lovely," Grace breathed. "How is it lit up like this?"

Nicholas shrugged. "I don't know. It just is. Always has been. And it's always the same temperature, like the most comfortable bath you've ever had in your life...not too hot, not too cold. No matter how much snow lays on the ground outside or how hot the summer is, it is always the same down here."

He sat on the beach and removed his boots, tossing them aside along with the keys.

"What are the stones for? They are so big and almost seem to be laid in a pattern."

"I don't know the answer to that either. They are a bit like the giant's road in Ireland. I'm sure you've heard of it. The road was created during a battle between two giants, and what remains looks like these stones. Some say this place was used for magic. That the nymphs and fairies, along with the spirits of the forest and the waters would meet here to make peace, to heal themselves after battle. For weddings and deaths and births. Are you taking off your boots?" He'd quickly lost patience with explaining ancient myths and rock formations while Grace wondered if fairies might be watching them now, peeking around the rocks, wings fluttering in a silent golden whir.

"Why would I take off my boots?" she asked, almost absently.

"Why do you think I would ask you to remove your boots?" Nicholas parried, standing up and gaining her attention. "Remove them, Grace. And your shirt. Correction. *My* shirt."

Grace sank down onto the sand. Her fingers trembled as she began unlacing the riding boots. Although the air was cool in the cavern, she wasn't chilled. No, she was very warm, shaking with thoughts of what Nicholas intended to do with her. And how much she wanted it.

Peeking up at him from beneath her lashes, she watched as he peeled off his breeches and his own shirt and promptly forgot to breathe. His body was truly a work of masculine art. Not that she had many male bodies to use for comparison. There was no fault to be found in the slabs of muscles lining his ribcage and abdomen, the sharp cut vee defining his lean hips. His biceps flexed in the lamplight, reminding Grace how he held her hips so tight in his hands just a few hours before. That strength was a powerful aphrodisiac; she felt dizzy just looking at him and the broad shoulders which still bore evidence of her fingernails, little half-moon marks gleaming dull pink on his bronze skin.

While her fingers fumbled with knots of the boots laces, her gaze traveled even further, down the impossibly wide chest, the bunching muscles there and the flat, copper colored discs of his nipples. His thighs were perfectly sculpted, unmarred, save for the wound caused by Sebastian's pistol. On his back, the crisscrossing of white scars from his father's riding crop gleamed in the lantern's light.

On his temple and hand, the scars from the fire were dark smudges.

Grace's heart swelled. With love. With shared pain. With sympathy and anger. She wished she could hurt those who'd hurt him. Make them suffer as he'd suffered. Make him understand she loved him enough to share his burdens with him. Have him love her enough to share them willingly.

"Don't look at me like that."

Her eyes flew to his at the roughness of his voice.

"Like what?" she stuttered, tossing her boots aside.

"Like you want to heal me." He strode across the sand, hooking his hands beneath her arms and pulling her up onto her feet. "I want you looking at me in an entirely different manner." He began unfastening the buttons of the shirt, staring down at her face with the oddest expression. "We came here to make love." Pressing a kiss to the tip of her nose, he whispered, "Shall I remind you what I'm capable of?"

Grace swayed against him as the shirt was drawn away. "I remember."

"Good girl." Nicholas's eyes glittered, containing more light than the water behind them. Reaching out, he swept her hair off her shoulders so it lay in a waterfall down her back, and Grace's eyes fluttered shut as he traced the line of her collarbone with his forefinger. "You're so delicate. So sweet and soft. And yet, you face me with the bravery of ten men. No fear. No dread of what I might do."

Grace allowed herself a tiny smile. "That's not true. Most of the time, I am in a state of panic over what you might do."

His finger circled her nipple, and as it tightened with his touch, Grace sucked in a breath, her eyes opening to meet his. "Are you alarmed right now?" His tone was deceptively calm, but she caught the tense undercurrent of it. He was as affected by her as she was by him, the fire between them burning so hot and so bright, it scorched them both.

"Yes," Grace admitted softly. "I'm terrified of what I feel for you. And that you will grow bored with me."

He stared at her while Grace steeled herself for one of his cutting, distant remarks. Instead, he brushed a kiss over her mouth and murmured, "Turn around."

She rotated, hands at her sides, as he took her hair, gathering it into a rope he held in his fist. His other hand slid around her waist, and he pulled her flush against his body. Her insides twisted into knots of anticipation. Shameful creature that she was, after just one bout of their bodies joined in exquisite passion, she was eager to repeat the experience. Spanning the graceful flare of her hip, Nicholas positioned her so her bottom sat cradled against the hardness of his sex.

Pressed against the muscled solidity of his chest, his breath whispered hot against her neck, sending shivers racing through her. He held her like that for a long moment, and Grace savored how cherished she felt.

"I won't tire of you, Grace. I promise you that."

Nicholas turned her back around, his smile heat and sin and wicked promises. The jutting arousal of his erection rubbing her belly drew Grace's curious eyes down, and when her gaze jerked away, he chuckled.

Taking her hand, he walked them both to the lake's edge. The warm water was soft and silky. A slight curl of steam rose from the surface, disappearing into the air. Nicholas entered first, and she followed until the water reached above her waist. He ducked under, wetting his body completely, and Grace did the same, slicking her hair so it lay sleek and wet down her back.

Neither said a word, Grace's eyes wide with excitement, Nicholas's glinting with desire.

"Come here, Grace." An undercurrent of steel threaded his softly spoken command.

At that moment, he resembled nothing less than a rogue

pirate ordering a captive wench to do his bidding. And Grace was willing to be that wench.

She slipped through the water until she stood flush against him, her hips and legs fitting between his wide spread thighs. His arousal prodded hard against her belly as she brought one hand up against the muscular expanse of his chest, her face tilted to his. In this position, her breasts were flattened, and they tingled with the contact. Every nerve ending in her body was electrified, her breath mingling with his harsh exclamation as their flesh molded together.

"Put your arms around my neck," he ordered, his voice raspy.

Grace complied. Her fingers laced together at the back of his neck, and because he was so much taller, she stood on tiptoes, the water providing buoyancy but no leverage. She could only drape against him, feeling a bit helpless. When did giving up control become so bloody exciting?

A triumphant smile flitted with Nicholas's next words. "Now, kiss me."

CHAPTER 36

*G*race hesitated before obeying him. Parting his lips as he'd taught her, her tongue slipped inside his mouth before she drew back and nibbled the inside of his lower lip.

Nicholas did not place his arms around her. No. He simply stood there, accepting her attention as if he were a sovereign king and this was his due. Grace ruffled the wet silk of his hair, the strands shifting through her fingers, and she kissed him again with growing urgency. Without conscious thought, her lower body undulated against his shaft.

Still, Nicholas did not embrace her.

Piqued, Grace shifted, concentrating kisses on his neck instead. Splaying her hands on his chest for support, she slid until her mouth reached his hard, flat nipples. Hesitantly, then with greater boldness when he remained still as stone, Grace licked them in turn, the point of her tongue gently teasing. Feeling his cock swell, she drew one nipple fully into the heat of her mouth, swirled her tongue around it and gave it a sharp nip with the edge of her teeth.

Nicholas's entire body jerked into awareness, his low growl

hot and gratifying to her ears. Vindicated, she continued on, trailing further south, tracing the line of his bisected abdomen with her mouth.

Each horizontal contour created by ribs and the muscles overlaying them was explored as she slowly drifted, sketching the path of dark gold hair that led to the straining length of flesh beneath the water's edge. Before she went under, a quick peek revealed Nicholas now gripping her shoulders as if she were a lifeboat in stormy seas. Eyes closed in desperation, his jaw clamped tight.

He no longer appeared to be the indolent pirate.

As she slipped beneath the surface, instinct told Grace what to do, told her to slide her hands over his firm buttocks to anchor her position. With a wickedness she was still surprised to discover existed inside her, Grace sank to her knees, opened her mouth and swallowed most of his thickness for the space of five heartbeats. The mingled flavors of warm flesh, some undefined spice and the sweetness spring water swirled on her tongue.

"Bloody hell!"

Even muffled under water, Nicholas's curse sizzled her ears. He yanked her off him, scooping her up as easily as if she were a minnow in a tiny teacup.

She flashed wet and gold as he hauled her against him, his palms under her rear, lifting her until Grace instinctively wrapped her legs around his waist. Locking her arms about his neck, their mouths fused together in a heated tangle of tongues as he carried her, sloshing through waist-deep water until he reached one of the rocks. She'd not noticed this one before. It wasn't really a rock at all, but something formed more in the shape of a narrow table, rising from the water, constructed of the same dark stone

Not a giant stone, but an altar of some sort.

Setting her down, Nicholas spun her so she faced away from

him. He knocked her feet apart, fitting himself between her thighs. "Do you trust me, honeybee?"

"Yes. Always. Forever."

"Hold on to the rock. Don't let go."

The order was harsh. A growl. A muttered plea.

"Nicholas—"

"Don't let go."

She did what he said. Her fingers gripped the edge of the table-like surface, positioned by his rough hands so she was bent over with just her forearms touching the hard stone. A moment later, his fingers parted her folds, ensuring she was ready for him. Then his cock thrust into the honey heat of her body with unerring skill, his fingers moving up, gripping her buttocks.

The quickness of his possession, the exquisite slide of his rigid flesh into her aching center stole her breath. It pushed her forward until the rock, slick as glass, flattened her belly and her fingertips gripped the opposite edge of its surface. And there Nicholas held, for a long moment, until she pushed back against him with a low moan and he slid out and into her again. Leisurely. Patiently. Until he couldn't seem to help himself.

Grace gasped at the intense lust surging like molten fire through her veins. Nicholas was both violent and gentle. Taking and giving pleasure. There was nothing teasing or coy about this possession. On the contrary, it became quick and hard and wild, and that made it all the more exhilarating.

When she tightened about him, when the fury became almost overwhelming and she frantically bucked beneath the onslaught, Nicholas understood. Surging deeper, widening his stance, he easily tilted her hips upward, helping her roll them until he was buried inside her as far as he could go. Voracious and greedy, he did not stop until Grace trembled around him, the shock waves of her impending climax rippling and shimmering over him. He hit a spot deep inside her, so sweet and tender, she could barely breathe.

"Say my name, Grace," Nicholas demanded, in a voice full of darkness. There was a lost, haunted quality flitting through its undercurrents that broke her heart. "Tell me you love me..."

"I love you," Grace whispered.

Nicholas bent over her, licking the skin between her shoulder blades. When her hand slipped on the rock, he nipped her sharply on the sensitive spot where the curve of her shoulder met the line of her neck. She quickly regained her hold, the bitemark stinging, her insides on fire and melting all at once. Another helpless, greedy moan escaped her, and after a moment of hesitation, Nicholas' teeth marked her a second time. Quick, striking. Just enough to send her tumbling over a black edge of desire.

"Again," Nicholas hissed, pulling her slightly away from the rock.

One hand snaked over the flat plane of her belly, dipping low between her thighs and finding the button of nerves that made her whimper. His other hand fisted tight in the mass of wet hair streaming down her back. Controlled in such a manner, Grace was anchored in place, her back arching in ecstasy, her hands still gripping the rock's edge.

"Say it again," he repeated, giving her hair a sharp tug.

She gasped in shocked delight. "I love you, Nicholas. I love you... I love you...." Then she couldn't speak as he drove into her with renewed frenzy. She was exploding into a million stars, and he was the spark igniting her. The wildfire spreading through her. The tornado overtaking her and obliterating everything except her need for him. Her love for him. He was the storm and she...*I am but a raindrop...a rain cloud...a lightning bolt...*

The thoughts scrambled in her mind as Grace flew apart and Nicholas put her back together with his crushing grip, his bruising fingers, his needy embrace. His sweet kiss.

"Oh, god. Grace...Grace...I... love...*fuck*...I need you. You're mine. Mine...*mine*..." The words sounded ripped from his tortured soul. A soul as brutal as he was, but tender and generous too, for all that he tried hiding it from the world.

When Nicholas peaked with her, sucked into a paradise painted in dark, intricate swirls of desire, lust and love, a secret, underground world of turquoise water and diamond lights where only the two of them existed, Grace sobbed aloud. She held the edge of the rock as if it were his heart.

She trusted.

She loved.

And she never let go.

Nicholas slowly eased out of Grace's body, holding her up as she half slumped atop the slick surface of the rock. Where he held her, his large hands tight on the sleek curve of her waist, he felt her pulse beating beneath the skin, the double time thumps of her erratic heartbeat. *One-two, three-four, five-six...*

"Sweet hell, I did not mean to be so rough." He was rueful but not sorry. He would never be sorry for what they did together while making love.

"I did not mind."

Her voice was a husky murmur he strained to hear.

"I was too rough..." he muttered again, convincing himself. She was spineless in his hands. As if he'd pounded all the life from her body.

Damn it. She wasn't used to all this sexual activity, and beast that he was, he'd taken her in a manner reserved for mistresses of long-standing. His jaw clenched. "Did I hurt you?" *Fool. Of course, you probably hurt her. You've treated her in the coarsest, most demeaning of ways...*

"I loved it," Grace said in a tiny voice. "It was perfect."

Nicholas spun her about so her face was visible, the lights reflecting as flickering flames in her golden eyes. His stare was disbelieving. "You loved it." Repeating her words, he realized he could count her heartbeats by the pulse in her neck. Hers was returning to normal, while he was positive his had accelerated.

Grace's eyes were glassy. She was still coming down from her orgasm, her mannerisms dreamy, floaty. "I never realized there were so many places we could make love. I want to try them all with you."

An image of her, sleek and wet, between his thighs, slipping beneath the water, taking him into her mouth, seared Nicholas's brain. The memory of her perfect, golden bottom bearing the imprint of his palms, the marks of his fingers, sent a surge of giddy possessiveness ricocheting through his blood. His groan was a mix of amusement and undiluted lust.

He swept her into his arms, licking droplets of water from her jaw, from her throat, from her lips.

"Grace," he murmured, eyes closing in a belated effort of gaining a bit of sanity, "if someone else doesn't accomplish the task, I swear you'll be the death of me."

CHAPTER 37

*T*he next few days were ones of idyllic bliss. Days of searing heat and pleasure and sinful kisses. Other than those two encounters the first night, Nicholas was careful in using the contraceptives each time they made love. After much giggling on Grace's part and heated whispered instructions from Nicholas, they even managed using the sponges. Grace preferred those. There was nothing between them when that method was utilized, but sometimes, Nicholas was too impatient to wait for their precise placement. Instead, he would hurriedly roll on a condom, taking her in a flurry of fierce possessiveness that left Grace breathless.

Wrapped in a cocoon of blindness to anything other than their insatiable need for one another, neither would admit aloud the paradise would surely end soon. They spent nights indulging their passion, and hours in the sun laughing, teasing and touching, heedless of the staff who watched their master in a state of confused awe. Indeed, the first afternoon following the cave interlude, Teaks rushed to Nicholas's aid during tea, thinking he was choking. The butler was waved away from the parlor by the duke, who was laughing so hard, he couldn't catch his breath.

"And you were how old? Nine?" Nicholas asked.

Grace nodded. "Yes. In my best dress, with new velvet ribbons and pins holding this dratted straight hair of mine in place. We were on our way to meet the new village pastor, but my parents weren't ready to leave, so I snuck outside. Instead of visiting the stables as I usually did, I went to the little brook behind the house. The day before, I'd read most of Shakespeare's *A Midsummer's Night Dream,* and I'd convinced myself a society of fairies resided there at the water's edge among the lily pads.

"At first, I stood on the banks, like a good girl. Soon enough, I inched my way further into the shallows and began hopping from stone to stone. I was an enchanted frog, you see, hoping a frog prince would find me. Or maybe one of the fairies, with gossamer wings spun of golden spiderwebs and wearing a crown made from dewdrops." She giggled, warmed when Nicholas smiled too. "There were dragonflies. And butterflies. And robins calling to one another. Alas, no fairies. Then, in a patch of sunlight, I saw a flash of green and gold in the water. I leaned over for a closer look and slipped. I tumbled right in. Completely. Drenched head to toe. The water was not very deep, but it was so cold, and when I sat up, a very real frog sat perched atop my head, singing a ballad only frogs must know. He was hopelessly entangled in ribbons and my hair."

In-between their mutual laughter, Grace continued. "I trudged home, my frog riding along, bellowing the entire time, and explained to my mother the circumstances of how I found my prince. Her shrieks echoed through the house every time that poor frog blinked. It took her and Mrs. Cooper some time to cut the poor fellow loose, and either he was terribly frightened or very brave, for he did not move or croak once after making all that racket on the trip to the house. Afterward, I insisted Father carry him back to the brook, and that was the last I saw of my prince. I'm quite sure he and the fairies had a jolly laugh at my expense."

They collapsed against the settee, and Nicholas tugged Grace into his arms. He wiped a tear of amusement from his eye. "It is a good thing you've not set your standards very high since then. I could never compete with such a stoic nature." He traced a finger over the modest neckline of her rose-pink gown, flicking the lace edging the bodice almost thoughtfully.

Grace wrinkled her nose and half-heartedly shoved his chest. "Perhaps you are my frog prince come to life after all these years. Seeking revenge for that bit of time trapped in my hair ribbons." She blushed, thinking of their time in the lake beneath the castle and knew he was thinking of it too when his lips lifted in a secret smile. "Now, you've stolen and bound my heart instead."

Nicholas sobered, drawing her closer until their noses almost touched. At this proximity, she could discern all the variants of green that made up his eyes. A sparkling array of emerald and jade and soft moss green. A bit of gold edged the irises, his lashes so long and thick, any woman would be jealous of them. She was reminded of that green-gold burst of color she saw that day in the brook, just below the water's surface. As a child, she believed something magical existed there.

That same wondrous, beautiful flash was here now, just beneath the glittering wariness in Nicholas's gaze. Falling into the depths of his eyes didn't frighten her. She would capture that elusive beauty, although she knew Nicholas would be horrified knowing she could plainly see what was within his soul, the yearning for something just beyond his grasp. A chance at happiness he believe he didn't deserve.

"But, you've nothing in common with so placid a creature." Grace's head tilted as she regarded him and the way his expression turned slightly defensive. "I think instead, you are a golden wolf prince from deep within the forest. Wild and untamed. Savage, yet clever enough that you came for me while I waited in a civilized hedge maze. No... not a frog at all. But a wolf. My own wild, wicked wolf.

"I wish..." Nicholas began thickly, then swallowed. "I wish

things were different. I wish I'd done things differently in the beginning with you."

Grace smiled gently, caressing his jaw. "They are different now, and that's all that matters, Nicholas. The past, the beginning...they mean nothing to me at this moment. I only care that you want me."

"I want you." The words were nearly a growl but not of a sexual nature. It was a sound of frustration and stubborn resistance, and acknowledgment of the emotions between them, their connection, his reluctant affection for her.

Grace pressed a soft kiss on the center of his lower lip, snuggling against him.

"I stole your heart without your consent. I surely don't deserve it," he said, almost regretfully. "And I don't deserve you. You'll realize that one day."

"Perhaps. But not today."

Grace pressed her mouth to his, silencing any further dissent, willing Nicholas to kiss her in that wonderful, all-consuming way he always did, to touch her until she forgot everything other than the two of them. Until he forgot as well.

And while he wasn't looking, she wiggled a little further into his heart.

A few nights later, while lying in bed, watching the fire burn down to embers, Nicholas brought up the subject both had so carefully avoided.

"You must go soon."

He was on his side, Grace nestled against him, her body echoing his, her bottom curving into his groin. She lifted one of his hands, resting snug in the valley of her breasts, and kissed his fingers one by one, as if thinking of a way of responding.

"Yes," she finally agreed.

Nicholas was quiet for a moment, then said, "You will go to Beaumont for the Ravenswood Ball next week. I will follow you there once I've seen to your stable's progress. The men and materials should arrive at Bellmar Abbey any day now. Possibly as early as tomorrow."

"Sebastian may be there when you arrive."

"If he is, it is of no matter. By now, he knows I am the one covering the expenses. It won't be that unexpected that I've come to check the rebuilding progress."

Grace shifted until she faced him. "I don't want to go to Beaumont. I don't want to dance and make polite small talk with men I've no interest in. I want to stay with you."

Her chin lifted, a gesture of defiance. It was adorable, and Nicholas loved it. He kissed the heartshaped point of her chin, then nibbled it until she giggled.

And then, because he was so in love with this infuriating creature he could barely rationalize it, because he worshipped her more than anything else on God's green planet, and because there was no occasion for his abrupt declaration other than the fact they were cozy in their bed, watching the flames of the fire dance merrily in the hearth, and her heart fluttered like a bird's wing against his chest, Nicholas revealed his soul.

"I've no wish for you to be anywhere without me, honeybee, and I particularly have no wish for any man to engage in any manner with you, polite or otherwise. But I fear Sebastian might burst a blood vessel if we appear on his doorstep together, and I would very much like to do this properly. After all, we will be spending the rest of our lives together, and I would hate having him as a disgruntled relative."

Grace froze, her heart evident in the golden-brown depths as she gazed up at him. "You never do the proper thing, Nicholas. What are you talking about?"

"Well, this is one occasion I will. I will ask your cousin for your hand in marriage, of course. And explain the shortcomings of my father and my own stubborn nature in keeping secrets for so long from my best friend." Nicholas's voice was soft but unwavering. He tangled a hand in the silk of Grace's hair, gently tugging her head back so he could look deeply into her eyes.

"Nicholas, I am content being whatever you wish me to be. Your mistress...your lover...your friend—"

"I will have you as my wife, Grace Willsdown. And as my lover. My friend. My mistress in our bedroom... Do you understand?"

"No... I don't understand. You said you would never wed, but now...are you sure?" she asked softly.

Nicholas winced. He'd hurt her so very badly, she could not trust the words when he said he cared for her. He must do more in convincing her. Taking a deep breath, he gave up the shield surrounding his heart. And when he let go of that burdensome object, it was amazing. As if he'd suddenly stepped into sunlight after centuries of darkness. Grace's sunlight. Blindingly bright and smelling of lemons and heather. Of rainstorms and hay.

His Grace.

"I've never been more certain of anything in my life. I'm tired of sharing you with the rest of the world. You belong to me, and every day apart from you is a day wasted." He gave a helpless laugh. "There is a hole inside me. An emptiness only you can fill."

"Perhaps you are merely hungry," Grace replied with her typical pragmatism.

"I am hungry," Nicholas agreed, his mouth set in a firm line. "For you. Your smile. Your laughter. Your touch, your kiss. Everything that makes you what you are, I crave it constantly. Goddamn it. I even want watercress sandwiches. You've bewitched me. I cannot settle for bits and pieces of you. Having you in tiny increments of time. Away in the shadows. Not anymore. I want all of you. I want everyone to know you are mine and I am yours."

His mouth swooped down, covering hers, and Nicholas knew

beyond any doubt Grace was the sweetest, finest thing he'd ever tasted. "I'll never get enough of you," he muttered between kisses.

When he finally leaned away, tears sparkled in her eyes even as she smiled somewhat sadly. Cradling her face in his hands, his lips swallowed up a salty drop before it could slide down her cheek.

"Do not cry," he ordered, helplessly. "You are in my blood, beneath my skin, deep in my very bones." Nicholas kissed her again and again, now almost frantic in confessing the depths of his love. "I cannot survive without you."

"Nicholas," Grace choked. "I beg you. Do not play games with me..."

"Grace. I love you. Only you." Nicholas rolled into his back, pulling her along so she sprawled across his chest. "Tell me I have your heart, love. Tell me you belong to me. Tell me that no matter how cruel I am, no matter the ugly, hurtful things I've said and done, you forgive me. I can be the man you deserve. The man you need. As long as you trust me and love me, I can be that man. After all I have done to you, I do not deserve it, but for God's sake, tell me it is not too late. Tell me you..." His breath caught; he steadied himself. "Tell me you still love me. Promise you will never stop loving me."

With a small cry, Grace pressed her mouth to his, kissing him with a fierce wildness that shook Nicholas to his core.

"I've always been yours," she said, breaking off the kiss. "When you took my hand in that gazebo, I was yours. Every moment from that first moment, I've loved you with every thread of my soul, with all that I am. I've fought for you, and I will always fight for you. And I will love you until the day my heart stops beating. Even then, I will love you from beyond the heavens. I am your Grace, and you are mine."

CHAPTER 38

Beauty unraveled
A heartbeat at a time
I unravel too
Surrender
To her
I'll never be the same.
I am hers.
~Nicholas August Harris March
Ninth Duke of Richeforte

$\mathcal{N}$icholas's heart twisted, finally understanding the reality of what Grace had given him. Herself. All that she was. He understood at last because now he wanted to give her the same. Everything.

Taking her wrist, he pressed his lips to the underside of it, where the skin was so fragile, so thin, and her veins traced blue in a network of tiny lines beneath the gold bracelet.

"You are mine, aren't you?"

"Yes." She smiled. "I am yours."

He pulled her nightgown over her head and quickly discarded the sleeping pants he wore. "And you love me."

"Yes. I love you. You love me too."

"God. You have no idea how much." His hands skated down her flanks, smoothed over her hips, then gripped her plump buttocks. Pulling her firmly against his erection, he whispered, "I want to make love to you."

Grace sighed in agreement. "Yes. I want that too. Please, Nicholas." Her mouth sought his, hungry and wild and sweet while he rubbed against her body. The friction, the glide of flesh against flesh, hardened steel against soft heat intensified the longing burning so bright between them.

"Sit up, my love," Nicholas murmured. "Climb on top of me."

When she was situated just as he wanted, her legs spread, straddling his muscular thighs with his cock rising against her lower belly, he sucked in a breath. He'd never seen a lovelier sight in all his life than Grace astride him, her eyes heavy with pleasure and anticipation, her magnificent breasts rising and falling with each shallow breath. She waited patiently for his instruction, her strong, yet delicate hands braced against his chest, and Nicholas found his mind so full of imagery, he was momentarily struck dumb.

"Nicholas?" Her tone held the slightest uncertainty, her brow furrowed just enough to cause a crease.

"Shhh," he admonished, smoothing a hand down the valley between her breasts, pleased when she closed her eyes on a shuddering exhalation, swaying slightly with his touch. "You've no idea how incredibly gorgeous you are. How you make the blood sing in my veins just looking at you. Grace, Grace, Grace. Somehow, you became my everything when I thought I needed nothing."

She smiled at him, lashes lowered just enough so he could see the kaleidoscope of gold in her eyes.

"Touch yourself, Grace. Imagine your hands are mine, your fingers my own. Caress every inch of you that belongs to me."

His husky whisper made her eyes widened. She bit her lower lip, and when Nicholas nodded encouragement, her hands lifted. Cupping her breasts, her fingers spread to support the plump weight.

"Sweet fires of hell."

Nicholas's choked curse spurred Grace on. With a shy smile, her hands molded the firm globes until peachy hued nipples peeked between her fingers. When she squeezed, gently at first, then harder, whimpering as sensations coursed through her body, Nicholas moaned, remembering the first time he envisioned this. That night on Calmont Down's garden terrace, when she boasted of her outstanding riding abilities. Nicholas had imagined her then, riding him, pleasuring herself. And now it was a reality.

"More," he croaked, hoping she understood his garbled direction.

Grace hesitated, but her hands glided down the planes of her body obediently, encountering the tip of his cock before reaching the junction of her thighs. Forming a circle with her palms, she watched him while she caressed and molded his hardened flesh, encircling the crown, trailing fingertips down the underside of the shaft until Nicholas thought he might lose all control or die from pleasure.

"Stop. Bloody hell, you must stop before I take you right now," he muttered, reaching up and tucking her hair back behind her ear. "Touch yourself, Grace. I want to see you touch yourself. Your fingers on your folds, between your thighs, in the midst of those sweet, golden curls. Yes, love. Like that...just like that...don't stop until I say..."

Nicholas watched in rapt fascination when her thick, sable eyelashes fluttered down, brushing the tops of her flushed cheeks as she watched her own hands. She couldn't keep her gaze away from the space between her legs. She was wet, so wet she glistened in the firelight, fingers shimmering as if dipped in morning dew, shadows and light dancing across her body as she transported herself dangerously close to an orgasm. Nicholas knew she was close, he knew her signs, the erratic pattern she breathed, the pretty flush suffusing her skin, the unfocused, dreamy look her golden eyes contained, the tense softness in her bones, as if she were held together with the softest of feathers. Jesus, he was going to come just watching her.

He could take no more. Threading their fingers together, he dragged both their hands through the soft curls and the damp, silky folds of her sex. Controlling her fingers with his, together they pinched the tiny, swollen bundle of nerves hidden there. Grace cried out his name in release, falling forward against his chest, her lush mouth finding his and sharing a ravenous kiss.

"The condoms..." he finally said, but Grace's head lolled side to side, her words running together in a delirious chant while pressing kisses to his throat and chin.

"No, no. I want you inside me. All of you. Just you, nothing else. Please, Nicholas. Please."

Immediately, Nicholas lifted her, resettling her so his sex thrust inside her body. She was still riding her climax when he sheathed himself inside her, her flesh so snug and tight around him, he felt dizzy. He felt her stretch in accommodation, felt her pulsating, her heartbeat struggling to find its rhythm, and the knowledge made him swell even larger. Harder. God above. He was about to burst, and Grace was whimpering in delight.

"Oh god. Nicholas...it's so...oh.... oh god."

"Yes, love. I know. I know. Move like this. Let me show you.... here, like this." He pushed her so she sat completely upright, then slid her forward until that sensitive little button of nerves hidden behind the curls hit just the right angle on his body. The resulting friction sent a shower of sparks down upon them both. "Yes...Grace...yes..."

His words became more guttural, but it was all so delicious

and wondrous and magical, he couldn't stop from rocking her hips again and again over his. Over and over until her inner channel clamped greedily about him and all the blood in his body rushed to that area where he invaded her.

He might have held on to his sanity had she not whispered, "Nicholas, my very own winter wolf, I love you," just before she shuddered, threw her head back and sobbed in yet another orgasm. And because he loved her so much, Nicholas surrendered himself.

Their lovemaking was a tender whirlwind, so sweet and all-encompassing, it eclipsed anything they'd shared before. Pulsing inside her, he took everything she gave him and poured himself back into her until they collapsed together in blissful exhaustion.

"You are my everything, honeybee," Nicholas murmured as Grace drifted asleep, in his arms. "My everything, forever."

CHAPTER 39

The whirl of excitement surrounding the return of the Earl of Bentley and his new wife allowed Grace the opportunity of fading into the background at Beaumont. Oh, there were murmurs of sympathy for the loss of her stables and her horses, and Celia practically strangled her with an embrace and a choked sob of sorrow, but the majority of attention was firmly fixed on the couple of honor.

Tristan kept his distance, his dark eyes unreadable, face set as if made of stone, and that alone created its own brand of gossip. Normally, the viscount tagged close at her heels, now he only approached with polite greetings. Speculation was rife as to the reasons why after his dogged pursuit, but Grace determinedly ignored the whispers.

People had been gathering for days at Beaumont and surrounding estates for the ball. With so many guests milling about, it was difficult finding a private spot for any type of discussion, but on the third morning, Celia successfully cornered Grace in the library. In her typical forthright manner, she didn't contain her curiosity.

"Is it true, Grace? Richeforte risked his life saving your horses?"

The tale had spread through the *ton,* and Grace saw no reason she should deny it. Everyone should know of Nicholas's bravery. They should all know he wasn't the monster they thought he was.

"It it." Grace placed the book she was reading aside and made room for Celia on the settee. "He would have died had Sebastian not gone in after him."

Celia chewed her lips for a moment, then blurted out, "Has the duke fallen in love with you, then?"

Taking a deep breath, Grace nodded. "He has. I'm so sorry, Celia. I know you have carried an affection for him this season. I never meant for this to happen—"

"Good. I'm so happy for you."

"You are?" Grace knew disbelief was evident in her tone.

"Of course! If anyone is to be his duchess, it must be you, Grace. You will love him as he deserves to be loved. Wholeheartedly and without reservation." The smile Celia gave Grace was one of deep affection. "I knew this would happen the night you two danced at the Calmont Downs' fete'. He was completely fascinated by you, and I told Mother she needn't worry about my pursuit of the duke because you'd already caught him."

"It's a wonder your parents did not lock me away to keep me from Richeforte's path."

"They are the most absent of guardians, I know, but then again, you are the most unusual of wards. I think they realized early on there was no hope of containing you. You truly are a Cornwall storm. You whirl in, do as you please, and whirl back out with a sunny smile, leaving others glad for the rainbow you left behind. Would you have allowed anyone to keep you from Belmar Abbey and your horses?"

"No. Never," Grace whispered.

"The duke, I expect, will give you anything you desire. Allow you to go wherever you please. And be right at your side while you do it." Celia patted Grace's hand, leaning toward her with a cheeky grin. "How you tamed the Winter Wolf is a secret I hope you share one day. It might help me find my own husband."

Grace sighed. "I fear Tristan will never forgive me. We did not part on good terms when he left Bellmar Abbey."

Celia leaned back against the settee, a small frown creasing her brow. "Tristan will be fine. When he sees you and Richeforte together, how you are, how you look at one another, he will understand. Perhaps now he will look for someone who loves him in that way as well. He deserves it so. I do wish Violet's parents were not pursuing an engagement for her to that awful Lord Gadley. She's loved Tristan since we were children, although he's never so much as spared her a second glance. She would be so good for him."

Celia sighed with disappointment before smiling fondly at Grace. "Do not worry about him, Grace. Tristan will find his own happiness, if he allows himself."

With a squeeze of Celia's hand, Grace conveyed her gratitude. She hoped her friend was right.

If she'd not been able to discuss the matter of Sebastian and Nicholas with Ivy and Sara, Grace was sure she would have cracked apart from the anticipation of waiting for Nicholas to arrive. Sara, of course, squealed with glee.

"I had my suspicions all along His Grace was not that bad," she exclaimed, hugging Grace. "Well, he does have the reputation of being quite wicked when it comes to women, but I never truly believed he was completely without honor."

Grace blushed. "Oh, he is wicked, Sara. Terribly so, I'm afraid."

Sara waved her hand. "You know what I mean, darling. His

father was downright hateful; it did not seem fair his son should follow those footsteps, even with his notorious reputation. I'm so happy for you, Grace. So very happy. Isn't this just wonderful for our dear Grace, Ivy?"

Ivy nodded. She was much more cautious. "For her sake, yes. She has fallen in love, and the duke loves her. But there is still Sebastian and Nicholas and everything driving the spike between them. Provided they do not attempt to finish what they began nearly six years ago, if they will listen to each other, hear each side of the story, I believe there will be a happy outcome to all of this. We must do all we can to keep tempers at bay. Sebastian can be so terribly hotheaded. It's a blessing the duke is known for his rather icy demeanor. If they both lose their tempers, I fear the results will be disastrous."

Seeing the stricken look on Grace's face at that distressing thought, Sara hugged her again. "They will discuss matters like rational men. Alan will be here, he can help. Ivy," Sara turned to the other girl, "are you sure Richeforte will come? You did invite him, and there was no mistake of his welcome here?"

"I specifically invited him. Of course, Sebastian has no idea, but we'll cross that bridge later."

Grace piped up, no small amount of pride evident in her voice. "Nicholas will come for me. Wherever I am on this Earth, he will come."

IT WAS AN AWFUL CRUSH OF PEOPLE.

Three hundred guests swarmed Beaumont's grounds and the elegant mansion. Not only were the top echelons of society present, the Dowager Duchess of Richeforte, newly returned from Ireland, had arrived that afternoon. She had yet to make an appearance, but everyone was abuzz regarding her appearance, the first since her husband's death some six months prior.

Her potential future mother-in-law was somewhere in a chamber overhead. Knowing this had Grace so nervous, it was amazing she could breathe at all, even withstanding the confines of a corset and the new ice-blue silk ballgown procured by Lady Darby specifically for this occasion. "A gift, my dear," she'd said, with a hug and a kiss to Grace's cheek. "Think nothing of it."

Beautifully constructed, with dropped shoulders and ropes of tiny stones that glittered like jewels adorning the low neckline, sleeves and back, it was a gown unlike anything Grace had ever owned. She'd never felt so much like a princess before now, and the thought occurred that as a duchess, it would be expected she dress like this all the time. No more breeches and tearing about the countryside on a horse's bareback, something she would gladly give up for Nicholas, although her heart clenched painfully with the realization that she would never ride Llyr in that manner again.

"Darling, you look as though you might throw up," Sara said, linking an arm through hers. It was the first instant since the ball began that the new countess and Grace were able to speak with one another. Ivy, on the other hand, was so busy, she'd not yet found a free moment from her duties as hostess. In the middle of introductions between two elderly ladies, she gave Sara and Grace a cheerful wave from across the room.

"I'm merely contemplating the fact that Nicholas's mother is here, somewhere, and she has no idea she might soon acquire a daughter-in-law," Grace remarked solemnly.

"Ah! Think how happy she will be when she finally meets you! That you are the one who has captured her son's heart! She will adore you, Grace. How could she not? Everyone does."

Grace swallowed hard. "Perhaps she will believe I've tricked him into an offer of marriage. I'm sure there are women aplenty who have tried."

"And none who succeeded. If what Ivy says is true, Richeforte loves you, Grace. And the Dowager Duchess will too."

"It is absolutely true. I love her madly."

Grace gave a muffled scream, clapping her hand over her mouth and whirling about. Nicholas stood behind her, devastatingly handsome in severe black evening attire, his rakishly long tawny blonde hair curling over the collar. While she struggled to maintain a measure of dignity and not leap headlong into his arms, Nicholas had no such qualms. He swept Grace up, crushing her so his scent surrounded her, that wonderful, amazing aroma of mint and sandalwood and spice that always made her head swim.

"How I missed you, honeybee," he whispered in her ear. "It has been at least a century since I held you. My God. You are a vision in this dress. The most beautiful thing I've ever seen."

"Only a week," Grace replied in a shaky voice. "But a century, if you insist."

He refused to release her, even when Sara giggled with a roll of her blue eyes, "I suppose this answers any question as to whether or not he adores you."

"Nicholas, people will talk. Blast, everyone in the ballroom is watching us..." Grace wailed in embarrassment. She almost mentioned his mother, but her chest was too tight, her relief at seeing him overwhelming.

"I don't care." His arms tightened, a note of desperation shading his tone. "I can't let you go right now." Hands cradled her jaw, thrusting into the intricate upsweep of her coiffure, tilting her face so he could kiss her. Right there in front of God and everyone. "Not even if my life depended upon it." His lips were just inches from hers...

"Shall we test that?"

Sebastian's hard voice came from a faraway distance, floating down, wiggling into the tiny spaces that somehow existed between Grace and Nicholas's bodies. She heard a low hum, which seemed to surround them from all sides. Heard Sara's gasp of surprise and something that sounded like glass shattering.

Burrowing into Nicholas's chest, she squeezed her eyes shut, hoping it would erase the impending disaster.

The violence of Sebastian ripping her from Nicholas's embrace sent Grace stumbling. She landed on the floor, sprawled flat on her stomach, the breath knocked from her. Before she could push herself up onto her knees, she heard two things simultaneously; Ivy, screaming at her husband that he must stop at once, and the other, an unfamiliar sound. The likes of which she'd never heard before. A roar...frightening and savage.

Wild rage.

Nicholas.

Sara was at Grace's side almost immediately, helping her stand. "Darling, are you all right?"

Grace could not answer, watching as Nicholas launched himself at his former best friend with all the fury a crazed bull would have for a tormentor.

The ensuing brawl was one the gossips would relate for years. Right there, in the midst of Beaumont's elegant blue, silver, and gold ballroom, the Duke of Richeforte and the Earl of Ravenswood traded vicious punches, rolling about on the inlaid parquet floor as if they were commoners scrapping it out in a Whitechapel alleyway. No amount of screaming from horrified ladies, nor attempts by other gentlemen at breaking up the fight, dented their bloodlust in destroying each other. Lord and Lady Darby stood just feet away, as shocked as everyone else. Celia pushed through the crowd, her mouth agape in horrified shock, with Tristan joining her.

Alan attempted inserting himself in the midst of the melee and for his efforts came away with a busted nose. Sara squealed in distress.

"Bentley! Darling! Oh, no!" She frantically waved a lacy handkerchief in his face, blotting at the injury.

Alan took the piece of cloth, swiped the blood away and reconsidered how he might break up a fight between his two best friends. "If only Gabriel Rose were here to assist," he muttered, referring to Sebastian's unorthodox man of affairs, "I'm sure between the two of us, we could end this madness."

The brawl continued, grunts of pain punctuating the noise of the ballroom as guests crowded closer. Some murmured this was years in the making. It was only a surprise it took this long in exploding. And speculation escalated as to what set the brawl off.

"I told you, if you so much as touched her, I would kill you," Sebastian panted at one point, glaring at Nicholas from an eye still relatively unswollen. He winced slightly, rotating the shoulder he'd suffered a gunshot wound in months before.

"And I told you," Nicholas spit out, wiping blood from a cut on his cheek with the back of his hand, "you should heed your wife's advice and let it be. Grace made her decision. She loves me, and I love her."

"Love? Love?" Sebastian sneered. "Do you love her as you loved Marilee? Or will Grace find herself as ruined as that girl? Dead because of your actions."

"You don't know what you are talking about. And if you ever lay a hand on Grace again, I swear by all that is holy, I will tear you apart. You goddamn bastard. Do you have any idea—"

Before Nicholas finished the sentence, Sebastian swung a fist, injured shoulder forgotten, connecting with his jaw and setting off the fight once more. For several more moments, they tussled, while Grace, Ivy, and Sara embraced one another, recognizing there was little sense in attempting to stop the violence. It needed to play itself out before a rational discussion could take place. Other guests now understood Grace was at the center of the quarrel. Somehow, she was the catalyst. Word spread like wildfire through the ballroom. The Duke of Richefort was in love with Lady Grace Willsdown. Yes. Lady Grace Willsdown. The Cornwall Storm. Impossible. But true.

"*Boys!*"

The female voice struck like a whiplash. Soft, genteel. But a whiplash, nonetheless.

All eyes turned toward the source. Incredibly, Nicholas and Sebastian ceased trading blows, their fists lowering. Tristan rushed in, grabbing hold of Nicholas's arms while Alan did the same with Sebastian. Both men heaved like hounds after a fox hunt. They were bloodied and bruised, elegant evening clothes hanging awry, cravats ripped, hair tousled. A pair of diamond cufflinks lay scattered on the gleaming wood floor. Ivy scooped them up.

"As usual, there's never a dull moment when you three get together." Brianna March, the Dowager Duchess of Richeforte, said sternly from a circle of glittering and elegantly dressed guests. She was quite beautiful, tall, and graceful, with a head full of dark gold, grey-streaked hair, and mossy green eyes.

She smoothed a hand over the stomach of her exquisite, dark maroon ballgown, a network of black jets across the bodice glittering in the gaslights of the chandeliers and said, "Now. We shall take this someplace a bit more private and discuss in a rational manner why you are trying to kill one another in the midst of Lord and Lady Bentley's coming home ball. I'd also like to know why my son did not inform me he has chosen Lady Grace as his duchess."

CHAPTER 40

Sins of the past
Wiped clean
Fresh start
Fresh day
With Grace
For Grace
Because of Grace
I am free.
~Nicholas August Harris March
Ninth Duke of Richeforte

"*L*et go," Nicholas snarled at Tristan, trying to snatch his arm from the other man's grasp. But Tristan held tight, and as others chattered around them, he spoke for Nicholas's benefit only.

"Is it true?" His eyes searched Nicholas's. "Do you love her? Or is this a game to you? Is she just another conquest?"

Nicholas's laugh was a bark of disbelief. "Does this look like a game? Of course, I love her. I'm insanely in love with her. Now, let me go before I break your arm. I must see to her. She looks as though she may faint."

Tristan glanced at Grace, then smiled, a bit sadly, but a smile nonetheless. It was evident at that moment he was releasing his love for Grace Willsdown, conceding victory to the man she'd chosen. Stepping back from Nicholas, he executed a slight bow. "A word of advice, if I may. That girl has never fainted before in her life." A moment of hesitation, then Tristan said, very softly, "Take very good care of her, Nick. For all her strength, she's as fragile as silk."

Nicholas nodded at the man who stayed his friend when all others had abandoned him. Reaching out, he impulsively shook Tristan's hand, squeezing it tight until the viscount smiled in understanding.

Spinning on his heel, Nicholas quickly made his way to Grace, gathering her close with a deep breath. She trembled against him, her hands searching his body, assuring herself he was all right, despite his battered appearance.

"I told you it would be an ugly scene if Sebastian and I ever tried discussing our issues," he laughed in her ear.

"Do not make jokes of this," Grace replied, her voice dangerously shaky. "That was horrifying to watch....and your mother..."

"Dear God. I forgot about her," Nicholas breathed. "Come along. The others are going on ahead, my mother leading the way. I suspect the destination is the library. There is room for all of us there. And should we start fighting again, we can push the settees up against the walls."

"Don't you even dare think of it," Grace cried.

"Will you doctor me?" Nicholas teased. "Will you put cold cloths on my wounds and tend to all my aches and pains?" His arm wrapped about her waist as they exited the ballroom and walked down the corridor. The musicians began playing again, guests chattering with excitement about the evening's surprising events while servants rushed about, cleaning up splatters of blood, broken glass and spilled champagne. "Shall I come to your room tonight, or will you come to mine? Strictly for medical purposes, should anyone ask."

"Behave, Your Grace," was her prim reply. She was a bit dazed by Nicholas's lighthearted manner. It was as if the vicious brawl erased the last remnants of the icily controlled duke she'd fallen in love with. Was it possible that pounding fists into another man's face could somehow erase all feelings of hate and betrayal? Could it have some type of cathartic cleansing of old emotions for Nicholas?

She couldn't help grinning when he laughed softly and said, "I love how you use my title when you believe it will sway me. When you are my duchess, I will try the same tactic and see if it works on you."

When they were all gathered in the Ravenswood library, Ivy and Sara poured drinks while Nicholas fondly embraced his mother and introduced Grace.

"You may call me Brianna, dear. At least until the wedding. And then Mother will do just fine, if you are inclined to call me so. You are a dear little thing, aren't you? Nicholas chose well. I feared he would never wed. His father and I set a rather horrible example of married life, I'm afraid."

Sebastian scowled at the duchess. "Do you really believe it will come to that, Your Grace? There are matters here no one understands. It makes a wedding between these two impossible. And I'll never allow someone I care for to marry a man like him."

"Sebastian, my love." Ivy handed him a glass of brandy. "Listen to what the duke has to say. You will understand, I promise."

"Let us start from the beginning, shall we?" Nicholas said slowly. He took a deep breath, taking Grace's hand, grateful when she gave his a tiny squeeze, flashing him a smile of encouragement. "Sebastian, I was not the father of Marilee's child. My own father was responsible for the deed."

Sebastian frowned. "What are you talking about?"

"It's true. He seduced her, or she seduced him, I'm not sure on that point. I suspected for some time she was making a fool of you with someone. I didn't know who until it was too late. When I refused to marry her and claim the baby as my own, the Duke threatened to disown me. I told him he could take his title and the entire dukedom straight to the devil. I would never marry that girl, nor would I betray you. When Marilee discovered her plan had failed, and not only had she lost her chance at becoming a duchess, but also any hope of becoming your countess, she was so furious. She vowed she would destroy us both. That she would have her revenge. And she did."

"How do I know this is the truth?" Sebastian asked, taking a deep swig of his brandy. He appeared lost, holding Ivy's hand tight. "Why did you not tell me this before? Why did you let me believe—"

"Why did you automatically assume the worst of me?" Nicholas interrupted savagely, slamming a fist down on a table. "You and Alan both. You believed me capable of such betrayal, even after our years of friendship. You turned your back on me as if it meant nothing to you. As if I meant nothing. All on the word of a woman who had already proven she could not be trusted. I could not say anything because I was ashamed. Of my father. And yes. Ashamed of my lineage, which let that inkling of doubt creep into your mind. You thought the cruelty and wickedness of my father had finally leached out through me."

Until this moment, Brianna sat in a chair near the fireplace, silently listening to the exchange. Her heavy sigh drew everyone's attention.

"It's the truth. The old duke did those awful things. He was a horrible man. He beat his son. He beat me. Took advantage of people, used them, seduced women, willing and otherwise, and generally made life miserable for those who knew him. Marilee's family owed him some manner of debt. He used her to pay it off, and somehow, she made my husband promise that if she became pregnant, he would make her a duchess, that he would force Nicholas to marry her. And the duke was becoming so desperate for a grandson, he agreed. Marilee used him just as he used her. They were both greedy, conniving creatures."

"Sebastian, my dear, sweet boy. Nicholas is telling the truth. You knew his father. You saw for yourself evidence of his cruelty, witnessed the beatings he'd give Nicholas when you boys came for visits. I kept Nicholas's secret regarding Marilee, thinking it was his to tell you, that after the death of his father, he would do so in his own good time. That time finally came."

Sebastian did not say anything for a long moment. He swirled the remaining liquid in his glass while Nicholas stood rigid, waiting to see what the outcome of this revelation would be.

"How did you come to realize you loved Grace, Nicholas? And why are you paying for the restoration to her stables? Before I could make arrangements on her behalf, you had already handled it. And when I was in London, I received letters from your barristers, inquiring as to a secret encumbrance. What do you know of that?"

Grace moved until she stood directly between Nicholas and Sebastian. "I learned of the encumbrance, Sebastian. I made a bargain with Nicholas before the fire occurred."

"What manner of bargain, Grace?" Sebastian asked softly, head tilting. Alarm filled his eyes.

For a moment, Grace was unable to speak, then her spine straightened. "The kind men have preferred for centuries. Myself in his bed. Five nights for my estate, my horses and my stables." Her chin lifted high. "Before we could complete our agreement, Nicholas ceded it all. He forfeited the encumbrance, dissolved the contract, and gave me his prized stallion because I lost Llyr. More importantly, he swore his love to me."

Sebastian's features tightened, his fists curling. The glass he held was in danger of being shattered. "He never held an encumbrance, Grace. Not in a true sense, anyway."

Grace was puzzled. "What do you mean?"

Nicholas frowned. "My barristers are still looking into the matter. Tristan is the one who first informed me of its existence. He wanted Bellmar, hoping it would force Grace into marrying him."

"Oh, Nicholas," His mother said sadly, disappointment evident in every word. "What have you done?"

"Nothing I did not insist upon, Your Grace. Nicholas is not to blame for my stubborn nature." Grace quickly assured the dowager duchess.

"The encumbrance was only on the land itself. Not the stables or the manor. Nor the horses. When Grace turns twenty-one, the whole of it becomes hers. The Earl of Willsdown skillfully negotiated with the old Duke when he borrowed the funds for those Irish horses, realizing he needed a way of safeguarding Grace's inheritance. Even if she marries, Bellmar Abbey and all related with it remains in the Willsdown name by a special Royal Decree. I have the necessary documentation to prove it. It has been in my possession for the past six months. When your father died, it was somehow sent it to me. I imagine for safekeeping." Sebastian's cold fury cast a chill in the warm library. "It's why your father never attempted collecting the debt. He was outfoxed by Lord Willsdown. So, you see, it was never yours to bargain with, you heartless fiend. But you knew that. Grace, he used you. He knew exactly what he was doing to get what he wanted from you. It's what he does. Uses people. Lies to them. Betrays them for his own selfish gain."

"Sebastian!" Ivy hissed. "Stop it. This instant. Oh! You stubborn man! Open your eyes and see. The truth is right before you. Nicholas did not know. He would not have used Grace so callously."

"Sebastian..." Alan sighed. "I believe him, too."

Nicholas was stunned. He never had the right to bargain with Grace? There was never an encumbrance giving him an excuse to have her? To kiss her? To make her his own?

Would she believe he lied to her? That he used her? Taking her shoulders, he turned her.

A hint of doubt shadowed the gold of her eyes, a tear sparkling in the depths. She caught a deep breath, snagging her bottom lip between her teeth and biting it. He could see the struggle inside her. How she was torn between believing the worst and believing in him.

Trust me, little bee. God above. Trust me and my love for you. I don't give a damn if no one else believes me, as long as you do.

Grace sighed. She smiled and gripped Nicholas's hand tight. He saw the cloud clear, the happiness as it spread over her features. The love for him shining through her until she glowed with it. Grace never doubted him. She would always believe in him.

"Nicholas did not know. He couldn't know. He fought so hard against the contract, and I insisted upon it. After he ceded it, I seduced him and he fought me on that too. The encumbrance? He'd already sent in a paper dissolving it before I decided he would be mine forever. So, yes. I believe him. I believe him now, Sebastian, as you should have believed him all those years ago. Let go of the disappointment you still carry, because it is disappointment in yourself and your lack of faith in his honor. Nicholas never failed you. You failed him. You and Lord Bentley turned your backs on a friend, and now you have much to make up for. You both still love him. As a brother loves another brother. Sebastian, you entered a burning stable and pulled him out. You saved his life. In your heart you believe him, so please, for my sake, and Ivy's, Alan's, Sara's, the Duchess. Most of all, for Nicholas and yours. Make your amends now."

Nicholas couldn't stop staring at the beautiful, wonderful woman holding his hand, defending him and stating her faith in him, her eyes shining with conviction and love. He wanted to haul her against him, kiss her senseless and shout from the rooftops that this incredible creature belonged to him and would be his forever. Her impassioned words had the entire room in tears.

Even Sebastian. He slowly reached out and laid a hand on Nicholas's shoulder, squeezing it hard, saying without words everything that needed to be said between them.

Nicholas nearly sagged with overwhelming relief. When Alan stepped closer and did the same to his other shoulder, his knees almost buckled with gratitude. He heard his mother sobbing softly and knew she was remembering the three of them as little boys, always into mischief. He understood how difficult it was, balancing the line between duty as a duchess and wife and her duty as a mother in protecting him from his father. They'd both suffered equally under that man's heavy hand. Nicholas hoped she would now find her own happiness in life. She deserved it as much, if not more, than he did.

The three men stood still, Grace caught in their midst. His chaotic fairy, his little whirlwind, his Cornwall storm, who managed to bring them all together. Ivy and Sara joined their group with a cry, tears streaming down their cheeks.

"I'm glad this is resolved. I can reveal now it was my decision to send the original encumbrance to Sebastian," the dowager duchess said in relief. "I believed it best nothing could be leveraged between the two of you before working out your differences. I never thought Nicholas would learn of the encumbrance. Since it would dissolve on Grace's twenty-first birthday, I thought it an insignificant point. The duke's barristers gave it to me before his death, and I instructed my own solicitor that it should end in Ravenwood's hands only. I'm sorry, Nicholas and Grace. I believed I was doing the best for all involved."

Grace flashed the duchess a blinding smile. "You did just

what I would have done, Your Grace, in order to protect those you love most. No one can fault your decision, especially myself."

Tears gathered in Nicholas's eyes. Tears he'd held for an eternity. Tears he'd never shed before. Tears he never knew existed within him. With their release, he was free. Cleansed. Joy fluttered within him. A sense of wonder for what the future would bring. A future with her. His Grace. A lifetime of happiness and light and laughter with her at his side. It was so much more than a man of his caliber deserved. Silently, he thanked God for her. For her determination in sweeping away the dark memories and all his dark corners until it was as though they never existed.

He knew his nightmares would be no more. And his habit of writing those nightmares down when he first woke? Done and over. He'd have Grace to tell his thoughts from now until forever.

Their gazes caught and held, and the love shimmering between them was so powerful, so magical, there was not a person in the library left unaffected.

"A winter wolf found me in a garden maze, and I fell in love with him. Somehow, he fell in love with me in return. Once, I thought all I wanted in this world were my horses and books and a quiet life alone. I was so terribly wrong. Spending a lifetime with someone you love is worth more than any treasure." Grace leaned up and kissed Nicholas softly. "Now, if you will excuse us, I think we will retire to our rooms and clean off a bit of this blood so we may celebrate Alan and Sara's homecoming properly. I'm sure they did not expect so eventful a welcome."

As they exited the library, Nicholas heard Alan remark in that wry way of his, "As an occasional betting man, I wager we've seen the last of those two tonight."

A spate of laughter followed that, then Her Grace said, a smile evident in her tone, "Knowing my son, I would say you are right, Alan."

CHAPTER 41

Neither one said a word until they reached Nicholas's bedroom.

Grace found cloths by the washbasin, wetting them with cool water from the pitcher. Nicholas sank into a chair before the fireplace, easing out of his jacket and unraveling the cravat. While she dabbed the cut on his cheek, he unbuttoned his shirt.

She didn't realize her hand was trembling until he gently caught hold of her wrist.

"Sweetheart, there's nothing to be frightened of now. Everything is resolved." His tone was teasing but sympathetic. He understood the latent emotions coursing through her. The tremendous wave of reactions she rode as the events replayed in her mind.

"He could have hurt you. And all because of my foolish bargain..."

"That foolish bargain brought us together. I'm not sorry for it. Are you?" His head cocked, waiting for her answer.

"Of course not! Only, you may not want a wife after all is said and done. Now, you're backed into a corner and—"

"Oh, Grace!" Nicholas threw back his head and laughed. "You amaze me."

"Stop laughing at me. This is not funny," she said between clenched teeth, dabbing at some blood on his chin.

"No. It's not funny. I'm just astonished that after all this, you could possibly think I would not want to marry you. You won't get rid of me that easily." He tugged her into his lap, and Grace went willingly, full skirts spilling over his legs. Bending his head, he nuzzled the curve of her neck. "Did I tell you how gorgeous you are in this dress? How the color makes your eyes sparkle like rare topazes? And that your skin glows like the sweetest of honey?"

Grace smiled, angling her head so he could kiss the spot below her ear. "No. You didn't."

"I didn't tell you how beautiful you are in it?"

"No."

"Liar." He nipped her neck, causing a rumble of approval low in her throat. "Should I tell you something else instead?"

"What is that, Nicholas?"

"You are even more beautiful out of this gown."

"Do you think so?" She gasped when his tongue traced across the swells of her décolletage. "But, I'm here only to nurse your wounds, Your Grace."

"Trying to sway me again? Won't work." His fingers danced nimbly on the buttons down her back. "If you keep squirming in my lap, a lesson will be in order."

"What manner of lesson, Your Grace?" Grace asked, with an innocent batting of her eyes, her mouth curving in a sinful grin.

"The kind you like, obviously. Now, help me get you out of this dress and me out of these blasted trousers before I go crazy with wanting you. And after I'm done proving how much I adore you, we have a ball to attend with our friends."

TWO MONTHS LATER

"You, darling, were magnificent."

Grace grinned at Nicholas as she removed the pins holding the lace and pearl-studded veil in place. "I merely repeated what the priest said. You, on the other hand, acted the part of besotted groom as though you've done it a hundred times."

"There was no acting involved." Nicholas took the veil from her hand, tossing the delicate bit of lace aside. "Come here, wife. That chaste kiss at the altar wasn't nearly enough for me."

Grace giggled. "Chaste? I believe we nearly singed the hair off every guest in the front rows. Sebastian and Alan appeared ready to leap up and break us apart. You," she poked him in the chest with her forefinger, grinning, "were overly enthusiastic, Your Grace."

"As were you, Your Grace." Nicholas wrapped his arms around her, kissing the tip of her nose.

"Then it is agreed. We are incorrigible together."

"It seems so. How fortunate that my mother adores you. A lesser woman would have a hard time of it." He nuzzled her neck until Grace arched her head to the side, allowing him better access.

"She knows my struggle keeping you in line. Now, behave, Nicholas. For a few moments more, at least. Anna will be here soon to help remove my gown."

"I can help you with that. In fact, I prefer it."

"If you wish." Grace gave his cheek a quick peck. Their wedding was a grand affair, large enough to include people expected when a duke got married and small enough that the people they both held dear were present. Personally, Grace thought the entire event too long and pompous, but she swallowed her misgivings when she saw the pleasure on the dowager duchess's face and the loving pride on Nicholas's standing at the end of the aisle. When he lifted the veil to kiss her, her heart nearly stopped at the look of completely adoration in his eyes.

"I wish your parents could have been there today to see you. You were so incredibly beautiful. They would be so proud of the woman you've become." Nicholas's words quiet against her hair.

Grace nodded, her eyes momentarily filling with tears. "They would have adored you. My father, especially. He would love how you take me in hand and do not allow me to run wild over you."

A knock came at the door, and with a kiss to Grace's forehead, Nicholas briefly stepped away so he could inform her maid they did not require her services.

Sauntering back, he grabbed two flutes of champagne from the bucket set up near the fireplace, grinning ear to ear.

"What is that look about, you devil?" Grace asked, taking one of the offered flutes and sipping the bubbly liquid.

"I told Anna we would not need her for at least two days. Possibly more." He spun Grace about, his fingers tracing the pearl buttons marching in a delicate line down her spine. One by one, he slipped them free of their moorings until he reached the last one resting in the small of her back.

Grace choked on the champagne, laughing. "Are you mad? What do you plan to do in this room for two days?"

"Hmmm. Can't you guess?" Nicholas whispered against the nape of her neck.

Grace shivered. "Your Grace..."

"Duchess..."

"You won't become bored?"

"Are you joking? Never in a million years." The dress loosened enough so it fell forward, and holding her hand, Nicholas assisted her in stepping out of the puddle of ivory satin. "Turn around, love. Let me see you."

Still holding her loosely by the fingers, he whirled her until she faced him, clad only in petticoats and the corset and chemise constructed of the same ivory-hued material as her wedding gown. The corset was a confectionary bit of fluff intended to be more pleasing to the eye than for support purposes. It was a lacy, delicate artful contraption of ribbons, ribbing and pearls, and the mere sight of the cups pushing her breasts to quivering heights was enough to make Nicholas groan in appreciation.

Equally filmy, thin stockings were attached to it, held up with delicate garters. It was like vanilla icing on a cake; the whole effect accented by exquisitely heeled shoes, ivory-hued and studded with the same pearl buttons.

"You look delicious enough to devour," Nicholas breathed, taking her champagne and setting their glasses down on a side table. "The money on your bridal trousseau was well spent."

"It was an exorbitant amount. I could have used the funds on the purchase of a few new fillies."

He grinned, tipping her chin up with a forefinger. "Now, no pouting. Did I not tell you you'd have your fillies as well? You know I can't deny anything you ask of me. It doesn't come as easy to me as it does to you...God's blood, Grace. Why have you made me wait these past eight weeks to have you? I'm mad with wanting you..."

"We needed something traditional in this unusual courtship of ours. And believe me, waiting was just as difficult on my part."

Grace sighed as he ran a hand up her arm, along her collarbone, and further until he reached the heavy rope of pearls he'd given her as a wedding present. When she touched his chest, her palms flat against the heavily muscled planes there, the Richeforte Diamond, all seven carats of it and the matching band of emeralds and gold glittered on her finger. And on her wrist, always on her wrist, was the bracelet he'd first given her.

Grace kissed him until his grip tightened about her waist. Her vow was a velvety heated promise.

"Forever, Nicholas. I love you forever. Do not ever doubt it."

"You brought me out of the darkness. My life, my heart. Everything is yours. My Grace, forever."

Grace's smile turned mischievous as she began working on

his cravat, twisting the silk between her fingers in a suggestive manner. "You mustn't be so docile, Nicholas. Do you suppose I might try taming you this time?"

"I going to make love to my wife while she's wearing only these gifts and the ring I put on her finger," he kissed her softly, intent on fulfilling his promises first. "I want to worship her and adore her and coax those little moans from her that heat my blood. I shall use my fingers, my mouth. My tongue. My body. All of me to make all of you mine."

EPILOGUE

BELLMAR ABBEY, CORNWALL

SEVEN MONTHS LATER

"*N*icholas. Wake up."

Nicholas shot from the bed, wild-eyed, naked, hair sticking up in all directions. Grabbing the first article of clothing nearby, he threw it on before belatedly realizing it was Grace's nightdress and would go no further than his neck.

"Jesus!" he bellowed, yanking the garment off and hurling it aside. "What is the matter? Are you all right? Is it the stables? Is someone hurt?"

Grace stood calmly at the foot of the bed, already dressed and wearing breeches and boots. Her hair was pulled into a braid. The fringe of bangs sweeping across her forehead revealed shining gold eyes.

"It's time! Come on! Or we'll miss it!" She threw on a light coat because even though it was early June, a recent cold spell meant the predawn hours were chilly.

"It's the middle of the goddamn night, Grace," Nicholas muttered, throwing on one of his shirts.

"No, it's not, grumpy. It's almost dawn. The sun will be up soon. If you don't hurry, we'll miss everything."

"I am hurrying. Give me a second."

Grace sprinted ahead, taking the stairs two at a time, holding onto the bannister for balance. She was out the front door and halfway to the stables before Nicholas even made it as far as the top stair landing.

The new stables were well-lit, with gas lanterns outside each stall, open and airy fretwork between the stalls themselves and high, beamed rafters allowing movement of air and light to pass. It was beautiful and modern and the most well-equipped stables in Cornwall. Indeed, in all of southern England. While Grace and Nicholas traveled across the continent and Ireland for their honeymoon, an army of workers and the Queen's famously gifted architect worked tirelessly at rebuilding the entire structure.

They had spent the last two weeks at Bellmar Abbey, waiting for the first crop of foals to be born. Nicholas considered this a continuation of their idyllic time together. They slept in late every morning. Rode in the afternoons. Made love in the shade of the Abbey ruins. Twice they swam in a hidden spring that hugged the coast, frolicking in waters as warm as the sun and clear as crystal. At every available chance, they shared a touch, a kiss, or a smile.

"Have we missed it, Hugh?" Grace called out, opening one of the roomiest of the box stalls and slipping inside to stand beside the stablemaster.

Nicholas made his way through the numerous stable boys and groomsmen. They parted respectively for him with nods and murmurs of "Your Grace" as he leaned across the half-door. He watched his wife kneel beside a gorgeous black mare breathing heavily through contractions. She did so with no panic, just a steady, calm resolve that was admirable. It was her first foal, and she was doing a magnificent job.

"Ach, nay. Still big as she was last night. Won't be nigh long."

The mare groaned, half rising, then stretched back in the straw, her stomach rippling with movement. A low chatter of excitement from the gathered stable hands behind Nicholas swept the aisles and Hugh gave Grace a big grin. "Och! 'ere we go, lass! That's the way, it is." He murmured softly to the mare, smoothing her neck and motioning that Grace position herself nearer the horse's head.

"You are doing so well, Cadence.... there you go, beautiful girl," Grace whispered, and Nicholas was sure her encouraging words helped as the contractions suddenly intensified. With a squeal of pain, the mare squeezed with everything she had within her. And her foal decided it was time to make an appearance, slipping out of the mare and onto the straw, all gangly legs and big eyes.

The next few minutes were filled with claps and congratulations as the mare was taken care of and the foal was tended. Grace hugged Hugh until the elderly man blushed. When the foal was cleaned and finally standing on his feet, looking at his mama and his mama looking at him, Grace gave Nicholas a smile so wide, he thought her face might split in two.

"It's a colt. And the spitting image of Llyr," she exclaimed. "Look...completely black, with one rear white stocking."

The foal wobbled for a moment, and Grace reached out a hand, steadying him. He stuck his muzzle in her palm, licked her, then with a flick of his stubby, little tail, stumbled on long, spindly legs to his mother, rooted around her flank with a little whinny of impatience and began nursing.

Grace followed Hugh from the stall and reached for Nicholas. She didn't realize she was crying until he swiped tears from her cheeks with a low chuckle.

"Will it be this way each time a foal bred from last summer is born?" he teased gently.

Nicholas understood why she was so emotional. It was the first one born after the fire. The first of Llyr's last season. And that this first foal was an exact replica of her beloved stallion, meant more than Grace could articulate.

"No." She laughed. "I'm just being silly."

The others slowly drifted away from the stall, laughing, slapping each other on the backs, saluting, or touching Llyr's halter where it hung in a place of honor at the entrance of the stables. Eventually, only Nicholas and Grace stood at Cadence's stall.

Watching the mare and her foal, Grace leaned into her husband with a sigh. Wrapping her arms about his waist, she rested her head on his chest.

"I will have bouts of unreasonable emotions over the coming months that have little to do with foals being born."

"Why is that, honeybee? Tell me what would upset you, and I'll see to it at once." Nicholas pressed a kiss to her forehead. "I'll not have you unhappy for any reason."

"This particular matter will resolve in about seven months. Even then, it will truly be just the beginning of things." She grinned, keeping her cheek pressed to his heart. "But it shall make us both extremely happy."

Nicholas didn't move for a full minute as her comments soaked in.

"Are you saying...Grace...for the love of God...are you...are we...?"

Grace tilted her head. "We shall have our own little one soon. Sometime after the new year, I think. I'm afraid I shall become as big as Cadence here. Will you still love me if that happens?"

A wave of dizziness overtook Nicholas. And fear. And exhilaration. And overwhelming love for the woman in his arms.

"You wonderful, beautiful woman. I swear, you will be the death of me. God above...you took those stairs like a whirlwind. Damnit, you will not argue with me on this. You will not leave our bed until this baby is born, do you hear me? You won't lift a finger unless I—"

"There you go, trying to control everything. I've no objection to staying in bed for a while, provided you are in it with me. But I've no intention of being treated like a hothouse flower while I carry your child. You'll take care of me. I'll take care of you." Grace stood on tiptoes and kissed his nose, as he was so fond of doing to her. "We'll take care of each other. Do you remember saying once you despised children? I hope you've changed your mind."

"A very foolish, stupid man said that. I will adore our child as much as I adore you."

Nicholas squeezed Grace tight, overwhelmed with happiness and love. It threatened to swallow him whole and leave him a blubbering heap. He, the Duke of Richeforte, a man once as cold as a winter storm, now leveled and brought to his knees by the sunshine of this girl's smile.

He reined in his careening emotions. "I want a girl. So I can spoil her most obscenely, ride her around on the back of Skye and demand everyone treat her like a princess. I'll have Cook bake lemon tarts and chocolate eclairs for her. She'll have anything she wants...and I will love and worship her forever. Just as I do her mother."

"If you love our baby as you much as you do me, then she will be very spoiled. And very lucky." Grace ran her hands through her husband's mane of hair, tracing the faint scar on his forehead. "I love you, Nicholas March."

"And I love you, Grace March. Thank God you tamed me." He brushed her lips with his.

In her mischievous way that never failed in heating Nicholas's blood, Grace whispered, "I wouldn't say I completely tamed the Winter Wolf. Take me back to bed and we'll disprove that claim. And then..." she nipped his lower lip with a husky, little laugh, "you may have a turn at taming me."

THE END

A WORD FROM THE AUTHOR

You can find me on the following media sites. I'm always having fun giveaways or doing takeovers with the awesome authors I've become friends with. If I happen to be at a book signing near you, come on by so we can meet in person! I'm warm and cuddly and always willing to sign a book or two!

Facebook:
https://www.facebook.com/authoraprilmoran

Facebook Reader Group April's Honeybees:
https://www.facebook.com/groups/aprilshoneybees

Goodreads:
https://www.goodreads.com/Author-AprilMoran

Instagram:

https://www.instagram.com/aprilmoranbooks

Twitter:
https://www.twitter.com/aprilmmmoran

Website:
www.aprilmoranbooks.com

If you love my books, please leave a review on Amazon, Goodreads or both. Every time you share, review or recommend an author or a book, you are helping an author reach new readers. We all appreciate it so much!

Taming Ivy ~ Book One of the Taming Series
    Available on Amazon
    https://amzn.to/2HWrt1j

The Untamed Duke ~ Book Two of the Taming Series
    Available on Amazon
    https://tinyurl.com/ya7ntgxm

Stay tuned for the next novel I have planned! You don't want to miss the angsty heartache and steamy romance in a contemporary rock and roll romance that will have you wishing you could slap some sense into the main guy and give the heroine a big hug!

I'm also currently writing the third book in the Taming Series. If you were hoping Tristan, the Viscount of Longleigh, finds true love at last, you won't be disappointed. It's shaping up to be a swoony, romantic, dashing love story. And our heroine will steal your heart so quietly, you'll understand how she steals Tristan's!

ABOUT THE AUTHOR

April has been writing since she was in elementary school. She still has those old notebooks, and for a giggle, might let you read them. Her style has sharpened since then, but the belief in the power of romance never changed. Readers will always find a happy ending at the end of her novels - but only after their favorite characters endure great angst!

April lives on Florida's Emerald Coast and has been married for 30 years to her high school sweetheart. They have one grown daughter, Alyssa, who they love dearly. April is tolerated by a sassy Quarter Horse mare and suffers severe rock-n-roll addiction. When not writing romantic tales about dashing, alpha heroes and confident, loving heroines, she and her husband attend concerts and plan trips to Disneyworld and Nashville with their daughter and son-in-law.

Made in the USA
Lexington, KY
07 June 2019